EM of WAR

Volume 1

Desire and Despair

Lesley Lever

This is a work of fiction. All the characters and incidents portrayed and the names used therein are fictitious and any similarity to the names, characters or history of any persons, living or dead, is entirely coincidental and unintentional. Even where recognizable names appear, their actions are fictitious.

First published in 2014 by Moreton Street Books

Revised second edition published in 2017 by Marylebone Publishing

ISBN-10:1978394241
ISBN-13:978-1978394247

For Paul

CONTENTS

PART THREE

ACKNOWLEDGMENTS

I would like to thank the people of Saint-Agrève and its surrounding villages for inspiring this story. To make its context as realistic as possible I have benefitted greatly from the wealth of information contained in books written by local people and the many excellent websites, historical accounts and novels concerning *La Grande Guerre*.

The cover has been designed by Peter Pope and Claire Monk of Peter Pope Associates. It has been a pleasure to watch an initial concept become an elegant reality.

The cover photograph is by Henri Pol, a photographer who lives in the Ardèche, website www.henripol.fr. His latest book (in English and French) is called *Global Troutter* on fly fishing in New Zealand.

Finally I would like to thank my husband Paul who has patiently and perceptively read version after version, listened endlessly, supported and encouraged me throughout the years it has taken to write *Embers of War*.

PART ONE

Chapter One

June 1914

'You do love Philippe, don't you?'

'Of course I do. You know we've always loved each other.'

'Then why d'you seem so miserable? Tomorrow should be the happiest day of your life. Everyone's excited about the wedding except you.'

'Please, Hélène! ' Agathe brushed her hair more fiercely. 'Stop telling me what to feel.'

Deflated, Hélène picked up her shawl; at the door she hesitated, shook her head with incomprehension and slipped out into the soft summer night. At the end of the terrace she jumped down from the stile, clenching her fists as she strode upwards over the tussocky grass. Hélène resented being excluded from the preparations which so preoccupied her sister and was frustrated by Agathe's lack of imagination which undermined all her romantic notions.

In the limpid moonlight Hélène clambered from terrace to terrace and soon reached the wind-knotted pines at the top of the hill. Dropping her shawl and kicking off her clogs, she climbed onto a large boulder. A slight, straight figure, she looked west to where the mountain of the Mézenc and the primeval dome of the Gerbier de Jonc loomed in inky blackness; turned towards the undulating waves of the Cévennes, whose interwoven crests emerged from hazy valleys; then to the east, where the icy peaks of the Alps glimmered in a fine glittering line. Exhilarated by the expectant beauty of the night, Hélène flung her arms wide and cried out, 'I want to be free, to love, to live!' She whirled round and round. 'I swear my life will be full of excitement, romance and adventure.' Her vow soared up to the indifferent moon and startled the shuffling animals as they went about their nocturnal lives.

Hélène sat for a long time, soothed by the murmur of the river far below, before sliding off the rock and bounding down the hillside. She walked warily across the farmyard, afraid the clattering of her clogs on the cobbles would wake her parents. As she reached out to lift the latch, she could hear Agathe saying her prayers. Hélène paused, not wanting to interrupt her.

'Finally, dear Lord, I want to be a loving wife to Philippe and give him many children, please help me endure the coming days - and especially the nights. Amen.'

Hélène sank down on the stone step, shaking her head, whispering to herself, '"Especially the nights!" If it was me, I'd long to make love to my husband, couldn't wait to be held in his arms.' Her body quivered involuntarily and her cheeks flamed as she remembered the salacious conversations of her classmates and the panting gropings of couples who believed themselves unobserved. 'Damn the Curé, Agathe shouldn't take any notice of his sanctimonious sermons.'

She let herself into the kitchen where the pine walls glowed, warm and comforting in the light of the fire. As they lay side by side, Agathe spoke wistfully, 'I'll miss you all so much. After tomorrow nothing will be the same.'

Hélène took her hand. 'But it'll be really exciting. A husband, children of your own, a new life. I'd love...' She stopped abruptly; Agathe would never understand her own passion for adventure, her sister had always resisted change. 'I know living with the Faugerons might be a bit frightening at first but...'

Her sister turned away brusquely. 'I don't want to talk about it.'

Hélène gave her hand a squeeze. 'Go to sleep – you have to look your best tomorrow.' Agathe groaned.

Hélène lay looking through the open doors of the box bed into the moonlit kitchen. Tomorrow she would see Roland again. Too excited to sleep, Hélène tried to imagine her emotions if she was to marry him tomorrow. She giggled as she remembered how he had kissed her on the way back from church. Savouring the delightful sensations of this unique experience, Hélène finally fell asleep.

***

In the dappled shade of the lime trees, the wedding guests gossiped and joked across a long table haphazardly constructed by Francis, Hélène's twin brother. The bunches of wild guelder roses Hélène had picked that morning were now drooping in the heat and many of the older men were surreptitiously loosening the scarves they wore as neckties. There was a lull in the proceedings while Hélène and the other young women cleared away the bowls of *poule en sauce* and brought out more bread to go with the *picodon* cheeses, which the family had saved for the occasion. When everyone was seated, Philippe's father, known as Faugeron even to his wife, banged his knife on the table. 'Well, son, we all want to hear what the bridegroom has to say on his wedding day.'

Philippe rubbed his hand across his face and reluctantly got to his feet. He kneaded the brim of his hat while the guests stamped their feet and banged the table; it was well known that Philippe was not a man to talk more than was necessary. 'It's no secret I've always loved Agathe.' He smiled down at his bride, took a gulp of wine and cleared his throat. His voice strengthened. 'I've waited a long time for today and in a year or so I hope I'll have put aside enough for us to buy our own farm up here on the Plateau where we both belong.'

'Don't overdo it or you won't have the …' – Monsieur Faugeron's gesture was graphic – 'to produce all the sons you're going to need.' This crude interruption caused more hammering on the table. Philippe blushed and he could feel Agathe stiffen.

Philippe shook his head and grinned. As he looked down the table at the familiar faces, their strong features weathered by harsh winters and the summer sun, he was overcome by a wave of affection and amazement at his own good fortune. 'Thank you for your good wishes. And to Emile and Mathilde Vernot, my new parents-in-law, thank you for giving me Agathe – you know I'll always look after her and do everything I can to make her happy.' He paused, searching for words. 'There's nothing more I can say.' Philippe sat down with a thump, took out his handkerchief and wiped his forehead. He turned to Agathe and whispered, 'You make me very proud.'

She blushed and smiled at him but he wished she would show more of the joy he felt – there was a deliberation, a restraint in her manner, which made him uneasy. He examined his bride closely, but she continued to look away, playing with the watch and chain he had given her as a wedding gift. He squeezed her hand and returned to discussing the prospects for the rye harvest with his father-in-law.

Small children, freed from their mothers' laps, ran out into the sunlight to play, while the older guests had reached the stage of contented somnolence that comes from a full stomach and copious red wine. As the white bonnets of the old women wilted, every aspect of gossip exhausted, and the men reached for their tobacco pouches, all that could be heard was the melodious buzzing of insects busily sipping sweetness from the lime flowers. This agreeable repose was interrupted by the arrival of the photographer, thirsty and crotchety after lugging his heavy equipment all the way from the village.

The wedding photograph had been Philippe's idea, a surprise for Agathe. Neither the Faugeron nor the Vernot family had been photographed before but after half an hour – as the photographer bullied and fussed – the novelty turned to irritation. The sun was in everyone's eyes; the men in their serge Sunday suits complained about the heat, Hélène was cross she had not been allowed to wear her hat, neither of Philippe's infant nephews would sit still and their mother's scolding made them cry. Madame Faugeron stared dourly at the perspiring photographer, who had given up encouraging her to smile, and Mathilde Vernot's eyes watered uncontrollably as she did not dare blink. Confidently seated between their respective mothers, Philippe continued to grin proudly at the camera, firmly grasping Agathe's hand. At last the photographer emerged from under his black cloth and the group quickly scattered.

The afternoon sun was still strong. Young children ran around the grassy terrace playing a noisy game of hide-and-seek, watched by mothers who had retreated under the shade of the trees. Madame Faugeron and a few of the older women renewed their endless knitting. The older men sat smoking at one end of the table, their gnarled faces shaded by brimmed Sunday hats, clasping glasses in various states of emptiness. The table was now exposed to the blinding sunlight: scattered bottles, ends of sausages, rinds of cheese and crusts of bread lay in disorder amidst seeping stains of Rhône wine, while under the trestles hens scratched contentedly for crumbs.

A wiry man wearing remnants of the traditional local costume energetically played the accordion while Philippe and Agathe led the younger guests in a *bourrée*. Despite the skirling music she moved sedately, careful not to dislodge the light brown hair that her mother had pinned up earlier that morning. It was generally accepted that Agathe had been the prettiest girl in her class and Hélène envied her sister's womanly figure. Philippe was not much taller than Agathe and already the years working on his father's farm had tanned his face and carved out its structure so he looked older than his twenty-two years. His hair was beginning to break free from the oil he had applied so copiously that morning and stood in a tousled crest as he brushed away the sweat from his forehead. As they circled arm in arm, he whispered to Agathe words that made her blush.

Hélène was watching the dancing as she chattered to her friend Lucinde. Neither her mother nor Agathe approved of Lucinde, whose 'bad end' was spitefully predicted by the village women, but their acerbic comments only fanned Hélène's admiration for her friend's independence and unconventional behaviour. Lucinde was eighteen, two years older than Hélène, and enjoyed teasing the local boys by flaunting her flamboyant sensuality. Since the death of her mother, she had lived in the dormitory of the silk factory in Le Cheylard where she worked – a den of sin for girls with no morals, according to the Curé. Hélène envied Lucinde's shapely curves which she accentuated by wearing tight corsets that pushed up and forward her plumply ripe bosom.

Lucinde giggled. 'Don't you think Marius is the handsomest man in the village?'

Hélène made a face. 'I don't know about that! Philippe's not bad looking in a craggy sort of way. But I'd choose Roland – he's got such deep eyes.'

'Philippe's too serious – he seems old already. As for Roland, I saw you looking at him in church.' Lucinde nudged Hélène hard. 'You couldn't take your eyes off him.'

'Not true!'

'Liar! Don't try to deny it. But he's far too cocky. I hate the way he speaks French instead of patois like everyone else.' She turned on her friend. 'And I don't like his mouth, it's too red somehow. No, Marius's the best looking by miles.'

Hélène rolled her eyes heavenwards. 'What happened to Pierre? I thought he was the one.'

'Too boring.' The two girls kept casting covert glances down the track leading to the farm until, losing patience, Lucinde jumped to her feet, pulling Hélène with her. Both girls stood shading their eyes as they hungrily looked at the obdurately empty path. 'Where can they be?' Lucinde slumped down on the bench. 'I wish the boys would come; it's incredibly dull without them.' She turned to Hélène impetuously. 'I'm so in love with Marius.'

'You're always in love!'

Lucinde laughed, and then sighed. 'But this is different. He wants us to get married.'

'But you've only been going out for a few months!'

'I don't care. I want him so much!'

Hélène raised her eyebrows. 'But what about his mother? I can't imagine she'd be overjoyed.'

'The old bag thinks her precious son's too good to marry anyone.' Lucinde sighed. 'And she certainly doesn't want him to marry me.' Hélène nodded thoughtfully. The sanctimonious Christianity of Marius's mother did not prevent her from being the most poisonous of Lucinde's detractors. 'But I'm going to marry him whether she wants me to or not.' Lucinde dropped her voice, 'There's something I can't tell you yet, but when she hears she won't be able to stop us.' Hélène was about to question her friend when there was a volley of gunfire, then another, from behind the house.

Lucinde and Hélène both yelped with pleasure. 'They're here!' Lucinde took Hélène's hand and they ran round the end of the barn where a group of young men, mostly in uniform, stood laughing, jostling each other as they stacked their rifles. They whooped and whistled as they saw the girls; two of them lunged towards Lucinde, picking her up and spinning her round as she struggled, squealing. 'A kiss before I put you down!'

Lucinde showered the young man with a hail of futile slaps as he nuzzled her full bosom. She looked round, frowning. 'Where's Marius?'

Hélène noticed Marius's expression darken as he came round the side of the barn and saw his two colleagues with their arms around Lucinde's waist.

He scowled as they swiftly disengaged and disappeared.

'I'm here.'

Lucinde walked slowly towards him. As she got close, she looked up at him from under her lashes, smiling. 'Where've you been Marius?' He frowned down at her as the youths whistled and catcalled. 'I've been waiting for you.' The other men laughed, shouting lewd comments as Lucinde took Marius's arm. As she led him away, Lucinde looked over her shoulder and winked at Roland. 'Hélène's dying to dance.'

Hélène flushed a fiery red, causing the young men to tease her until she did not know where to look. Roland laughed at her embarrassment, shouting, 'What about some wine? We need a drink after climbing that hill.' Before she could escape, a young man in uniform put his arm round her waist, and when Hélène protested, wriggling out of his grasp, they all burst into boisterous laughter. Hands shaking as the deep red wine gurgled from the spigot into the pitcher Hélène glanced surreptitiously across at Roland, thinking how handsome he looked in his red and blue uniform.

A violin had joined the accordion, the young men paired off with the eager girls and soon the terrace was lively with music and swaying skirts. After a while Agathe came to sit with her mother and the other older women, fanning herself with her handkerchief. Mathilde smiled contentedly at her daughter. 'You make a fine couple. I'm so pleased for you both.'

Madame Faugeron patted Agathe's knee. 'I've got three good sons; your daughter's lucky to have married one of them.' She looked round complacently. 'Saint-Agrève did us proud today; I don't believe any couple's ever had a better send-off.' She added loftily, addressing no one in particular, 'It shows the high regard they've got for the Faugeron family.'

Agathe bit her lip; living with Madame Faugeron was not going to be easy. 'They certainly were generous with the wine and cakes.' She paused. 'I wasn't looking forward to the procession back from the church.' Seeing the frowns of incomprehension on the women's faces, she continued stiffly, 'I know everyone means well, but the banging of pans and all that shouting, it's not … it's not very dignified.' Madame Faugeron shrugged uncomprehendingly. 'I was grateful Philippe carried me over the *cluasse*; I was dreading having to jump over the fire. I was scared I'd trip and bring bad luck on our marriage.'

Madame Faugeron laughed indulgently. 'That's just a silly superstition. I was surprised at Philippe, though. The bride's supposed to jump across to signify she's changed from a girl to a woman – the groom's not supposed to lift her over.'

Agathe spoke firmly in an attempt to impress on her mother-in-law that she was not easily intimidated. 'He did it because he knew I was worried about it.' Madame Faugeron looked sceptical. 'And I don't believe it is just a superstition. Remember Rosalie Neboit's wedding – she slipped, and within a year she'd had a miscarriage and her husband'd lost three of his fingers.'

Mathilde reproved her daughter gently, 'That must have been a coincidence. You shouldn't take these things so seriously, my dear.' As Madame Faugeron bridled, Mathilde took hold of her daughter's arm. 'Agathe, I need your help, let's go inside.' When the two women were in the kitchen, Mathilde shut the door and looked anxiously at her daughter, who was close to tears. 'Don't get upset, Agathe. She's all bark and no bite. I've known Véronique Faugeron for years; underneath it all she's got a kind heart.'

Agathe spoke like a petulant child, 'I don't want to go away, it'd be so much better if we stayed here. You and father are so much nicer than the Faugerons.'

Mathilde held Agathe's hand. 'My dear, you've got Philippe to look after you now. He's a good man, Agathe – you couldn't have married a better. He'll make sure his family is kind to you.' The two stood for a moment holding hands; as they moved towards the door, Agathe threw her arms around her mother and they held each other close. As she gently disengaged, the sadness in Mathilde's voice betrayed her words, 'You won't be far away. We'll come over for a *viellée* soon.' She kissed Agathe's forehead.

Agathe joined Philippe, who was talking to her father. Noticing traces of tears, Philippe put his arm round Agathe and walked to the end of the terrace where no one could overhear them.

'What's the matter? You don't seem at all happy.'

Agathe stood looking over the wooded valley. 'I am happy.'

Philippe remained silent: her reply was obviously untrue, but he had no idea what to say; Agathe's moods often confused him. He took out his handkerchief and held it out, but she waved it away. 'I don't understand, we've looked forward to our wedding for so long, yet now it's here, you seem sad.' He paused, not wanting to be disloyal to his family. 'I know it'll be a big change for you and it won't be easy living with Gerard and his wife - Sophie can be a difficult woman, but I'll talk to my brother about her. I'm sure we'll get used to each other in a few days.' Agathe still said nothing. Philippe struggled to reassure her. 'Agathe, you know I'll always take care of you. I'm not one for fine words, but you'll never need to be afraid while I'm around.' Agathe took his hand and laid her head on his shoulder.

As Hélène refilled the guests' glasses, she could not help but overhear the hectoring voice of Madame Faugeron. 'Forgive me for meddling Mathilde, but Hélène should leave that Lucinde alone. Look at her! That blouse's so thin it's hardly decent. She's a bad influence and it won't do your daughter's reputation any favours to be seen hanging around with that good-for-nothing.'

Marius's mother joined in, her thin voice acid with hate: 'That's what I keep telling my son, but he's infatuated with her. If only his father was alive, he'd have beaten some sense into him.'

Madame Faugeron changed her knitting needles with an aggressive flourish. 'I wouldn't worry about Marius – he's a good boy. He'll grow tired of her soon enough.'

Hélène defiantly went over to sit with Lucinde. Her friend glared at the old women, who continued their gossip, punctuated with malevolent glances aimed at the two girls. 'What're the old crows saying about me?'

Hélène made a face as she lied, 'It wasn't about you.' Seeing the disbelief on Lucinde's face, she shook her head. 'It was something that happened this morning. Maman allowed us to get dressed in her bedroom because there was so much going on in the kitchen.' Hélène blushed. 'Actually, it's got the only decent mirror in the house and,' she giggled, 'this is very embarrassing, I wanted to look at myself.'

Lucinde chuckled. 'You mean naked?'

Hélène grinned and nodded. 'After Agathe had gone downstairs, I took the mirror off the wall and propped it on the chest by the window.'

Lucinde sucked in her breath. 'Please don't tell me you broke it.'

''Fraid so. Maman was really upset.'

Lucinde looked shocked. 'Hélène, that means seven years' bad luck.'

'That's what Maman said. She didn't want Agathe to know about it because she's so superstitious.'

'But it won't be Agathe! The bad luck comes to the person who was looking in the mirror when it broke.'

'Then that's me! Honestly Lucinde, it's just an old wives' tale.' Lucinde looked unconvinced. 'It's stupid and I refuse to believe it.' Hélène touched the sleeve of her friend's blouse. 'Changing the subject, your blouse is really pretty. It's silk isn't it? From the factory?'

'Certainly is.' She leant towards Hélène. 'I stole it.' Her peal of laughter brought more sour looks from the women sitting under the trees. 'Don't look so disapproving – all the girls who work in the factory take enough to make a blouse from time to time.'

Hélène sighed. 'I envy you. It must be wonderful not having to clean out the animals and not milking three times a day. I don't want to even see a farm when I'm grown up.'

'Then join us. There are usually one or two vacancies for machinists.'

'No, that's not what I want. Next year I'm going to train to be a teacher. I've got my father to agree – at last.'

Lucinde pulled a face. 'I hated school. Couldn't wait to leave.'

Hélène smiled. 'I like learning new things.'

Lucinde pulled Hélène to her feet. 'Why're we wasting time when there are all these men around? Let's dance!'

Shadows were creeping along the terrace; the warm evening air was redolent with the smell of crushed grass and the heavy scent of lime blossom. Only a few couples continued to dance and when the accordionist said, once again, that he wouldn't play another note 'til he'd had something to eat and drink, the young men slapped him on the shoulder and sloped off to the edge of the terrace to smoke. They were chatting about hunting when Philippe joined them.

'Isn't that where you shot the boar?'

Philippe nodded.

One of the younger men whistled. 'They say you'd only seconds to fire.'

Philippe shrugged. 'I'd startled it.'

The young men looked impressed. 'They're big brutes, but they run really fast. And if you'd missed ...'

Philippe looked embarrassed. 'I was lucky.'

Roland sounded irritated, 'Everyone knows you're a good shot, Faugeron.' He lit a cigarette. 'Hunting's about the only exciting thing to do round here. I don't know how you yokels stand it: you work all day and when you've finished there's bugger all to do.'

'We're usually too tired to do much.'

Roland sniggered, 'That'll have to change.' The young men tittered. 'Countrywomen can be very demanding, I'm told.' Roland warmed to his theme, 'Look at your sister-in-law – three children in four years. You'll need plenty of stamina to keep up with your brother.'

He was about to continue, egged on by the coarse jokes of the others, when Philippe stopped him, 'That's enough, Roland.'

'Come on, it's your wedding day – can't we enjoy a bit of fooling around? Dammit man, don't be so ... buttoned up.' Roland pretended to undo the brass buttons on his trousers, encouraging his companions, whose jokes became louder and ruder until their laughter attracted the attention of the women sitting at the other end of the terrace, who smiled indulgently.

Philippe stood silently, waiting for the horseplay to subside. 'Okay, that's enough.' The laughter petered out in the face of Philippe's unamused calm. He threw away his cigarette. 'Let's join the others.'

Roland hesitated for a moment but then, with an ironic bow, walked past Philippe, whistling the chorus from '*Quand Madelon*', a tune popular with the soldiers in his barracks. The young men sat down and sullenly lit their cigarettes. The awkward silence was finally broken by an enquiry from their host, Emile Vernot.

'How're you young people enjoying military life?'

Those in uniform looked at Roland for a reply but he concentrated on rolling his cigarette, meticulously pinching off the tobacco fibres at each end, before he answered reluctantly, 'You get used to it.' He stretched out his legs, admiring the bright red of his trousers. 'And there're plenty of pretty girls in Privas who have a soft spot for soldiers.' The men laughed. Roland waited until they were quiet before growling, 'But what's the point of spending two years learning to fight if we never get the chance to do anything except fire at a few wooden dummies?'

Marius joined them. He spoke laconically, 'You're lucky it's only two years – we had to put up with three.' Marius leant so far back his chair almost overbalanced. 'Waste of time. Hated every minute of it.'

Roland glowered at him. 'That's not what I meant! France needs a well-trained Army. That was the problem in 'seventy; we weren't prepared, so the Prussians walked all over us. A complete disaster.' He spat on the grass.

Another youth, also in uniform, joined in, 'A war'd be a bloody sight better than being stuck in Privas, where there's damn-all to do.' Many of the young men banged the table enthusiastically in agreement.

Marius was scornful. 'You shouldn't swallow everything you read in *L'Action Française*. After forty years of peace, it's hardly worth starting a war for two *départements*.'

Young Francis stood up and leant across the table, his flushed face close to Marius as his words came tumbling over each other. 'You can't say that! Of course we must fight to get them back – it's a slur on our national honour that Frenchmen are living under German rule.' He began to stutter when he realised he was the focus of everyone's attention. 'I agree with Roland. War, glory, fighting for our country, all that sort of thing, would be a lot better than being stuck here. I wish I was old enough to do my military service.'

'Hold on, Francis, your time'll come soon enough.' Philippe smiled at the boy. When Francis opened his mouth to reply, Philippe gently took hold of his arm, shaking his head.

Roland threw down his cigarette. 'Young Vernot's right – the loss of Alsace and Lorraine's a national disgrace. Anyone who disagrees is either a traitor or a coward.'

Philippe intervened, 'For God's sake, Roland, don't be ridiculous. Marius's entitled to his point of view without being called a traitor.' This did not go down well with the others, who muttered angrily.

Marius got up slowly, standing with his hands deep in his pockets, defying the glares of the young men while the old men looked away, embarrassed. 'Fighting's just bloody stupid. Kill or get killed – where does that get anyone?'

Roland jumped to his feet and strode round the table towards Marius, an ugly expression on his face. He sneered, 'Scared of fighting, Marius? Or has the lovely Lucinde softened your balls?'

Marius threw aside his chair and lunged towards Roland. Philippe grabbed Marius, holding on to his arms while Roland stood in front of them, swearing, his fists clenched at chest level, ready to punch. Philippe pulled Marius away from Roland. 'Let him alone, Marius, he's only trying to provoke you.' With Marius still twisting and struggling in his grasp, Philippe turned on Roland. 'This is a wedding, not a barracks – decent women don't want to see men brawling.' Marius continued to swear and struggle, but by now the other men had forced Roland back to the other side of the table. He spat on the ground and sat down sullenly. Philippe glared at him, then took Marius's arm and walked him away, talking insistently under his breath.

Emile Vernot spoke in a placatory tone: 'In my opinion, a war's the last thing we need.' He turned to the older men for support. 'It's hard enough as it is to make ends meet on the Plateau. We need all the men we can get – especially as it seems many of you young ones can’t wait to leave for a soft life in the valleys.’

The men drank and smoked with a surly restlessness. Roland sat sulking.

One of oldest men roused himself, his reedy voice escaping through teeth worn to the gums by his beloved pipe. ‘In my experience, fighting wasn’t much fun. Marching from pillar to post. Being fired at all day. Bugger-all to eat, no wine to speak of and damn-all sleep.’

Roland jeered at him, ‘Come on, Grandpa, you can hardly talk – 1870 was a joke. No sooner'd you got to the Front and it was all over. Our Army just caved in!’

‘Don’t talk like that! You should show some respect for those who lost their lives. Chabert and Bellat died at Sedan.’

‘Okay, I didn’t mean to be disrespectful. ‘

Francis raised his glass. ‘To the glory of France.’

His father slowly got to his feet and solemnly removed the glass. ‘Francis, I think it’s about time you fed the pig.’ For a long moment Francis glared at him, his face swollen with rage and too much wine; he banged the table so hard the glasses leapt in the air and stalked off, muttering under his breath. His father looked after him, shaking his head. ‘War might seem a great adventure to you young ’uns, but I’ll feel a lot happier in a couple of years’ time when I’m off the territorials list.’

Philippe came back to the table. 'I agree.' He looked directly at Roland and then slowly round at the hostile youths. 'Don't get me wrong – I'll fight if I have to. I don't want to, but I will.' He poured himself some more wine. 'Anyway, I don't know why we're talking about war.'

Emile nodded. 'You're right, Philippe, there are more important things to worry about – like getting in the hay and the rye. We had a good summer last year; let's hope it'll be the same this time round.'

At a nod from Roland, the young men went off to tease a group of girls who had been making eyes at them for a full quarter of an hour. The older men sucked on their pipes, refilled their glasses and stared beyond the dancing couples at nothing in particular. Philippe sat looking absentmindedly at Agathe, who was chatting to Hélène. Emile followed his gaze and chuckled quietly. 'And today of all days, I expect you've got more cheerful thoughts on your mind.' Philippe looked down, embarrassed. 'Well, Faugeron, I think you'd better be getting the young couple home.'

Faugeron winked back at him and the men guffawed. 'Aye, they've a lot of hard work ahead of them tonight.'

The men spoke in unison, 'First the ploughing. Then the sowing. Then the making hay!'

Philippe got to his feet, his face bright red. The men drained their glasses and went over to the women.

Agathe looked pale and held her mother close as she said goodbye. Accompanied by the banging of pans and raucous music, the whole wedding party walked round to the waiting cart, which was decorated with leafy branches and wild flowers; even the bullocks were gay with ribbons on their horns and tails. There was much good-humoured teasing as Philippe lifted Agathe over the wheel to sit in state on her trunk. Agathe's sister-in-law clambered up, fussing and scolding her children; Madame Faugeron was manhandled into the cart and placed solidly on one of the benches. A gaggle of children ran gleefully in and out shouting incoherently, hitting each other with crudely made dolls. Emile shook Philippe's hand as Monsieur Faugeron led the bullocks down the track. Mathilde wept while the other women told her not to be so silly, her daughter had got a good husband. Agathe stood up to throw her posy to the jostling girls, but at that moment the cart lurched and the bouquet fell to the ground. Lucinde dashed forward and picked up the wilted, dusty flowers.

***

Dusk was falling as the party returned to the table. Women laid out the remaining *pogne* cake, the men called for more wine and the dancing began again in earnest. Lucinde and Marius stood out from the others; their bodies were close but not touching, held together yet apart by some mysterious charge. They moved in perfect synchrony, forward and backward, stamping their feet at each movement, arms raised, clapping rhythmically. Lucinde's thin blouse was damp under her arms and the fine silk clung to her breasts. They moved forward, stamped their feet, backward, stamp, forward again, faster and faster – turning but still keeping precisely the same distance apart. Their eyes never left each other, unblinking, unsmiling, intense.

Hélène was not dancing. Roland had flung off his jacket and was whirling round another girl from the village. As she moved between the seated figures carrying a pitcher of wine, Hélène spied the Curé sitting apart from the others. It seemed as though he had fallen asleep, both hands under his soutane, but as Hélène moved closer she saw his half-closed eyes were fixed on Lucinde, a nervous tick flickered at the corner of his mouth, his upper lip was beaded with sweat. As she bent to fill his glass, he got up so suddenly he knocked the jug to the ground, splattering wine over his cassock and, bent double, with a low moan, ran behind the bushes the men used when they wanted a piss.

The music became relentless, faster and faster. Lucinde and Marius kept time as they went forward, stamp, backward, stamp, until the piece ended with a downward flurry of notes on the violin and a drawn-out drone on the accordion. Lucinde dropped her arms around Marius's neck and they kissed voluptuously. There was an audible intake of breath from the seated women and Madame Nouzet imperiously called to her son. Lucinde disengaged herself from Marius, looked over her shoulder at the old woman, who was banging her stick with rage and, with a contemptuous flick of her skirt, ran off, pulling Marius towards the woods at the end of the terrace.

As the couples separated and flung themselves, hot and panting, onto the ground, Hélène saw Roland was on his own and dared to join him. Roland broke the awkward silence, 'So it'll be your turn to marry next?'

Hélène blushed. 'That's a long way off.' Then she looked at him, smiling cheekily, 'Why? Are you proposing?'

Roland laughed. 'Me? I'm not the marrying type. I want to see the world before I settle down.'

There was another silence, neither knowing what to say. When Hélène spoke, it was with an oddly formal politeness. 'What is it like living in Privas?'

Roland looked at her; Hélène was prettier than he remembered. 'It's not much better than here, full of country bumpkins.'

'Are the girls pretty?'

He looked at her again. 'Some of them. But there're some pretty girls here too. Or at least there's one.' It was amusing to see the colour rise in her cheeks.

Hélène looked down. 'Life must be much more fun in a big town.'

Roland took hold of her hand. 'I'd hardly call Privas big. My father wants me to study medicine at his old university in Lyon, but I'd much prefer Paris.'

Hélène smiled at him. 'So would I! I'd love to go to Paris.'

Roland threw away his cigarette. 'But I certainly don't want to be a doctor up here on the Plateau.'

Hélène spoke proudly, 'I'm going to be a teacher.'

Roland said nothing, staring at her, calculating. Hélène felt herself blushing. He brushed an invisible speck from his red trousers and spoke tentatively. 'How about going for a walk?' Hélène tried to hide her excitement; she nodded quickly. 'Wait for me behind that tree. It'd be better if your parents didn't see us going off together.'

The sun had left the sky and it was almost dark in the woods. The crumbled remains of last year's leaves deadened the sounds of their footsteps; slender branches intertwined above their heads, their leaves softly whispering together. Hélène spoke hesitantly, 'I hope there'll be a moon tonight.' Roland did not reply. 'Last night it was almost full. I went up the hill, it was so romantic.' She ran ahead before turning towards him, her eyes glowing. 'I love these woods – they're like a beautiful temple.' She lowered her voice further, 'A sacred place where we must speak in whispers so we don't disturb the spirits.'

Roland stooped to pick up a branch. 'I bet there's good hunting.' He snapped off the spindly twigs and leant on the wood to test its strength. 'Philippe must've killed the boar near here. Bit too self-satisfied, your new brother-in-law.'

Deflated, Hélène felt the hot blood rise to her cheeks. She had spent many nights dreaming of being alone with Roland, but this was not what she had imagined or hoped. She fell into step beside him; they walked along the path in a disjointed silence.

'I can't see how he can stomach that cowardly bastard, Marius.'

Reluctantly, Hélène replied, 'Lucinde says she loves him.'

'Love! That's called lust. She's like a cat on heat and he's enjoying it so much he can't think of anything else.' Roland hit out at some brambles. 'Love – that's girls' talk. I'd much rather go off with a troop of soldiers and fight.' He laughed. 'Give me a good scrap any day – or a good ...' He stopped abruptly.

Hélène walked on in silence, determined not to cry, ashamed she had let him into her secret thoughts – and disappointed Roland had made no move to kiss her. 'I'm going back. Maman'll be wondering where I am.' Her voice wavered.

Roland stopped; he sounded uncertain, 'Don't go. We've not been away very long.' He stared into her eyes until she could stand it no longer and looked down; he took hold of both her hands. 'No one will find us. There's no one around.' He drew her towards him and kissed her hair, then her forehead. Hélène felt herself wilting but stood firm, hands by her side. Roland kissed her with small delicate kisses all the way down her cheek to the soft skin between the collar of her blouse and her ear; it tickled in a delightful way. Hélène put her arms around him and he held her close, so close that she could feel his erect hardness under his uniform. She felt an urgent, painful – and pleasurable – flame shoot through her body.

Roland lifted her chin and kissed her lips. He slid his tongue into her partly open mouth; his lips were wet, which Hélène found disgusting but fascinating. One of his hands curved round her buttocks, holding her close, the other moved up to feel her breast. Hélène pushed his hand away, afraid he would despise breasts that were still barely more than buds. He kissed her again and pulled her closer. 'Let's find somewhere where we can lie down.'

He walked purposefully, towing her behind him, when suddenly he stopped. Hélène looked at him, confused. 'I can hear something.' Roland's whisper was guttural, low; he gave a quiet snort, 'I think someone else has had the same idea.' With his arm around Hélène's waist, they walked on tiptoe a few paces down the path then stood still, listening. When the noises started again, Hélène recognised Lucinde's voice: deep, urgent, 'Yes, yes.' Marius interrupted, murmuring indistinctly. Lucinde continued, 'It's okay, go on, go on, don't stop. Too late ...'

Hélène watched as a scornful smile crept over Roland's face. He grabbed Hélène's wrist and pulled her towards the sounds, which were becoming more rhythmic and insistent. He whispered, 'Let's watch them. Lucinde's quite a girl.'

For a moment Hélène did not understand what he meant – then, shocked, she pulled her hand free, rubbing her wrist. She stood immobile. In the stillness of the woods the breathing of the lovers became harsher, Lucinde's small exclamations intensified; there was the rustle of clothing and a quiet curse from Marius. To Hélène's disgust she saw Roland creeping forward, hiding behind trees as he closed in to get a better view. As she backed down the path, Hélène could hear Lucinde moaning with pleasure.

Hélène ran back to the farm almost in tears. She straightened her skirt and wiped her hand over her face as she reached the terrace. Groups of guests were taking their leave, the men looking up at a sky darkened by clouds, shaking their heads.

***

When the piles of dishes had been replaced on the dresser and the table scrubbed clean, the family sat for a while in the kitchen. The empty chair that had been Agathe's for so many years was tucked away under the table. Emile cleared his throat and, dropping a comforting hand on Mathilde's shoulder, went to the door. 'The weather's turning. I'm worried about the hay. Thank goodness tomorrow's Sunday – it'll give us a day for these showers to clear. Let's hope the weather holds for next week.' Nothing was said, but as she went to bed Mathilde, unusually, kissed Hélène on her forehead.

Alone for the first time in the rustling bed, Hélène could not sleep as contradictory and strange ideas chased through her mind. She kept confounding Agathe's fears for her first night with Philippe with the sound of Lucinde gasping with desire and could not understand how the two women could feel so differently. As for her own longing for love and romance, their walk in the wood had shown her Roland was not the hero she had spent so many nights inventing – but then she remembered the fascinating sensation of his kisses. She stretched out her arms in the big soft bed – her life was just beginning, there was so much to explore, so many things she would do. In the seconds before she fell asleep, Hélène missed her sister.

Chapter Two

July–August 1914

Released from the suffocating anxiety of her father and Francis' moods, Hélène ran most of the way to the town. It was a relief to hitch up her skirt, to feel the warm air on her legs and dash down the stony path. Since Sunday, when the men had left church arguing over France's reaction to the increasing antagonism between Russia and Austria, the rhythm of the family's daily life had broken down. Her father, normally so energetic and determined, now trailed round the farm with a numb indifference and their evenings were tense, awkward with long silences.

Hélène headed for the Café Mathieu, hoping to buy a copy of *Le Matin* for her father. As she trotted into the square, longing for a cool lemonade, her happy anticipation was jolted by the sound of raised voices. The café was crowded, unusual for a Thursday afternoon and, even more surprising; she could see several women moodily sipping glasses of sweet ratafia. Hélène frowned; women did not leave their homes in the middle of the afternoon.

‘I tell you, it’s good news. For the last few days negotiations have been going well.’ The speaker thrust his crumpled paper in the face of Monsieur Bernard, the café's proprietor.

A truculent voice came from the back of the café. ‘But the Russians are already mobilising, which means Germany’ll have to do the same – and then we’ll have to follow suit.’

‘And go to war! We’ve had enough of the bloody Germans, let’s ‘ave a go at ‘em and be done with it!’ Several of the younger men stamped their feet to show their satisfaction.

‘Why should we go to war because some wretch from a country we’ve never heard of has taken a potshot at some tinpot Archduke? What’s the point?’

‘The point is we’re itching for a fight. Our Army’s never been in better shape.’

‘Our governments shouldn’t’ve signed so many damn-fool treaties.’ Hélène recognised Monsieur Bernard’s placatory tone as he carefully refilled glasses with red Rhône wine.

‘To hell with treaties! Let’s face it, there’s never going to be a proper peace with Germany ’til we get Alsace and Lorraine back.’ Again the younger men shouted their agreement, their glasses banging on the zinc-topped tables making a great clatter.

A lone voice rose above the row, speaking plaintively, ‘But surely not now? It’s almost August, the height of the harvest season. It’d be madness.’

'The sooner the better. Get it over before winter sets in.'

The red eyes and inflamed faces told Hélène this argument had been going on for some time and she felt intimidated by the large angry men as she wormed her way to the counter. Monsieur Bernard smiled at her, relieved to be distracted from the discussion. Hélène could smell the wine on his breath as he told her there were no journals left – hadn't been since early morning. Disappointed, Hélène turned to leave and saw Marius sitting in a corner, sullenly staring at an empty glass, his handsome face warped by a sulky expression. Hélène asked if he knew what was happening. Without replying he reached into his jacket for a newspaper, stabbing his finger at the headline on the front page. Hélène read it swiftly and looked up at him. 'But this doesn't seem so bad. Perhaps it'll all blow over – like it's done before?'

Marius mutely shook his head and called for another glass of wine. He seemed so sunk in gloom that Hélène changed the subject. 'How's Lucinde?'

Marius's voice was slurred. 'I wan' get married. Make sure she's mine 'fore I leave.' He looked at Hélène, unsure whether to trust her. 'D'you know she's pregnant?'

Hélène sat down heavily, her hand to her mouth; the news was shocking but not surprising. Before she had time to think, she blurted out, 'Then you must get married.' An angry frown hardened Marius's features, so she continued quickly, 'I know Lucinde wants to. She's always saying how much she loves you.'

Marius made a sound between a sniff and a snort; he took a deep gulp of wine. 'Don't worry, course I'm going to marry her.' He looked up at the ceiling and sighed. 'But it'll be hell telling my mother.'

Hélène smiled wryly. 'She certainly won't be pleased.' She paused. Given Marius's sensitivity, Hélène was unsure how to continue. 'But if it's likely you'll be called up, you'd better not leave it too long.'

Marius swore under his breath. 'I've arranged with the Maire that we'll be married *en vitesse* this Saturday.'

'So soon!' Hélène leant forward. 'Can I come? Lucinde's my best friend.'

'No. We want it to be as quiet as possible. The clerk'll do everything that's needed.' He finished his wine. 'I hope nothing happens 'fore then.'

'But it's Thursday already, surely nothing can change in two days?'

Marius gesticulated towards the crowd still arguing round the bar. 'Listen to that lot! Whether people want it or not, it's too late. Things are happening that can't be stopped.' He spoke loudly so the others could hear, 'Whatever you say, war's inevitable.' Hélène shoved the paper into her basket and left hastily as the flushed, fevered faces turned their hostile glares on Marius.

Hélène walked home slowly, trying to make sense of her thoughts. The mood in Saint-Agrève had struck her as strange and disturbing, so unlike the lethargic tranquility of a normal Thursday; even the bustle of market day was quite different from this agitated inactivity. Hélène realised with a pricking of fear that the tension that had so affected her family was everywhere. No one knew what was going to happen, there was nothing anyone could do to influence it so they had to wait, filling the empty hours with wrangling or retreating into an isolated torpor. As Hélène dawdled along the familiar path, it seemed as though the whole of nature was also in suspense. The air was charged with anticipation: the intense sunlight was too bright, too brittle in its clarity; the thin brown grass, the leaves of the chestnut trees and the dusty white heads of the hedge parsley all stood strangely still; even the birds were silent. Hélène shook herself: she was being fanciful – it was the height of summer, this was normal. But she knew it was not: a brooding evil lurked behind this calm.

Although she would never dare speak her thoughts out loud, the enthusiasm of the young men in the bar had been contagious. Life on the Plateau was stiflingly monotonous; the seasons followed their cycles year after year and few events disturbed their inexorable rhythm – a war would bring change and new opportunities, it might even make it easier for her to leave the farm and take up teaching. But there was another side to the boasting and bragging of Roland and his mates that had gone unspoken – underneath his preoccupation with Lucinde, Hélène had smelt it in Marius – people were afraid. Even if the war was short and glorious, it was bound to bring death and destruction.

Hélène looked across at the tough Mézenc cattle, the flocks of sheep, the terraces back-achingly carved out of hillsides that yielded such miserable harvests with so much labour, and shuddered. How could her family manage without her father? The women in the bar had been fearful for their future; scared they would not survive without their men in the harsh conditions of the Plateau, where life was an unremitting battle.

The evening sun was still hot as Hélène walked thoughtfully over the hill and looked down at the farm below. As she ran down the path she could see her father and Francis still cutting hay in the bottom field, the long blades glittering as the two men swung their scythes in a measured, economical rhythm. As she hailed them, Emile immediately put down his scythe and strode up the hill; Francis yelled something but was too far away to be heard as he dashed towards her.

'What's the news? Have we declared war?' Francis snatched the journal out of her hands, scanning it quickly, before handing the paper to his father in disgust. 'Damn our bloody politicians, why can't they make up their minds.' Emile grunted as he read the headlines; he laid the newspaper on a wall, smoothing it mechanically as his eyes travelled slowly down the page. He pulled at his moustache and shook his head.

Hélène tried to reassure him, 'The news is more optimistic, don't you think?'

'It all depends on Russia; if it's true they are mobilising, war will be inevitable.' He stood staring down at the fields below and shivered. The sight of the two lower fields of rye still uncut seemed to shake him out of the apathy of the last few days. He straightened up. 'We'd better do as much as we can before it gets dark. Tell Maman to keep supper.'

In the kitchen Mathilde was grumbling as she stirred a big copper pan full of boiling red currants hanging over the fire. 'I don't know why Papa let you go to town today – there's so much to do, and Agathe's not here to help.'

Hélène sighed. 'Maman, he's so worried.'

'That may be so, but if we don't deal with the fruit, when winter comes you'll be asking what we were thinking of.' Hélène, irritated, was about to reply when Mathilde let the pan slip and the scalding liquid splashed over her hand and onto the hearth. This had never happened before: for thirty years Mathilde had made jam, handling the heavy pans with care so as not to waste any of their precious produce. Hélène felt a stab of panic as she watched the quivering shoulders of her stoical mother and realised Mathilde, too, was afraid.

***

The following day the family rose before dawn and went down to the bottom fields. Hélène and her mother tied up the sheaves of rye while Emile and Francis worked their way to the end of the patch, the cut swathes lying in neat rows behind them. The day was searing hot and Hélène was grateful when Emile signaled they could break for lunch. All four were covered in sweat, wisps of grass stuck to their bare arms and chests. Hélène pulled her floppy cotton bonnet down over her forehead to hide her face from the torrid sun. It did not take long to eat the substantial bread and cheese Mathilde had brought with her and when it was finished Emile took out his pipe, tapped it against his teeth, sighed, and put it back in his pocket. 'No time to sit idling, we need to get this finished before evening.' Francis complained but had no choice but to pick up his scythe and follow his father.

Stooping to tie up the rye was back-breaking work and the tough stalks rasped at her hands, so Hélène was relieved when to hear Philippe calling down from the farm. This was so out of the ordinary, especially in the middle of harvesting, that all four dropped their tools and ran up the hill towards him.

Hélène and Francis arrived first but Philippe, after greeting them, waited until Emile and Mathilde struggled onto the terrace, sweating and out of breath. Hélène would always remember that interminable, taut silence; the humdrum buzzing of flies intensifying her sense of foreboding.

'What is it, son?' Emile could hardly speak.

Philippe clasped his shoulder. 'Not good news I'm afraid.' They all looked at him intently. 'They came to take the horse this afternoon.'

Emile sank down onto the edge of the water trough. 'Requisitioned!' Philippe nodded. 'That's it, then.'

Again Philippe nodded. The group remained silent, taking in what he had said. 'I don't think there can be any doubt now. It can only be a matter of days before we're called up.'

Mathilde began to cry. 'Taking our men. And our animals too. How're we to live?'

Philippe put his arms around her. ‘It won’t be for long. Everyone’s certain about that. We’ll be back before winter.’

Francis burst in, ‘Can I go up to Saint-Agrève and find out the latest?’

Philippe shook his head. ‘No point. I came by the town on my way here. No one knows what’s going on. We’ve heard the Army was recalled to barracks yesterday evening, but no one can say whether it’ll just be the reservists who’re called up – which seems inevitable – or the territorials as well.’

Emile groaned. ‘If it’s the territorials then that’ll mean me. Dammit, I’m forty-four; two more years and I’d have been spared. There’ll only be Francis left to do any of the hard labour.’ He looked sadly at Philippe. ‘You’re lucky, your father’s a few years older than me, so he won’t have to go, and young Henri’s a bit younger than Francis, so you’ll have two men to work the farm.’ He shook his head. ‘It’s terrible to leave in the middle of the harvest. What’ll we live on if the wheat and barley lie rotting in the fields?’

They did not eat until late that night, Emile insisting they spend every minute of daylight in the fields. Francis found it hard to contain his excitement, but the overpowering gloom of his parents reduced him to silence and no one spoke as they pensively spooned up their soup.

Hélène could not sleep, restlessly speculating on what the effects of this momentous event might be. As she tossed from side to side, Hélène envied the young men who would go off to fight.

Convinced by Roland, she had no doubt the war would be a triumph, and vividly imagined the excitement of battle, the glory of killing the enemies of France, the rapturous gratitude of the population as their soldiers returned victorious. But the prospect for women and girls was much less clear and a lot less thrilling. Agathe and Mathilde would play their part supporting the men they loved, but unless she could persuade Roland he needed her, the cataclysm that was transforming the whole of France would simply pass her by. Hélène clenched her fists in frustration.

***

The following morning, Hélène was mixing a mash for the pig when she heard a voice that made her heart race; Roland was greeting her mother in the kitchen. After washing her hands at the pump and retying the ribbon round her hair, Hélène crossed the yard and stood out of sight, listening.

'We're on alert, ready to go. Serving soldiers have been given a couple of days' leave to get our things in order and say goodbye.' Hélène could not hear Mathilde's question. 'We don't know exactly when, but it's bound to be soon.' Roland laughed happily. 'Personally, I can't wait.'

Hélène sidled round the door. 'What brings you here Roland?' She was surprised and gratified to see him blush.

'I'm making the rounds to say goodbye. I thought I'd drop in.' Hélène tried to hide her satisfaction at the thought of the 10 kilometres he must have walked in order to 'drop in'. Roland looked nervously at Mathilde. 'I thought Hélène and I might go for a walk before I leave.' Hélène looked beseechingly at her mother, who seemed in two minds. Roland laughed nervously. 'Patriotic duty, speeding the soldier on his way – that sort of thing.'

Mathilde slowly nodded her head. 'I suppose so, but don't be long. Your father wants to get as much done as possible before ...' Hélène threw her arms around her.

Roland strode across the yard talking rapidly and proudly. Hélène did not take in what he was saying as he spewed out numbers – numbers of cannon, numbers of horses, numbers of cavalry, of infantry, battalions, regiments, units. As the incomprehensible words swirled over her, Hélène was swept up by his enthusiasm and trotted beside him, relieved to be away from the gloomy forebodings of her parents and flattered that Roland had come to see her. Roland's talk of the Army and of the dangers he would face – and, of course, overcome – bathed him in a romantic glamour that she found irresistible.

Hélène thought it wise to avoid the track along the hillside that would have brought them into full view of her father and brother, who were heaving sheaves of rye into the bullock cart, and chose to go straight into the woods, following the path leading to the bottom of the valley. Once they were hidden by the trees, Roland fell silent and took Hélène's hand. She said nothing, not wanting to disturb the gentle spell of the rustling leaves and quietly murmuring stream. Roland cleared his throat as though he was about to say something, then thought better of it. He let go her hand.

In the quiet peacefulness of the woods it did not seem right to talk of war, and as they walked side by side the silence between them became uneasy and then awkward. When he did speak, Roland's voice was too loud, his prosaic words puncturing Hélène's romantic daydreams. 'Marius and Lucinde were married this morning in the Mairie. Apparently his mother's furious – and so's the Curé.'

Hélène frowned. 'Why should the Curé be angry? Surely it's better they're married, especially as she's pregnant.'

'He was annoyed she hadn't confessed. I think the old bugger's miffed because Lucinde hadn't told him what she was up to. I get the impression he enjoys confessions of that sort. Anyway, in his eyes they're not married – only the Church can marry someone.'

'But there wouldn't have been time.' Hélène was silent for a moment; she did not want to spend these precious minutes arguing with Roland. She took hold of his hand. 'A secret wedding days before a soldier goes to war sounds very romantic.'

Roland snorted. 'It wasn't secret and there's nothing romantic about it! Obviously Marius is in an impossible situation, but the last thing he needs is a wife.'

'What d'you mean? They love each other, so it makes sense to get married.'

'It makes no sense at all. By saddling himself with Lucinde, he'll always be worrying what she's up to as soon as his back is turned. She's hardly the faithful type!'

This piqued Hélène. 'She may not have been in the past, but Lucinde's different now. She's changed; she loves Marius.' Hélène ignored Roland's raised eyebrows. 'When he comes back he'll have a wife and child waiting for him.' Hélène thought for a moment. 'And if he doesn't return, Lucinde'll have avoided disgrace and she'll have their baby.' She took Roland's hands and looked up at him, her wide mouth half-smiling, half-pouting. 'Why don't we get married?' She laughed to cover her audacity. 'There'd be just enough time.'

Roland laughed. 'Not on your life!' and bent to kiss her. Hélène stood still as he put his arms around her and drew her towards him. The same excited tingling crept over her that she had felt before when he kissed her. After a while she pulled away, saying with more confidence, 'I'm serious Roland, why don't we get married?'

He pulled her towards him again. 'Don't be such a fool.' Annoyed at seeing her fleeting dream evaporate, Hélène drew away and they walked deeper into the woods, scrambling over rocks where the path disappeared into the stream until they reached a glade where the sun dappled through a slender canopy of leaves and the grass sloped down to the sparkling water. Roland drew Hélène towards him and kissed her, his tongue flickering inside her mouth – this time she found the sensation wonderfully pleasant. He pulled her down onto the sun-warmed turf. Entranced, Hélène lay on her back, eyes closed, as he kissed her face, then down beneath her chin. She giggled. 'That tickles.'

He stroked her breasts through the rough cotton of her blouse. For a moment he hesitated, then his hand moved further down to caress between her thighs. The warmth of the sun on her face and the gentle brushing of his lips against her breasts were infinitely exciting. Roland looked up, questioning. Hélène murmured, 'Go on.'

Roland paused for a moment, then put his hand inside her blouse and fondled her breasts. Hélène lay with her eyes tight shut, her body quivering with new sensations. Abruptly Roland sat up, looking down at her. 'I assume you're still a virgin?'

Hélène lay looking up at him, hoping to see some tenderness in his eyes, but his face was in shadow against the translucent leaves. 'Of course I'm a virgin – but you're going away. I don't know when I'll see you again. You might even get killed.' She still could not see his expression as she said what she had so often dreamt of saying, 'I think I might be in love with you.'

Roland bent to kiss her forehead. 'That's ridiculous.' He ignored her open blouse and kissed her lips, then the soft place beneath her ear, which made her moan.

Hélène held him close, savouring the new sensations that invaded her body. She did not look at Roland, but said softly, 'I don't want to be a virgin any more. I want to know what it feels like to make love.' Hélène shifted to lie beside him; she kissed him, sliding her tongue through his parted lips. After a while she pulled down her camisole, took his hand and placed it on her breast, his touch made her sigh with pleasure. She kissed him again, moving closer so they were lying face to face. Hélène reached down and felt his hardness. Roland groaned and, as she embraced him, rolled over to lie on top of her. He wrestled with the buttons of his trousers while she lifted up her skirt and pulled down her knickers.

Roland whispered, 'Are you sure you want to do this?' Hélène nodded and opened her legs wide.

Suddenly he was inside her and it hurt. It hurt so much Hélène cried out with pain. Roland was pushing upwards, splitting her in two, pounding against her, oblivious. She tried to push him away, but she was pinned down by his insistence. The pain increased as his thrusts became fiercer and faster, and then suddenly he withdrew, his hand on his penis, groaning as a stream of thick warm cream spurted onto her thighs and skirt. Roland lay for a moment whimpering with pleasure, his hand still massaging his penis, which seemed repulsively long and red. He curled away from her and got up. Without a word he went down to the stream and washed himself, tucking in his vest and long shirt as he buttoned up his trousers.

Hélène lay watching him, but Roland would not look at her – and into this prolonged, now antagonistic silence came the distant sound of the Saint-Agrève siren accompanied by the melancholy tolling of bells. Startled, Roland jumped into the air yelling, 'That's it! We're off at last! Hallelujah!' He looked down at Hélène, still lying on the grass. 'I've got to go.' He saw the disappointment in her eyes and said quickly, 'Don't worry, you won't get pregnant.' Resenting her hurt expression, he added harshly, 'Not by me, anyway. I made sure of that.'

He had reached the edge of the clearing when a pang of decency made him turn back to her. 'Aren't you coming?' He took in her blood-stained skirt. 'Christ, you'll have to clean yourself up before you go home.' Still Hélène remained silent, looking at him intently. Roland shrugged his shoulders and impatiently squatted down beside her. 'Hélène, I've got to go. I've got to get down to the barracks in Privas before six.' Hélène nodded silently.

When he had gone, Hélène took off her skirt and rinsed it and her knickers in the stream. The wet clothes felt clammy and uncomfortable and even when she reached the meadows the late-afternoon sun was not strong enough to dry them. When Mathilde asked her what had happened, she replied laconically that they had been following the stream and she had fallen in; Mathilde was too preoccupied with Emile, who was restlessly pacing round the farmyard, to pay much attention. Hélène disappeared into the hayloft to be on her own.

She felt sore, terribly sore, but that was insignificant beside her sense of resentment and disappointment. That had not been what making love was meant to be, it was not what her friends at school had intimated, what Lucinde so obviously enjoyed. The way Roland had kissed and stroked her had awakened a new universe of delight, but the taking of her, the rupturing of her virginity, had been devoid of anything other than searing pain. Hélène felt humiliated and close to tears, she knew losing her virginity was no light matter; this had been drummed into her by the gossiping of the older women who were only too keen to brand any young woman whom they suspected as sluts – but now it had happened it could not be reversed. Hélène could not blame Roland, she had been more than willing, but she did blame him for his boorish insensitivity. Hélène shut her eyes, squeezing back tears. Below in the yard, her mother called her name. With a sigh, she slid down the pile of hay and, walking gingerly, went into the kitchen.

***

The following day was a Sunday and the Vernot family went to Mass in Saint-Agrève. There was a huge crowd round the door of the church, pushing and shoving to read the small poster giving details of the mobilisation. Francis elbowed his way energetically into the throng while the rest of the family stood round despondently. They watched as Philippe emerged; his face tight, eyes red from lack of sleep, he said something quietly to Agathe. They both glanced at Emile and walked over to the Vernots.

Philippe delivered the bad news swiftly. ‘I’m afraid they’re calling up everyone, territorials as well as reservists.’ He put his hand on Emile’s shoulder, who turned away to hide his dismay. ‘At least we’ll be together in the 86th Regiment.’

Mathilde choked, gasping for air, Hélène reached out to comfort her, but she collapsed into the arms of Agathe. ‘What’s going to become of us?

We can't manage without Papa.' Both women were sobbing. Even in the turbulence of her emotions, Hélène felt a small pricking of envy that her mother had, once again, turned to Agathe for support rather than to her. She moved away from her family, waiting for Francis to return.

Philippe took Emile aside. 'Agathe and I have been talking. She wants to come back to Les Laysses.' Emile shook his head, frowning, while Philippe shrugged and sighed. 'I've tried to talk her out of it. It hasn't been easy for Agathe to get used to living with us.' He paused as Emile nodded slowly, absorbing all that Philippe would not say. 'But she does have a point. Now the worst's come to the worst, we'll have more hands on our farm than yours. It'll be very difficult for Mathilde and the twins to do all the work on their own.'

Emile sighed. 'But it'll make it a lot harder for Agathe when she does have to go back.'

Philippe grimaced. 'That goes without saying. My mother can hardly bear to speak to her and the less said about Sophie, the better.'

Francis rejoined them, his face uncharacteristically grave. 'Papa, we've only got 'til Wednesday. You've got to catch the train for La Voulte at midday.'

The bell ended its lugubrious tolling and the crowd made its way into the dark dampness of the church. Most of the women dabbed at moist eyes while the men talked in lowered tones. During the intercessions the responses were given with quiet fervour and there was an air of anticipation as the Curé portentously mounted the steps of the pulpit to give his address. He paused before speaking, looking down imperiously at his unusually large congregation.

His sonorous, triumphant voice resounded throughout the church, 'Thanks be to God! This is a glorious day for our country. We are sending our strongest and our best to reunite our beloved France so we can hold our heads high once more and cry: Every Frenchman is free to live on French soil!' There was a quickly muffled cheer. Francis half rose in his seat but was pulled down by his father.

As the sermon continued, the mood sobered and many in the congregation became restless; their shuffling turned to murmuring as the Curé warmed to his theme. 'This war is a challenge sent by God. The men of France should be proud to fight for their country, for glory and for justice – and the wives they leave behind will be honoured by their husbands' sacrifices.' Raising his arms in benediction and recommending to all departing men the special Mass he would hold on Wednesday, the Curé ended his sermon and descended majestically into the body of the church. Most of the congregation lined up to take communion but with the sin of fornication unconfessed and weighing on her conscience, Hélène made an excuse and left the church.

Walking down the narrow street towards the square, Hélène could hear Lucinde's voluble chatter and Marius's reluctant replies, she found them sitting in the Café des Sports. Lucinde bounced up, hugging Hélène tightly before gesturing theatrically towards Marius, who sat looking pale and unhappy. 'Meet my husband, Monsieur Marius Nouzet.'

Hélène smiled at her friend's proud delight. 'Congratulations!'

'Yesterday morning.' Lucinde beckoned for another pitcher of red wine. 'I'm so happy!'

Marius continued to look moodily out of the window. Lucinde turned to him affectionately. 'Oh do stop worrying! Your mother'll come round in the end; she's bound to love the baby.' Marius sniffed, hunched over his glass. 'Anyway, as soon as this damned war's over we'll get our own house and she can go to hell.' Marius half shrugged and raised his eyebrows. Lucinde became irritated. 'For God's sake, Marius, don't look so bloody miserable! Everyone says it'll be over in a week or so.'
Marius spotted Philippe and Agathe standing by the fountain and escaped to join them.

Lucinde rolled her eyes and shook her head. 'He doesn't want to go.' Lucinde's expression darkened. 'Of course I don't want him to leave either, not so soon after getting married.' She turned to Hélène, all smiles once again. 'I can't tell you how wonderful it is to spend a whole night together.' Lucinde actually blushed. 'We didn't waste much time sleeping, even though we had to make love really quietly because of old Ma Nouzet.' Hélène looked at her friend inquisitively. 'It wasn't easy telling her, I can tell you. She raised the roof. A lot of rubbish about not being married in church meant we weren't really married in the eyes of God, et cetera et cetera. Then I told her about the baby. That sent her off into another fit – you can't imagine the language!' Lucinde was silent for a short moment. 'But it was water off a duck's back. We both knew how badly she'd take it. Anyway, I insisted that now I was her son's wife, I had the right to share his bed – and I must say the news about the war made that a bit easier. She can't really keep us apart when we've got so little time left.' Lucinde poured herself another glass of wine.

'So you'll be living with her – that'll be quite a challenge! What about your job?'

Lucinde shrugged her shoulders. 'I'm a married woman now; I don't need to work in the factory.' She pulled a face. 'Actually, I don't have much choice. I'll have to work in the shop, as there'll be no one else to do Marius's work. Spending all day and night with the old bag'll be grim.' She brightened up. 'But in five months I'll have the baby, Marius will be back and we'll find our own place.'

***

The summer weather held for the next two days and the whole of the Vivarais region seethed with families desperately getting in the harvest. This frenetic activity was a blessing, as it left only the grey hours before dawn prey to forebodings and fears.

On Wednesday morning the Vernot family set off in numb silence down the track to Saint-Agrève. The sky was overcast and heavy with impending thunder; the warm humid air made their best clothes, so recently worn for Agathe's wedding, prickly and suffocating. Swifts and swallows swooped close to the ground, bluebottles swarmed round the dead carcass of a hedgehog. The night's crying had drained Mathilde of all energy and she held on to Emile's arm, a public intimacy that unnerved Hélène, whose thoughts veered between sadness at her father's departure, which still seemed unreal, and conflicting ideas about what to do when she saw Roland. Should she be affectionate – or cold and unfriendly – the dilemma had kept her awake all night and was still unresolved.

It was only ten o'clock, yet it seemed all the citizens of Saint-Agrève were restlessly milling around the square. Too unsettled to wait at home, they had hours to fill – with nothing to do and nothing left to say. Monsieur Bernard had broached a barrel of his better wine and was standing outside his café filling and refilling the glasses of all the men who were about to leave for the Front. Most of the young men had downed several glasses by the time the Vernots arrived, and were becoming boisterous.

'Berlin by Christmas!'

'Christmas! By Toussaint, more like.'

'Dammit, what about the *vendange*? We'll have to be back for that. Even the bloody politicians in Paris won't want to lose a good vintage. We'll just have time to get up to Alsace, bloody their German snouts and be back again.'

Cheered on by admiring girls, the men became louder and more boastful. 'I'll bring back some fine German sausage for you.'

Roland swaggered forward, jacket open, shirt collar unbuttoned. 'Sausage! It's scalps I'll be bringing back.' He staggered slightly. 'They'll never dare put a Prussian boot on French soil again.' He waved his kepi in the air wildly.

The older townsfolk moved away from the loud, arrogant youths and their noisily appreciative girlfriends, muttering unhappily. There was some discussion amongst the men, who delegated Philippe to go over to the group; he spoke quietly to Roland, who shrugged sulkily and called for more wine.

Seeing Philippe talking to Roland, Hélène felt brave enough to follow him. With an effort at a light-hearted smile, she said, 'You will write to me, won't you?'

Roland raised his eyebrows, his voice thickened with alcohol. 'Why should I write to you?'

'Because ...' Hélène blushed.

Roland laughed dismissively. 'Don't be such an idiot. I'll have much more exciting things to do than to write letters to a ....' He stopped himself and, after a sardonic pause, continued, 'To girls.' The other youths began to gather round, made curious by Hélène's evident embarrassment.

Philippe took hold of her arm. 'Come away. They've all had too much to drink.' Hélène's cheeks flared an ugly red as the comments of Roland's comrades followed her across the street.

On the opposite side of the square, Marius leant over Lucinde, his hands spread flat against the stone on either side of her shoulders, speaking insistently in a low voice. Lucinde stood with her back against the wall, imprisoned by Marius, her expression mutinous. 'Stop going on, Marius. I've told you over and over I love you.'

Marius bent closer to her. 'Promise you'll be faithful.'

'We're married! Of course I'll be faithful. It's silly to promise.' Lucinde would not look at him, her tone truculent.

Marius shook his dark, curly hair out of his eyes. 'I want you to promise me.' He straightened up a moment and then bent over her again, his eyes insisting on a response, but Lucinde petulantly continued to look down at the handkerchief she was twisting in her hands. 'It isn't easy leaving you on your own. I need you to promise, Lucinde.'

'If it means you'll stop going on about it then yes, I promise.'

'And to look after the baby. Promise me you'll be careful.'

'Of course I will! I want our baby just as much as you.' She looked beyond him at the crowd filling the square. 'You're being really boring, Marius!'

All of a sudden Lucinde broke into giggles as she caught sight of Tomas, a simple-minded young man, who was being teased by Roland and his comrades. Roland filled Tomas's glass to overflowing then poured the wine into the boy's open mouth until it dribbled down his chin. Roland clapped him on the back, causing him to spit out most of the liquid. 'Never mind, Tomas, you'll be the only man in town by this afternoon. That'll be a great opportunity for you – and a great consolation for the girls we're leaving behind.' The crowd, including Lucinde, laughed. Tomas was impudently proud of his penis, which was almost always erect and startlingly large. He would expose this fine member to any female, however young or old, to the disgust of most of the women and the tolerant amusement of the rest. 'Taking over from the big boys, are you Tomas?' Roland pretended to grope his own crotch while the others laughed. The other young men jostled Tomas, making lewd gestures. Three youths, led on by Roland, got hold of him and pulled down his trousers; as usual, his prick stood high and magnificent.

Lucinde called over Marius's shoulder, 'Throw him into the fountain, that'll cool him off.' Marius swore at Lucinde and, grabbing hold of her wrist, pulled her after him towards his mother, who was sitting on a stone bench, banging her stick on the stone flags in frustration.

The youths dragged Tomas over to the fountain; four of them got hold of each one of his limbs and raised him once, twice, three times into the air before letting him go. Tomas's back hit the water with a great smack, he lost his footing and floundered, splashing his tormentors, who laughed as they prodded and poked him as he tried to clamber out. Eventually losing interest, they let him slope away and returned to the café, defiantly joking with each other as they met the disgusted looks of the older men.

The church bell tolled eleven. Family groups stood around uneasily, aware time was ebbing away. Some groups were silently miserable; in others the departing men gave frantic last-minute instructions to their families who stood listlessly, not listening. Francis replied sulkily to his father's long list of tasks, looking with envy at the young men in uniform as they jostled and joked with each other. Hélène stood beside her mother, who twisted and retwisted her handkerchief into a tight ball that she dabbed at eyes which were leaking tears. They were joined by Agathe and Philippe, who could not hide the sadness in his voice, 'It seems we're all agreed, Agathe will come back to the farm with you.'

Mathilde held Agathe tight. 'It'll be such a comfort to have you with us, my dear.' Hélène felt a pang of jealousy, hurt that her mother showed a greater affection for Agathe than for her.

Agathe turned to Hélène, smiling wanly. 'And we can share our own bed again.' Hélène tried to smile, to hide her resentment.

At quarter past eleven the Curé came out of the church and waited impassively while the disparate groups coalesced into a congregation before giving them his blessing.

The church bell rang out twice – half past eleven. Philippe straightened up slightly. 'I'm afraid it's time to say goodbye.' He walked beside Emile as they made the rounds of the other families, exchanging kisses and adieux. The mood in the square became even more sombre: women cried softly, low voices murmured final farewells and expressions of love. Finally returning to the Vernots, Philippe took Agathe in his arms and held her close.

Agathe wept silently as she unclasped the crucifix from around her neck, the crucifix she had been given when she was confirmed and had never taken off since. She kissed it and fastened it round Philippe's neck, making the sign of the cross over him. She whispered, 'May God protect you and bring you back safely.' Philippe bent to kiss the top of her head.

Hélène could not bear to watch them. Standing in the square, surrounded by all the people she knew, Hélène felt alone, detached and unwanted. Amidst the pain of others' partings, Hélène could only shed tears of self-pity.

One by one the family embraced Philippe and then Emile, who could hardly hold back his tears. Mathilde held on to her husband's arm until he tenderly unwound her fingers and placed her hand in Agathe's; after a moment's pause, he walked backwards for a few paces, committing to memory this final image of his family. Eventually Philippe gently took his arm and they disappeared into the melee of four hundred men who were chaotically lining up, ready to march to the station.

The church bell struck three mournful notes – quarter to twelve. A drum rolled, several of the men got out their trumpets, and the younger ones broke into the 'Marseillaise'. The mood lifted; the men straightened their backs and stood taller, they pulled together their suits and disheveled uniforms so they looked smarter, more military. They stood to attention, waiting impatiently. The Curé mounted the steps of the fountain. 'In the name of the Lord I give you His blessing. Fight bravely for the glory of God and of France.'

Girls in the crowd cheered, many threw flowers. For a few brief minutes the atmosphere was almost festive. The men tucked the flowers into the barrels of their rifles or in their buttonholes and marched off, even the older men making an effort to look like soldiers. As Hélène watched him march away, her father seemed older and frailer than the others, a faded version of the resilient farmer of a month ago. As the men made their way down the narrow street singing *Quand Madelon,* waving to their sweethearts, shouting, 'To Berlin,' and, 'Freedom for Alsace and Lorraine,' the women walked alongside, children and barking dogs running ahead and around the line of men. At the station the train peremptorily blew its whistle.

There was an amiable chaos as the men embarked and leant out of the wagons so their girlfriends could scramble up for a last kiss. Philippe reached down to hold Agathe's hand for the last time. Hélène, Mathilde and Francis stood watching, Mathilde's eyes red with spent tears.

In the last of the four trucks, Marius leant out to reach Lucinde. She tried to jump up to kiss him but failed; she tried again but fell back frustrated, near to hysteria. Marius tried to calm her. 'Stop it, Lucinde, think of the baby.'

Lucinde jumped again but missed him, her hands scrabbling at the wooden walls of the wagon as she slithered down. 'Make sure you come back before it's born.'

The train made a preparatory lunge forward. Marius tried once more to get hold of Lucinde's hand. 'Remember your promise, Lucinde! Your promise!' The men nearby laughed, joking about what this promise might be and elbowed him out of the way.

The train let off a jet of steam and slowly began to pull out of the station. There was a tremendous shouting from the wagons, 'We'll be back before Christmas!' 'Back before Toussaint.' 'Take care.' Handkerchiefs were waved, kisses blown into the wind, a few wilting flowers were thrown down to the prettiest girls. Lucinde and Hélène ran alongside the train as, with one last lugubrious whistle and wagons bristling with waving arms, it rounded the bend and disappeared.

Lucinde and Hélène ran out of the station into the road, and eventually the train reappeared, tiny and far away, crawling silently across the rolling fields until it finally became indistinguishable from the countryside.

'They've gone.' Lucinde's voice was low and flat.

Hélène spoke more to herself than her friend. 'The Army's taken them; it will decide what happens to them – and to all of us.'

The two girls linked their arms around each others' waists and walked slowly to join the cortège of women making their way back to the square. There was no trace of the raucous bustle of less than an hour before; three old men smoking impassively outside the café brought home to the women the town's desolate emptiness. One woman began to sob loudly; two others hushed her and hurried her home. As the women made their way through the Grande rue with its shuttered shops, they peeled off into the narrow alleys and their empty homes, while a few made their way to the church.

As the Vernots reached the crest of the hill, the sheets of rain, which had been moving steadily across the Plateau from the Mézenc, caught up with them and raindrops mingled with the tears of Agathe and Mathilde. Soon all four were soaked as they walked mechanically onwards, sodden, trapped in the numb misery of their thoughts. Hélène felt excluded from the loss that united Agathe and Mathilde, and as she trudged behind their bowed figures she felt nothing – nothing but an exhausted emptiness.

Chapter Three

Autumn 1914

After the men had left, a peculiar apathy settled over the Plateau. At Les Laysses it was not just that Emile was missing – at this time of the year he was rarely seen except at mealtimes – but the whole countryside seemed still and empty without the noise and bustle of men at work. The rye had been threshed and its straw stored, manure spread, their kitchen garden weeded and preserves bottled for the winter – but in spite of this obsessive activity Hélène found herself looking at the sun, surprised it was still morning, impatient it was not yet evening. The interminable hours after supper were the worst as the depleted family sat round the table, talking desultorily to hide fears they would not share.

It was late afternoon and Francis was expected back from the market. The September sun was still warm and the three women sat under the shade of the lime tree, whose branches were alive with the gentle thrumming of insects. They were shelling peas, wrapped in their own thoughts. Every five minutes Hélène ran round the side of the barn, anxiously examining the path from the town.

Agathe took out her watch and caressed it, its familiar face reminding her of her wedding and of Philippe. 'Stop fretting, Hélène, Francis's probably having a drink with his friends. He gets so frustrated – don't begrudge him.'

Hélène stamped her foot. 'All we do is wait - and I'm so sick of waiting! It's been well over a month and we've had no letters, no news, nothing!'

Mathilde gently put her hand on her arm. 'Try to be patient, Hélène.'

Hélène knew the other two were suffering, but could not help bursting out, 'It wouldn't be so bad if we knew where Papa and Philippe actually were.'

Agathe spoke pensively. 'If we'd retaken either Alsace or Lorraine, I'm sure we'd have heard.'

Hélène climbed the stile, looking for Francis, speaking impulsively over her shoulder. 'But Roland said the war'd only last a few weeks!'

'I never believed that.' Agathe looked sternly at her sister. 'And I wish Francis would stop going on and on about it.'

Mathilde sighed. 'I just hope they'll be back by Christmas.'

Agathe swept the pea pods into a pail. 'There's no point in speculating, Maman, we're in the hands of God.'

Hélène groaned and raised her eyes heavenward but, catching sight of Francis at the brow of the hill, she ran up the path towards him. When she got close enough to see his expression, she came to a sudden stop, her eager questions frozen by a sudden fear. Francis's face was white despite his summer sunburn. Hélène could smell the wine on his breath, but this did not account for his unsteadiness as he stumbled towards her. He caught hold of Hélène and pulled her behind a kink in the stone wall so they would be hidden from the women below.

'I don't understand it, Hélène! The news is unbelievable.' Francis pulled a newspaper from the lidded basket they used to take produce to market. 'We were all convinced our Army must be in Belgium and Alsace but now we're told the Front's no further than the Somme in the north and south of Nancy to the east – miles away from the border.' Hélène frowned, shaking her head as Francis paused to take a gulp of air. 'It seems things aren't going nearly as well as we'd imagined.' He sat down heavily on a stone. 'And that's not the worst.' Hélène crouched beside him and took his hand. 'Noel Chapelon's been killed. He died over a week ago in a big battle in Lorraine. Apparently thousands of men were killed – we don't know how many, but rumour has it there was an awful lot. And my friend Louis has had his legs shot away, he's in a hospital north of Paris.'

Hélène collapsed back against the wall, her hand to her mouth. 'That's horrible! Maman and Agathe will be terribly upset.'

Francis looked at her beseechingly. 'Can you break it to them, Hélène, you're much better at that sort of thing?' He was trying not to cry. 'Do we have to tell them about Noel?'

Hélène hesitated before shaking her head. 'He's a cousin, they'll find out pretty soon anyway.'

Agathe and Mathilde listened to what Hélène had to say in silence, staring sightlessly down the valley. On hearing of Noel's death, the two women crossed themselves and Agathe murmured a prayer. All four sat, unspeaking, until the sun sank down behind the hill and the air became cool and damp. Agathe shivered and went in to milk the cows, but Mathilde continued to gaze straight ahead, as the long shadows crept up from the valley and dimmed the golden bracken of the hillside.

As the sisters were preparing for bed, Hélène tried to talk about the day's news but Agathe simply turned away. Realising her sister did not want to share her thoughts, Hélène went outside, wanting to be alone.

A soft moonlight bathed the valley but the air was cold and Hélène wrapped her shawl tight around her. She tried to grieve for Noel but he was one of many cousins, only seen at weddings and funerals; she did not know him and soon gave up pretending to a sadness she did not feel.

Hélène's thoughts turned to Roland and she frowned, confused and irritated. She bitterly regretted her thoughtless impulse to lose her virginity, not so much for the deed itself, but because it had brought her so little of the pleasure she had anticipated. The fear that she might be pregnant had also added an acute anxiety to the maelstrom of emotions she had felt in those first few weeks and it had been a great relief when her monthly curse arrived. She told herself she hated Roland for being so uncaring, for hurting her, for taking her at her word but she mainly blamed herself, she had been foolish and reckless, carried away by the mood of the moment.

Soon the damp chill drove her back into the warmth of the kitchen. Waiting until she was sure Agathe was not still awake, she sat down and picked up one of the cats coiled by the fire and buried her face in its sleep-smelling fur.

***

September advanced, each dawn bringing colder, denser mists that rose in gentle wraiths to reveal the brilliant ochre, gold and russet hues of the autumnal woods. Working on the farm had been arduous in August but it now became punishing as the family struggled to harvest the potatoes and turnips. Emile had made the whole process seem easy, but however often Francis threw the *croc,* the bent iron fork that lifted the clods, or kicked them with his clogs, he did not succeed in loosening the tubers and it was back-breaking work hacking away at the recalcitrant earth with a pick and spade.

***

In mid September the Faugeron family joined them for a *viellée.* This was the first time the Vernots had had any visitors since the outbreak of war and, after weeks without Emile, Monsieur Faugeron seemed even larger than life. He kissed Agathe on both cheeks as he boomed, ‘Any sign of a grandchild yet?’ Agathe blushed, shook her head and hurried away to fetch the customary plum brandy. Her reply clearly disappointed the Faugerons and provoked Sophie, Agathe's sister-in-law, to recount in numbing detail how quickly she had become pregnant with her various children. The Vernot family sat in an embarrassed silence.

Irritated and bored, Monsieur Faugeron turned to Francis. 'Have you heard the latest?' Francis shook his head and the women fell silent. 'The government's left Paris.' There was a gasp of disbelief from Agathe and Mathilde. Monsieur Faugeron continued gratified to be the centre of attention: 'Left on the second of September for Bordeaux.' He banged the table in indignation. 'The spineless press daren't give us the full story, but I've heard rumours the Germans've got as far as Senlis.'

'My God!' Hélène's hand flew to her mouth. 'That's just outside Paris!'

'Thirty kilometres, to be exact. They've left General Gallieni to defend the capital. At least he seems to know what he's doing, thank God, which is more than I could say for most of our blasted generals.'

'So Paris is safe?'

'For the time being.' He sighed. 'Who knows? No one can make sense of the telegrams coming into the Mairie'. He tapped his pipe to dislodge the ash and shrugged. 'But one thing's clear, there's no sign of the government returning to Paris. Trust those buggers to look after themselves.' Monsieur Faugeron puffed out his chest. 'The last I heard our boys are dug in round the Marne, along with the British.'

Francis leaned forward, his voice breaking. ‘But this is terrible!’

‘There's no getting round it, we can’t hold out against the Prussians’ heavy guns, our seventy-fives don’t have anything like the same range.’

Agathe's voice quivered. ‘Have you heard from Philippe?’

Madame Faugeron interrupted tartly, ‘No one’s had any letters.’ She took a large bite of the *copetada* cake and patted Agathe’s arm. ‘You should take that as a good sign; they’re quick enough to tell a family if they’ve lost someone.’ She looked at her daughter-in-law with some sympathy. ‘Out of the four hundred or so fellows from Saint-Agrève, sixteen've been killed already.’

Agathe sat down and put her head in her hands. ‘In less than two months! That’s awful!' Her voice dropped to a whisper. 'Absolutely awful.’ There was silence, apart from the crackling of the fire and the sound of Monsieur Faugeron sucking on his pipe.

The alcohol emboldened Hélène to enquire about Roland. Monsieur Faugeron raised his eyebrows, ‘Your sweetheart, eh?’ as Hélène blushed.

Madame Faugeron fixed Hélène with a piercing look and snorted contemptuously. ‘Doctor Gounon’s made sure his precious son stayed safe in Privas.’ She took a stiff peg of brandy and continued sarcastically, ‘Roland Gounon’s far too valuable to be sent to the Front like everyone else.’

Francis frowned. ‘He won’t be pleased about that!’

'That's as maybe.' Madame Faugeron continued, glaring at Hélène, 'And I wouldn't go getting any romantic ideas about that young man. From what I hear, marrying's certainly not what he has in mind when it comes to girls.'

Hélène blushed bright red while Mathilde remonstrated gently, 'Now, now Véronique, Hélène's too young to be thinking about that sort of thing.'

After the Faugerons had left, Agathe and Hélène washed the dishes and put them away, Mathilde sat with her knitting lying idly in her lap, while Francis walked back and forth getting in his sisters' way, swearing softly. After sitting for a while, conscious of the gloom in the room, Agathe went to the wall cupboard and brought out four small glasses and a bottle of the chestnut liqueur that was saved for special occasions. As she sat down she said with a quiet satisfaction, 'I know we're all upset, but I've got some good news I didn't want to share with Philippe's family just yet.' She looked at them one by one and said proudly, 'I'm going to have a baby.' Mathilde took both Agathe's hands in her own, tears welling up in her eyes, Francis let out a bark of triumph and Hélène embraced her sister.

After Mathilde and Francis had gone to bed, the two sisters continued to sit by the embers of the fire. Hélène turned to Agathe. 'Why didn't you tell the Faugerons about the baby?' Without intending to accuse her sister, the words hung in the air, grudging and resentful.

Agathe sighed. ‘I couldn’t bring myself to do it.’ She looked away from Hélène’s questioning stare. ‘Somehow I can’t feel it’s anything to do with them.’

‘But it’s Philippe’s child, their grandchild.’

Agathe shrugged as she dropped her nightdress over her shoulders. ‘The Faugerons are terrible gossips and I know they’ll tell everyone. I’d hate it if Philippe got to know from them, not me.’

‘And what about me?’ Hélène’s voice was sharp. ‘Why didn’t you tell me?’ She bit her lip, offended that Agathe had not told her before the others. ‘We always used to tell each other everything.’

Agathe put her arm around Hélène’s shoulders. ‘I would’ve told you soon, but after I’d lied to the Faugerons I had to tell all of you this evening. If I hadn’t, it would’ve been on my conscience.’

Lying awake, Hélène tried to be fair to her sister. She was sad Agathe would not talk about the month she had spent with Philippe’s family - but she now had her own secrets and had never considered telling her sister about Roland. Listening to Agathe’s regular breathing, Hélène realised their relationship had subtly changed. Imperceptively, Agathe had come to take the place of their father, organising the work of the farm and making sure they all kept to the tasks she had allocated, especially Francis. Her determination to keep the farm going gave strength to them all, especially Mathilde. But the relationship between the two sisters was not as it had been; the exchange of confidences that had been such a pleasurable aspect of their sleeping together in the closeness of their box bed had ended with Agathe's marriage, and Hélène felt alienated by her sister's unaccustomed distance. There were many nights when Hélène would lie awake, conscious Agathe was also unable to sleep and unhappy, yet she did not dare comfort her, afraid her sister's sharp words would destroy her attempts to recreate their old intimacy.

***

Gathering dry oak and beech leaves to fill their mattresses for the winter was one of Hélène's favourite tasks and she was looking forward to going to bed surrounded by the comfortable rustle of soft new leaves. Long shafts of brisk sunlight turned the drifts of dry foliage into a glowing golden carpet, and between the skeletal trees Hélène could see beyond the interwoven valleys to the white crests of the Alps far away across the Rhône. The day was so beautiful that despite herself, Hélène sang as she stuffed the crisp russet handfuls into the clean cotton sacks and, carried away by her own euphoria, she turned impetuously to Agathe. 'I'm so glad you came back!'

Agathe smiled. 'I'm happy to be here. Les Laysses is my home.' She paused. 'It always will be.' She waved her arm over the long sloping hillsides with their woods, the whin-covered fields, the bracken and the dark green broom. 'This is what I love, the open space, the mountains, the views that go on forever. All those gloomy pine trees round the

Faugerons' farm hemmed me in – I felt as though they were crushing my spirit.'

Hélène nodded. 'I can understand that.'

She was about to say more when her eye was caught by the distant figure of the postman pushing his bicycle up the lane. For a moment they both stood still. Agathe whispered, 'Thank God, at last!' and ducked, laughing, as Hélène threw an armful of leaves towards her. Holding hands, the two sisters rushed up to the farm. As he handed the letter to Mathilde, the postman's kindly face was beaming, his eyes moist. 'At last they've set up the postal service to the Front – heaven knows why it's taken so long. It's been a terrible two months for everyone.' He smiled tenderly at Mathilde, who was turning the letter over and over before swinging his leg creakily over the crossbar. 'Let's hope we'll have the men home soon and they'll let me retire.'

Mathilde went slowly into the kitchen and opened the precious letter carefully; laying it on the table, she stroked it tenderly to smooth the almost transparent paper. She sat down, fishing for her spectacles in her apron pocket. The others stood watching her face. Mathilde was a slow reader and it took her a long time to get to the end of the short letter. When she had finished she sat back, crossed herself and said softly, 'Thanks be to God.'

Impatiently, Francis snatched up the scrap of paper and the two sisters bent over his shoulder to read their father's thin, scratchy writing. He described how they had marched across Paris to cheering crowds. Now he was at – here the name had been blocked out by the censor – and had been given the job of stretcher-bearer. He was glad about this as it meant he did not have to fight, but as the attacks were often at night, he didn't get much sleep. He missed them all, would Maman send him two pairs of thick woollen socks – and wanted to know if the potato harvest was in and reminded them they must kill the pig before winter. After they had finished reading, the whole family sat in silence, tears in their eyes. Eventually Agathe examined the envelope. 'The third of September. Over a month ago.'

Two days later a much longer letter arrived from Philippe, which Agathe read aloud. He wrote of bombardments that blasted the French positions day and night; four men in his company had been killed, including the corporal, a teacher from Le Cheylard whom Philippe had particularly liked. After this the regiment had been ordered to retreat. '*It was extremely tough with the Germans harassing us every step of the way. We couldn't rest or the Prussians would've caught up with us. We marched 40 kilometres one day under a baking sun; our thick uniforms make the heat unbearable.*' Agathe's voice faltered as she read out, '*You'd hardly recognise me, it's impossible to shave so I've grown a beard and a fine moustache – a real* poilu*! The good news is that I'm in one piece, as are Emile and Marius.*' Agathe blushed as she skipped to the end, saying, 'This part won't interest you.'

When Agathe had finished reading, Hélène looked at her sister, whose hand was trembling. Francis spoke pensively, breaking the long silence, 'So Faugeron was right. Our Army's had to retreat.'

Agathe shuddered. 'It sounds terrible.'

Mathilde put her hand on Agathe's arm. 'At least both of them are safe. That's what we must be thankful for.'

Hélène muttered under her breath, 'They may be alive, but I'd hardly say they're safe.'

The women sat in silence while Hélène made coffee, a rare treat at that time of day. Agathe reread her letter, folded it up and put it in the pocket of her blouse. She looked at Hélène. 'We need to decide when we're going to kill the pig.' This seemed such an incongruous remark given the circumstances that both girls dissolved in giggles. Mathilde smiled too; despite the letter's disturbing content, all three were relieved to have heard from their men and the celebratory *tuaille* when a pig was killed would be a welcome treat in the grim approach to winter.

***

The first snows had fallen and the ground was icy as the Vernots greeted Monsieur Faugeron, his son Henri and the two *saneres,* local experts on butchering pigs. The men stood in the farmyard tossing back glasses of red wine, joking and telling well-worn tales of recalcitrant hogs who had put up prodigious struggles before being killed.

As soon as she saw the strange men enter the barn, the old sow sensed her fate; squealing and honking, she barged out of her sty and made a run at Francis, who stepped out of the way of the furious creature. After a chase back, forwards and around the yard, the men cornered her in the angle between the farm and the barn and Monsieur Faugeron delivered a mighty blow to her head. The five men struggled to lift the 150 kilos of inert flesh onto the cart whereupon Gibert, the most experienced *sanere*, swiftly inserted his long knife into the pig's neck so her hot blood streamed into a pail held by Agathe. The smell of blood was overpowering and Hélène, who had been standing watching, had just enough time to catch the bucket before Agathe ran, retching and vomiting, to the edge of the terrace, a slimy slick of sick streaking the white snow. She staggered away into the farmhouse.

Throughout the long morning the men butchered the carcass while Hélène and her mother washed and cleaned the long ropes of intestines, turning the muddy slush of the farmyard a virulent crimson. Despite several jugs of red wine it was cold, wet work and it was a relief when the warm blood, mixed with fat and spices, was poured into the entrails and put on the stove to boil. Agathe sat moodily in the kitchen, irritated by the pleasantries of Monsieur Faugeron, who had been delighted by this evidence of her pregnancy. The men helped themselves to rough red wine while Mathilde served steaming, plump slices of black pudding, fried potatoes and hunks of fresh bread.

When the men had gone and the kitchen tidied, Hélène sat down beside Agathe, who still looked queasy and pale. 'What's the matter? Is it the baby?'

'No, that had nothing to do with it.' She sniffled into her handkerchief. 'It was the blood. The smell of it. The hot stickiness of it. The sign that life is leaking out of a living creature.' Hélène looked at her, not understanding. 'I couldn't help thinking of Philippe and our soldiers. Death must come to them in the same mess of blood, pee and shit as that pig. As civilised human beings we want to die in our beds with some dignity, but our soldiers die like animals: torn apart, bleeding to death, guts hanging out.' She shuddered. 'And with no one there to comfort them.' Hélène put her arm around her sister's shoulders, murmuring reassurances she did not believe.

***

The following Monday Francis and Hélène loaded the cart with joints of pork and a large basket of dried *saucisses*, which had to be taken to market to make space for all the new sausages now hanging from the beams in the kitchen. Because they had to go the long way round, it was still dark when they set off, Francis leading the bullocks by the light of a storm lantern. A sleety rain was falling onto icy slush, treacherous for the bullocks, whose shod hooves had little purchase. As they gingerly edged down the track, the twins heard Agathe calling after them, 'Only accept coins, not that useless paper money!' They giggled, excited at the prospect of being in charge of the cart, the first time they had been allowed to drive it on their own.

By midday they had sold their produce and went to the Café Mathieu for lunch. Now they were doing the work of men, women were beginning to enjoy some of their habits, and Hélène was not surprised to see as many women as men in the café, although each sex occupied tables at opposite sides of the room. Francis rather self-consciously joined the old men, who were poring over a tattered map of France. He tentatively asked if someone could show him Sarrebourg, and calloused, earth-ingrained fingers hesitantly moved across the map eastwards towards the German border.

One of the old men spat. 'Sarrebourg? You say your brother-in-law was there?' Francis nodded. 'Then he was lucky to get out alive. We've heard of three lads from the village that didn't make it. The 86th took a terrible pounding; thousands of men killed, lost almost all its officers. Bloody incompetent generals!'

Faugeron, followed by his son Henri, came into the café, shaking a scattering of snow off the sacks pinned round their shoulders. He came over and picked up the map. 'Forget Sarrebourg – things've got a lot worse. The 86th has retreated to just north of Paris; they're at Compiègne, as far as we know.' He drank deeply and poured himself another glass, making his listeners wait. 'But at least our lads've stopped the Prussians from taking the capital.' He stabbed the map again, taking a large gulp of wine. 'The last we heard from Gerard was that they're moving up towards the Somme.' He wiped his bleary eyes. 'Poor bastards, I hope they've been issued with decent boots, they've done a hell of a lot of walking.'

Irritated by the men's quarrelsome speculation, Hélène left the café and went to call on Lucinde. Madame Nouzet greeted Hélène with a sour face.

'Haven't you heard?' Hélène shook her head. 'She's in bed, has been for the past week. She lost the baby.' Madame Nouzet shoved packets of sugar from one side of the counter to the other, muttering angrily under her breath. Hélène ran towards the stairs as Madame Nouzet shouted, 'You can't see her – the Curé's in there.'

Hélène barged into the bedroom. Lucinde lay curled up close to the wall; unwashed, uncombed hair spread over the pillow; red, swollen eyes peered from a puffy, bloodless face. The Curé sat on the edge of the bed, his hand lying on the coverlet almost touching the exposed white flesh of Lucinde's shoulder; he glared at Hélène and quickly got up. As he bent over Lucinde, he patted her bare arm; she winced and pulled the bedclothes tighter around her. At the door the Curé turned. 'Don't forget, this is a punishment for your sins.' He paused and wiped beads of sweat from his upper lip. 'I'll come back tomorrow.' As Lucinde swore into the blankets, he made the sign of the cross over her. 'May God be with you.'

Hélène held her friend's hand as Lucinde burst into tears. 'What on earth's happened?'

Lucinde struggled with her sobs. 'I was almost eight months. It all seemed to be going fine 'til one day I couldn't feel anything, the baby wasn't kicking any more. I thought this was odd so I went to see doctor Tourasse.' Tears streamed down her face. 'I could tell he was worried, then when I started to have really bad pains, he had to take it out.' Lucinde could not go on, waves of grief shuddered through her body. 'He cut me open and took out the baby and...' She sobbed hysterically. 'Now I'll never have children.' Hélène looked aghast as Lucinde wailed, 'And Marius was so pleased that I was pregnant. We both wanted lots of children and now we'll never have any.' Lucinde buried her head on Hélène's shoulder.

After a while Lucinde calmed down a little and Hélène gave her a drink of water, steadying her friend's shaking hand. 'I can't tell you how cruel my damned mother-in-law's been. She never stops telling me I shouldn't have married Marius, that I've ruined his life. She goes on and on about how Marius'll come to hate me because he'll never have a son. Then she says it's God's punishment, same as the damned Curé.'

Hélène frowned. 'Does he visit you often?'

Lucinde made a face. 'Practically every day, he sits by my bed for hours going on and on, telling me this is all my fault. He gives me the creeps, just sitting there staring at me – his smell makes me feel sick.' A flicker of her old fire returned. 'Filthy old man!' She turned to Hélène, tears starting to flow again. 'But how can I break the news to Marius? I can't put it off much longer or the old bag'll tell him.' Lucinde moaned, 'I'm so miserable, I just can't bring myself to do it. D'you think Agathe might mention it in a letter to Philippe and he could tell him?' The distraught girl looked utterly washed out. 'I'm so worried: he never wanted to go back into the Army and I've heard things are really tough. This'll be a terrible blow...' Lucinde lay whimpering, wiping her nose with a corner of the sheet.

Depressed and helpless, Hélène sat with her friend until, exhausted, Lucinde slid down under the goose-feather quilt.

Once outside, Hélène was dismayed to see the sky had the yellow tinge that warned of snow and the light was failing fast. She hurried over to the café to find Francis asleep, his head on his arms, a half-full glass of wine in front of him. He was grumpy when Hélène pulled at his sleeve, annoyed she had been so long.

The bullocks climbed slowly up the road out of town and it was dark when they turned onto the track leading down to the farm. They still had 4 kilometres to go and Francis urged the bullocks onward, but they would not hurry their stately pace. By now the snow was falling thickly, the bullocks' hooves kept slipping on the icy track and Francis was finding it difficult to keep his feet. Hélène, who was sitting in the cart, called out. 'We're almost at the bridge; keep to the outside of the bend!' But the thick snow muffled all sound just as it shrouded the path ahead. Francis took the cart too close to the wall, the left-hand wheel grated against the stones of the bridge and the cart came to a jolting halt. There was a moment's silence; Hélène hauled herself over the side of the wagon and clambered down.

They both slid under the cart – the end of the axle was trapped between two large rocks. It could not move forward and the shafts of the wagon were at an angle that made it impossible to roll it backwards.

Francis swore. ‘What the hell can we do? The wheel’s completely jammed.’

‘Why don’t you go on and get some ropes. We should be able to pull the cart backwards and get it onto the track.’

Francis snorted. ‘Agathe's going to be furious!’

Hélène winced. ‘That can’t be helped. She’s bound to be worrying by now anyway.’ She looked round; the snow was still falling steadily. ‘I’ll stay here and make sure the animals are okay.’

‘You’ll freeze to death.’

Hélène shivered. ‘Don’t worry, I’ll get in the cart and pull the tarpaulin over me.’ She gave him a hug. ‘Be as quick as you can.’ Within seconds he had disappeared, obscured by the fluttering snow.

Hélène felt afraid and alone. She had no means of telling how long Francis had been gone and she was numb with cold. To pass the time, she stamped her feet and flailed her arms to keep warm; she tried singing to keep herself company, but it only made the oppressive silence worse. As Hélène stroked the snow from the eyelashes of the long-suffering bullocks, flakes melting as they landed on their glistening muzzles, it occurred to her she might be able to lead the animals backwards, forcing the wheel away from the bridge. Tentatively she took hold of the yoke and pushed hard, forcing the animals back, slipping and struggling to keep upright. The animals made an effort and the wagon moved a little but not enough to free the wheel.

As Hélène stumped up and down an idea formed in her mind. There was a plank in the cart that they used as a bench; if she could lodge it between the wheel and the wall, she might be able to lever the wheel free. Lifting the corner of the heavy tarpaulin, she tugged at the plank, which came away too quickly and she fell backwards into the soft snow. Shaking off the white powder, Hélène looked underneath the cart to see where she could get a good purchase. The best solution would have been to push the plank in from the front, but the bullocks made that impossible, so she decided to try from the rear. Pushing aside some snow-covered brambles, Hélène crawled under the back of the cart. She shoved the piece of wood as far as it would go between the wheel and the stones of the bridge. Using all her strength, she pulled its end towards her in an effort to prise the wheel away. She felt something give, the wheel shuddered for a moment, she experienced a surge of elation – until the plank broke and she fell forward into the snow. The sudden noise alarmed the bullocks, who jerked against their harness, shifting the cart so the wheel moved back a fraction, trapping Hélène's arm beneath it. She screamed in agony.

Hélène lay pinioned, the searing pain shooting along her nerves. She tried to pull her arm clear but the agony was so great her cry descended into gasping sobs. Forcing herself to ignore the pulsating throbbing Hélène pushed at the wheel, hopelessly, knowing it would not budge. She dug at the snow under her arm in an effort to create some space, but the icy ground was stony and hard. Hélène bit her lip hard to stifle a scream which would frighten the animals and make the situation worse. She wept, choking with frustration and pain.

Hélène closed her eyes; she had to wait for Francis and Agathe to rescue her. She called out, 'Agathe, Agathe. Help me, help me.' The snow continued to fall silently, impervious. She pleaded with the icy blackness, 'Please, Agathe, please come quickly. Come quickly. Hurry!'

The snow underneath Hélène was melting, the icy water seeping through to her skin. It was cold. The pain was intense. As Hélène closed her eyes, she thought she heard voices – a murmuring multitude of voices groaning: calling for warmth, for water, for sleep. In this indistinct cacophony Hélène thought she recognised her father; his words coming and going. As the pain numbed her into unconsciousness, a thought drifted into her mind. 'This is what our soldiers have to endure.' Irrationally angry, she called out, 'But you have each other! I'm alone in this silent, black night.'

Emile gave her a sad smile. 'Be grateful for the silence and a night sky that's not lit by shells.'

Hélène whispered, 'No, there are no bombs here, Papa.'

A host of white flakes danced ever downwards, downwards.

'But it's so cold. So cold. Cold ... Cold.'

Chapter Four

Autumn 1914

Philippe stretched out his stockinged feet towards the smoking fire. After weeks marching across France, the three days spent in this decrepit barn had seemed like heaven. Philippe twisted his boots to loosen the caked mud, trying not to think about tomorrow, when the regiment would move back to the Front.

Marius kicked open the door, the icy blast provoking a volley of curses. He threw his knapsack on the floor and hunkered down, glowering at the circle of men round the fire.

Firmin, a comrade from Saint-Agrève, who was picking lice out of the seams of his shirt, growled truculently. 'Where's our dinner?' Marius shrugged. 'I thought you'd gone to find out.'
Marius replied reluctantly, 'It's coming.'

'Why're you always so bloody miserable? We've got hot grub on the way. Honestly, there's no pleasing some people.' He turned to the others and winked. 'Spoilt by his new wife. Can't be happy without her loving arms around him.' Firmin leant over Marius and made smacking kissing noises.

Philippe spoke sharply, ‘Lay off Firmin. Let’s enjoy what we’ve got while we can.’

Firmin went over to the door. ‘Where in hell’s name’s the fucking booze? I’m parched.’

As he spoke, there was a clatter of pans as the rolling canteen arrived. The men jostled with each other, mess tins and mugs at the ready.

‘No need to push and shove, there’s plenty for everyone.’ With a smile of pleasure, Philippe recognised Emile’s voice and clapped him on the shoulder. Emile beamed. ‘I made sure your section was my last stop so I could eat with you.’

Marius interrupted roughly, ‘D'you have a letter for me?’

Emile looked crestfallen and said pacifically, ‘Let’s eat this nosh while it’s more or less hot.’

‘Yes or no?’ Marius barred Emile’s way into the barn.

Philippe took his arm. ‘Let the man in – he’s walked miles to bring us our rations.’

Marius glared at Emile as he emerged into the firelight. ‘Damn you!’ He grabbed his food and sat on his own, his back to the others.

Philippe spoke in an aside to Emile. ‘Lucinde’s going to have a baby and he’s desperate to know if it's arrived.’ The other men started to tease Marius, but Philippe shook his head and there was peace as they concentrated on eating the warm rice and watery stew.

After they had finished, Emile asked Philippe to follow him outside and handed him an envelope with a broad smile. 'I think you'll be pleased at the news.' Philippe raised his eyebrows as Emile nodded. 'I've already heard it from Mathilde.' Emile's smile faded and there was an aching longing in his voice. 'They seem to be more or less managing.' He stood head bowed, then sighed deeply. 'I'd better get going.' Emile seemed to shrink into his waterproof. 'I'm tired, Philippe. I'm dead beat – it's worse than harvest time.' He pushed his cart onto the muddy track. 'It's all this walking that does for me.' He shook his head. 'But I'd rather deliver food to the men than scrape up the sick and dead.' He shuddered. 'I've seen terrible things, injuries so awful you can't imagine – the poor souls'd be better off dead.' He smiled sadly at Philippe. 'Still, I mustn't complain.' After a long pause, Emile continued, 'I just hope the fighting here won't be as bad as it was in Lorraine. We lost so many good men.' Philippe stood watching as Emile disappeared into the lightless night.

Philippe waited until the others had bedded down before he opened the precious envelope. In the three months since they had left Saint-Agrève, Philippe had had two letters from Agathe, while Marius had not received any news from Lucinde. Philippe felt sorry for him; his moodiness did not irritate him as it did the other men; he understood why Marius was worried about Lucinde and why Firmin's smutty jokes must torment him.

When he was sure the others were asleep, Philippe crept out of his corner and crouched beside the embers of the fire, blowing on a handful of straw until it burst into flames. He silently slit open the envelope and stared with pleasure at Agathe's neat handwriting that tidily covered both sides of the paper. Philippe shut his eyes and held the letter close to his cheek; it still held a hint of Agathe's freshness and he could imagine her bent over the paper, biting her tongue with concentration as she wrote. Unable to wait any longer, his eyes ran rapidly over the page. The news that they were about to have a baby hit Philippe with a joy so powerful he could hardly breathe. Philippe read and reread the letter, searching for proof beyond the words themselves; her description of feeling sick each morning filled him with confidence, that she could no longer wear her usual skirts shook his heart with reassurance. Closing his eyes, he felt his whole body ache with an unbearable homesickness for the farm and for Agathe.

Fumbling in his eagerness, Philippe pulled out the worn photograph taken at his wedding. Agathe and the family group stared back at him. Philippe wished he had a photograph of his wife on her own; her picture was too small and in its distant stare there was little of the graceful contentment he loved. Tenderly, Philippe put the photograph and letter back in his pocket. He closed his eyes as images of their wedding flooded into his thoughts.

Their first night together had not been at all as he had imagined or wished. Once the family had left them alone which had come as a relief to them both, instead of falling into his arms as Philippe had hoped Agathe had walked up and down the room restlessly. The distance he had sensed in her throughout the day seemed to intensify. Agathe had then spent a long time saying her prayers and although Philippe knew she was devout, this had confused and unmanned him. When she did come to bed and at last he held her in his arms, Agathe's whole body stiffened, she became tense and unyielding. He had kissed her, tried to soften her rigidity with gentle words and caresses, but her anxiety only increased. Philippe became embarrassed by his upright penis and turned away. After a while, unable to suppress his fierce desire, he took her once more in his arms and held her close. He lay on top of her, but the stiff, taut body beneath him would not melt and he was afraid of hurting her.

Philippe kissed her gently. 'Don't worry Agathe, don't worry.' He lay beside her, listening to her dry sobs, holding her hand, murmuring, 'It'll be all right. Don't worry; we just need time to get used to each other.'

During the long night Philippe made several attempts to make love to Agathe – always thwarted by the same frigid response. In the morning they were forced to endure the family bringing the newlyweds soup, according to the traditions of the Plateau, and listen to their rough, well-meaning ribaldry. It was only after three such tormented nights that Agathe said to Philippe, 'Please do what you have to,' and their marriage was consummated. Since that time Philippe had tried to awaken in Agathe some of the passion he felt for her but had reluctantly come to realise that Agathe only submitted to his lovemaking because she saw it as the unavoidable duty of a wife. In the weeks he had been away, he comforted himself with the thought that they had only had a month together; after the war it would be different.

Philippe turned on his side, determined to get some sleep – and groaned. Agathe had written to say that Lucinde had lost her baby and asked him to break the news to Marius. Philippe sighed; it was difficult enough to prevent Marius from acting in ways which would lead to trouble, the death of his child was certain to make him even harder to manage.

Their corporal, Preyssat, woke the section well before dawn. 'Decent coffee, a sure sign there's going to be hell to pay.' Firmin swore as he downed the hot liquid. Philippe winced as the straps of his heavy pack settled on sore shoulders made more sensitive during the respite of the last three days. The men threw their coffee grounds onto the remains of the fire and reluctantly filed out into a cold, wet drizzle; all that could be heard was the clink of billy cans against spades and the squelching of boots on the muddy road.

It was ten o'clock before the long line of men was allowed to pause in the shelter of a small wood. The rain had cleared and the unploughed fields were steaming under warm sunshine, an apparently normal morning except for the distant booming of big guns. They stood smoking, there was nothing to eat and the men were tired, hungry and thirsty. Philippe half moved towards Marius but thought better of it; everyone was preoccupied, fearful of the imminent attack. A runner came up to the group of officers and the men watched intently as they read their instructions, pointing at a farm some 400 metres away, outlined against the sky on the crest of a small hill.

Firmin took a final drag at his cigarette before throwing it on the ground. 'I bet that'll be where we're headed.'

Philippe narrowed his eyes. 'God help us if there's any Boche in there. There's bugger-all cover.'

There was a ripple of movement as the men readjusted their packs and picked up their rifles. Preyssat came over. 'Our orders are to take that farm. Strategic position, et cetera, et cetera. The 1st and 3rd Companies'll make the first attack, then we'll follow.'

'Any sign of the Prussians?'

'We've got cover from our seventy-fives that should blast them to hell, then we'll go in.' As he spoke, the artillery from the rear of the wood opened fire and the soldiers watched as great chunks of masonry crumpled as the farm sustained shell after shell. With a great yell, the first wave of infantry set off across the fields, running and jumping across ditches. They had reached about half way when an involuntary gasp burst from the waiting men as a machine gun started to shoot from the door of the farm, mowing down the line of soldiers as easily as a scythe cuts through grass.

'Bloody hell, oh sweet Jesus!' Firmin's voice was barely audible over the deafening cacophony of the bombardment and the pattering of the machine gun.

Their corporal took a deep breath. 'Okay, boys, time to go. Run, take cover, then keep running.'

Philippe's mind went blank, he started to jog forward as fast as his heavy pack would allow. He could hear the staccato spitting of the machine gun, three men in front of him fell; he passed them without looking, his only thought to keep going. There was a sudden rush of air past his ear; the shell hit the ground several metres behind him. A small part of his brain registered this as good; he was safe from the German bombs, at least. To his right he could see the thin streak of bullets as the machine gun panned towards him. Men fell to their knees and Philippe hurled himself flat on the ground, hearing the uncanny whistle of the bullets as they passed over his head. He got up and ran on; stumbling over the bodies of men sprawled on the tussocky grass. He threw himself on the ground again and looked up at the farm, still 100 metres away. Five of the first wave of soldiers were sidling round the farmhouse wall towards the doorway; as they lobbed in their grenades there was a great rush of dust and debris and the machine gun was silenced. Philippe got to his feet and raced up the slope. A bullet whistled by, he heard a scream and one of his companions fell sideways, clutching his thigh. Philippe kept on running.

Around the farm there was a low wall; Philippe crouched in its shelter along with Firmin and Marius, all three breathing heavily. Peering over the bodies of two dead soldiers, he saw a German sharpshooter firing, his gun steadied on the sill of a first-floor window. Sliding his rifle between the two corpses, Philippe took aim and saw the German's arms fly up as he crashed backwards.

The interior of the farm was now silent. There was a shout, 'We've made it, lads,' and the men got up, stumbling over the rubble, hugging and slapping each other.

The rear half of the farm's kitchen looked strangely normal – a sideboard with copper pans, a print of the Virgin Mary tacked to the wall – the rest was devastation. Three Germans lay dead, their bright blood still oozing across the stone floor, their machine gun a tangle of mangled metal.

Philippe ran through the house, recognising with a shudder the corpse of the sharpshooter he had killed. From an upstairs window Philippe looked down over the fields back to the wood where they had stood smoking less than an hour ago. He held on to the lintel of the window and retched. The pale autumnal sun shone, the tranquil scene appeared peaceful, but bodies lay everywhere, their bright red trousers standing out against the gold of the uncut corn. When he returned to the kitchen, Philippe heard Preyssat giving the men their instructions.

'We've got to dig in, dig in deep and fast. The Germans are bound to attack as soon as they can, before they think we can get established.' He looked round, and bit his lip: only eleven men stood before him. 'Is this everyone?' He did not dare wait for an answer. 'Any sign of a cellar?'

Philippe pointed to a door. 'It's not very big.'

Marius spoke with cold fury, 'We can't hold on. There's not enough of us. We need to fall back.'

Firmin signaled to the men, who threw down their rifles. 'Let's get the fuck out of here.'

Philippe stood in their way. 'Don't be so bloody stupid. If you leave, you'll be killed before you've gone twenty metres. We've got to stay put 'til our artillery's cleared the German line ahead of us.'

As he spoke, the ground shuddered and the men dived into the cellar. A shell hit what remained of the roof of the farm; it was quickly followed by another, and another, the building above them disintegrating in suffocating blasts of dust. For an hour the bombardment continued, each shell remorselessly tearing away at the fabric of the farm, the noise so loud it was impossible to think, dust caking mouths and suffocating nostrils, rubble drubbing on the floor above them, making it creak and bow ominously downward. For two hours the eleven men sat jammed together, their knees up to their chins, unable to speak or move.

When the bombardment appeared to have ended, the men remained where they were, ears alert to the unnerving silence. At last Marius made a move. 'I'm getting out of here.' Preyssat tried to restrain him but Marius elbowed himself free and crawled out. 'Fucking hell! There's bugger-all left.' One by one the men struggled out of their shelter, limbs creaking from cramp as they stretched. All that remained of the farm was a heap of rubble, the odd black pan and the bright white of broken crockery the only indication that it had once been a human habitation. The air was thick with dust; each man was covered in a ghostly powder through which stared raw red eyes. Marius got hold of the corporal by the arm. ‘We can’t stay here. We’ll be slaughtered.’

The corporal waved his hands over the fields that lay between the remains of the farm and the French positions hundreds of metres down the hill. The setting sun shone tenderly on the bright uniforms of the corpses, occasionally a groan could be heard or a hand waved feebly. ‘That’s our alternative, Marius.’ He looked round at his men. ‘We’ve got to make a better shelter – and wait for night to fall. I’m sure the regiment’ll make contact.’

All night the exhausted men crouched, cramped and crowded, heads grazing the beams above, unable to sleep. The corporal tried to raise their spirits. ‘Someone from HQ’ll soon let us know what’s going on.’

‘Like when?’ Marius’s voice was truculent.

‘And when’ll they bring us some fucking food and water?’ Firmin's voice was hard and bitter.

The corporal tried to sound encouraging. ‘If they don’t come tonight, they’re bound to come tomorrow night.’

‘Tomorrow night!’ Marius’s voice rose an octave. ‘I don't want to die like a bloody rat trapped in this blasted pit.’ The atmosphere in the tiny space was murderous.

The corporal looked at his watch. ‘Time for the next two to go on lookout. Marius and Firmin, it’s your turn.’

Firmin swore. Philippe said quietly, ‘I’ll swap with Firmin, if that’s okay.’ The corporal nodded, relieved, and the two men wriggled their way out of the entrance.

Philippe and Marius took up their posts, grateful for the chill evening air and a damp mist which soothed their dust-caked throats. They stood back to back for several minutes without speaking, Philippe looking across at the German line, an almost indistinguishable shadow across the field ahead, Marius looking back down the slope, still dotted with the dark forms of dead men.

Philippe cleared his throat and spoke gently, 'Marius, it's no good upsetting everyone, it just makes the rest of the chaps angry and then it's worse for all of us, including you.'

'If they can accept what's happening, I can't!' Marius paused for a moment as both men stared ahead into the darkness, when he did speak his voice was low and determined. 'I can't stand it.' Philippe did not reply. 'It's not that I'm the only one who's afraid – we're all afraid, or we should be.' Marius waved his hand towards the inert corpses. 'Look at those poor bastards. We've every reason to be shit scared.' Again he paused. 'It's that I can't see any sense in all this destruction.'

Philippe took time before replying, 'I agree there's no sense, but we haven't a choice, Marius.'

'Everyone's got the choice to live or die. I don't have the words to explain it properly, but where is this liberty that we were taught is so important when we're ordered to walk to our deaths, to be mowed down by a machine-gun?'

Philippe sighed deeply. 'It's best not to think about it.' He gave a cynical laugh. 'I try hard not to think about anything except how to survive another day.' He paused, 'If I allowed myself to question why we're here, I'd go mad.' The two men watched the moon coming and going behind the clouds. 'Marius, we've no choice. We're soldiers and have to obey orders. If we don't, everything'll fall apart and we'll all get killed.' He waited for a reply but none came. 'Don't aggravate the situation, Marius. You can't go it alone.'

'Bugger the others.' Marius was terse. 'I don't give a fuck.' He was quiet for a while, then said softly, emphasising each word, 'I can't take much more of this.' He paused again, 'I have to get back to Lucinde.'

Philippe did not reply and the two men continued to watch as the moon came and went, illuminating the desolate landscape, then plunging it into darkness. Philippe remembered the letter in his pocket; his fingers sought the envelope. Touching it, he felt safe, it was his talisman against evil. He frowned as he remembered Agathe's other message and looked across at Marius, his back straight against the moonlit sky. Philippe hesitated, wondering how many times he would have the opportunity to talk to Marius away from the suffocating closeness of the patrol. He opened his mouth to speak, then thought better of it. He could not bring himself to add to the despair of his comrade; he must wait until they were somewhere calmer, safer – a place where a man had the space to begin to think rationally.

It was just before dawn when they heard the sound of footsteps. The regimental runner handed a note to the corporal, who read it and blenched. He did not meet the eyes of the men staring at him.

'We're to push forward to clear the lines ahead.'

The men swore. Marius stamped his feet with incomprehension. 'I don't bloody believe it!'

The corporal dropped his voice, muttering under his breath to the dispatch bearer. 'We've lost about a hundred men – we simply can't do it.'

The soldier replied briskly, 'We'll be sending up reinforcements. The best way to defend this position is to attack. We need to clear the area around it; otherwise it'll become a sitting target.'

'Too bloody late, it's already a fucking sitting target.' Firmin swore.

Preyssat demanded tersely, 'Why isn't our artillery returning fire?'

The runner shook his head. 'Too dangerous. Because you're on a hill and the Germans are so close, the chances are our shells would hit you and not them. They won't take the chance. It'll have to be an infantry charge, there's no option.'

More footsteps were heard and a low shout. 'Anyone want some grub?' The men scrabbled to get out and found three men struggling to clamber over the rubble, loaded with sacks of bread and jerry cans of water. Emile smiled with relief when he saw Philippe. 'Thank God you've made it. I was really worried when I heard what'd happened to the 86th. Sorry we couldn't get to you boys earlier.'

The men bustled round him, tearing off chunks of the tough bread and stuffing it into their mouths. Emile's eyes moistened as he caught sight of

Marius and reached into his pocket, waving a pale blue envelope in his face. 'At last, the letter you've been waiting for.' He beamed as Marius snatched it from him.

Philippe's heart sank; he wished he had made more effort to prepare Marius for the bad news. For a moment, as he watched Marius hungrily read the first few sentences, he hoped the letter was simply a love letter written in happy anticipation of the baby's birth, but as Marius's face suddenly contorted, his agonised expression told Philippe he had learnt the worst. Marius pushed aside the bread Emile was holding out to him, flung himself away from the group and stumbled across the rubble to the remains of the barn. Philippe watched as Marius bashed his hand against the jagged stones until blood came.

The other men stood watching. 'What the hell's got into him?'

Philippe shook his head. 'His wife was expecting a baby, I expect it's to do with that.'

Firmin shrugged. 'Is that all? Why's he making such a fuss, there'll be plenty of time to fucking make babies if we get back from this lot with our tackle in one piece.' The other men sniggered.

Philippe went over to Marius and put his hand on his shoulder. 'Bad news?'

Marius turned towards him. 'Bad as it can get. Lucinde's lost the baby and,' he paused, struggling to control his emotions, 'she can't have any more. Finished.'

Firmin called over, 'So what's so bad about that? From the way you're taking on I thought she'd run off with someone else.' He turned to the others. 'Anything's better than finding your woman's been playing around and not knowing whose bastard you've been landed with.'

To prevent more trouble, Preyssat called out, 'Eat up, men, these fellows have to get back.'

Emile hurriedly collected the empty cans. 'We've been told to pick up the rest of the poor buggers tonight, but I'm afraid we'll be lucky to find any alive. Hot days and cold nights does for them pretty quick.' Emile grasped Philippe's hand. 'Good luck, son. See you soon.' Looking back at Marius, Emile said sadly, 'I wish I hadn't brought that godforsaken letter. It's really upset him.' Philippe could hear the clattering of the cans for some time, then silence.

***

Philippe hoped the corporal would send him on lookout with Marius again, but he was allocated a later watch with the young soldier, Jean, who was barely conscious with fear. It was a relief to be outside the foetid shelter and Philippe took several deep breaths to clear his lungs. The sky was an impenetrable void and occasional clouds floated in a dignified fashion across the moon. The night looked like any other, but all Philippe's senses were vibrating. He crawled on his belly to the crest of the rubble, his eyes probing the darkness where each shadow hid a danger and the gentle breeze brought with it a strong whiff of putrefaction. On the slope leading down from the farm towards the French lines, Philippe could just make out shadowy figures moving from place to place. He smiled, thinking of Emile with affection; he had come to respect and love the gentle ways of his father-in-law. As time wore on, the stretcher-bearers moved towards the crest of the hill, bending to collect their load and moving slowly back down the hillside with their burdens. The night was eerily still and the earth exhaled a silent sigh as the mist rose from the still-warm ground into the frosty air. Lulled by the melancholy calm, a mixture of nostalgia and exhaustion swept over Philippe. He sat, distracted by his thoughts, as the moon sailed from behind a cloud, clearly illuminating two men silhouetted on the brow of the hill; they were crouching down, linked together by the black mass of their wounded colleague on its stretcher. As Philippe focused, there were two quick shots and the men fell to the ground. Cocking his rifle, Philippe fired. For a moment there was silence, a stillness broken by an enemy machine gun spattering the intervening no-man's land with bullets.

In the glittering moonlight, Philippe looked for the two fallen men and heard a cry he knew must come from Emile. Without thinking, he put down his rifle and started to clamber down the rubble when he felt a hand grasp his belt and pull him back.

'What the fuck's happening? What's all the noise about?'

Philippe glared at his corporal, their faces inches apart. He could only stutter, 'The bastards, the bastards. Can't the swine let us collect our bloody dead and wounded?' Preyssat shook him; Philippe swore. 'I'm sure they've got Vernot, my father-in-law. I've got to get him.'

The corporal tightened his grip. 'Don't be such a bloody idiot, Faugeron. You'd be killed before you'd gone ten metres.' Philippe continued to struggle until the corporal punched him hard in the stomach and he bent over in pain. 'You're not going anywhere. I need everyone I've got for tomorrow.'

Philippe lay on the damp ground, clutching his belly. In the silence he could hear a long-drawn-out groan he was sure was uttered by Emile. Philippe struggled to get up, but the corporal still gripped him. His voice softened, 'I'm sorry, Faugeron, but there's no point in getting yourself killed as well.'

Philippe could not hide his tears. The corporal squeezed his shoulder. 'The Germans're expecting an attack; they probably thought they were firing at some scouts.' He took hold of Philippe's rifle. 'Come with me, Faugeron. It's time for the next watch.'

Philippe could not sleep. With his rational mind he knew it was impossible, but he could hear Emile calling his name, crying for help. He silently cursed the corporal, who slept across the entrance to the dugout.

Before dawn Preyssat woke the men and they took up positions behind the remaining fragments of walls; it was cold and damp, there was no moon. With a sharp blast of his whistle, the corporal gave the order and the men ran forward, bayoneted rifles at the ready. After 50 metres Philippe saw two of his comrades felled by the bullets raining around them. He dropped to the ground, searching for some cover, crawling forward with Firmin on his left, Marius on his right. As Philippe looked up he saw the corporal hurl a grenade into the enemy's trench, now only 30 metres away. The ground around him shuddered with the force of the explosion and when the dust had cleared, Philippe saw Preyssat spread-eagled on the ground. Firing was now coming thick and fast from the German line. Two men from his section were making their way back to the farm; one fell screaming, another clasped his head – but there was no head to clasp.

Philippe lay as close to the earth as he could, his mouth full of mud and grass. He edged his head upwards and saw Firmin and Marius crawling backwards, leaving him behind. He tried to shout at them, but the staccato clatter of small-arms fire, now backed by the visceral booming of big guns, stifled his words. Philippe too began to crawl backwards, trying to find some cover against the crepitating volley of bullets. His feet came up against something soft and he heard a groan. Twisting round, Philippe found himself lying beside Emile, who put out his hand. 'Save yourself, Philippe. I'm done for anyway.'

The noise was terrifying. Shells burst into the hillside, sending up huge spurts of earth and rock. Philippe slithered round Emile, took hold of his boots and tried to pull Emile behind him as he crawled up the hill. A man ran past, screaming, 'They're coming, they're coming!' Philippe looked up; ahead, a straggling line of men was advancing towards him, already close enough for him to see their faces, glistening bayonets leveled. Philippe looked round quickly; the farm and its precarious defence was still over 50 metres away, Emile groaned at his feet. He bent down and tried to pick up Emile, who moaned with pain. Philippe knew he would never make it if he carried the wounded man back with him. He looked ahead at the advancing enemy, now so near Philippe could hear their panting breath. Philippe let Emile down gently and, with a roar of frustration and rage, ran as fast as he could up the hill to the farm. As he threw himself behind the rubble, he fired his rifle, killing the German soldier who was about to step over Emile. In a wild fury he fired again, another German fell. He scrambled backwards into the cellar as a French machine gun opened fire and two more Germans tumbled forward, covering the body of Emile.

Chapter Five

Winter 1914–Autumn 1915

'It's too dangerous. What if you got trapped too?' Francis shivered as he looked at Hélène's motionless body.

'Don't be so feeble! If we don't get her out soon she'll die of cold – and I'm not strong enough to hold the bullocks.' Agathe was already sliding under the back of the cart. Francis twisted the rope round his wrists and urged the animals forward. 'Pull as hard as you can.' There was silence as he tugged on the rope, his feet sliding across the icy snow, the bullocks unable to find a purchase on the slippery ground.

'I can't get a grip!'

'Keep trying. It's our only hope.'

Francis despaired, long minutes passed until he heard Agathe's muffled cry, 'She's free! For God's sake don't let it drop back.' Francis's heart bounded with relief when he saw Agathe's bulky form emerge, pulling an inert Hélène after her.

'How is she?' In the light of the lantern Hélène's face was a livid white, her eyes closed, an unresponsive bundle of dark clothes against the drifts of snow.

Agathe felt her sister's pulse. 'Alive but unconscious. Let's have one more go at freeing the cart, see if we can avoid carrying her all the way home.'

They made a few attempts to get the cold, frightened animals to press backwards but still the end of the axle would not budge. The snow continued to fall in thick sticky flakes as Francis struggled to lift Hélène's dead weight onto his shoulders. Agathe unharnessed the bullocks and they set off down the hill, the small pool of light sending long darting shadows that confused and frightened the animals. Agathe edged forward slowly; fearful she would fall and damage her precious baby. The darkness beyond the wall of illuminated snow was disorientating, the soundless night pressed in on them.

Francis laid Hélène on a pile of blankets by the fire and Agathe pulled off her coat, its sleeve stiff with blood. She tenderly ran her finger along the thin arm and knew at once the bone was broken. 'Get the goose down quilts and Maman's smelling salts.' Agathe gently swathed her sister in the soft duvets and held her in her arms, trying to thaw Hélène with her own body's warmth. 'Now warm up some milk and put in a good drop of brandy.' Bright yellow flames flew upwards as Francis threw more logs on the fire.

Hélène winced as the sting of ammonia hit her nostrils, Agathe and Francis looked at each other with relief. As Hélène opened her eyes and saw her sister's face bending over her, she began to cry. 'Agathe, thank God!' Her teeth chattered. 'I thought I would die. My arm hurts. It was so cold.' Hélène sobbed into her sister's bosom while Agathe fondly stroked the springy, wet hair away from her forehead

***

The snow had given way to a persistent penetrating rain, which swept down from the Mézenc. Every day Agathe and Francis wrestled with the heavy clods of earth, wrenching turnips and beetroot from the sodden soil. Each evening Agathe would sink heavily onto a chair, too exhausted to speak as she sat supporting the weight of her unborn child. Watching her, Hélène's heart twisted with guilt, fretting at the encumbering splints on her arm.

Hélène was the first to spot the Maire as he pushed his bicycle up the track to the farm. As the acrid taste of vomit soured her lips, Hélène leant against the barn for support. Everyone knew it was the duty of the Maire to tell a family of a death and in the last five months dozens of families around Saint-Agrève had received his dreaded visit. Unblinking, mesmerised, , Hélène stood watching as he propped his bicycle against the gatepost, wiped the sweat from his brow, gulped down a swift swig of brandy before pulling a slim envelope from the inside pocket of his coat. It was only when she saw him straighten up and walk steadfastly across the terrace that Hélène came out of her trance and ran into the byre.

Her white face and huge eyes told Agathe the news. The pail of pigswill fell over, the smelly mess dribbling over the straw. She gasped, 'But who?' Both girls tottered into the farmyard. Hélène could see Francis on the far hillside piling up branches; she waved at him until he dropped his load and started running. In the kitchen Mathilde was kneading dough, her arms white with flour. When she saw the bloodless fear in her daughters' eyes she sat down, a cloud of flour rising, then settling softly over the table. All three women fixed their gaze on the door. They waited an eternity until the Maire knocked and came in; the envelope in his hand. There was a long moment of stillness; none of the women would take the proffered letter, piercing him with their stares. This unearthly immobility snapped as the Maire walked towards Mathilde and laid his hand consolingly on her shoulder. She tautened and shrunk away, letting out a long diminishing wail, 'Oh no. Please God, no!' The Maire gently placed the envelope on the table in front of her and sat down.

'I'm so sorry Madame Vernot. Emile was a good man. One of the best in the whole area.'

Neither sister spoke, hypnotised by the fragile pale blue envelope. Mathilde repeated over and over in a low monotone, 'Oh God, please don't let it be true. Please God. Please God.'

Francis burst into the kitchen. Hélène took his arm, saying softly, 'Papa.' He let out a groan and burst into tears. Agathe brought out a bottle of cordial and handed glasses of the strong spirit to Mathilde and the Maire.

The four Vernots avoided looking at the envelope, which remained unopened until long after the Maire had left. Eventually Francis rose and, picking up the flimsy paper, carried it to the light of the window. He read softly, '*Emile Vernot, fallen in battle on the night of the 20th November. He died for the glory of France.*' He slapped the flimsy paper. 'That's all. "Died for the glory of France."' He swung round, gripping the doorpost. 'Glory, what bloody glory?'

For hours they sat round the table unspeaking, unmoving, except for Agathe, who refilled their glasses with cordial and their mugs with strong coffee. Eventually Agathe drew herself up. 'We'll have to prepare the wake. And there'll have to be a Mass.'

Hélène was querulous through her tears, 'What's the point of a wake when Papa's not going to be buried here?'

Mathilde, who had remained dry-eyed, staring down at hands still white with flour, covered her face and began to cry, terrible wrenching sobs. 'Never to see him again. Lying so far from home.'

Tears streamed down the faces of Hélène and Francis, while Agathe tried to comfort her mother.

Later that evening groups of neighbours came to sit with them. Little was said; even Madame Faugeron was subdued as she recounted the grim tally. 'Almost fifty dead from here or hereabouts. And another thirty badly wounded.' She shook her head. 'So many good men lost in such a short time. God help us if this continues much longer.'

A week later a letter arrived from Philippe. It contained little apart from condolences and praise for Emile, whom Philippe had come to love as a father. When Agathe had finished reading, Hélène frowned through her tears. 'Why hasn't he told us what happened to Papa?'

Agathe folded the letter carefully. She spoke softly so Mathilde would not hear. 'Perhaps he thinks it's better we don't know. Remember Francis might be called up.'

'But that's more than a year from now!' Hélène whispered violently. 'The war's bound to be over by then.'

Agathe shook her head sadly. 'Only God can tell.'

***

It was almost April. The cherry blossom filled the valley with their soft pink clouds, and the chestnut trees, haughty and magnificent, held aloft their pale candelabras. Agathe was big with child. She pumped the butter churn slowly up and down, moaning with the effort – suddenly she sat down, clutching her swollen belly. Mathilde rose from her chair by the fire and, half walking, half stumbling, went to find Francis, who was with Hélène sowing rye in the only field they had managed to plough.

'Get Madame Bret quickly, Agathe's started.'

Francis set off up the hill at a jog while Hélène ran into the house. Mathilde's bed was prepared with fresh hay covered by old sheets. When it was ready Agathe went upstairs and laid down, her forehead was beaded with sweat as she grasped hold of her mother's hand and moaned piteously. Hélène busied herself below heating cauldrons of water.

Three hours later Agathe's cries were fierce and frequent. Night had already darkened the sky when Hélène finally caught sight of Francis as he helped Madame Bret down the steep slope, carrying a bundle of cloths and a large canvas bag. With the curtest of greetings, the midwife went straight to Agathe, and a few minutes later Mathilde came down into the kitchen, smiling wanly, her eyes tired. 'She'll be fine. These things have to take their course.'

From time to time Madame Bret called for more hot water. Agathe's shrieks of pain came faster and faster. Then suddenly there was a new sound, the long wail of an infant inhaling its first distasteful breath of air. Hélène rushed up the staircase. 'Is it a girl or a boy? Can we come in?'

Madame Bret's voice was stern. 'You wait 'til we're ready.'

As the family trooped into the bedroom, Madame Bret stood beside the bed, her hands on her hips. 'It's a girl.'

There was something in her tone that made Hélène frown. 'We're very happy it's a girl.'

Madame Bret returned to folding the unused sheets, making sure there was a disapproving crack each time she shook out the folds. She muttered to herself, 'Let's hope she'll have better luck next time.'

Hélène felt a stab of envy as she saw her sister lying with the tiny infant on her breast. Agathe looked pale and utterly spent, but her satisfied smile made Hélène wince. Annoyed with herself, Hélène rushed forward to kiss Agathe and gently moved aside the soft woollen blanket wrapped round the new baby. ‘She’s so pretty! Can I hold her?’

Clicking her teeth, Madame Bret shooed the family out of the room. ‘You leave the child alone; it needs to be with its mother. And let her rest, she’s exhausted.’

Francis grumbled under his breath, ‘And let’s have something to eat.’

Mathilde had gone to bed. Madame Bret was asleep on a chair upstairs, packed and ready to leave as soon as it was light. The twins sat in the glow from the fire, a pitcher of wine on the table between them. Hélène spoke wistfully, ‘It must be wonderful to see your baby and hold it for the first time.' She lowered her voice. 'After all the unhappiness we've been through it's even more of a miracle.’ She nodded towards the end of the table. ‘It’s so sad Papa’s not here. He’d have been so happy.’ Hélène cast a quick glance at her brother. 'I still can't accept he won't be coming back.'

There was a long silence. Francis sighed. ‘Having a baby may be wonderful, but it'll make everything much harder. Now the worst of the snow’s over, the ground’s beginning to soften and soon the really heavy work’ll be about to begin.’ Francis looked across at Hélène. ‘It's hard to believe this time last year Papa and I did it all while Maman did the cooking and Agathe looked after the animals.’

Hélène added softly, 'And I sneaked off into the barn to read.'

Francis gave her a rare smile. 'We didn't mind. We were proud of how well you were doing at school.' Hélène looked deep into the fire. Her education had ended when the men went away; there had been no question of it being otherwise. 'Everything's changed. Papa's no longer with us, Maman sits grieving all day – and now Agathe's got the baby to look after.' Francis carried on talking in a forced, determinedly neutral tone, 'And next spring ...' but his lips quivered and he could not continue.

Alarmed by his distress, Hélène took his hand. 'I'm sure it won't come to that.'

Francis looked away, shaking his head. 'Better not think about it.'

Hélène glanced across at her brother, his face illuminated in the yellow gleam of the fire, noticing for the first time how much he had changed; the chubbiness of boyhood had melted away and the planes and shadows of a man's face had appeared. Her brother had become a good-looking young man – Hélène felt an overwhelming rush of pride and love for him. She said softly, 'We'll manage.'

Francis clasped her hand. 'We'll have to.'

***

A year had passed since the women of Saint-Agrève had said farewell to their men. There was no more talk of an early end to the war, and a besieged hopelessness had crept over the countryside. A special Mass was held to mark the anniversary.

The Curé's voice resonated round the church, remorseless and interminable. He commanded the assembled women to be as courageous as their brave men serving at the Front; he paid tribute to the 'blessed' soldiers who had made the supreme sacrifice so France would emerge a better, more Christian, more Catholic country. It was an extended version of the sermon he gave every week and Hélène was bored and irritated. As she looked round the cheerless church with its rows of bowed hats and headscarves, Hélène thought she caught a fleeting smile light up the face of Nathalie Peyrard, who was sitting across the aisle. Intrigued, she bent forward, looking out from under the brim of her hat, and intercepted a rapid exchange of glances between Nathalie and her brother. Hélène could not help smiling to see how the girl's cheeks flamed as she quickly buried her head in her prayer book.

Outside the church, Hélène made a point of nodding to Nathalie as the couple stood in tongue-tied silence at the bottom of the church steps and decided not to join Mathilde and Agathe as they made their way from family to family, receiving sympathy with an embrace and murmured acknowledgement.

Hélène found Lucinde sitting on the edge of the fountain swearing at Tomas. 'If you pinch me again I'll beat you black and blue!' Tomas stuck out his tongue and loped off, smirking. Lucinde threw a pebble after him and sat swinging her feet backwards and forwards, clearly in a foul mood.

'Life's so bloody dreary.' She looked dolefully at Agathe, who was surrounded by women admiring the newborn. 'Every baby reminds me of the little boy I lost.'

Hélène nodded sympathetically. 'Berthe's lovely, but she's my sister's child not mine.' The phrase emerged tinged with a bitterness she had not intended and Hélène fell silent, not wanting to put into words the growing envy she despised in herself.

'It's hard to accept someone else's happiness.'

Hélène squeezed her friend's arm, 'Agathe's hardly happy, Lucinde. She worries all the time about Philippe.'

'And I worry about Marius. I don't know what to make of his letters. He seems so angry with everyone; he even says nasty things about Philippe, who's supposed to be his friend.' Lucinde looked sideways at Hélène and changed tack. 'He keeps saying he can't stand it any longer and wants to come home.' There was a long pause; Lucinde sighed deeply. 'A year's such a long time.' She laughed emptily. 'How're we supposed to manage without sex for a whole year?' There was another heavy silence, she bent towards Hélène and lowered her voice, 'Not everyone's living like a nun, y'know; in fact, some girls are enjoying themselves while their husbands are out of the way.' Hélène looked shocked; Lucinde gave a dry, humourless laugh. 'Don't look like that – we're young, it's natural to want a man.' Her voice dropped even further, 'Solange, Firmin Arsac's wife, is banging the blacksmith whenever his wife's back's turned.'

Hélène looked disbelieving. Lucinde nodded vigorously. 'Everyone knows about it.' She continued, 'And Florence Dufour's pregnant, anyone can see that, but no one knows who's the father. Could be one of three or four possibilities, as far as I can tell.'

'That's dreadful! What'll their husbands do when they hear about it?'

Lucinde shrugged. 'Why should they hear? No one's going to tell them.' She stood up, suddenly resentful. 'Our lives are so bloody hard, we're doing all the men's work as well as our own, surely a little bit of fun isn't too much to ask.'

Hélène looked sharply at her friend – and bit her tongue.

Lucinde pulled Hélène to her feet. 'What about you? No point in waiting for that Roland, he's got plenty of girls running after him in Privas from what I've heard.'

Hélène looked away from her friend to the empty square, deserted and dusty in the summer sun. She said pensively, 'I'm fine. I've no time to worry about that sort of thing anyway.' As she walked home, Hélène admitted to herself that neither of these statements had been true.

That night Hélène dreamt she was alone with the blacksmith in the sweltering heat of his smithy, his long sinewy arms holding her naked body close to his bare chest – and awoke aching with the same feverish desire Roland had aroused in her. As the dream faded, Hélène was overcome with disgust - sex should be an expression of love, not some animal urge that could be satisfied by any male. She remembered with revulsion her painful, banal encounter with Roland and was angry that he had taken her without any pretence at either affection or romance. She did not regret the loss of her virginity – the passing of time had made it seem irrelevant – but resented the fact that this pivotal event had been so disappointing and unsatisfactory. As Agathe murmured in her sleep, Hélène turned away in irritation; she could not imagine her sister having carnal cravings and, as for Philippe, it was inconceivable he would ever be unfaithful to Agathe.

***

In September, over a year since they had left for the Front, the soldiers of the 86th were allowed their first 'permission' – six days' leave when they could return home. By the time the news reached Les Laysses, their arrival was imminent and, in spite of Madame Faugeron's insistence that Philippe (and Agathe) should stay with them, Agathe was adamant Philippe should spend his leave at Les Laysses. A plump chicken was killed, everything that could be scrubbed was scrubbed, Agathe baked furiously; Francis grumbled half seriously as he swilled the yard that it would be a lot more useful if he threshed the corn.

Agathe insisted on going on her own to fetch Philippe from the station – the walk back to the farm would give them a little time to themselves after a year of separation. Hélène understood her reasons – but resented being prevented from taking part in the town's welcome for its returning soldiers. She reluctantly followed Francis to the threshing floor, moodily watching out for the couple. At last Francis let out a yell, 'He's here!' Hélène threw down her flail and ran impetuously down the track; as she got closer she could see Agathe and Philippe had their arms around each other and did not appear to be particularly pleased to see her.

As Francis and Hélène circled round the couple like two eager dogs welcoming their master, Hélène was shocked to see the changes a year at the Front had wrought. Philippe was no longer the gauche young man of a year ago; he looked thin and wiry, his face gaunt, the sun burnt cheekbones contrasting with the pale, shadowy areas where his chin and cheeks had been recently shaved. His mouth smiled often but there was a distant sadness in his eyes. As they reached the gate of the farmyard he gently disengaged from Agathe. 'You've kept the most important person to the last! Where's my baby girl?'

Mathilde stood on the threshold holding Berthe, dressed in her christening robe and wearing a fine lace cap for the occasion. Philippe bent over, tickling her chin, afraid to take the precious burden that Mathilde held out to him.

He turned to Agathe, his eyes full of tears. 'I daren't hold her. After a year's soldiering I'm afraid to handle anything more delicate than a rifle or a sixty-pound pack!' He kissed Agathe and turned again to his daughter, a brown finger tracing the soft roundness of her cheeks. Hélène felt a deep pang of jealousy as she saw the tender lovingness in the eyes of Berthe's parents as they held hands, gazing with delighted awe at their daughter. She turned away, grasping the rough stones of the wall for support as the force of her envy made her feel faint.

Before the family sat down to eat, Agathe asked Philippe to sit in Emile's chair. Philippe stroked its worn back and shook his head; there was a long silence, which became awkward as Philippe stood, his head bowed. He looked across at Mathilde, his eyes red. 'I'm so sorry Emile's not here with us.'

Throughout the meal Philippe could not take his eyes off Agathe and Berthe, from time to time a small smile flitted across his face. Hélène felt excluded as the husband and wife exchanged glances, their looks turning simultaneously towards the crib where their child lay, her tiny hands gesticulating pointlessly.

After they had finished eating, Philippe lit his pipe and Francis leant forward, stumbling over his words in his eagerness. 'Tell us what it's really like?' He gave a deprecating laugh. 'Remember last year, when I was so keen to go to war?' Philippe did not reply but turned away slightly, his expression closed. 'After Papa died, that all changed.' Francis stopped. 'Actually my feelings had altered long before that - but when we got the letter,' again he paused, glancing at his mother who sat in silent grief, staring at the fire, 'and it's talk of "glory", it made me feel sick.' He stood up abruptly, his voice breaking, 'In six months I'll be called up -

unless it's all over.' He leant over Philippe. 'What d'you think are the chances?'

Philippe winced, his face tight, eyes partly closed, and Agathe told Francis sharply to leave him be. 'We don't want to spoil these few days of happiness.'

Philippe took her hand. 'It's so good to be here, I don't want to think about anything else.' He smiled gently at Francis and both men went out to check the animals were safely inside for the night.

***

On the afternoon of the fourth day, Lucinde burst into the kitchen. Agathe, who was feeding Berthe, looked at her in astonishment, Lucinde never walked farther than the shops in Saint-Agrève without a good reason. Hélène and Francis dropped their bags of newly threshed corn and jostled round the kitchen table, curious to know why she had come.

'I want to talk to Philippe. I want to know if Marius's telling the truth or just trying to frighten me. He says such dreadful things I can't believe they're true.'

'He's over at the Faugerons'.' Agathe's tone was cool, 'But Philippe won't talk about the Army.'

Francis interrupted, despite his sister's warning look, 'I wish he would! I want to know how our father died.'

Lucinde opened her eyes wide in amazement while Hélène kicked Francis hard under the table.

Mathilde struggled to get out of her chair and went up to her room.

Lucinde's face was pale. 'Marius's just the opposite; he won't stop talking about it. He says it's terrible. They're always scared, all of 'em, even if they try to hide it. And thirsty. The food's disgusting. They live in holes filled with filthy water and mud. The stink's appalling. He goes on and on.' She began to cry. 'And he says it's all for nothing. They fight back and forward over the same ground, with more and more men being killed each time.' Lucinde dabbed her eyes and lowered her voice, 'So Philippe hasn't told you how your father died?'

At this point an uncanny silence filled the room. Philippe stood in the doorway, his face white, eyes black with anger. He strode into the kitchen, grimly grasped Lucinde's arm and marched her out into the yard. She struggled to keep her feet as he dragged her into the barn. He glared at her, arms folded. 'What've you been telling them?' Lucinde looked down, rubbing her arm. Philippe waited for an answer then continued his voice cold with contempt, 'What gives you the right to worry Agathe unnecessarily and scare Francis so he'll dread what's facing him in a few months time?'

Lucinde tossed her head, her eyes narrowed as she ignored his question. 'So, what Marius says is true. It must be as bad as he makes out.'

Philippe looked at her with disgust. 'If that's what you wanted to know, you should've asked me, not frightened my family.' He banged his fist on the wooden manger. You've done more damage than you can imagine.'

Lucinde shrugged. 'By telling them the truth?' She looked straight at Philippe, throwing his anger back at his stony face. 'At least I didn't tell them you let their father die so you could save your own skin.'

Philippe winced, his eyes narrowed. 'Is that what Marius told you?'

Lucinde replied, resentful but partly contrite, 'He didn't say that exactly. But that's what I think he meant.' She continued to look defiant as Philippe held on to the wall of one of the stalls.

When he did eventually speak, his voice was measured and severe, 'Lucinde, there are many things you can't understand that've happened to Marius and me over the last year. If Marius wants to share his experiences and opinions with you that's his choice, but I don't want to share mine with my family. I want to protect them from the horrors we've been through.' He looked away. 'As for my father-in-law, I loved him and would've given anything to save him if I could. That's all I have to say about that.' His voice rose. 'Now get the hell out of here and stop spreading gossip in the town. I say this for your own good – and for Marius's.' When she had gone, Philippe walked to far end of the terrace and lit a cigarette.

Back in the kitchen Philippe sat down calmly, saying only that Lucinde had had to hurry back to town. Hélène stared at him, frowning, Agathe busied herself with Berthe. There was a long silence until Francis spoke, his voice high pitched with anxiety, 'Philippe, was Lucinde telling the truth?' Philippe did not reply; Francis stood up, bending over him. 'I've always imagined it's worse than they say it is in the papers, but I want to know what I'm letting myself in for.'

Philippe sighed and took his arm. 'Francis, I'm not going to talk about it. I've only got two days left – let me enjoy being here with you all.' He paused while the others stared at him intently, then turned away, his tone irritated and sharp. 'I haven't got the words to describe it and I don't want you to worry any more than you are already. Let me be.' He stalked out into the crisp autumn evening.

***

Philippe's last morning dawned clear and bright, the glorious colours of the trees glowed on the hillside opposite the farm. In the gloom of the kitchen the Vernot family breakfasted in melancholy silence. The brilliant sunshine of late September mocked their sombre mood as they walked slowly up the stony path towards the town. At the crest of the hill Mathilde embraced Philippe and said, weeping, 'I'm sorry I can't come any farther – it's too painful to see you go.' For a while Philippe stood watching as she walked haltingly back down to her home.

In the town Lucinde stood at the door of her mother-in-law's shop; when she saw Hélène she ran towards her, looking distraught. 'Marius won't go. He refuses to put on his uniform.' She glanced at Philippe. 'He's been drinking since yesterday morning. He can't leave. He's not fit to go anywhere.'

Philippe glared at her. 'Don't you understand? He hasn't a choice.' He started to walk quickly towards the shop entrance, Lucinde scurrying beside him, grabbing at his arm.

'He can't go! He's in a dreadful state. He refuses to go.

'Where is he?' Philippe was climbing the stairs three at a time. Marius could be heard bellowing at his mother; there was the sound of slamming doors.

Lucinde screamed, 'Let him stay. You can't make him go!'

Philippe marched into the sitting room; Marius was slumped against the wall, unshaven and undressed. Philippe pulled him to his feet; frog marched him into the bedroom and hurled a shirt and a pair of trousers at him. Lucinde stood at the door shouting, 'Leave him alone! Leave him alone!'

Philippe said nothing until he had got Marius more or less into his uniform; he snatched up the heavy canvas haversack and crammed it with the kit that was strewn over the floor. Marius clung to Lucinde, crying with drunken, slobbery sobs. Philippe took hold of Marius's arm, but Lucinde held tightly to him. Philippe stood away from the couple and spoke directly to Marius, ignoring Lucinde's gabbling, 'Marius, pull yourself together. You know you've got no choice. You've got to come with me.'

Marius wiped the tears and mucus from his face. 'I'm not coming Faugeron, I refuse.'

Philippe spoke with fury; time was running out and he resented spending these precious moments with Marius rather than with Agathe and Berthe. 'If you stay here you'll be arrested as a deserter and shot. Is that what you both want?' He glared at Lucinde. 'That's what'll happen if he doesn't come with me.' He took hold of Marius's arm and dragged him down the stairs. At the shop entrance he shook Marius. 'Don't make a spectacle of yourself, straighten up and walk like a man. We'll go by the back street.' Supported by Philippe and Lucinde, Marius stumbled through the town. When they reached the station Hélène noticed that Marius was not the only soldier who was so drunk he had to be manhandled onto the train. The groups on the platform stood silently, staring up at the sad faces filling the train windows. This time there was no band, no fanfare, no flowers, just a handful of families standing weeping as the train carried away their men.

The return of the men to the Front left behind a pervading depression. No hope lingered in the hearts of those who had watched their men leave for a second time, afraid they would never see each other again. After a year of anguish, there was no sign the agony would ever end.

Chapter Six

Autumn 1915–Spring 1916

In the weeks after Philippe's departure, Hélène became increasingly alarmed by the dramatic change in her twin's behaviour; during the day he worked with an obsessive frenzy, after supper when there was nothing to be done, he would sit staring silently into space. One evening when the others had gone to bed, she dared to ask him what the matter was. Francis did not reply but moodily gathered up a handful of twigs, snapped them into small pieces and threw them onto the fire.

Hélène continued to take the husks off a pile of boiled chestnuts. 'Is it Nathalie?'

'That's none of your business.' Francis sat frowning, and then said less aggressively, 'That's all over.'

Hélène looked up at him sharply. 'Why? She's such a nice girl.'

'That's why.' Francis twisted round on his chair. 'I can't allow her to get tied down.' He swore. 'She's only sixteen; she's all her life ahead of her.' He got up and paced round the room. 'In five months I'll be gone and God knows whether I'll come back - or in what state.'

Hélène looked at him, her eyes full of tears. She chose her words with care. 'Nathalie may not look at it like that. She may want to be "tied down".' Hélène continued, 'Other girls of her age are getting married.'

'That's exactly what she said. I told her they were stupid. And that it would be selfish of me to marry her.'

'She has a right to her own opinion, Francis.' Hélène reached across the table to take his hand but he pulled away. 'Try not to be so pessimistic.' She shook her head, trying to find words that might raise his spirits but, after glancing at his closed expression, she gave up and remained silent.

Francis pushed back his chair and strode towards his room. 'I've made up my mind. I've told Nathalie it's over. That's the end of it.' He clicked up the latch. 'Now leave me alone.'

***

Agathe was preoccupied with Berthe and did little work outside the house, but she constantly nagged the twins over what they must do, and how, and when. There were frequent rows.

It was late October and the sickly heat of the autumn sun was not strong enough to melt the frost on the puddles in the yard; Hélène slipped on the icy cobbles and fell, spilling all the morning's milk. As she sat rubbing her ankle, Agathe flew out of the kitchen. 'How could you be so careless?'

'Can't you see it was an accident?' Hélène banged the empty pail. 'You're always finding fault with what we're doing!'

Agathe stood with her hands on her hips. 'Someone has to! Francis spends all his time in another world and since your accident I can't trust you to be sensible.'

Hélène threw down the bucket. 'Not that again! When will you stop bringing it up?'

Agathe glared at her. 'We almost lost Les Laysses because of you.'

Francis emerged from behind the barn. 'That's not fair! Hélène and I have done all the heavy work since Berthe was born.'

'And who's supposed to look after her?'

'I'd love to look after Berthe but you won't let me.' Hélène was close to tears.

'But you're not her mother!' Agathe turned on her heels and went back into the kitchen.

Francis put his arm around his sister's shoulders. 'Don't let her upset you.'

Hélène spoke angrily, 'She's so selfish – she won't even let me hold Berthe.' She sat on the side of the trough, hiccoughing through tears. 'What's going to happen, Francis? I'm scared I won't be able to manage the farm when you've gone and it'd be the end of Les Laysses if Agathe went back to the Faugerons.'

Francis laughed cynically. ‘Pigs will really have to fly before that’ll happen.’ He bent down to pick up the empty bucket. ‘Anyway, it might not be such a bad thing.’ He smiled bleakly. ‘It'd mean you could get away from here. You’d be free to become a teacher, as you’ve always wanted.’ He shook his head vigorously. ‘But forget it – Agathe’ll never leave here.’

Lunch was eaten in an awkward silence, broken by the postman bringing a letter for Francis, who laid it by his bowl unopened. Francis had never received a letter before and after minutes of silent curiosity, Agathe asked brightly, in an effort to lighten the tension, ‘I suppose that’s from Nathalie?’ She continued to soak crusts of bread in milk for Berthe. ‘I’m glad you two have made it up.’

After turning the envelope over several times, Francis tore it into pieces and threw them into the fire.

Hélène looked at him, shocked. ‘Why d’you do that?’

Francis got up. ‘If I’d read it, I’d have replied,’ he said, and went rapidly out into the farmyard.

***

A ritual had emerged around Philippe’s letters; Agathe would read it first and after the evening meal she would read it out to the others. In the monotony of their existence its arrival was something to celebrate. That evening Hélène filled the glasses with plum brandy and Francis put another log on the fire. As Agathe smoothed out the fragile paper, she said solemnly, 'It seems something's happened to Marius.'

The letter started with Philippe's familiar grumbles about the idiosyncrasies of his comrades; it then continued, '*"I'm afraid I've bad news about Marius. As you saw when we were on leave, he hates being a soldier and I've always been afraid he'd do something foolish. Anyway, a week ago he got a letter that really upset him. He wouldn't say what was in it and I'm pretty sure it wasn't from Lucinde. After that he became very irritable and was even more difficult than usual. (Actually, one of the men had a go at him– his swearing was stopping any of us from getting to sleep, and I had to lash out a bit to prevent a fight.)"'*

Francis snorted. 'It'd be about Lucinde. I bet someone's told him what she's been up to.'

'If that's true, I imagine it was probably from Marius's mother – she hates Lucinde.' Hélène looked across at her sister. 'What else does he say?'

'*"One night we were on our way to the second line, pretty thankful to be away from the fighting for a few days. It was dark and as we were crossing a canal we were attacked. There was a lot of confusion, a lot of shelling and some of our chaps were killed. We never saw Marius after that. It's possible he was shot and we never found the body – although we found all the others who'd not made it and buried them. Some of the men from Saint-Agrève think he's—"*' Agathe looked up. 'This bit's been blanked out. I imagine he must mean he's deserted. Anyway he continues, "*I've told them not to say anything as it'll cause a lot of problems for his mother – and Lucinde – if the townsfolk think that's what he's done, so please don't say anything, as it's only gossip and rumour.*"'

Agathe folded up the letter and put it back in its envelope. Hélène sat looking into the fire. 'Poor Lucinde.' The others said nothing.

***

The whole family trooped down to Saint-Agrève for Toussaint. The market square was almost as it had been in the days before the war, apart from the absence of men. Agathe bought sprays of chrysanthemums and they walked with the other families to the graveyard. The cemetery was a desolate sight; groups of black-clothed women and children kneeling by each family's grave, some swaying back and forth, keening with grief even though the object of their sorrow was buried far away. Mathilde and Agathe bent to kiss the lichened granite; Hélène and Francis stood by, their faces stony, eyes sore from too much weeping. The church bells tolled solemnly and the dark-clothed forms straightened up, knees aching, and the doleful cortège made its way into the church.

The Mass was long and the church cold. The Curé's sermon was interminable. To pass the time, Hélène looked out for Nathalie and eventually found her sitting at the front of the church, safe from the sight of Francis. As Hélène half-listened to the Curé's threadbare themes, she surreptitiously watched her brother, his head lowered, pulling at the band of his hat. Hélène felt pity wringing her stomach, knowing he was counting each month, each week, each day until the dreaded, the inevitable, summons would arrive.

Halfway through the sermon, Hélène heard the church door open and, turning round discreetly, saw Roland enter. Despite so many nights spent despising him, even of hating him, her heart leapt. She knew Roland had treated her badly yet she could not suppress a flutter of anticipation at seeing him again. A nervous excitement competed with shame, with resentment as she willed the self-important priest to end his long-winded harangue. After the service, her heart beating violently, Hélène wormed her way through the file of women slowly moving towards the porch; outside in the square, surrounded by a group of boys, she caught sight of Roland smoking and laughing. As Hélène hesitated on the steps of the church, he nodded and stared intently at her as he chatted. Making an effort to appear unconcerned, Hélène walked towards him.

Taking care not to sound reproachful, she said, 'It's been a long time since I've seen you.' and held out her hand.

Roland looked her up and down appraisingly. 'First time I've been able to get up here. I've a few days leave before I join your dear brother-in-law's company. At last I'll see some action!' He glanced at the black ribbon tied round her sleeve and added quickly, 'Sorry to hear about your father. He was a good man.'

There was an awkward pause. Hélène stood silent in the hope Roland would say something that might rekindle a little of the romance she had once felt for him, might say some affectionate words she could cherish while he was at the Front - but he said nothing. To fill the uncomfortable silence she said coldly, ‘I hear you’ve been stuck in Privas all this time.’

Roland shrugged. ‘Bloody boring. Couldn’t get out of it – my father insisted.’ He laughed cynically. ‘But there are some compensations for living in a town where all the men are away.’ He winked at Hélène, which she found repugnant. He moved closer to her. 'Perhaps we could go for a walk this afternoon.' He paused. 'In the woods.' He smiled at her cynically.

Hélène recoiled and glared at him with contempt. For a moment they stood facing each other. Francis quickly came across the square and stood beside Hélène. 'Is anything the matter?' He looked belligerently at Roland.

'No, nothing.' Hélène turned on her heel and walked away rapidly. Roland’s mocking laughter followed her, grating on her nerves.

The day was dark and damp. The grieving women in the graveyard had revived all the desolate thoughts Hélène tried hard to subdue. She remembered the gentle ways of her father and the pain of missing him was cruel and intense. Roland’s crudeness and indifference had extinguished any flickering dream of finding love. Hélène tried not to cry as she walked with her brother towards the market square feeling as though her life had no purpose and brought her no joy.

Lucinde was installed at a table inside the café with Florence Dufour and Solange Arsac. Francis stopped abruptly. 'I'm not going in there. No man's safe around those three.' Hélène looked at him with surprise. Francis shrugged. 'None of us'll go near them.' He frowned at Hélène. 'And you should steer clear too – they won't do your reputation any good.'

They were both on the point of walking away when Lucinde called out, 'Vernot come and join us. Hélène, tell your brother to come over here and liven us up.' Francis glared at her for a moment and quickly walked away.

Before she could escape, Lucinde took hold of Hélène's arm. 'What's got into him?' She called for another pitcher of wine and a glass for Hélène. 'We're trying to drown our boredom. Life in this bloody hole's so sodding miserable.' Lucinde's eyes were swollen and red. 'I heard the Maire made another visit yesterday. I went out with Anton Hubert for a while - he was sweet – another one who won't be coming back. It's all very well for the damned Curé to say this war's a punishment for our sins, but Anton was only eighteen – and a virgin.' Lucinde continued, muttering under her breath, 'Damn his sanctimonious soul, he's worse than any of us, the lying hypocrite!'

Florence banged her glass on the table. Monsieur Bernard called from the bar, 'I've told you before Lucinde, if you and your friends don't behave, I'll throw you out.' Florence replied with a rude gesture. Outraged, Monsieur Bernard threw down his dishcloth and stalked across the room.

Suffused with shame, Hélène pulled at Lucinde's sleeve. 'Let's go. I want to talk to you on your own, anyway.' They walked past a group of women who were sitting in a corner of the cafe enjoying the disturbance, their black-scarved heads bent together, hissing with indignation. The two girls climbed past the church and reached the terrace at the top of the Chiniac; in the distance wraiths of mist partially masked the mountain of the Mézenc and gusts of rain swept across the Plateau. A watery sun emerged and in its brief, unforgiving light Hélène looked at Lucinde, noticing the puffy face, the over-full bosom barely covered by the straining blouse and felt a rush of pity for her friend. A soul that had been full of optimism and happiness a year ago had been coarsened by the strains of misfortune.

'I don't know what's happened to Marius. It's weeks since I've had a letter. He used to write every fortnight.'

Hélène put her arm around Lucinde's shoulder. 'The post isn't very reliable.' She shook her friend gently. 'If the news was really bad, you'd know by now.' Her tone was unconvincing.

'I think she's done what she always threatened to do.' Lucinde turned to Hélène, her eyes sore and inflamed. 'His damned mother's told him.'

Hélène asked quietly, 'Told him what?'

Lucinde shrugged and sighed. 'That I've been unfaithful, of course. All the time he was on leave she kept making snide remarks. I told him they weren't true and I think he believed me – while he was here.' Lucinde looked across at the distant hills.

'But a few weeks ago we had a row, a really bad one. She was being so bloody poisonous; she said she'd had enough of Marius being made a fool of by me. I said some things I shouldn't have – I was so fed up with her – so I bet she did write.' Hélène did not respond. Lucinde wailed, 'But what're we supposed to do? I can't live like a nun year after year. It's been fifteen months! No one can expect us to sit around waiting and waiting. Life's so bloody tedious.' Some of Lucinde's old fire returned. 'God dammit, I'm young, I want to have fun, I want to make love. And why shouldn't I? I didn't make this war happen.'

Hélène replied bitterly. 'The war's ruined everything. At least you've got Marius. My life's just work and more work. I've nothing to look forward to – all the men who're left are too old, too young or have something wrong with them.'

Lucinde looked at her sideways. 'There's nothing wrong with Romano.'

'Who's Romano?'

'A gypsy. Lives in the woods over by Saint-Romain. He scrapes a living out of making charcoal.' Noting Hélène's disapproving expression, Lucinde said aggressively, 'I'm not the only one. Quite a few of us visit him. I can tell you where he lives if you like.' When she saw Hélène's look of horror, Lucinde said roughly, 'Don't pretend you're any different – you need a man just like the rest of us. You should have some fun, not stay stuck in that miserable farmhouse with two women and your snotty brother.' Hélène shook her head fiercely and the two women parted, irritated and dissatisfied.

As Hélène walked home, a thin wind was blowing the last leaves off the trees. Kicking her way through the rotting mat of vegetation, she felt a sneaking sympathy for her friend’s unfaithfulness. At night Hélène's dreams betrayed her – ravished by some unknown man, she would wake, aroused, panting with frustration. As the sun set and night overcame the dying day, she wondered if Lucinde was right – that all women were the same, incomplete and unsatisfied until inseminated by the male. For a moment she was tempted to ask Lucinde where she could find the gypsy but, as she looked towards the hills faded now into gloomy shadows, she shivered. She would not compromise – she was young; she would wait for love.

***

The mood in the farmhouse darkened as the months before Francis was called up shortened into weeks. During the day he worked frantically; at mealtimes he ate in silence; after the evening soup he would go to his room, shutting out the others.

March arrived and with it the dreaded letter. Once more the family made their way to the station where a handful of young men stood surrounded by their silent families. Hélène held Francis close and tried to smile. ‘It’ll probably be over by the time you’ve finished training.’ Francis said nothing, his face grim.

Farewells over, the family stood in subdued silence, waiting for the final moment when Francis would have to board the train. This awkward hiatus was broken by Nathalie Peyrard pushing her way through the knots of relatives. She ran towards Francis, looked up at him for a moment, and then threw her arms around him. She held him tight, saying over and over, 'I love you. I'll always love you. I'll wait.' Francis kissed her and held her close for a long time; Hélène could see his dark lashes were wet with tears. He disentangled himself but kept hold of Nathalie's hand until the train arrived.

Mathilde crossed herself, repeating, 'God bless you and keep you safe.' Tears crept down her lined cheeks. The train hooted mournfully and the young men climbed up the high steps, reaching down for a last clasp of the hand. With a jolt the train pulled away, the men waving, the women standing in groups, empty, tearful. Minutes after the train had disappeared; the silent shells of women and children slowly abandoned the station to its desolate emptiness and made their way home.

***

Mathilde's hand shook as she took the mug of warm milk, kissed her daughters and slowly made for the door. The two sisters listened to her faltering footsteps as she climbed the stairs to her bedroom.

Hélène's heart ached with the pain of missing her twin; since the birth of Berthe, Francis had replaced Agathe as her confidant and she felt terribly alone. Her thoughts went back an eternity to

Agathe's wedding, to the broken mirror and its curse of bad luck. The last two years had brought bitterness beyond her imagining and Hélène shivered with fear at what the next five years might bring.

Hélène looked across at her sister. Agathe was sitting close to the fire on Emile's old chair, which she had appropriated, saying it was the most comfortable for feeding Berthe. The child lay cradled on her lap, suckling at the alabaster breast whose gentle curve glowed in the firelight. Berthe sneezed and lay gurgling, the small mouth moving, seeking to reconnect with the darkened nipple. Agathe guided the tiny head towards her breast, gently smoothing away the soft dark hair, a smile of pleasure and satisfaction illuminating her face as the baby sucked contentedly.

Suddenly a stabbing hatred transfixed Hélène; from nowhere a loathing for her sister took her breath away. Suffocated by the fierceness of this emotion, Hélène scraped back her chair and went outside, desperate for air. Agathe shouted after her crossly, 'Shut the door! You'll give Berthe a cold.'

As Hélène leant against the wall of the barn, an agonising jealousy overwhelmed her. 'Of course Agathe can smile – nothing, not even this bloody war, can take her baby away. Why should she have everything she wants?' Tears ran down Hélène's face as the piercing anger slowly ebbed away, leaving an exhausted desolation. She stood for a long time, soothed by the soft sound of rain falling on the fledgling leaves.

Chapter Seven

February–March 1916

'One fucking day early! We're entitled to one more day, but oh no, corporal what's-his-face declares we're leaving tomorrow. I could fucking throttle him!' Firmin continued to swear as he stuffed his kit into the lumpy haversack.

Philippe came into the kitchen of the farmhouse where the platoon had been billeted; he nodded to Francis, who sat disconsolately by a pile of crumpled clothing. 'Back to the Somme?'

'No, they're bloody sending us somewhere else.'

'Any idea where?'

The atmosphere in the room was taut; the men muttered angrily. Firmin pounded his fist hard on the table. 'How the hell should I know? We're only the bloody soldiers who're fighting this sodding war. Why bother to tell us anything?'

Francis asked, a hint of hope in his question, 'Surely it can't be worse than where we've come from?' Snorting cynically, the men returned to their packing.

Over supper a desperate boisterousness possessed the men as the wine flowed abundantly. Firmin had insisted as they were losing a day of R and R, the least the quartermaster could do was to give them their full two days' worth of rations. Even Francis, who had only been with the platoon for two weeks, had joined in the banter around the table. Philippe's heart warmed as he looked across at his brother-in-law chatting to Joseph, a rare smile on their faces, their cheeks rosy with wine. 'They're both still boys,' Philippe thought to himself, glad to see that Francis, for an hour or so, had lost the pinched pallor of the last fortnight.

'What's her name?'

Francis blushed bright red. 'Nathalie.'

Firmin boomed down the table, 'Nathalie Peyrard? I can't believe she's out of primary school. Pretty, though.' He did not wait for a response. 'Dammit, all women look good when they're young. As soon as they've got us hooked, they give up and go to seed.'

Francis looked pleased at the attention; he drank off his glass and called for more wine. The men laughed as he drank rapidly, refilling his glass and teasing him.

Supper was almost over when Roland burst into the room, stamping his feet, his cheeks red and shiny. 'Bloody cold – almost froze my balls off.' He took off his overcoat and flung it into a corner. Beaming with self-satisfaction, he stood in front of the fire, holding up the flap of his jacket to warm his backside. Firmin was the first to ask where he had been. Roland smiled at him smugly. ‘With Rosalie, the rather sweet young girl in the boulangerie. We've just had a very pleasant time banging away in the storeroom.’

The men put down their knives and sniggered with envy. Firmin snorted with derision. ‘I don’t believe you. Only whores go with the bloody infantry – the nice girls save themselves for the officers.’

Roland grinned, patting the crotch of his pants. ‘Some of us’ve got what it takes, officer or not.’ He turned round, presenting his rear to the company as he made a show of warming his hands over the fire. ‘And I’ve another rendezvous tomorrow!’

As the guffaws died down, Roland looked round, puzzled. One of the men said mildly, ‘’Fraid you won’t be able to meet your new “friend” tomorrow – we’ll be on our way, destination unknown.’

Roland swore long and imaginatively while the others laughed, arguing over the remains of the cheese.

Firmin refilled everyone’s glasses and, nudging his neighbour, turned to Roland. ‘Go on, tell us what you and your fair Rosalie got up to.’ He turned, grinning, to the other men. ‘We’re always keen to learn new tricks.’

Roland tipped his chair backwards and lit a small cigar, exhaling with satisfaction. ‘For a country girl she knew a thing or two.’

Philippe got up, irritated. ‘Put a sock in it, Roland, we’ve had enough of your stories.’ He took Francis by the arm and moved away from the table.

‘And where d’you two prigs think you’re going?’ Roland sneered at Francis. ‘Your young ears too delicate to hear what grown men get up to?’ He blew a smoke ring and said ruminatively, ‘I bet he’s still a virgin!’

‘He’s been telling us about his girlfriend.’

Francis flamed red with embarrassment.

Philippe said crossly, ‘Leave him alone, Roland.’ He moved away from the others, who were slumped round the table, while Francis stood dithering.

Roland took his arm. ‘So, you’ve got a girlfriend?’ Francis nodded, looking down at the floor. Roland stood in front of him, legs straddled, arms crossed. ‘So are you or aren’t you a virgin?’ Francis shook his head dumbly. There was a hoot of laughter as Roland forced him down onto a chair. ‘Eighteen and still a virgin! What a waste!’

As the evening wore on the wine brought on a darker, more destructive atmosphere and the tales of sexual exploits became wilder. Roland turned to Francis, his eyes small and red with drink. ‘What’s your problem - ’fore I was eighteen I’d had dozens of women ’round Saint-Agrève.’ He refilled his glass.

Alarmed by Roland’s sneering tone, Philippe looked up. ‘I said, leave him alone, Gounon.’ He looked sternly at Francis. ‘You’d better get ready for tomorrow.’

Roland minced round the table, repeating what Philippe had said in a high-pitched voice. 'Get your satchel ready for school, Francis dear, there's a good boy.' Francis reddened and frowned. 'How's Mummy's boy going to manage with all those howwid bombs and nowhere to clean his teeth?'

Francis lurched forward, fists high; Roland danced away, taunting him, 'Mummy's boy. Eighteen and never been fucked.'

He ducked as Francis punched and missed. The other men stumbled backwards out of their way, braying for a fight, banging the table. Roland pranced towards Francis, throwing out punches, feinting to right and left so that Francis, unsteady with drink, lurched from side to side.

Philippe stepped in and caught Roland's arm. 'For God's sake, stop it!' Roland continued to jeer; the others stamped their feet and banged the table louder and louder, faster and faster. 'Leave the boy alone.' Philippe twisted Roland's arm, making him yelp with pain and let him go.

Roland stood swearing angrily, his face red with rage, his eyes narrowed and malevolent. 'Talking of girls in Saint-Agrève, some of them can't have enough of it. Your sister, Hélène, for example – couldn't wait to get my trousers off. Begged me for it.' Francis and Philippe were now coming at him fast, but he made sure the table was between them. Roland jeered, 'Pity she was so bloody useless.' Keeping his eyes fixed on Philippe, he swayed, leering at him, satisfied his words had struck home.

Francis pushed aside the intervening men who staggered back, happy to enjoy the entertainment. He jabbed at Roland, who caught his arm and the two fell to the ground, overturning chairs and kicking out at the table so bottles and glasses fell shattering on the floor. The two men struggled and squirmed, legs lashing, so tightly knotted together Philippe could not separate them. The noise of the fracas attracted men from the rest of the building who piled into the room, eager to watch the fun – until the corporal burst in, swearing furiously. He stood over the two men and grabbed the back of Roland's jacket, pulling him upright.

'That's enough of that. Haven't you bloody idiots had enough fighting?' He pulled Roland towards him so their faces were almost touching and shouted, 'Gounon, if we weren't leaving tomorrow, I'd lock you up for a week with no bloody rations.' Seeing the blood oozing from Francis's lip, he said curtly, 'You'd better get yourself cleaned up.' He turned to Philippe angrily. 'I don't know what's got into you, letting him get into trouble.' He took in the smashed glass and broken chairs. 'And all of you'd better get this lot straightened up, smartish.'

***

'My bum's numb with the rattling of this damned train.' Firmin's voice came grumpily from the other side of the truck as the train jerked once again to a stop.

'It's got to be Épernay.' Roland stood on tiptoe, stretching to peer out of the gap between the roof and the sides of the cattle truck. The train juddered into action. 'And we're still going east.' He crouched in a corner, staring fixedly at Philippe and Francis who were desultorily playing a game of bezique. Roland worked his way towards them and said under his breath, 'Sorry about last night.'

Philippe laid down an ace. 'Ten points.' He played another couple of tricks.

'I was totally pissed.'

Philippe and Francis continued their game. Irritated, Roland shrugged. 'Fuck you! I've said I'm sorry.'

Philippe put down his cards and looked Roland straight in the face; he spoke quietly but with menace, 'Given we're in the same section, we can't avoid each other but I'm warning you, Gounon – keep out of my way.' Roland climbed over the others, opened the door a crack and had a piss.

Francis kept his head down as he shuffled and reshuffled the pack of cards. In the gloom a stray beam from the dying sun caught the unshaven down on the boy's chin and Philippe sighed; looking after Francis had turned out to be more of a responsibility than he had counted on, but he accepted it for Agathe's sake, and because he liked the boy.

Francis whispered, 'D'you think it's true about Hélène?'

Philippe did not reply at once. 'What does it matter? He shouldn't have said it.'

He did not trust either Roland or Firmin to keep quiet about Hélène and he knew very well what damage such rumours would wreak in the narrow streets and narrow minds of Saint-Agrève. The men restlessly shifted their packs and greatcoats in an effort to get comfortable, grumbling at the lack of food and the icy air, which stung like a needle as it whistled between the rough planks of the wagon.

***

After a sleepless night, the men jumped down from the train to find themselves in a churned-up field along with thousands of men already chilled to the bone by a fine rain. To the north another mass of men were slowly being marshaled into a long line that snaked all the way to the horizon.

‘At last, hot coffee. My bum’s a block of ice.’ Firmin dipped the hard bread into his coffee. ‘Where’re we going, anyway?’

The corporal looked at him with an odd expression on his face. ‘Verdun. The battle’s been going on for about three weeks. Sounds tough.' He sighed. 'And the really bad news is we’ve got a seventy-kilometre march to get there.’

Halfway through the afternoon they passed a group of men coming in the opposite direction. As the men trailed past, Firmin muttered, ‘What the hell’s got into those buggers?’ He called out, ‘What regiment?’ The men did not reply but lurched onward, eyes dull, leaning on their rifles. Firmin and Philippe exchanged looks and Philippe nodded towards Francis, who was staring at the ragged straggle of men, his face pale.

It was punishing work marching in the sleety rain; eventually the captain ordered a halt and with relief the men slipped the soaked leather straps off their shoulders. Firmin went over to the captain. 'What was that company we passed a few kilometres back?'

The captain looked at him closely. 'Why d'you ask?'

'They looked done in. Most of 'em could hardly walk – surely you must've noticed.'

The captain nodded. 'They seemed in pretty bad shape. That was the fourth battalion of the 109th.'

'What d'you mean a battalion? There were hardly enough to make up a platoon!'

The officer shrugged. 'We'd better get going.'

The next day a drab dawn brought more steely rain and a meagre breakfast of cold coffee and hard bread. With blistered feet and aching limbs, numb with lack of sleep, the men assembled into a ragged line and set off. Staggering in the opposite direction, they met more bands of returning soldiers, many with bandages stained with rusty blood and clothes so caked with mud they were unrecognisable as uniforms. Eyes, huge, dark and expressionless, stared out from faces so gaunt one could see the skull's outline beneath their dirt-encrusted skin. After a while the two columns, one inexorably creeping towards the battleground, the other crawling away from it, passed without even an exchange of glances.

Late in the afternoon, there was a sudden shout, 'Take cover – plane!' Philippe looked up as the fragile contraption sped rapidly towards them, the noise of its engine shrill and menacing over the deeper throbbing of the lorries on the road nearby. He ducked quickly, pulling Francis down onto the muddy grass. He could hear the sharp rap of the machine gun as the airplane dipped low over the road, the crash of a lorry as its driver lost control, then the whine of the returning plane and sharp cracks as the spray of bullets hit the metal casings of guns and the flanks of vehicles. As the drone of the engine faded, they could see the damaged lorry was already being dragged off the road and the moving line of trucks continued uninterrupted as grimy soldiers mechanically shoveled gravel onto the pitted surface of the track.

When night fell the platoon looked round for a place to bivouac, but there was nothing to protect them against the icy March rain. A wood ran along the crest of a nearby hill and although its wintry branches provided no shelter, its carpet of dead leaves offered an illusion of softness and a respite from the pervading mud.

'They're certainly warming the place up for us.' Firmin's attempt at a joke fell flat. The men, chewing on their corned beef, sat staring ahead, their eyes riveted on the dull red glow that traced the horizon. Frequent flashes lit up the lowering clouds and an occasional trail from a red or green flare fell lazily to earth; as the sounds of the day died away, the distant booming of guns grew more distinct. Their meagre meal over, the men sat smoking silently, glowing points of light waxing and waning in the darkness. Philippe wanted to say some comforting words to Francis but could think of nothing that might ease the boy's misery, so he wrapped himself tightly in his cape and lay down on the wet earth. Francis continued to sit, hunched up, knees to chin, staring at the flickering lights over to the east.

Philippe woke as dawn was breaking. Francis was still sitting in the same position but was writing laboriously on a piece of paper. When he became aware of Philippe stirring, he hurriedly folded his letter and put it in his inner pocket, surreptitiously wiping his sleeve across his face.

Approaching the ruins of Verdun, the landscape changed from fields – where it was still possible to imagine men ploughing, planting, reaping corn – to a sea of endless mud where any trace of life had been blasted and beaten into the shattered earth. As the men ate what remained of their rations amidst piles of charred rubble, their corporal laughed humourlessly. 'So this is what we've been told we must hold.' Philippe felt a cold shudder run down his spine. 'Our orders are "whatever the cost, Verdun must not fall".'

Beyond the ruins, their route lay through tangles of twisted metal. The long shafts of gun carriages reached up to the glaucous sky, broken cases spewed trails of rusting ammunition, heaps of every form of wreckage intermingled with rotting corpses – mules, horses, bullocks. The sound of guns, which had been a sinister rumble, had now become the distinct roar of individual howitzers and mortars whose explosions, still too far away to be dangerous, shook the ground. The earth, as far as they could see, had been scraped clear of any sign of life; its contours and landmarks made and remade each hour of each day by rockets, shells and bombs. There was no escaping the nauseating smell, the unmistakable stench of death. As the men staggered onwards, clutching handkerchiefs to their faces, their captain called out incessantly, 'Keep moving, keep moving.'

As they moved forward, the bombs became so frequent the men no longer had the time or the energy to throw themselves down. They walked bent double, as though this pathetic, instinctive response would make them less vulnerable. The bombardment was now so intense that nothing else could be heard and thinking became impossible. Soon the column of men could not avoid the human corpses that lay in their path, their boots sliding and sinking into a congealed slime that could not conceal the unspeakable.

It was dark when the corporal came down the line. He shouted over the din, 'We're almost there. We're breaking into platoons.' He signaled to Philippe and the others. 'Follow me.'

Philippe and Firmin exchanged glances, alarmed and confused. Firmin took hold of the corporal's arm, shouting in his ear, 'Where the hell are we going? Where are the trenches? There's bugger-all here.'

'We're to follow this dyke and find the company we're relieving.' The men gave up trying to make themselves heard and sullenly crept along the wet ditch, trying to keep under cover. Twenty minutes later they found four men huddled together.

'Company and regiment?'

'15th company, 158th regiment.'

'We're taking over. We're your relief.'

The men did not reply, but struggled to get by, swearing as they slid into the water at the bottom of the gully. As they jostled past, Firmin asked, 'What's it like here?' The first three men did not reply, like phantoms determined to escape before dawn, they vanished into the dusk. Firmin took hold of the last man's arm. 'Tell me, you snotty bastard, what's it like?'

'Fucking awful.'

'Where're the others?'

'Dead, mate. Or as good as. Let go! I'm getting out of here.' The man pushed past roughly and within seconds had also disappeared.

Suddenly a flare lit up the sky, trailing an elegant spiral of light as it fell to earth. The men flattened themselves against the sides of the ditch, swearing as the vile-smelling water swamped their boots and puttees. As the flare faded, the only light came from enemy guns firing at irregular intervals, their shells landing some hundreds of metres away; from a much closer position came the intermittent patter of a machine gun. It was impossible to sleep and an interminable drizzle formed rivulets that wormed their way beneath clothes that were already soaked. Illuminated by the occasional flare, Philippe could see Francis, his dilated eyes staring, isolated by the deafening racket. Philippe attempted to light a cigarette, but his matches were too damp; he swore.

Gradually the sky lightened and the irregular bombardment became more intense. Philippe inched his way up to the rim of the hollow and looked out over a landscape that chilled his marrow. To his left were the blasted stumps of some trees – the only features left in a morass of mud. A few yards away a great plume of earth and stones shot upwards, higher than a church tower; the debris clattered down on Philippe's helmet.

All that day and the following night the men hunkered down, starving and desperately thirsty. Roland and the corporal volunteered to go back for victuals and returned hours later with some tins of sardines and a welcome jerry can of water. The corporal had also brought their orders.

Firmin glared at him. 'Move forward – to what?'

'Some abandoned trenches. We're to regroup there after dark and wait.'

'Anything's got to be better than this sodding ditch.' Firmin turned accusingly towards Roland. 'This water tastes funny.'

Roland swore at him, 'That's the last fucking water you'll get for a while, so be bloody grateful. I'm not making that trip again.'

That night a thick greasy fog covered the ground, making it easier to evade the sights of the machine-gunners. As the men crawled forward, a shell whistled past Philippe's ear; he dived into a bomb crater and, a moment later, Francis joined him. They crawled up the side of the hole and ran forward until they found Firmin, Joseph and Roland lying in another depression. Firmin waved them down. 'This's the best we can do tonight.' The corporal joined them, struggling for breath.

The foggy light of morning revealed the front parapet of the dugout was a tumbled pile of decomposing bodies, their arms hanging down as though asking for help. One body in particular was stretched out on top of his colleagues as though relaxing in some remembered sunshine; the face was still intact: a strong, sensitive mouth apparently smiled at his new, living companions. Francis vomited, the other men swore as this new mess splashed over their boots and leggings.

Far over to the right the sound of a whistle reached them; the corporal gingerly looked out over the rotting cadavers. 'It's an attack, let's go!' The men scrambled upwards, dislodging their dead comrades, who tumbled drunkenly into the pit below. The men tried to run forward, their feet gripped by the cloying mud, bending low to make a smaller target for the bright, spitting bullets. Thrown off balance as the ground around them shook, the group carried on running as the earth to their left was thrown high into the air. There was a long low whine followed by a scream – many screams – and Philippe and Francis were thrown to the ground. For a moment they lay breathing rapidly and then moved forward again. Another bomb screeched past, the falling debris drumming hard against their helmets. Again they clambered into a hole.

Roland threw himself beside them, his face bloody, then the corporal and Joseph slid down to join them. The corporal muttered, 'Got to get back.

Let's wait 'til dark and make a run for it.' Firmin scrambled in, swearing wearily.

The four older men lay smoking, trying to take cover below the shallow edges of the crater, cursing occasionally as an exploding shell covered them in filth. Francis continued to sit upright, staring down at his feet. The corporal offered him a cigarette, but he just shook his head. Philippe passed Francis his water bottle, but there was only a drop of the brackish water left. In the late afternoon there appeared to be a break in the bombing and the five men tentatively wriggled over the top of their hole into a world that had undergone its daily transformation. They crawled back over the terrain they had covered that morning, past many bodies, some of whom they recognised. A soldier moaned pitifully as they crawled past, calling for water. Philippe muttered, 'Sorry mate, none left.'

It was getting dark as the men crawled into a shallow depression barely deep enough to hide them from the binoculars of the enemy. Francis sat, shivering with misery, his lips blistered and swollen with fruitless licking. The men elbowed each other to find room at the bottom of the crater as the bombardment started again.

The morning dawned with a bright indifferent sunlight, but the cheerful sun only intensified the smell of decay and their desperate thirst. Francis sat immobile, his lips moving soundlessly; Philippe thought he was praying, but then realised he was repeating over and over, 'Maman, Maman.' In the light of a flare he saw tears running down Francis's face. Philippe put his arm around him but the boy did not appear to notice; Philippe let his hand fall.

A shout arose from the blasted earth around them. 'Attack! Boche!' The men struggled to their feet, pulling helmets tight, grabbing their rifles. Francis remained seated, his whole body quivering. Philippe bent down and pulled him up but Francis resisted, tugging away, his eyes wide with stark, overwhelming terror. Philippe shook him hard.

'We've got to get out, follow me!' The noise of the barrage intensified, drowning his words. A screaming shell rushed by their ears, the vibrating air making the two men stagger. Francis broke free and ran forward, towards the oncoming enemy. Another bomb exploded to their right. Francis continued to run. Philippe tried to catch hold of him but Francis was already too far away; he sensed that Francis was shouting, but he could not hear over the din. Philippe lurched forward but Francis was still ahead of him, the line of German soldiers now clearly visible. A great plume of earth rose to their left. Philippe saw Francis stumble then stagger on.

They both felt the soft rush of air as the shell came towards them. Philippe tried to shout but the words hung empty as he saw Francis's body, still apparently running, leap into the sky. It flew upwards, arms and legs still moving gracefully as though he was effortlessly sprinting up the hill behind Les Laysses. Philippe watched as the upward flight ended and the heavy haversack dragged its owner down to the ground, while Francis's rifle gave one, two, elegant arabesques high in the air, and then fell to earth. Philippe knelt down by the boy; Francis's eyes stared up at him while a lungful of blood burst from between his crusted lips.

A German was closing in on him; Philippe could hear the rasp of his breath. He struggled to his feet, his rifle with its bayonet stretched out before him. As the two men clashed, Philippe stepped sideways, jabbing his bayonet into the other man's belly, and heard him groan as he sank to the ground. Philippe stood over him, knowing his enemy was fatally wounded; he still raised his bayonet high and stabbed it into the soldier lying helpless on the muddy earth. He saw the fear in the man's eyes cloud over as his life left him. Philippe stood for a moment, then turned and ran back, tears streaming down his face.

***

Several days later, what remained of the company assembled outside the foetid tunnel where they had spent three days, sheltering from the bombs. Philippe breathed deeply, sucking in the clean, damp air and looked round at his companions. Of the thirty men who had jumped down from the wagon at Bar le Duc, only eight now remained. An unfamiliar captain marshaled the remnants of two other platoons, which had been equally decimated. The men's faces were unhealthily pale and they leant for support on their rifles whenever the captain looked the other way; the days and nights cooped up in the stinking underpass had done almost as much to drain their resources as the preceding days.

Philippe sighed as the order was given and the exhausted, enfeebled men prepared to set off to the fortress of Vaux.

It took six hours for the men to reach the fort, a distance of 3 kilometres, throwing themselves to the ground as the shells rained down, crawling from crater to crater. When they arrived they were put to work filling sandbags with earth to reinforce the defences of the battered fort. At nightfall their captain led them down through a stony ravine ending in a network of trenches. The barrage was relentless. Unable to sleep they sat smoking, watching the moon tranquilly slip in and out between the clouds. From time to time Philippe spat out the accumulated dust in his mouth and slapped ineffectively at the lice in his trousers.

As the red glow of the guns began to fade against the golden light of dawn, the men stretched their numbed limbs into action. A call went up, 'Attack, attack!' Almost indistinguishable against the grey ground, Philippe could see swarming hordes of soldiers pouring towards them, the pale sun glinting on their bayonets. The captain shouted, 'Hold fire. Hold it. Fifteen paces then let 'em 'ave it!'

Philippe steadied his rifle against a sandbag and took aim, his finger was trembling on the trigger; he shook his hand and grasped the gun more firmly. When the order came, Philippe saw the line of men falter, many fell, but the rest came on, running up the slope, fumbling with their grenades. He fired again. A German threw his grenade in a wide, arching movement, the small projectile hovering in the air then falling over to Philippe's left. The explosion knocked him over as he heard Roland scream with pain. The Germans were now upon them. Philippe smashed his rifle down on hands grasping at the sandbags. A head appeared and Philippe hit out; the man disappeared, falling backwards. The Germans were now pouring over the defences; another grenade detonated, flinging earth into Philippe's face. He ran into a communication trench where the rest of his platoon had taken up position, firing back down the gully now teeming with Germans. The captain was behind him, ordering the men to fall back. Philippe reloaded and took aim, covering his colleagues as they backed away. A grenade went off behind him, blocking his retreat. Philippe continued to fire but made no impression on the press of Germans ahead of him. He pulled out the pin of his grenade and threw it directly at the leading soldiers, metres away. There was a deafening bang and Philippe's world went dark.

Chapter Eight

Spring–Summer 1916

Hélène read the letter again, brushing away tears of relief, her finger caressing Francis's schoolboy handwriting.

'We've had a terrible march to get to this place; we passed men who looked as though they'd gone through hell. We're about to go into a big battle at a place called Verdun. I can see flashes from the artillery even though we're still a few kilometres away, so the guns must be just as big or bigger than they were in the Somme.' The writing became more irregular and Hélène's heart gave a twist as she imagined her brother chewing on the stubby pencil before resuming. '*Philippe tries his best but there isn't much he can do, each of us has to find our own way through this godforsaken mess. I can't tell you how much I miss you all and wish I was back on the farm. I'm afraid I'll never see your dear faces again. I can hear the others waking up, so we'll be on our way shortly. A thousand kisses, Francis.*'

Hélène laid the precious paper on the table, stroking it gently. The letter was dated three weeks ago. It was now almost six weeks since they had heard from Philippe. Hélène looked out of the window; the sun was high, the time for the postman had passed; another day of waiting.

***

In the sun the air felt soft and warm but in the lee of the barn the night's frost still staked its long white shadows. Agathe bustled out of the barn, Berthe strapped to her back; Hélène abruptly headed away towards the fields.

'Don't rush off! One of the bullocks has lost a shoe. You'll have to take him down to the blacksmith's tomorrow.' Hélène nodded quickly. 'I'll come with you.'

Hélène bit her lip; the weekly trip to the market was the only time she was able to get away from Agathe. All winter they had been cooped up together and now, as the weeks passed with no news of Francis or Philippe, the slightest misunderstanding often flared into an ugly quarrel. She tried to be diplomatic. 'You don't need to come. I can manage easily.'

Agathe bridled. 'I'm coming with you.'

'Then you go on your own. I can look after Berthe.'

Agathe looked at her with exasperation. 'No! You'll have to deal with the blacksmith and the market. I must talk to the Curé. And I want to light a candle for Philippe.'

'And Francis. Whatever good they do!' Seeing Agathe's pain, Hélène wished she had kept silent. She reached out. 'I'm sorry, Agathe. Of course we'll go together. Who knows, there may be some news.' She gave Agathe a quick hug, gently pinched Berthe's rosy cheek and fled down to the fields.

***

Hélène left the bullock in the smithy, embarrassed by the gaggle of young girls who stood whispering and giggling as they watched the blacksmith swing his hammer, showing off his sweating, sinewy body and sending his admirers suggestive smiles as he plunged the red hot iron, sizzling, into the pail of water.

Hélène went into the church to collect Agathe but she was still kneeling in prayer. For a while she sat outside on the low wall of the church but the clear spring air held no warmth and she reluctantly decided to wait in the café and run the risk of meeting Lucinde.

At the door, Hélène hesitated; she could see Lucinde sitting at the back of the café, her listeners gazing at her wide-eyed.

'Even though I'd confessed, he still wouldn't give me the Sacrament.'

Solange Arsac looked at Lucinde with astonishment. 'You confessed?' Lucinde nodded. 'You confessed everything?' Solange sat back in disbelief, 'I wouldn't dare. I haven't been to Mass for over a year.' The other women giggled.

Lucinde laughed cynically. ‘Believe me, I tell him everything. All the details – when, where and how!’ Lucinde lowered her voice so that the women had to bend their heads close to hear. When she had finished, they fell back in their chairs, screaming with laughter, hands over mouths.

‘He didn’t! Are you sure?’

‘I could hear him!’

Florence squawked with salacious delight, ‘The dirty beast!’

Annoyed by the noise, Monsieur Bernard came over to their table. ‘That’s enough! You’re scaring away my decent customers.’

Lucinde smiled at him sweetly. ‘But we’re your *best* customers, Monsieur Bernard.’

He made to chase her, flicking his dishcloth as the three women made their way to the door, laughing. Grumbling to himself, Monsieur Bernard retreated behind his bar. ‘This is the last time, Lucinde. I won’t put up with all your nonsense.’

Hélène went back to the church, where Agathe soon emerged with a group of women, their faces sallow and strained. She spoke in a hushed voice, 'In the last month three men from Saint-Agrève have been killed. And Roland Gounon’s on his way home – he’s lost both legs.’

Hélène gasped. ‘Poor Roland. That must be dreadful!’

As the two sisters walked down the path to the farm, Agathe said bitterly, ‘I can’t stand this endless waiting.’ Her voice broke. ‘Philippe’s last letter was in February and it’s now almost May!’

‘But Francis wrote in March.’

'It's still far longer than we've ever had to wait before – and they hadn't even got to this damned Verdun.' She dried her eyes. 'I suppose we'd better put a good face on it for Maman.'

As soon as they entered the kitchen, both women saw the envelope lying on the table and their hearts stopped. Mathilde sat by the fire, her back to them, her voice less than a whisper. 'My son. They've killed my son.'

***

As each woman wearily went about their daily tasks, Hélène found it impossible to believe her twin brother was dead; she saw him everywhere, heard his voice, was pierced by his laughter.

After another week of fruitless waiting, Agathe insisted Hélène must ask Roland if he knew anything of Philippe.

Hélène walked along the path; the fields sparkling with gay daffodils jarred against her gloomy thoughts. She moodily broke off a branch heavy with crab-apple blossom, swishing it from side to side until the battered flowers hung sad and bruised. She threw it into the stream.

Preoccupied with her thoughts, Hélène did not notice Lucinde until she felt a tug at her arm. Hélène frowned; she did not want to see or be seen with Lucinde. She tried to pull away but Lucinde held her tight, her eyes shining strangely. 'I've been looking out for you. Come up to the Chiniac; there's something I've got to tell you.' As they ran up the cobbled alleys, Hélène took a sideways look at her friend; she looked younger, fresher, more like the old Lucinde. As they sat on the stone bench looking out over the Plateau, Hélène said without enthusiasm, 'It must be Marius. He's come back.'

Lucinde laughed delightedly. 'How d'you guess?'

Hélène shrugged. 'The way you look.' She bit her lip; from the depth of her own grief her friend's delight was hard to stomach.

'I'm so happy!' Lucinde made a face. 'I couldn't tell those other cows, they can't keep a secret, but I trust you Hélène. Promise you won't tell anyone.' She shook Hélène's arm, suddenly serious. 'Promise! Marius's life depends on it.' Hélène nodded wearily.

'Last Wednesday I was woken up by stones hitting the shutter. I thought it must be Romano – but it was Marius!' She giggled. 'I've got terrible bruises on my back from the floor of the store – those flagstones are really hard! He's hiding in the attic. Even his mother doesn't know. Serve her right – she's always so nasty to me.'

Hélène tried to show some interest. 'It's been a long time since he …' She hesitated.

'More than six months.' Lucinde stretched luxuriously. 'I hope he won't have to stay in hiding much longer. I've told him there are other deserters in the valley over by Rochepaule and no one minds about them.'

Hélène looked at Lucinde with horror. 'But those aren't local men. Of course he'll have to stay hidden – no one would accept a deserter. At best they'd give him up to the police; at worst they'll kill him.' Hélène stood up and looked down at her friend. 'And they'll soon become suspicious if you carry on looking so pleased with yourself. As soon as I saw you I knew Marius'd made an appearance.' Irritated, Hélène picked up her basket. 'Be careful, Lucinde. You must pretend nothing's happened.' She turned away. 'I've got to go.'

Hélène lifted the heavy knocker of the Gounon's door; for a moment she was tempted to sneak away, but she let the brass handle fall, the sound juddering along the deserted street.

Roland was sitting by the window, a checked blanket over his lap. He did not turn as she entered but continued to stare at the shuttered façade of the house opposite. Hélène stammered some sympathetic phrases which appeared to provoke Roland who replied angrily, 'Forget it! You've no idea what it's like to be a cripple, so you can keep your pity.' He motioned with his stick to a chair. 'Sit down. I can't bear people standing over me.' He paused before saying grudgingly, 'I'm sorry about your brother.'

Hélène did not reply at once but looked directly at him; his face was still scored with livid red lines, a white triangle of bandage held his left arm to his chest and the blanket could not hide the emptiness beneath. She cleared her throat. 'The telegram came last week.'

Roland frowned. 'That took a long time. He died well over a week before I copped this lot. As I said, I'm sorry.'

Hélène nodded; she continued coldly, 'My sister sent me to ask you about Philippe. We haven't had a letter from him for months and she hoped you might have some information.'

Roland turned to look out of the window. 'I don't know any more than you do. We were penned down in a gully leading back into Fort Vaux. A grenade went off and that's what did for me. Faugeron was firing at the time, I remember that. Then there was another explosion – a grenade I suppose. I've no idea what happened next.'

Hélène became fascinated by the tic that flickered under the tight, pale skin of his cheek. 'But we'd have heard if he'd been killed, wouldn't we? We heard about Francis.'

Roland shrugged. 'That depends. Faugeron reported the boy's death, but if there's no one there to see it – or anyone alive to tell someone – then who's to know?' His tone became harsh and sarcastic. 'Don't imagine a battlefield is nicely tidied up every night and all the poor buggers who've bought it are buried with little wooden crosses at their heads.' He spat on the floor. 'But Faugeron can look after himself if anyone can. For all I know, he could be fighting somewhere on the Front, holed up in some godforsaken hospital, or dead. I haven't a clue.'

Shocked by the intensity of his bitterness, Hélène sat in silence. 'Thank you.' She got up. 'I'd better be going.'

Roland glanced at her quickly, softening a little as he took in her sad white face. 'Try talking to Solange Arsac. I saw Firmin briefly before I was carted off to the relay hospital at Bar-le-Duc. That's if the bitch ever bothers to read his letters, the poor bastard!'

At the door of the café Hélène braced herself and was relieved to see it was empty apart from Monsieur Bernard washing glasses. He beckoned to her. 'Come in, come in.' A large gentle hand guided her to a seat. 'You look as though you could do with something strong.' He poured her a glass of cognac and sat down beside her. 'I'm sorry about your brother. He was a good lad.' Hélène began to cry. There was a long silence. 'Terrible. Terrible for your mother to lose them both.'

Hélène wiped her eyes with the ball of sodden handkerchief. 'She sits all day. Doesn't cry, doesn't speak, just sits.'

'Terrible!' Again there was a long silence. Monsieur Bernard turned to Hélène, 'Were you looking for someone?'

Hélène nodded. 'Solange Arsac. I wondered if she'd any news of my brother-in-law.'

Monsieur Bernard pursed his lips and raised his eyebrows; he slowly took out his watch. 'Quarter-past one. Madame Lafont ...'

Hélène interrupted, confused, 'The blacksmith's wife?'

'Madame Lafont, the blacksmith's wife, will now be at the rue de l'église giving her bedridden mother her lunch.' He paused. 'Therefore it's a safe bet that Madame Arsac will be on her back in the shed behind the smithy.' He snapped shut his watch and carefully replaced it in his waistcoat pocket. 'She's a disgrace!'

Hélène finished her cognac – its fiery heat had been comforting – and fumbled in her pocket for her purse, but Monsieur Bernard shook his head. He stood watching as the small black-clad figure walked disconsolately into the dazzling glare of the midday sun.

Hélène felt sick as she neared the farmhouse. From the top of the hill, she could see Agathe looking out for her, so she walked deliberately slowly to warn her she had nothing to say. In the kitchen a sulky fire heated a pan of thin porridge.

'No one has any news, I'm afraid.' She paused. 'Roland seemed bitter and angry, but I suppose that's hardly surprising.' Hélène got up. 'I posted the letter to the Ministry but I don't imagine it'll do much good. Have you milked yet?'

Agathe shook her head as she put Berthe down in her cot. Hélène felt a pang of irritation: when Agathe was not looking after Berthe, she spent the rest of her time praying, which left all the work to Hélène. She grabbed the pail and clattered out to the barn.

Agathe trailed after her. 'I'm sorry, Hélène. I can't believe God is listening; He knows my heart's too full of resentment. Tomorrow I'll go and talk to the Curé.'

Hélène said with exasperation, 'But what about setting the potatoes? That's got to be done while the weather's fine.'

Agathe had tears in her eyes. 'I'm sorry, but it doesn't seem important.' Hélène rolled her eyes and slammed the barn door after her.

***

As the two women turned into the square, Hélène spotted Roland sitting outside the café. She tugged at Lucinde's arm. 'Let's go round the back way.' Lucinde looked at her with surprise and burst into laughter. 'So you're still sweet on Roland?' She shuddered. 'I can't imagine making love to a man with no legs.'

Before they had reached the corner Roland had spotted them. 'Hey Lucinde, come here!' When the two women did not stop, he called out again, more loudly, 'Don't worry I won't jump on you.' The men around Roland sniggered. 'Has your coward of a husband come home yet?'

Lucinde shot free from Hélène and marched towards him, towering over Roland's chair as he looked up at her smirking. 'Don't you dare say things like that!'

'Tut, tut, something I've said must've hit a chord.' He sneered up at her, enjoying playing to the crowd, which was rapidly gathering. 'Go on. Promise you'll open your legs for me – the local war hero!'

'I'd have nothing to do with you even if you had the best legs in the whole French Army.' Hélène tried to pull Lucinde away.

'Ah, then it must be your deserter husband that's making you so touchy.' Roland paused, calculating his effect. 'Perhaps he's found some other woman to shag.' Seeing an expression he could not interpret flit across her face, he continued,

'Or he's turned up and put paid to your fun and games.'

Lucinde reached over to slap him; Hélène managed to catch her hand as the crowd gasped. Roland looked round pleased to be the centre of attention, before continuing, his tone low and menacing, 'Let me give you some advice. If the coward has turned up, he'd better watch out. I'll make it my business, legs or no legs, to ensure he gets exactly what he deserves.' He ducked, sneering as Lucinde aimed another blow at him. 'Pity it's the wife that's got all the spunk. You'd have done a lot better in the Army than your darling Marius, and we'd both've had a lot more fun.'

Hélène leant over him. 'Shut up, Roland, that's enough!'

As she walked away, Lucinde shouted over her shoulder, 'Cripple!'

Hélène shook her friend. 'For God's sake, Lucinde, be careful! I know Roland provoked you, but people are bound to take his side.'

'I don't care what they think.' Hélène swore under her breath as Lucinde flounced into her mother-in-law's shop.

***

Shadows edged across the flank of the hill. Hélène ran faster, determined to be back before dark so Agathe would not notice her absence. When she reached the tumbledown hut, she found Marius sitting in the gloom; his teeth gleamed white as he smiled at her.

‘Am I glad to see you! I’m absolutely famished.’

Hélène put down the basket and started to unpack its contents rapidly. ‘It’s dangerous for Lucinde to come here often – and for you. I’m sorry I couldn’t come sooner.’

‘She shouldn’t have asked you.’

‘That's okay.’ Hélène made a face. ‘But I'm afraid we’ve very little food left - and my sister's got sharp eyes.’ She looked anxiously at Marius. ‘I won’t be able to come very often.’

‘You won’t have to. I’ve got to leave here.’ Hélène looked at his drawn face and saw the sadness in his eyes. Marius walked over to the door of the hut. ‘It’s far too dangerous to stay around here, if any of the townspeople found me I hate to think what they’d do to me. Even Lucinde could see it wouldn’t work after that spat with Gounon.’ He took the loaf and broke off a chunk. ‘She's desperate to come with me, says we could make a new life together.’ He shrugged his shoulders. ‘But I'd never make it to Switzerland with Lucinde in tow.’ He sighed. ‘You’ve no idea how hard it’s been!’

‘I'd love to know what happened.'

Marius looked at Hélène closely. ‘Lucinde said you can keep a secret.' Hélène nodded. He spoke quietly, 'There was an attack; it was all very confused so I took a chance and swam down a canal as far as I could and laid low all the next day. Then I struck lucky! I managed to find a field of turnips that hadn’t been harvested so I dug out as many as I could; they kept me going for a good few days. Of course I was still wearing my uniform so I reckoned my best bet would be to find a woman living on her own and frighten her or persuade her to give me some civilian clothes. I eventually found a woman struggling to get in her crop of potatoes; I reckoned only a woman on her own would try to do that. When she got over her fright I offered to help on the farm in return for some clothes. I stayed a couple of months. She risked a lot. If anyone found out, her life would've been ruined – and I'd have been shot. She was a good woman.'

'Will you ever come back here?'

There was a long pause. 'I don't think so.'

Hélène nodded slowly. 'I don't believe people here will forget or forgive.' She paused before asking softly, 'But what about Lucinde? It'll be awful for her. She needs you.'

'I know.' For a moment Marius leaned his head against the door jamb. 'I'll send for her as soon as I can. There's nothing else I can do.' He turned and looked straight at Hélène. 'You won't need to come again.' He smiled and Hélène felt her body respond to the appeal of this handsome man. She put her arms round his neck, holding him for longer than she should, entranced by the intoxicating feeling of his arms around her. Slowly Marius disengaged himself and kissed the top of her head. 'Thanks for the food, Hélène. I hope you don't get into trouble.'

As Hélène ran down the hill, she knew she would never see him again.

***

Two days later Lucinde came panting into the farmyard, her hair undone, blouse patched with perspiration. She tugged at Agathe's arm, who looked at her with disgust. 'Where's Hélène? Where I can find the lying ...!' Agathe pointed contemptuously towards Hélène, far down the hill hoeing their plot of vegetables. Lucinde pushed past her.

'Where is he? Where're you hiding him? You bitch!'

Hélène recoiled and tried to defend herself. 'What on earth are you talking about?'

Lucinde thrust her face close. 'Where's Marius? You keep away from him.'

Hélène pushed her away. 'So, he must've gone.' She looked at Lucinde wearily. 'Don't be such a bloody idiot! Of course he's not here, there's nowhere to hide.'

Lucinde looked at Hélène closely and burst into tears. Hélène took her arm and walked with her into the woods, away from the watchful eyes of Agathe. 'I went to the hut on Wednesday and when I left he said "*adieu*", not "*au revoir*", so I realised he'd probably be leaving soon.'

'Without even saying goodbye. Nothing!' Lucinde was sobbing hysterically.

Hélène put her arm around her. 'He probably felt it was the kindest thing to do.'

'But I would've gone with him! I told him I didn't want to stay here.'

'That's what he was afraid of. It'd be impossible if he took you with him.' Lucinde continued to cry noisily. Hélène stood looking at her with resignation. 'Come on, Lucinde, I'll walk with you up the hill, but don't let Agathe see you like this. Whatever she thinks, it'll most likely lead to another row.'

***

The long-awaited letter arrived in mid June, not from Philippe but from the Ministry. It informed them brusquely that Private Faugeron had been wounded, was currently recuperating at a military hospital in Lyon and would be coming home in two weeks' time for a period of convalescence.

***

Hélène urged the bullocks to walk a little faster, but they ambled on at their own imperturbable pace. She looked back at her sister and Berthe perched high on the cart they had filled with straw and blankets, relieved the waiting was almost over.

At last they heard the train's whistle, a lugubrious sound that brought back dismal memories; instinctively the two sisters grasped each other's hand. It took the train a long time to come to a halt and an eternity for Philippe to ease himself down from its high step, supported by two soldiers. Agathe kissed him gingerly and stood back, taking in the bandaged head and leg, the clothes that would not fasten over the wadding around his waist, the crutches on which he leant heavily. She crossed herself. 'Thank God you're here.' Philippe smiled, a reassuringly familiar expression in a face so white and emaciated it was almost unrecognisable. The two women gently led him away.

After supper the family sat outside watching the light retreat from the shadows of the valley. Breaking into the peaceful silence, Hélène muttered, 'Four long months.' Shocked at having spoken her thoughts out loud, she glanced surreptitiously at Philippe, whose eyes were closed. Agathe put her finger to her lips, glaring at Hélène.

Philippe opened his eyes. 'It must've been hard. 'Specially after the news about Francis.'

Agathe patted his hand. 'Don't upset yourself. You're here now, that's all that matters.'

Hélène sprang up and stood at the edge of the terrace, facing them. 'But why didn't you write? Or at least get someone to write for you.' Ignoring Agathe's exasperation, Hélène stood over Philippe. 'Not knowing was dreadful. Waiting every day, worrying every night.'

Philippe nodded, sighed heavily and put out a hand to silence Agathe. 'For months I couldn't remember anything. I was in hospital at Lyon but I'd no idea how I'd got there or who I was; my papers had got lost when they'd taken me to the dressing station and had had to cut me out of my jacket. Then one day a nurse ran up to my bed, she was very excited, waving something at me. It was our wedding photograph! For some reason she'd been sorting out a bag of belongings and had recognised me in the photo. As soon as I saw it, things started to come back.' Philippe took a pull at his pipe. 'Unfortunately that included the bad as well as the good.' He took Agathe's hand. 'As soon as I remembered my name, they got in touch.'

That night Hélène was awakened by Philippe shouting. Through the thin wooden floor came the sounds of a struggle, a crash and a yelp of pain. Agathe shouted for help; Philippe was lying on the floor, moaning and clutching his side. Eventually the two sisters manhandled him onto the mattress where he lay, shivering in agony and drained of all colour.

Every night they were woken by Philippe's nightmares.

Hélène and Agathe were in the high field reaping their meagre crop of rye. 'It's always the same. He's searching for Francis; he keeps calling his name, saying he's going to bury him.' Agathe straightened up, leaning on her scythe. 'I hope the war hasn't affected his mind. Over in Le Cheylard two men came back completely crazy.'

Hélène shook her head. 'He's been through terrible suffering. I'm sure his memories will dim in time.'

Agathe brushed away a tear. 'The wound in his side's almost healed and I'm sure if he's allowed to stay, his leg'll get better eventually.'

Hélène frowned. 'What d'you mean "allowed to stay"? Anyone can see he's not fit to go back to the Front.'

'The hospital authorities apparently told him he can only stay here until he's well enough to rejoin his regiment.' She leant on her scythe, weeping. 'How can they do this to him – to anyone?'

Hélène patted her sister's shoulder. 'Don't worry; it's bound to be a long time before they reckon he's fit.' She snorted. 'Perhaps the war'll be over by then.'

'I can't believe it'll ever be over.'

The next week a letter arrived informing Philippe that he was to report to an Army doctor in Privas to assess whether he was fit to return to the Front. There was a profound silence in the kitchen as the letter was passed from hand to hand. Agathe looked at Philippe with tears in her eyes. 'You can't go! If you attempt to do anything you're exhausted within minutes.' Philippe pulled at his pipe, saying nothing. Agathe ran outside sobbing. Hélène could think of nothing to say and sat looking at Mathilde who stared, as she always did, into the embers of the fire.

***

Two years after his first departure, Philippe left for the Front once more. Hélène, Philippe and Agathe, carrying Berthe, walked without speaking along the path leading to the town. The path was gay, bordered by cornflowers, cow parsley and red campion; a dazzling sun beat down on the group, causing Philippe to sweat in his thick uniform and lean more heavily on his stick. The streets were deserted and at the station they were the only group waiting on the platform. The train arrived; Philippe held Agathe a long time in his arms, kissed Berthe and Hélène and clambered laboriously into a carriage. As it crept along the platform, the two women were still and silent, only little Berthe waved and smiled at the hand clutching a forage cap as it grew smaller and smaller. They stood as the train disappeared, stood until the signal clanged down and stood until the stationmaster bustled up to them, hustling them out onto the road. Hélène put her arm around Agathe's waist as they wearily walked home.

***

It was September, late in the afternoon, when Hélène came rushing into the kitchen. 'Get the animals inside. There's a huge black cloud over the Mézenc and it's coming this way. Hurry!'

Agathe ran outside; the wind had risen, the sky loomed a jaundiced grey and over on the hill the woods were already dark and menacing. Agathe shooed the cow into the byre; Hélène scuttled round the yard catching the hens and shoving the squawking bundles into the barn as the first hailstones fell. A cockerel who had indignantly evaded Hélène cackled with rage as the ice hit him, flew clumsily at the two sisters and was thrown ignominiously into the kitchen. Hélène and Agathe stood on the threshold as hailstones bigger than marbles bounced high off the cobbles.

After half an hour the storm had passed and the sun shone innocently in a serene blue sky. The two women looked out on a world as white as midwinter, except for the battered trees, whose remaining leaves stood out, incongruously colourful against the snowy blanket covering the fields.

Hélène ran down to the vegetable patch she had been tending all summer; she scrabbled away at the icy particles lying ten or more centimetres deep, exposing the shattered leaves and broken stalks. Tears running down her cheeks, Hélène walked heavily into the kitchen. 'Carrots, beet, cabbages – all gone. Everything's ruined.'

Agathe crossed herself and fell to her knees. 'Oh God, why have you forsaken us?'

PART TWO

Chapter Nine

July 1919

Hélène twisted her hair into a loose knot, jabbing long pins into the unruly auburn curls. She twirled round and smiled, satisfied the pleats of her new dress would swing gracefully when she danced and quickly went out into the sunlit morning to look for Philippe, who stood at the edge of the terrace, smoking.

'It's time to go.' She held out his heavy uniform jacket, brushed and pressed by Agathe ready for the victory parade.

He hesitated before taking it. 'I didn't want to wear this ever again.'

Hélène glanced at him sympathetically. 'Try not to be so gloomy. Today's a day for celebration. All France is saying thank you to our soldiers.' Philippe sniffed as Hélène tugged at his arm. 'You should feel proud!' Philippe shook his head as she rattled on, 'It's been so long since we've enjoyed ourselves.' She spun round, laughing. 'I think the last proper dance I've had must've been at your wedding. Five long years ago!' Hélène threw out her arms. 'What a lovely day. The whole world's putting on its best face for you.'

Philippe's wry smile broadened as they turned the corner of the farm and he saw the cart that was to take the family to Saint-Agrève draped in tricolours, the curved horns of the bullocks decorated with red, white and blue ribbons. Hélène grinned. 'Don't they look smart! I bet you'll see nothing finer on the Champs Elysées today.' Philippe tossed his jacket into the cart and helped Mathilde and the heavily pregnant Agathe into the wagon, finally handing up Berthe, who was scolded by her mother for getting mud on her new dress.

Hélène scampered along beside Philippe, who held a steadying hand on the harness of the bullocks. 'I haven't felt so happy since we heard the war was over. That was the best day of my life – until today!' She looked sideways at Philippe. 'And for you too, I bet.' She quickly glanced up at Agathe, who was leaning over, shaking her head. Philippe caught their exchange of looks.

'It's all right, Agathe, talking about the end of the war won't give me nightmares.' He thought for a moment before smiling up at his wife. 'I think our wedding was the happiest day - but it certainly was a great moment.' The women held their breath; since his return Philippe had never spoken about the war. 'We'd heard rumours on and off for weeks that things were drawing to a close but actually the German bombardment was as heavy, perhaps even heavier, than it'd been for some time. Arsac said he thought the Germans were dumping as much ammunition on us as they could so they'd have less to leave behind when they scarpered. Anyway, things were pretty much as normal until eleven o'clock on the eleventh, when we heard a trumpet sound the *cesse feu*. That was extraordinary in itself, but then there was silence – the guns, all of them, just stopped.' He stopped walking and stood looking towards the distant line of the Alps. 'You can't imagine just how astonishing that silence was – no sound of gunfire after four years. Four years when every day, all day, even at night, there was always the noise of guns coming from somewhere. That stillness was uncanny, eerie, almost sinister. Then, from far away on the left, rushing down the trench came a great shout, '*Vive la France*!' and we all yelled as loud as we could. We climbed over the parapet and looked at the enemy; they were coming out of their bunkers too. Some threw down their guns, some held up their hands, others just turned and walked away. It was an unbelievable sight.' He grinned at Hélène. 'Then we sang the "Marseillaise" – it'll never sound as moving or as powerful as on that day.' He turned away, his voice breaking. 'It was a great feeling.'

Hélène ran ahead and walked backward, looking at Philippe, her words coming quickly, 'It was lucky it was market day, so I was down in Saint-Agrève. Like you, we'd heard rumours but they never seemed to come to anything.' She turned round, her voice carrying back to them on the soft summer air. 'There was a peculiar atmosphere that morning, people were going about their business but in an absentminded way – every now and then they'd forget what they were saying and stand still, listening. After I'd sold all my cheeses I joined the crowd in front of the Mairie, but nothing stirred. Then, all of a sudden, the bells started to peal and everyone went mad!' Hélène whirled around, her arms outstretched. 'We were all hugging each other, shouting, crying. Someone started to sing the "Marseillaise" and we all belted it out at the top of our voices. Monsieur Bellat went to get his accordion, Hubert took out his violin and everyone just danced around the square – the animals looked at us as though we were totally out of our minds! Monsieur Bernard dished out free wine, people hung flags out of their windows, and all the time the bells kept ringing and ringing until your head was spinning!'

Agathe shouted down, laughing, 'And it wasn't 'til late afternoon you remembered me and came back with the news.'

'Oh, I knew you'd hear the bells!' Hélène stopped, her eyes glistening. 'Surely that was your best moment too?'

Agathe thought for a moment. 'Of course it was a tremendous relief, but it also seemed unreal. Perhaps because I was on my own, the bells weren't enough to convince me. Then we heard about the Spanish 'flu and that really scared me; I kept thinking how dreadful it would be to have survived the war only to be killed by a stupid illness.' Agathe leant down to take her husband's hand. 'It was only when I saw you walk up to the farm that February morning wearing civilian clothes that I felt really happy. Then I knew the nightmare was over and we could pick up our lives where we'd left off. That was the best day for me.'

Philippe grinned. 'It certainly took long enough! We thought we'd be home before Christmas.'

Because everyone was in such high spirits, Hélène took the rare liberty of teasing Philippe. 'I bet you stayed away deliberately just to miss the worst of the winter. When you heard we'd a metre of snow on the Plateau, you men decided you'd rather stay in a comfy barracks than be up here, shoveling snow.'

Philippe threw his cap at her, laughing, while Agathe crossed herself and said gently, 'Thank God. Life's getting back to normal and we can forget about the war.'

Hélène was close enough to hear Philippe mutter to himself, 'If only we could.' In the silence that followed, all three cast surreptitious glances at Mathilde, who sat staring ahead, tears gently running down her cheeks. Agathe put her arms around her mother as Berthe hid her face in her skirt.

The square in Saint-Agrève was already crowded. The church bells rang relentlessly, flags hung from every window and paper bunting dangled limply between the trees. Agathe walked ponderously from group to group, keeping an eye out for the Faugerons, whom she wished to avoid. A group of old women dressed in black were huddled in a knot outside the entrance to Madame Nouzet's shop, where she stood leaning on her stick, casting baleful glances at Agathe's burgeoning belly.

At the opposite side of the square a group of men were gathered round the door of the café: some stood with their uniform jackets flung over their shoulders, their shirts already stained with patches of sweat, others sat with trousers and sleeves neatly tucked over absent limbs. Philippe joined them, looking round uncertainly. Firmin Arsac came over with a glass of wine. 'Haven't seen much of you since we got back – how're you finding things?'

Philippe grinned. 'Bit of a change.'

'Faugeron, Arsac – you buggers'll have to come over here, these new fucking legs are killing me.' Roland made an effort to stand, splayed out on crutches and aluminium legs. He swore and sank back onto a bench. 'I'll be damned if anyone's going to wheel me to the bloody church' – he wiped the sweat from his brow – 'but these sodding things hurt like hell.' The three men stood drinking until their stilted conversation tailed off into an awkward silence.

Hélène could not avoid Lucinde, who was standing by the fountain, glaring at the men who had repossessed the café. Lucinde looked appreciatively at her friend, 'You look pretty – that dress really suits you.'

Hélène twirled round. 'I copied it from a magazine – it's the latest fashion in Paris.'

Lucinde looked wistfully down at the smooth white breasts that strained at the low neck of her blouse. 'I've put on so much weight I can hardly get into any of my clothes.' She lowered her voice. 'I still haven't heard from Marius. It's terrible on a day like today to be on my own.' Hélène nodded, embarrassed.

A trumpet called the men into line and Hélène wriggled her way to the front of the crowd, tapping her foot as the town band enthusiastically played '*L'Arc de Triomphe*', the victory march composed for the celebration. Five years ago over four hundred men had marched to war, out of step but upright and strong; now only half that number shuffled to form a column. Roland swayed unsteadily on his crutches, a few had to be carried on chairs, others led their blind colleagues, many more supported those who were weak and disorientated. As they made their way through the narrow streets the crowd cheered lustily, throwing handfuls of flowers, but the men marched slowly and in silence, as though they shared the efforts of their damaged colleagues. Halfway down the Grande rue a handful of men led by Firmin Arsac turned off towards the Protestant temple, while the rest continued up the hill to the church.

'Let us give thanks.' Illuminated by a shaft of multi-coloured light, the Curé stood looking down with satisfaction at the crowded church as he delicately adjusted the gold-embroidered stole he only wore when the Bishop paid a visit. He laid his hands reverently on the tricolour hanging from the pulpit, and paused for a moment, relishing the fading echoes of his sonorous voice. 'We are here to celebrate a glorious victory. The treaty signed two weeks ago finally brings peace to our beloved country. Through the Grace of God we have vanquished our enemies and put an end to war in

Europe. France has paid a terrible price, but it is a worthy sacrifice to be able to say to our children and grandchildren: we have made the world safe for you.' As the Curé paused there was a ponderous silence, broken by a wheezing cough that rasped on and on.

Resisting the emotional weight of his words, Hélène looked up at the dust dancing in the shafts of sunlight, then down to the restive congregation. Many were in mourning, anonymous and drab, but others wore their best clothes, ill-fitting finery exhumed from closets and reeking of mothballs. To distract herself from the Curé's orotund platitudes, Hélène tried to remember the names of some of the missing men: Louis Bellat, who could scythe a field faster than anyone; Anton Chapelon, whom everyone called when a cow was sick; Jules Montelimard, usually to be found in a bar while his wife did all the work ... According to Madame Faugeron, almost 150 men had not returned. Hélène shut her eyes tight, trying to not to cry at the memory of her beloved father and brother.

But she could not ignore the soldiers sitting in the choir facing the congregation. A few looked up at the priest, backs erect, shoulders straight; others sat bowed by some inner defeat, gazing sightlessly at distant battlefields where their comrades lay; others sat quaking with an unforgotten fear. Many were more obviously damaged – neatly pinned sleeves, empty trousers flapping, dressings covering eyes that could not see, bandages hiding wounds that had healed but were too terrible to be looked upon. She shivered. 'How could God have allowed so much suffering?'

The Curé's stentorian voice broke into her thoughts. 'On the eleventh of November, the name day of St Martin, the patron saint of France, our beloved country became whole again. At last we can hold our heads high as a united nation after forty-seven years of division and oppression.' A soldier in the front row could not stifle his cough, his red eyes weeping yellow mucus. The Curé continued, his voice filling the church, 'This was a just war and a war justified by God. It was a war sent to purge us of those odious practices that are an affront to our Lord. Our Father saw we had become lustful and vile. He abominated our sins of the flesh. In France, in this town, even sitting in this congregation today, there are those who fornicate, commit adultery, and indulge in lascivious practices abhorred by God - this war was a punishment to show us the error of our ways.' He turned to the soldiers beneath him, opening his arms wide, embracing them by his gesture. 'These valiant men sitting here today return not only as heroes but also as saviours. We must learn from them the virtues they practised for four long years – patriotism, courage, self-sacrifice and, above all, chastity. These virtues will make our country great again and bring to each of our firesides the wisdom and charity of Our Lord.'

A soldier staggered to his feet, handkerchief clasped over his mouth, unable to stanch the gasping cough wracking his feeble frame. A colleague led the stumbling man up the aisle and led him outside. His retching could be heard through the closed wooden doors.

'We owe this victory to God.' The Curé paused majestically. 'We have expiated our sins and, thanks to Him, have emerged purified and ready for our greater duties to our faith and our country. We must keep fresh in our hearts the demanding virtues of our soldiers and deny ourselves the sweet-smelling sins of peace.'

Hélène wove her way past the throng of those wishing to take Communion and escaped into the cleansing sunlight. She paced impatiently round the square until the Curé emerged, smiling graciously at each member of the congregation as they passed from the darkness of the church into the light. Hélène winced at the beatific smile on her sister's face as she bent to kiss the Curé's ring. Agathe walked towards Hélène, one hand lying lightly on the rounded sphere of her belly, the other clasping Berthe, who was rubbing her eyes, grizzling and querulous. 'What a wonderful sermon! Our Curé really rose to the occasion.'

'No he didn't!' The sharp anger in Hélène's voice caused people to turn their heads. 'You saw the state of the men sitting there in front of us – is all that suffering truly a "price worth paying"? And what about all the others who didn't come back? Did Papa and Francis have to die to "purify" France?'

Agathe's lips tightened, but she said nothing, conscious there were people looking at them, murmuring. Hélène continued, speaking loudly, 'Heroes I would agree with, but saviours? How can he call Roland Gounon, who's so bitter, and Firmin Arsac, who's such a bully, saviours?' Not waiting for her sister's angry reproach, Hélène stalked off down the road.

The freshness of the morning had been burnt away by the pitiless midday sun; she jammed her hat back on her head and slowed down, not wanting dark stains of sweat to spoil her new dress. As her anger evaporated, she regretted her outburst; she did not want to ruin this special day by arguing with Agathe.

It was cooler in the barn and the huge room was full of bustling activity: small girls laughed as they made two long tables cheerful with paper flags, boys clambered up ladders to hang loops of bunting along the craggy walls, members of the band fiddled with their instruments. Feeling superfluous, Hélène returned to the sunlight. Looking for some shade, she spotted Nathalie Peyrard sitting under a tree, twirling her hat on her finger.

'How are you?' Hélène held out her hand.

Nathalie smiled briefly, pleased to have company. 'I'm fine – I suppose.'

There was an awkward pause; the thoughts of both women turned to Francis but neither was willing to speak his name. Hélène broke the silence. 'Have you any plans now ...?'

Nathalie played with the ribbon of her hat, her eyes sad. 'Yes, I'm going away. This September I'll start my nurse's training in Valence. There's nothing here for me.'

Hélène was silent for a while. 'What about your family?' Nathalie was an only child.

Nathalie smiled ruefully. ‘Of course they’ll miss me and I’ll miss them, but you can’t live your life for the good of others. You have to take your own decisions, even if it’s hard to break away.’ She looked closely at Hélène. ‘Francis told me you wanted to be a teacher – are you leaving too?’ Her face brightened. ‘It’d be wonderful if you came to Valence.’

Hélène shook her head slowly. ‘It doesn’t seem fair to leave Agathe with a new baby on the way and Philippe’s not really fit yet.’ She shook herself; if Nathalie could leave her parents, surely she could leave Les Laysses. A wave of resentment at the younger girl’s determination left Hélène feeling irritated and demoralised. She stood up quickly. ‘Good luck and *bon courage*, Nathalie.’

Clusters of people were now gathered round the entrance to the barn, the women surreptitiously wiping perspiration from between their breasts, men throwing off their heavy jackets. Roland arrived on a chair, lashing out with swipes from his crutches. ‘I don’t need your fucking help. Let me alone, damn you!’

Finally the company sat down to eat. As the hours of the afternoon drained away, the thin barley soup was followed by trout in an anaemic sauce – after another long pause chicken stew and boiled potatoes were doled out by a swarm of sweating girls. The wine had done little to soften the resentment between the two sisters and their attempts at conversation only made things worse. To pass the time, Hélène kept refilling her glass with red Vivarais wine and Philippe smoked his pipe. After toying with a leg of chicken lying queasily in its greasy sauce, Hélène pushed back her chair and went outside.

The long afternoon had softened the glare of the sun and its mellow light soothed her spirits. Hélène stood under the dappled shade of the trees; the steep hillside was shorn of its rye and beyond the ribs of stubble Hélène could just distinguish the hazy outline of the Alps. She breathed in the gentle air and smiled; soon the dancing would begin.

In the doorway Hélène was hit by the heavy smells of food, sweat and the reek of rough wine. The barn was now reverberating with raised voices, faces were flushed, shirts yawned open, women's skirts were discreetly loosened. Detached from the raucous hurly-burly, Hélène stood watching as the young girls scurried round serving the crowns of *pogne* cake and spilling over-full flagons of wine.

On her right Faugeron was holding forth to a group of old men who nodded sleepily, eyes rheumy with too much drinking. 'At last things are getting back to normal.'

An old man grunted, 'Normal, what d'you mean by normal? The Plateau'll never be the same. Too many farms are lying empty and no one's willing to buy 'em.'

'The women can't manage on their own so they're leaving to find work down in the valleys. In Devesset the Mazets and the Roches have both left their farms – just walked away.'

Philippe pulled at his pipe. 'I don't blame them – it's a hard life up here. But Agathe won't hear of leaving – and I can't imagine a life away from the Plateau.'

One old chap looked at him sideways. 'You'll find it hard with only yourself to do the work. It'll be a long time before you'll have a son to help you.'

Philippe smiled. 'There's my wife – and Hélène – we'll get through.'

The conversation meandered into grumbles about the weather, diseased crops, the cussedness of pigs and Philippe smiled inwardly, reassured his life was subsiding into the rhythms of five years ago. He relit his pipe and pulled on it contentedly as he watched his wife and daughter out of the corner of his eye.

Not wanting to sit with Agathe, Hélène walked on past the Faugeron family. She paused for a moment, wrinkling her nose at the sight of Sophie, who was scolding her eldest child, slapping vainly at two daughters who ran round her chair while bouncing a squalling infant on her lap. Gerard Faugeron sat smoking beside his wife, a smug smile on his face; thanks to his post as quartermaster he had returned from the war unharmed, rotund and self-satisfied. The youngest Faugeron, Henri, lay back in his chair, pleased with the impression he was making on the four simpering girls sitting nearby, who tittered whenever he spoke. Henri had arrived at the Front just as the war ended and had seen just enough fighting to brag about it. He stood out amongst the young men, exuding a rude healthiness and an insolent cheerfulness that the other youths of his age had already lost. A distance had grown between the two families ever since

Agathe had refused to leave Les Laysses – a frostiness that had intensified after the deaths of Emile and Francis. It was not that the Vernots envied the Faugerons' good fortune, but the Faugerons had taken it upon themselves to resent their imagined envy.

Hélène joined Mathilde, who sat forlorn and silent amongst the older women and helped herself to some cake. 'Now the men're back at least they've put a stop to some of the goings on.' Lucinde's mother-in-law nodded towards Solange and Firmin Arsac, who sat gripped in a frigid silence. 'Someone must've told him what she'd been up to.' She cackled with satisfaction. 'They say she got a good beating.'

Madame Faugeron spoke loudly, 'Serve her right. If more men did the same it might make some of the others behave themselves.'

Mathilde intervened gently, 'That may be true, but Arsac goes too far. You can see he's given her another black eye.'

'She deserves it.'

'She won't stay if he keeps treating her like that.'

'Who cares!'

'And as for my daughter-in-law, God damn her!' Madame Nouzet helped herself to a glass of wine and a large slice of cake. Hélène thought angrily of the thankless hours Lucinde spent looking after the cantankerous old woman. Madame Nouzet ostentatiously dabbed her eyes. 'I wish my son'd never set eyes on her. He'd be at home now if he hadn't married her.'

The other women muttered in embarrassed agreement. Madame Faugeron pursed her lips. 'It's not only Lucinde – it's the others she leads on. Adrienne Escomel's gone completely off the rails – and that Florence Dufour! Everyone knows she's had another baby. Passing it off as her mother's never fooled anyone.'

'Doesn't seem to have stopped her – just look at her now.' The women's heads swiveled towards Florence, who was leaning over one of the Rousson brothers who had lost an arm, while Lucinde held his good arm pinned behind him. Florence had a piece of cake balanced on the voluptuous ledge of her breasts. Having eaten the cake, the young man insisted on licking the remaining sugary crumbs from the soft skin of her cleavage. Roland and a group of youths egged them on, laughing.

'Sickening! The Maire should do something about it.' Madame Faugeron turned to look complacently around the room at her three sons. 'Thank God there's nothing like that in my family.'

Feeling the need for more cheerful company, Hélène flopped down beside Lucinde. The tablecloth in front of them was now wrinkled and stained, littered with crusts of bread soaked in gravy and crumbs of *pogne* cake. Lucinde pushed a half-full glass of wine towards Hélène and waved her hand round the room. 'Look at them all.' Couples who had seemed content with each other five years ago now sat silently staring at nothing, unconcealed contempt souring their expressions. Lucinde shoved the pitcher of wine towards Hélène. 'Help yourself.' A hard, brooding expression on her face warned

Hélène to be careful. Lucinde swore. 'This is no bloody fun. I'm sick of stuffing myself.' She called out to the *cabrette* player, who was running his fingers over his chanter, the weary drone emerging from his bagpipe contrasting with the cheerful scales of the accordion and the violin. 'When's the dancing going to start?'

When the meal was finally over, a restless atmosphere permeated the room. Men went outside to relieve themselves, women stood up, adjusting their clothes and shaking crumbs from their skirts. At last the musicians started to play a lively polka and Hélène felt her spirits rise. Not wanting to be seen to belong to Lucinde's group, Hélène walked across the barn to sit with Agathe, swishing her skirt in time to the music, surreptitiously searching for prospective partners. It was not long before several couples got up to dance and Hélène began to feel the irritations of the day fall away, the bright tune made her feet tap, her body responding to the quick rhythms of the accordion. As the musicians got into their stride, pairs of girls danced together, darting hopeful glances over their shoulders at the handful of men who stood joking by the door, eyes narrowed as they inspected and assessed.

Agathe appeared to relax and Philippe turned to his wife, smiling. 'How about a dance? It's been such a long time.'

'Our wedding!' Agathe patted his hand as she shook her head, laughing. 'How can you even think of me dancing? I lumber about like a great heifer with calf.' Philippe grinned and pressed her hand for a brief moment.

Hélène looked at Philippe. 'But I'm dying to dance.' Her eyes sparkled as she leapt up and stood in front of him. 'You could dance with me.' She reached down and pulled him to his feet.

Agathe spoke quickly and cruelly, 'No he can't!' Both Philippe and Hélène looked at her, incredulous. 'Have you forgotten his leg? You know it's not properly healed.'

Philippe raised his eyebrows and sat down again. Hélène stood in front of her sister, her hands on her hips. 'It can't be that bad, he would've danced with you.'

Agathe tossed her head, her face set tight. 'My husband's not going to dance with anyone but me – it isn't right.'

Hélène flung herself down on her chair, Agathe, grim-faced, jogged Berthe up and down on her knee, Philippe looked down at the floor. As Hélène seethed with frustration, Roland came over, an arm propped up on one of his crutches, the other supported by an Army mate. He stood swaying in front of Philippe, his eyes small, red and glittering. 'Why aren't you dancing, comrade? You've got two good legs and two pretty women to dance with.'

Philippe frowned but said nothing.

Roland's lip curled. 'You don't realise how lucky you are, Faugeron. Two women and one man shacked up together can't be bad. I hope you're making the most of it.' Winking at Philippe, he sniggered. 'While one's knocked up, there's always the other.'

'That's enough Roland! You're disgusting.' Agathe attempted to get up.

Philippe restrained her, saying menacingly, 'Clear off and mind your own bloody business, Gounon.'

Roland staggered and almost fell onto Agathe's lap. She pushed him away; he was pulled upright by his friend and stood teetering in front of Philippe. 'You're a miserable sod, Faugeron.'

Hélène felt near to tears; the relentless cheerfulness of the music grated on her nerves. After a while Agathe nodded frostily in the direction of the Faugerons. 'Why don't you dance with Henri?'

On hearing his name, Henri turned towards them, his eyes sliding past Hélène, not registering her existence. Hélène felt a rush of blood to her cheeks as she saw the sixteen-year-old girls tittering behind him and heard one of them whisper behind her hand, 'He'll never dance with her, she's far too old.' Hélène felt a tightening in her chest, a stab of panic; she tried to shrug it off but the words had wormed into her thoughts.

She spat out, 'Nothing would make me dance with him!' and flounced away to join Lucinde at the other end of the hall.

Sullenly, the two women watched the dancers as they linked arms, changed partners and worked their way up and down the room in a lively cotillion. Lucinde nudged Hélène. 'Look at Lafont.' The blacksmith had hold of his wife's arm and was pulling her onto the dance floor. She tried to get away, her face twisted with anger, but his grip on her arm tightened and she was forced into the dancing throng. Lafont laughed in her face as he stamped his feet, linked arms and swung round with another woman, leaving his wife behind.

'Look at her!' Lucinde nodded towards Solange Arsac, who was watching the blacksmith with unconcealed lust. She shoved aside her glass. 'Let's dance. I'm sick of sitting here feeling miserable.'

As Hélène hesitated, Lucinde took her hand and dragged her into the middle of the room. The cotillion was exhilarating: the musicians played faster and faster as the dancers jigged backwards and forwards, linking arms, swapping partners and whirling off again, skirts flying. Tomas capered in and out, pinching the women's bottoms and trying to put his hand up their skirts – until he was marched outside, where he could be heard whimpering. Hélène felt her spirits rise as the wild rhythms of the music, the stamping feet, the clapping hands became wilder and fiercer.

The dance ended and the *cabrette* led the accordion and violin into a waltz. Lucinde grasped Hélène close; the sickly sweetness of Lucinde's perfume mixed with sweat and her hot breath, foetid with wine was nauseating. Lucinde whispered, 'D'you see the Curé?' Hélène looked round and caught sight of the priest standing by the door watching them. She nodded. 'Watch this.' Lucinde took out a handkerchief and paused for a moment, facing the Curé as she thrust the scrap of cloth deep down into her cleavage to mop the sweat trickling between her breasts and bent forward so that her voluptuous curves almost escaped from her blouse.

The Curé gasped and left the barn. Lucinde burst into giggles.

Hélène chuckled. 'You shouldn't tease him like that!'

'He should know better.'

As the two women waltzed past Madame Nouzet, Hélène overheard her saying acidly to Mathilde, 'You'd better keep an eye on Hélène, she's getting as bad as the rest of them.' Hélène tried to loosen Lucinde's hold, but the other girl just laughed and held her more tightly.

As they whirled past Roland, he shouted sarcastically, 'Don't those two make a lovely couple? No guessing what they get up to when they're on their own,' to the delighted cackling of his entourage.

Hélène blushed and forcefully freed herself from Lucinde's grasp. 'Let's sit down, I don't like this tune.'

At last the waltz ended and the hot, perspiring dancers returned to their seats. Hélène said sulkily, 'No one's asked me to dance. Not once this afternoon.' The accordion player announced the next dance would be a mazurka – and it would be the ladies' turn to choose their partners.

'Well, now's your chance.' Lucinde looked round the room, eyes narrowed thoughtfully. 'Who shall I choose?' Her face brightened. 'I'll ask your brother-in-law – I can't imagine why he's not dancing.'

Hélène snorted. 'Forget it. My sister won't let him dance with you.'

'Why not? What's wrong with me?'

'Because she won't let him dance with anyone except herself and she won't dance 'cos she's pregnant.'

'All wives are so bloody selfish!' Lucinde giggled. 'Then I'll choose Arsac – so Solange can ask Lafont. But what about you?'

Hélène's expression was sullen. 'There isn't anyone I want to dance with.'

'Rubbish! Why don't you ask Henri Faugeron?' Lucinde turned to Florence. 'And you go for Gerard. That'll piss off that cow Sophie.'

As the violin scraped a preliminary chord, Hélène walked quickly across the hall but saw she was already too late: the four girls who had been ogling Henri all afternoon were jumping up and down, begging him to dance. Henri stood up, preening his small moustache, keeping them in suspense as he eyed each of them from head to foot. As he held out his hand to the prettiest the three rejected girls subsided into acrimonious sulks. Frustrated, Hélène bit her lip and turned towards Roland's group, hurriedly asking a man she did not know for a dance, blushing with humiliation as his companions bent double with glee. As he got up awkwardly with a delighted expression, Hélène paled; her chosen partner had a heavy orthopaedic boot on his left foot, attached to a leg that was far shorter than the other. They manoeuvred clumsily into the throng of dancers, trying to avoid treading on each other's toes.

Lucinde stood in front of Firmin Arsac, arms akimbo. 'Who're you calling a slut?'

'You! All the filth that's been going on while we're away's down to you.'

'Go on Arsac, tell her!' Roland's voice carried across the room.

Lucinde stood for a moment looking down at him, her eyes narrowed. 'May you rot in hell, Arsac.'

Above the music, Sophie Faugeron's sharp voice reached Hélène. 'There's no way my husband's going to dance with the likes of you. Leave him alone.'

Florence stood her ground. 'I didn't ask you. I'm asking him.' She held out her hand to Gerard, who blushed and stood up.

His wife got up too, scattering children. 'Don't you dare, Gerard!'

Hélène moved out of earshot as the music became faster and fiercer, her feet suffering from the missteps of her partner, who was sweating profusely. Tomas, excited by the swirling music, capered in and out of the dancers. He pinched Hélène's bottom hard and she lashed out at him. Glimpses of couples came and went: the blacksmith and Adrienne swooped past, their faces close; Henri bounced by, his strong arms holding his swooning partner tight. As the dancing couples whirled faster and faster, Hélène's partner could not keep up so she let him limp off to his companions and went to lean against the wall, glaring furiously at the frenetic, spinning dancers.

Sophie Faugeron and Felicitie Lafont had gathered round Agathe. They stood scowling at Lucinde, who had retreated to her seat, a full glass of wine in front of her. The venomous voice of Sophie Faugeron reached Hélène. ‘Those women are determined to seduce all our husbands. They’re disgusting.’

‘And spoiling the party for everyone.’

'I'm going to put a stop to this.'

At the far end of the room, Lucinde sat brooding, doggedly refilling her glass and tossing back the harsh red wine. As she stood wondering whether to join her, Lucinde’s voice blared out, strident and hoarse, cutting across the racing trills of the band and the stamping of booted feet on the stone floor. ‘Stop the bloody music!’ The music tailed away; the dancers, muttering and confused, came to a ragged halt; all eyes, some hostile, some amused, turned towards Lucinde, who rose to her feet.

‘You’re drunk! Sit down and shut up.’ Felicitie Lafont’s sharp voice shrilled down the hall.

‘I’ve had enough of this!’ Sophie Faugeron rose to her feet and strode across the floor, drawing a trail of women behind her. They converged into a malignant pack in front of Lucinde. ‘This is supposed to be a victory celebration – to thank our men who’ve sacrificed so much.’ She leant forward, spitting her words into Lucinde’s face. ‘A sacrifice your husband wasn’t prepared to make.’ Roland cheered loudly. ‘Don’t you dare spoil it for the rest of us.’

Lucinde moved back. Straightening up, she spoke with a ringing authority which reached all corners of the room. ‘This isn’t a celebration, it’s a wake. Use your eyes. The Curé can call these men heroes, but they're not a patch on the men who left us. Just look at them.' She waved towards the group surrounding Roland and their pitiable infirmities. She scowled at the women braying with indignation at her. 'And just because you've got husbands, you haven't the right to tell us what to do.'

Roland shouted out, 'Who says you haven't got a husband?'

Lucinde turned on him. 'At least he'd the guts to say what he thought about the bloody war.'

There were cries of outrage. A woman's voice rose high and sharp, 'Don't you dare compare my husband with yours. My Anton died fighting bravely for his country.' The women massed in front of Lucinde bayed with rage and shook their fists.

As the women surged forward, shouting, the Curé tried to intervene. He took hold of Lucinde's arm in an effort to lead her away but she pulled free. 'Get your hands off me, you filthy hypocrite.' The Curé recoiled and stood breathing heavily in a corner of the room.

Madame Faugeron called out to the Maire. 'Put a stop to this! She's drunk.'

The Maire signaled to the band to start the music again; the musicians made a half-hearted attempt to play over the din, then fell silent. The Maire spoke to Lucinde, but she only swore at him in reply.

Madame Faugeron pushed the Maire aside; she put both hands on the table and leant over so her face was close to Lucinde's. 'Shut up, Lucinde Nouzet. There are plenty of better women than you who've been widowed. They put up with it – why can't you?'

Felicitie Lafont broke in, her voice raw with rage, 'And leave our men alone. We know what you and your friends get up to ...'

'All whores!' The voice of Lucinde's mother-in-law echoed down the barn.

Florence stood beside Lucinde, facing the accusing women. 'Stop blaming us – your men wouldn't stray if you gave them what they wanted.'

There was a seething agitation in the room, many of the men gathered their families together and made for the door, shouting indignantly that the whole day had been spoilt. Madame Faugeron flounced back to her seat. The Maire once again attempted to intervene. Lucinde sat down and began to cry.

Hélène looked at the mob of self-righteous women towering over the slumped figure of Lucinde; Florence stood behind her friend, hands on hips; Tomas knelt on the floor, clutching Lucinde's skirt, whimpering in sympathy – and between the two groups stood the sinister figure of Roland, arms supported on crutches, spindly metal legs splayed out like some demonic spider. Hélène said fiercely to Agathe, 'What Lucinde said is true.'

Agathe frowned imperiously. 'Don't talk nonsense!'

'Look round the room. Where are the men I could marry? There aren't any. They're dead, married already, or like Roland.'

'So what can be done about it? Nothing!' Agathe picked up Berthe, preparing to leave. 'The

Curé was right: this is God's will, so you'll just have to learn to put up with it.' She moved towards the door. 'And you'd better stay away from that Lucinde – she's bad news.'

Philippe helped Mathilde to her feet, saying sadly, 'This isn't what we fought for.'

'The whole day's been dreadful,' said Agathe. She would not meet Hélène's eyes.

They joined the many families who were muttering angrily, jostling against each other in their eagerness to leave the room.

On the way home no one spoke and Hélène trailed behind the others. The evening sun still shone over the hills but its soft light did nothing to calm Hélène's mood. She felt drained; nauseous from the wine, food and emotion – and overwhelmingly sad. She was young and pretty, she had hoped the day would have been fun, had even imagined there might be a romantic adventure. But it was all empty foolishness – the carefree past could not be brought back. She remembered the words 'too old' and shuddered - at twenty-one she was condemned to the life of an old maid. Tears of self-pity crept down her cheeks.

When they reached the farmhouse, Agathe put Berthe to bed, her lips taut with disapproval and went upstairs; a short while later Philippe finished his pipe and silently followed his wife. Hélène took off her new dress and crammed it into the chest, hating the hopes it had represented. She went outside.

Hélène slowly made her way up the fields to the crest of the hill. She tried to tell herself that she loved her sister - but she hated her narrow-minded optimism and blind faith. As she climbed upwards Hélène's resentment of her sister's happiness grew. Agathe had the life she had always wanted – Philippe, Berthe, the farm. The disappointments of the day had told Hélène her own future would hold nothing she had longed for. It would be lonely, desolate, hopeless.

She looked at the familiar outline of the Mézenc, crisp against the cold blue of the sky. The moon stared down at her unblinking; the crystal points of the stars shone infinitely distant and indifferent. Impenetrable shadows surrounded her, full of phantoms. This beautiful landscape, implacable and pitiless, was her prison. She whispered into the night, 'I must leave this place. I have to get away.'

As Hélène walked across the farmyard, she could hear Philippe's muffled shouts – another nightmare.

Chapter Ten

September 1919 –July 1920

‘You can’t leave! I’ve got Berthe and Maman to look after and Philippe can’t run the farm on his own. I’m so sick of arguing with you.’ Hélène stood facing her sister with hands clenched, while Philippe scraped back his chair and went outside. Agathe banged down the dishes she was carrying. ‘It’s your fault he can’t bear to be in his own kitchen.’

Hélène replied tartly, ‘Obviously he prefers to sit in the barn drinking.’

‘What he does is none of your business.’ Agathe picked up the plates and stacked them noisily on the dresser. She sat down heavily, careful of her swollen belly and wiped back a damp lock of hair. ‘You can leave after the baby’s born.’

‘But by October winter’ll be coming and it’ll be much harder to find work.’

Agathe closed her eyes and sighed. ‘I can't understand why you are so desperate to leave.' Philippe and I both want you to stay. We can have a good life here, like our parents and grandparents.’

Her voice hardened. 'Why can't you accept what God has sent you and be thankful?'

Hélène replied sulkily, 'I've told you so many times. I want to make something of my life.'

'Our father should never have encouraged your fancy ideas. You only think of yourself. What about me, what about Berthe – what about your mother?'

'It's not me that's being selfish, it's you! You want everything to stay the same; you won't allow anything to change.' Hélène fell silent; both women listened to the weary clumping of Philippe's clogs as he made his way up the outside stairs to the bedroom. Agathe put her head in her hands; she could not understand why Philippe drank himself into a stupor most nights and what she did not understand upset her. Hélène bit her lip. 'I'm sorry Agathe; I didn't mean to hurt you.' She put a tentative hand on her sister's shoulder. 'I'll stay – 'til the baby comes.'

Agathe gave her sister a hug. 'And for a while afterwards? Babies are such hard work at the beginning.'

Hélène felt her hackles rise. She said sharply, 'I've said I'll stay 'til October.'

When she was alone, Hélène stood by the fire, angry with herself for giving in to Agathe once again. In her bare bedroom she took out of her chest a well-thumbed copy of *Le Petit Echo de la Mode* and, as she turned the pages of the treasured magazine, imagined herself as one of the young women it pictured walking nonchalantly through the streets of Paris or drinking coffee in a busy café. She unhitched the small mirror from its nail and carefully opened a small tin box, brightly decorated with flowers. Using a clean handkerchief, she dabbed the powder over her face, smiling as the freckles she hated almost disappeared. As she looked in the mirror, her smile faded and she snapped the box shut so hard the pale pink powder floated in the air to land gently on her nightdress. 'What's the point? I'll never go to Paris. Damn Agathe, damn the new baby.'

***

The two women in the church shook their heads. 'You'll find him at Madame Nouzet's. She's poorly; the Curé's gone to visit her.'

Hélène was surprised to find the Nouzets' shop closed and hesitated before gently pushing open the door. She could hear the hectoring tone of the Curé and Lucinde's truculent replies. Unseen in the gloom of the entrance, Hélène stood watching as Lucinde reached for her cardigan, the Curé, anticipating her, picked it up from the counter and held it out. As Lucinde put her arms into its sleeves, Hélène watched as the Curé's hands moved round and lightly caressed Lucinde's breasts. The two stood transfixed, Lucinde's back leaning against the Curé, his arms around her; she moved forward slightly so his hands were cupped over the yielding flesh. For a moment they both stood, absorbed by this peculiar embrace – until the priest leapt back, arms flung out. Lucinde turned slowly, her face uplifted, her lips open; their eyes locked together and Lucinde swayed forward so their bodies made contact, the rounded firmness of her breasts pressed against the Curé's chest as she shut her eyes. This lasted a long moment until, as though released from a spell, the Curé staggered backwards and a terrible groan escaped him. 'May God forgive you, you ...' He looked down and Hélène saw the concupiscent swelling under his cassock he could not conceal.

Lucinde looked at him with contempt and, as the Curé rushed towards the stairs leading up to Madame Nouzet's apartment, shouted after him, 'You'd better not let her see you like that! She might think you're after her.'

Shocked, Hélène retreated into the cleansing autumn sunlight and the everyday bustle of the market. She waited until the Curé had left before going back into the shop, where she found Lucinde calmly pouring raisins into bags.

'Don't bother going to see him! After Marius left, I asked the Curé if he could help me find somewhere to go; it was driving me mad cooped up with the old harridan, waiting on her hand and foot.' She moved the blue packages to one side, sighing. 'He was no bloody use. Read me a lecture about how I'd a responsibility to look after the old cow. Told me he wouldn't help me even if he could.' She stuffed a handful of raisins into her mouth. 'Then the sanctimonious bastard had a go at me – all the usual stuff.' Hélène waited, curious to hear if Lucinde would mention what had just happened, but she said nothing.

Hélène frowned. 'Then he'll probably tell me to stay and help Agathe too.' Lucinde nodded with a wry smile. 'What about the silk factory in Le

Cheylard – might they have any vacancies? I'd rather find a job where I could start my teacher training, but I'd be prepared to go anywhere just to get away.'

Lucinde made a face. 'You could try, but when I spoke to them they said they didn't want girls over twenty. Too much trouble. They're hiring sixteen-year-olds – if they hire anyone. They say there's not much business. It's the same here; no one's buying much these days.' She came out from behind the counter and took off her apron. 'But it's a beautiful day, why don't you come with us? I'm going to shut the shop, get hold of Adrienne and Florence and we'll all go to the woods and pick some *ceps*. Old Pilat says there're lots around this year.'

'I don't think ...' Hélène hesitated. She disliked the other two girls and did not want to be seen with them, but she was lonely: Philippe rarely spoke to her and Agathe's conversation was almost entirely focused on babies – when they were not having rows.

Lucinde grabbed her arm. 'Don't be silly. You'll have to hang around 'til the market's over and your brother-in-law's had his lunch anyway.' She was already locking the door. 'Have some fun for a change.'

The four young women walked laughing and singing down the road towards Intres. Just beyond the forbidding mass of the Domaine de Rilhac, Florence led them deep into the dank woods. The girls called out to each other as they darted from place to place, plucking the smooth shafts out of the soft fragrant moss. But it was cold in the shade and

Hélène was relieved when Lucinde called out, 'I've had enough. Let's go to our usual spot and have some lunch.' The four young women ran along a path until they reached a secluded glade where the enclosing trees were bright with golden leaves and beams of sunlight warmed a bank covered in ferns. Lucinde threw herself on the ground and took a bottle of wine from the bag she had slung over her shoulder. The others settled themselves comfortably, their backs against the lichen-covered trees.

'So what's new?' Lucinde looked at Florence and Adrienne expectantly and giggled.

Adrienne laughed, a guttural, self-satisfied sound. 'Have you seen the new boy who sells ribbons and stuff? He seems sweet.'

'Called Micaelo, he's Spanish.' Florence looked daggers at Adrienne. 'Leave him alone, I got there first.'

Lucinde laughed. 'How is he?'

Florence stroked her thighs luxuriously. 'Keen, energetic, very satisfying. Need I say more?'

'Yes, tell us, we want all the details!'

Adrienne made an imperceptible nod towards Hélène who had flushed bright red; Florence tittered, Lucinde shrugged and the three fell silent.

'What about Romano?'

Lucinde made a face. 'What about him? There's a woman from Les Eyres who seems to have caught his eye. I'm more interested in the Italian who's working on the Faugerons' farm.' She licked her lips. 'His eyes are so dark; the muscles on him make me feel faint.'

'Have you ...?'

Lucinde laughed. 'Give me a chance – he's only been around a week!' She turned to Hélène. 'What about you?' Hélène wished she could sink into the earth. Lucinde nudged her. 'Don't be shy, you can tell us – we tell each other everything.' She leant forward. 'What d'you do when,' she giggled, 'you get the urge? What about that attractive brother-in-law of yours? Now your sister's in the club, he must be desperate.'

Hélène got to her feet, her face flaming. 'Don't be ridiculous! There's nothing like that going on.'

Adrienne turned onto her stomach. 'Don't get so excited! We're all young, we're all normal – stands to reason we need a man. It's a fact of life.'

'When men chase women no one bats an eyelid.'

'They enjoy it and so do we.'

Lucinde turned to her friend. 'Are you telling us that you only do it to yourself?' She turned to the others. 'That's terrible!'

Florence spat out a stalk of grass she had been chewing. 'If the worst comes to the worst there's always Tomas. He'll happily oblige. Give him half a loaf of bread and he'll bang away all afternoon round the back of the church.'

'That's disgusting!'

'Oh don't be so prissy! What d'you want – a handsome hero, wedding bells, love ever after? I'm telling you, Hélène, that ain't going to happen up here on the Plateau.'

'I want to leave.'

'And what makes you think it'd be better in the valley? The war killed men from down there just the same as here.'

Lucinde sat up, waving the second bottle above her head. 'Who wants the rest of this wine?' The other two fell on her, rolling together on the grass, arms around each other, giggling, a squealing mass of bodies twining and heaving. Adrienne held Lucinde in her arms while Florence held her by her waist. 'Should we?'

Lucinde looked over at Hélène, who was sitting watching them, fascinated and horrified. She sat up, pushing the others away. 'Better not.' She clambered to her feet, straightening her clothes. 'We should be getting back. I promised the old biddy I'd make her a fricassée of *cèps* for her *gouter,* tho' I won't get any thanks for it.'

Hélène had intended to linger behind, but Lucinde and Adrienne linked arms with her and together all four young women careered wildly down the road. As they entered the town, the others sang more loudly and walked with a more determined swagger. Hélène was conscious of unseen eyes watching them and blushed with embarrassment. Women turned their heads as they passed, whispering behind their hands, their glittering eyes following them. Men subtly turned their backs, shrinking closer together as though for protection. Conscious of this, the three women laughed louder, their comments became more outrageous and they pretended to be tipsier than they were. A group of men outside the café watched them, their lascivious eyes narrow and moist with wine. Hélène could not hear their comments, but there was no mistaking the contempt in their gusts of laughter. This attention seemed to further stimulate the three women, who stooped to rinse their hands, blackened by the fungi, in the cool water of the fountain. They dabbed at their necks with wet handkerchiefs, bending over to expose their fine cleavages to the admiring males.

Florence was splashing water over her face when Tomas, who usually lurked by the fountain, goosed her from behind. Conscious of the men sitting outside the café, she turned towards Tomas and flicked up her skirt so he could see her drawers and slapped him hard with a wet cloth. The men whistled, Tomas ran away and the women chased him, splattering him with water. When he was at a safe distance he turned round, jigging up and down, rubbing his crotch as the women imitated his gestures and jeered at him.

As Hélène had feared, Roland soon appeared from inside the cafe, tottering as fast as he could on his crutches, his eyes lit up when he saw the women. He called across the dusty square, 'Had a good time in the woods, girls? Hope you've come back satisfied and relaxed – doing it yourself takes the pressure off us men.' He raised his eyebrows as he noticed Hélène. 'I spy a new addition.' He staggered toward her, she blushed fiercely. 'So how d'you find it in a foursome? I bet you've learnt lots of tips from our experts here.'

Hélène turned away, swearing at him, while Lucinde ran off, calling over her shoulder, 'Shame you couldn't join us, Gounon, we'd have taught you a thing or two.'

Hélène could not hide her disgust; she pushed past the cackling men and went into the café to find Philippe.

He was joking with a group of farmers, his cheerful laughter was quite different from the taciturn moodiness he showed at Les Laysses and Hélène saw, with some surprise, that when he smiled her brother-in-law was an attractive man; his sun-browned skin taut over high cheekbones, his dark blue eyes clear and direct. As he turned and saw her, Philippe's expression closed, he drained his glass and stood up slowly.

On the way home Philippe said nothing, his thoughts apparently far away. To break the silence, Hélène asked him what the men had been laughing at in the café. Philippe shrugged. 'Just farming matters.' He continued to look straight ahead as he said in a neutral tone, 'I saw you with Lucinde and her gang.'

Hélène blushed. 'I feel sorry for her.' She spoke sharply, ashamed of her embarrassment.

Philippe raised his eyebrows. 'She causes a lot of trouble.'

'She wouldn't be like this if Marius was around – or her baby hadn't died. Life's been unfair to her – it's no wonder she's unhappy.'

Philippe looked at Hélène. 'Unfairness is no excuse. And lots of people are unhappy.'

Hélène looked straight ahead. 'That's true.' She paused. 'Life seemed so carefree before the war. Remember the way Lucinde and Marius danced at your wedding?' Philippe grunted and Hélène continued, 'It all seemed so simple then – and the sun shone all the time.' She laughed to cover the break in her voice. 'It's all so far away.' She turned to Philippe. 'Don't you ever talk about the war – with Arsac or the others you were with?'

Philippe was silent for a long while. 'No, there isn't much point. It's all over.'

'That's what Agathe says: forget it, it's in the past.'

Philippe smiled ruefully. 'Sadly I can't forget it, even though I try.' He shook the reins. 'But I don't want to talk about it; and Agathe has a point, it's better you don't know what it was like.'

Hélène said nothing, thinking of the long days Philippe worked, exhausting himself until long after night had fallen – then sloping off to the barn to drink on his own until he was numb enough to fall asleep. They reached the farmhouse in an uncomfortable silence.

***

The baby was born at the end of October: another girl, to Agathe's obvious disappointment. Philippe had comforted her, saying 'Don't worry, there'll be plenty more,' which had sent a shiver of envy down Hélène's spine. Cécile was a sickly child who needed a lot of attention and it soon became clear there was no question of Hélène leaving the farm in the foreseeable future.

Winter set in early and, although there was not as much snow as the previous year, December was cruelly cold. The track leading to the farm was treacherous and it took all Philippe's strength to break the thick crust of ice that formed on the water trough each night. Unable to escape to the market, Philippe became increasingly moody and his nightmares more frequent. The cries of the new baby made the kitchen especially claustrophobic and the whole family had to endure long, interminable days where the only diversion seemed to be rows between the two sisters.

As the wearisome winter trailed into February, Mathilde's health deteriorated rapidly. She no longer sat by the fire but lay in the box bed, wisps of white hair straying from her cotton cap and her hands, clasped on the crocheted coverlet, shook convulsively.

Hélène felt her forehead; it was burning with fever. When Philippe came in from watering the animals, the two sisters spoke to him in whispers. 'She's much worse. We must send for the Curé.'

Philippe raised his eyebrows. 'It's pretty bad outside.' He bent over Mathilde and nodded. 'The sooner I get going the better.'

Hélène held her mother's limp hand in her own, the feeble pulse barely perceptible; she glanced across at Agathe, who was suckling Cécile. 'Surely he'll be back soon, he's been gone four hours?' She went to the window. 'It's still snowing, and getting dark.'

The two women sat waiting in the flickering light of the fire, whose occasional flames sent silent shadows scuttling into corners; Mathilde's wheezing breath the only sound. At last Hélène heard a noise outside and cautiously opened the door to find Philippe and the Curé kicking ice off their boots and shaking the sacking from their shoulders, solid with snow.

The Curé knelt by Mathilde's bedside and intoned the last rites. After he had made the sign of the cross, he joined the others by the fire as Agathe poured the cordial saved for special visitors into a tiny glass. The Curé's bulky form was a brooding presence in the small kitchen and cast a dark shadow over the bed where Mathilde lay. In the firelight Hélène thought he looked jaundiced and pale, his jaws sagged with apparent tiredness; for a moment she felt some sympathy for him, but as he held out the hem of his snow-soaked cassock to the heat of the fire, the musty smell of church, unwashed clothes and his unloved body nauseated her.

Agathe offered the Curé some stale cake left over from a *viellée* two weeks before; he gobbled it down, and then asked sharply for a bowl of the soup bubbling over the fire. Agathe looked at him askance. 'It's only *garbure*.'

'For our supper,' Hélène added pointedly.

The Curé ate greedily, the warm liquid running from the corner of his lips, his chins glistening in the firelight. Agathe refilled his bowl and Hélène began to count the small glasses of cordial he tossed down.

The two sisters took it in turns to leave the warmth of the fire to sit holding their mother's hand. Just after midnight Mathilde opened her eyes, her voice barely a thread on the air. 'I'm coming,

Emile.' There was a harsh rasp as the final breath left her body, a long shudder convulsed her fragile frame, the Curé made a sign of the cross, and it was all over. He closed her eyes and folded her hands on her breast.

The Curé prepared to leave, filling the room with his sour smell. He briskly expressed his condolences; in a hurry to leave, he said tersely, 'There's no question of a burial at the moment, the earth's frozen solid. I've already got old Chalfont and Madame Beal lying in the sacristy.'

Agathe looked at him with desperation. 'But we must say a Mass for her.'

'As soon as the weather permits.' He made a sign of the cross over the weeping women, swiftly helped himself to two more glasses of cordial and went out into the eddying snow.

The following day the snow had stopped falling but lay over a metre deep in the drifts banked against the walls of the track leading up to the road. Philippe brought some planks from the barn and fashioned a coffin for Mathilde. When it was finished, Agathe used one of her best linen sheets to line the rough box and Mathilde's corpse, laid out in her best clothes, was tenderly placed within it. After a prayer together, Agathe looked at Philippe. 'How're we going to get Maman to the church?'

'At the moment it's impossible. The snow's too deep and too soft.' He took Agathe's hand. 'We'll have to put her in the hay barn.' Agathe shuddered and began to cry.

It was five days before Philippe brought out the sled and roped the coffin securely in place. Hélène watched as Agathe and Philippe dragged the wooden box containing the remains of her beloved mother down the snow-filled track. After they had disappeared, she stood for a long time at the corner of the house, eyes full of tears. Back inside, the kitchen felt wonderfully empty and peaceful; Berthe chattered happily to herself as she played with some bobbins and Hélène gathered Cécile from her cradle, humming softly to the sleeping child.

After a while Cécile began to cry, an urgent wail demanding food. Hélène kissed her soft hair and, moving aside her shawl, opened her blouse and placed the tiny head against her naked breast, feeling a surge of pleasure as the tender mouth nuzzled round the unfamiliar curves. The delicate lips searched and found the small hard nipple and began to suck, as Hélène held her close a new, pure happiness overwhelmed her - but the nipple was too unrewarding and the infant began to whimper. For a while Hélène held the crying baby to her breast, cooing and cradling her, enraptured by her soft searching and gently flailing fists. She kissed Cécile and closed her blouse reluctantly, dipped a clean rag in the mixture of warm milk and honey she had prepared and gave it to the baby to suck. It took a long time until the exhausted child lay back in her arms and with a satisfied sigh fell asleep. Hélène sat with the baby on her lap, talking to Berthe as the little girl rolled the wooden bobbins in a complicated game only she knew how to play, overcome by a feeling of completeness and contentment, a longing to have a child of her own.

***

Hélène straightened up for a moment, looking across the broad, sloping field to the line of reapers. The five men had taken off their shirts; the sweat running down their bodies glistened in the sun. She watched as they swung their scythes, strong sinews relaxing and contracting in a hypnotic rhythm as they cut their way through the upstanding grass, and five long snakes of mown hay extended behind them. Her gaze kept returning to the last man in the line. Hélène watched the Italian as he strode forward, his muscular shoulders swaying, the sweat collecting at the base of his back where it disappeared into loose trousers held up by braces.

Hélène mopped the sweat running between her breasts and loosened her blouse: the only sounds were the buzz of insects and the hiss of hay severed by the slicing blades. The smell of fragrant grass mixed with the strong scent of sweat was intoxicating in the heat of the June day. Agathe caught up with her, sending forkfuls of grass flying into the air to lie in a neat row behind her.

'Haymaking's the best time of year. I'm going to miss it.' Hélène leant on her pitchfork. 'It must be nearly lunchtime – I'm exhausted and famished.' She shaded her eyes and was pleased to see Madame Faugeron and Sophie struggling across the stubble with two large baskets. The men reached the end of the field, threw down their scythes and made for the shade of the chestnut tree where the Faugeron women were laying out lunch.

Madame Faugeron sat down, panting with the effort, and undid the top buttons of her blouse. 'My God, it's so hot!'

'Better not undo that much further or I'll be tempted to carry you off into the bushes!'

Madame Faugeron gave her husband a hearty slap. She looked round complacently at the men of her family, all strong and healthy, smelling of hay. 'All of you, put your shirts back on if you're intending to eat, you smell ...' She tried not to smile, disarmed by the grins on their faces. 'Well, it's indecent.'

Gerard, who had lost his wartime corpulence after two years working on the farm, drained his glass and held it out for more. 'Come on, Maman, honest sweat never did anyone any harm. As for the bushes' – he nudged his wife – 'it was at haymaking, a few years ago now, when Sophie and I did a little business over there, as I recall.' He waved his glass towards the woods up the hill. 'And little Bernard was the result. Haymaking's the time to make hay.' The others groaned and laughed, except for Sophie, who flapped a napkin at the wasps circling the soft balls of cheese and snapped at an errant child.

Bored by their banter, Hélène broke off some bread and went to sit under a nearby tree. Through half-closed eyes she watched as the group ate, joked and gossiped. She smiled in anticipation; in two days' time she would be starting a new life, away from these people whom she knew too well and who's every word and action were minutely predictable.

Madame Faugeron looked round. ‘Where’s Henri?’

Sophie slapped one of her daughters in irritation. ‘I don’t know where he’s got to – there’ll be no lunch left if he doesn’t come soon.’

With tight lips, Agathe nodded towards the wood and the Faugeron men tittered as Henri emerged, his arm around young Floralie Nugent, both looking hot, rumpled and sheepish. ‘Are those two engaged?’

Madame Faugeron snorted. ‘Not as far as I’m aware.’ She glared at her youngest son who shrugged, winking at his father. ‘And not if I can help it. Sloping off into the woods indeed! You should wait ’til you’re engaged, at least.’

Monsieur Faugeron laughed heartily. ‘You’re showing your age, Véronique. In this heat who can blame a young man for wanting to go courting a pretty girl?’

‘Courting! Is that what you call it?’ Madame Faugeron paused to help herself to some more cheese. ‘Speaking of which, have you heard?’ She turned to Agathe. ‘Solange Arsac’s run away. Hasn’t been heard of for two weeks.’

‘She’s no loss! Anyway it's hardly surprising; her husband made her life a misery.’

Sophie pursed her lips. ‘Then she should’ve been more careful. Apparently she kept pestering the blacksmith even though he’d lost interest. God knows what she’s doing now.’

‘Probably joined that Florence Dufour, wherever she’s got to. Another baby on the way and no chance of passing it off as her mother's now she's a widow.'

'They say she's run off with the pedlar; he must be a good ten years younger than she is.' Sophie turned to Agathe. 'So Hélène's leaving?'

Agathe nodded and made a wry face. 'She was absolutely determined. She'll be staying in Valence with Nathalie Peyrard.' She hauled Berthe back from the pot of honey. 'I didn't want her to go; it'll be very difficult without her.'

As Hélène sat dreaming of her new life, her pulse quickened as she saw the Italian gracefully rise to his feet and saunter towards her. As he drew near, his eyes penetrated hers so deeply she blushed. He sat down facing her, still staring at her intently. He picked a long stem of grass and brushed it lightly along the length of her bare leg; it tickled and Hélène laughed. He smiled, a knowing, lazy smile, as he said, 'You're pretty,' and again Hélène blushed. This seemed to encourage him and he moved closer. Hélène began to speak, but her words came out in the wrong order and she blushed some more. He shook his head. 'No understand.' They sat looking at each other until Hélène was unable to meet his dark, dangerous eyes and stared instead at the black hairs on his chest, which became silky and fine as they snaked down below his waist and into his pants. Following her gaze, the Italian laughed softly. Embarrassed, Hélène said she wanted to join the others and tried to stand up; he helped her to her feet and took her arm, edging her towards the woods that ran beside the field. 'You be my friend?' He gazed down at her, his eyes infinitely dark, liquid, commanding; he smelt of hay and the powerful tang of a male ready for sex. Hélène looked up at him and smiled, her knees weakened beneath her.

Sophie interrupted her husband's cheerful grumbles. 'Now what's going on?' The group looked towards Hélène and the Italian.

Monsieur Faugeron got to his feet. 'I'll put a stop to this.' He strode over to the Italian, who removed his hand from Hélène's elbow. 'Leave the girl alone. If there's any more trouble with women, you'll be sent back where you came from!' The Italian shrugged, hesitated for a moment, winked at Hélène and walked off whistling towards the farm.

Monsieur Faugeron sat down again, joints creaking. 'He works well but I'm not sure he isn't more bother than he's worth. He's got women for miles around drooling after him.'

'Did you hear, there was a fight between Lucinde and Adrienne over him, both drunk of course, and he just stood with his arms crossed, laughing at them.'

'He's an insolent bugger.' Monsieur Faugeron raised his beaker and looked across the field with satisfaction. 'We've finished here, thanks to everyone. Splendid crop again this year.' He turned to Philippe. 'We'll be over at your place this afternoon – just give me an hour to get my wind back.' They all laughed as he pulled his hat over his face, crossed his hands over his chest and fell asleep.

***

The barn was stiflingly hot. Dust choked the air as Hélène lifted another heavy forkful high, twisting it deftly so it flew upwards to land neatly in the upper part of the hayloft. She could not see Philippe but she could hear the steady rasp of his breathing; Hélène smiled – they worked well together.

Their tranquil rhythm was interrupted by Philippe's angry cry, 'Clear off, I don't want anything to do with you.'

Hélène peered to one side and saw Lucinde standing at the top of the ladder. She staggered unsteadily and lurched forward, her momentum forcing Philippe down onto the pile of dry grass. He tried to push her away but the yielding hay gave him no purchase and Hélène watched with disgust as Lucinde kissed Philippe full on his lips and straddled him. Philippe swore violently and struggled to shove her away but she held him tight. Philippe fought more fiercely, still reluctant to hit a woman, but her weight pinioned him beneath her.

'Bugger off. What the hell d'you think you're doing!'

Hélène grabbed hold of Lucinde's feet and pulled hard. 'Get off him, leave him alone.'

Philippe kicked out at Lucinde and the pair slithered down to the ground below.

Alarmed by the noise, Agathe appeared in the open door of the barn, a black figure against the streaming sunlight. 'You bitch!' She seized hold of a rake and began beating Lucinde. 'You cow, you slut – get off my husband, you whore!' She continued to beat Lucinde as hard as she could until

Lucinde let go of Philippe and dropped to the floor, groaning, wrapping her arms around her head to protect herself from the blows.

Hélène scrambled down the ladder and grabbed her sister's arm. 'Stop it, Agathe. You'll kill her.'

'It'd be better if she was dead, the filthy whore.'

Lucinde crawled towards the door, whimpering, blood seeping through the back of her blouse. Hearing the creaking of the hay wagon, Hélène ran outside. 'The cart's coming!' She looked back. 'We can't let them see her like this. Help me.' Hélène took one of Lucinde's arms, Agathe took the other and they hauled the limp body round the farm and into the hut used for the bread oven.

Lucinde lay on the beaten earth, groaning. 'My back's hurting. My God, I need a drink. What's going to become of me?' She curled up on the dusty, beaten earth, her hands over her ears as Hélène closed the door so the others would not see her.

That night Agathe and Philippe had an argument, a rare row with raised voices, which Hélène could hear despite the pillow she held over her ears.

'You must've encouraged her.'

'Of course I didn't! How can you think that? We joke in the café that no man's safe around her, but I never imagined she'd try it on me.'

'You must've done something.'

'Don't be silly! I bet she was after the Italian and when she saw he wasn't here, she came after me. She was terribly drunk – you must've smelt it.'

There was silence for a while, until Philippe said gently, 'Agathe, you know you're the only woman in the world for me. I can't imagine making love to anyone else.'

Overhead there was silence and Hélène winced, bracing herself for the familiar sounds of their lovemaking, sounds that had become an obsession over the last few months. She listened intently, imagining the actions that initiated each change in tempo, each muffled moan – involuntarily her hand moved down between her legs. The squeaks and grindings of the old bedstead accelerated into an urgent rhythm and came to a rapid conclusion with Agathe's quickly suppressed cry of pleasure.

Hélène shook herself. In two days she would be out of this room, away from the farm, free to live her own life. She caressed the stout, studded trunk, packed and repacked with her belongings over the last two weeks, stroking its rough surface. 'One more day and then ...'

***

Hélène stood watching nervously as Philippe hauled the huge chest up into the cart. She steadied it as it teetered on the wooden side of the wagon, balanced on the edge.

From the corner of her eye she saw Berthe dash round the corner of the farm, caught a flash of white dress as she chased one of the hens. The startled oxen moved back in their harness, the wagon jolted, Hélène instinctively pushed the chest upwards, afraid it would fall back onto her. It swayed back and forward for a moment then crashed down into the cart. She heard a sharp yelp of pain.

Agathe ran out of the house, clambered up to peer into the well of the wagon and subsided, her head in her hands. 'May God help us! What have you done?'

Hélène stepped backward; she could feel the sharp protuberances of the stone wall tearing at her jacket as she slid downward. When she finally reached the ground she took off her hat.

Chapter Eleven

Summer–Autumn 1920

Hélène strode to the edge of the terrace. 'Stop pretending! Who's going to get in the potatoes, stack the wood, plough the bottom field?' She turned on her sister. 'You know I can't leave 'til Philippe's leg's better.' She faced the couple who sat mute and tense on the bench outside the farmhouse, impervious to the soporific buzzing of insects and the pale beauty of the evening sky as it deepened into darkest blue.

Shivering slightly as the cool shadows crept from under the trees, Philippe winced as he moved his leg in its heavy splint off the stool on which it had been resting. 'Hélène's right, she can't leave just yet - and she's going to need help; she can't do everything on her own.' He turned to Agathe. 'Why don't you talk to my family? They might be able to spare someone.'

'I don't think that'll do any good.'

'We haven't got much choice.'

Hélène turned away from the valley, a gleam in her eye. 'Perhaps they'd lend us the Italian?'

'Only if we paid him.'

Hélène had not forgotten the man's insistent gaze and the fine hair that snaked down over his taut brown body. 'There's the money we put aside for Valence. We could use that if we had to.'

Agathe stood up, frowning. 'I hate asking them favours.'

'Then I'll go!'

Agathe snapped, 'Don't be stupid, they're not your relations.' She bent down to help Philippe to his feet. 'I'll go tomorrow - as you both insist.'

Hélène lay on her bed; the night was insufferably hot and the small room was stuffy. She kicked the sheet away and lifted up her nightdress, fanning herself with an old magazine. Her thoughts turned to the Italian and she smiled in the darkness. If he came to work at Les Laysses there were bound to be times ... Hélène made an effort to think of other things, but her imagination would not be diverted: she quivered with pleasure at the thought of stolen embraces, passionate kisses, the promise of fulfilment that lay deep in his seductive eyes. She reached underneath her nightdress, feeling for the moistness where the aching delight was centred. A stab of pleasure made her groan as she stroked herself gently. Afterwards, feeling the familiar mixture of incomplete satisfaction and disgust, she turned on her side, inventing a romance that ended in marriage and children, the Italian silently adoring, enfolding her in his strong arms.

Hélène's hopes evaporated as soon as she saw Agathe's face. 'I knew it would do no good.' Agathe slammed down her basket. 'Your mother! Plenty of pitying looks and sympathetic noises for her "poor son", but when I asked if they could help, she gave me one of her condescending smiles.' Agathe mimicked the old woman, shaking her head, '"You know it's impossible. We've got far too much to do here."' Then Sophie joined in with her usual snide remarks about how much bigger their farm is than ours and crowing because she's pregnant again.' Agathe flung herself down on the bench. 'I hate the lot of them!'

Hélène dried her hands on her pinafore and sat down beside the other two. 'What about the Italian?'

Agathe snorted. 'Gone! Sent away. Sophie said he was a nuisance because there were always women hanging around. I wouldn't be surprised if she wasn't a bit taken with him herself. My dear father-in-law said making a pass at you, a respectable girl, was the last straw.' She fanned herself violently with her hat. 'In my opinion they got rid of him as soon as the rye was in because they didn't want to pay him over the winter.'

Another dream extinguished. The flickering scenario that had comforted Hélène overnight had faded into another foolish fairytale. She ran inside and fell onto her bed. In the darkness she cried until there were no more tears.

As Hélène dabbed at her inflamed face with water from the stoop on the windowsill, she overheard Agathe talking to Philippe. 'Gerard was saying Madame Cellier couldn't stand another winter up here on her own and the Legrand sisters couldn't pay anyone to cut their wood - so they've both left.' There was a short silence. 'I'm afraid,

Philippe. I know Hélène doesn't want to stay, but I can't see how we can manage without her. Who knows when you'll be back to normal? Or whether you'll be able to do everything you used to?'

Philippe hesitated a long time before replying, 'Agathe, you must face the fact that we may have to leave. Lots of families have gone.'

'Never! I don't care what it takes. I'll never abandon this place.' Agathe burst into tears. 'This is my home. I won't live anywhere else.' Hélène shuddered.

There was a long silence. 'Then we'll have to manage somehow,' Philippe's tone hardened. 'And we'll all have to make sacrifices – you and I as well as Hélène. Try to be kinder to her, Agathe. It's hard for her to give up all her hopes, especially as she was so close to leaving.'

The nights were warm and Hélène had taken to walking outside in the cool evening air so she did not have to lie awake listening to her sister's lovemaking. She sat down heavily on the bottom step of the stile. Hélène knew she had to put aside the romantic notions that flared fleetingly before fading into frustration. She had to find a way to bear her imprisonment on the Plateau. 'A husband?' Hélène shook her head. 'I've been through this so many, many times. There's no one, absolutely no man I could marry.' She shuddered, remembering her partner at the dance, now unhappily married to one of her old schoolmates. She plucked a long stem of grass and sucked its sweet sap; she smiled, thinking of time she had spent alone with Cécile and Berthe. 'A child!' Hélène sat for a long time mulling over the notion – a child would give her someone to love, to fill the void of her loneliness, it would give a purpose to her life. Hélène looked up at the stars. ‘My own child,’ she challenged their icy aloofness, ‘I don’t care what people will say: I must find a way.’

***

‘Can you spare me a few minutes, Roland?’ Hélène stood barring his way home, her smile too bright, hands sweating with embarrassment.

‘What for? You saw me in the café; you could’ve spoken to me there.’ Roland hitched himself more securely on his crutches and came straight towards her, hobbling as fast as he could.

Hélène turned and trotted after him. ‘I didn’t want to talk to you in the café.’

Roland groaned. He pushed open the front door with his crutch and led her into a small dark room. He stood facing Hélène, who blushed and looked at her feet, stammering, ‘I don’t know how to begin.’

Roland looked her up and down and began to laugh, the cynical sound reverberating in the confined space. ‘Don’t worry. I know why you’re here.’

Hélène looked at him, eyes wide. ‘That’s impossible!’

Roland signaled to a chair, Hélène sat down while he perched on the desk, propped up by his crutches. ’Look at you. A dress I haven’t seen before, probably new. Hair all done up.’ He sniffed.

'A touch of scent – a bit too sweet for my taste. It all gives the game away.'

Hélène's cheeks burned. 'I don't know what you're getting at.'

Roland sighed. 'You're not the first – by a long way. The speech you're about to make goes like this. "I've loved you, been attracted to you ever since – in our case – since our fuck six years ago. I've thought of you every day – et cetera, et cetera."' Roland continued in a mincing monotone, '"I've only just managed to pluck up the courage to ask you for—"' He paused. '"For any one of the following – singly or in combination – a good shag, my very own baby or to marry me so I can have some other husband's brat without a scandal. The fact that you haven't any legs doesn't matter, provided you've got a fully functional cock."'

Hélène gasped, putting her hand over her mouth. Roland stopped to savour her mortification. 'Of course you'd never have said that last part, but it's the one bit that's actually true.' He flicked a cigarette out of its packet and lit it. 'Out of curiosity, which one do you want?' He inhaled as Hélène sat, face aflame, not knowing where to look. He shrugged. 'Don't bother. The answers to all three are no, no and no.'

There was silence in the room. Hélène got up, humiliated and hopeless. She walked wearily towards the door. Her hand on the doorknob, she dared to look back, hoping for a reprieve, but Roland was smoking fiercely, staring hard at the floor. He looked up, chin high in the air, their eyes met, but he quickly turned away.

After she had left, Roland hopped over to the cupboard. As he reached for the bottle of brandy, one of his crutches slipped on the stone floor, he fell heavily to the ground and the bottle shattered, the oily liquid suffusing the stuffy room with its sickly, seductive smell. His mother hurried in, alarmed by the noise, fussing. As she helped him to his feet, Roland swore at her. 'I've told you to not to put it away.'

His mother tried to brush the dust off his jacket but he pushed away her hand. 'If I didn't, you'd drink it.'

'So what? Who the hell'd care?'

His mother sighed but made no reply, she looked sideways at him. 'What did Hélène Vernot want?' She spoke softly, 'She's a nice girl.'

'No nice girl should have anything to do with me, you know that! But I suppose you're hoping someone else'll look after this rotten, fucked-up body? That's what you want, isn't it?'

His mother stood for a moment, not responding to his taunt, helpless in the face of his frustration. In a flat voice she said quietly, 'Lunch is ready.'

'I don't want any sodding lunch.'

His mother went to the door; she turned and looked back at the bowed back of her son, her heart aching with pain and sadness. She hoped he would say something, but he continued to stare down at the broken shards of glass; for a long moment she hesitated, and then left the room.

When the he heard the door close, Roland put his head in his hands and sat, rocking back and forward, muttering, 'Poor bastard, poor bloody bastard.'

***

Hélène walked slowly along the empty street to the café where she had left her shopping. Her hand trembled as she opened the door. Monsieur Bernard glanced at her and pushed forward a chair; Hélène was too upset to return his kindly look and asked for a small cognac. He poured out the dark gold liquid, patted her shoulder and returned to his conversation with Firmin Arsac and one of the travelling salesmen who visited Saint-Agrève from time to time.

'She was behind all the goings-on while we were away.' Arsac spat on the ground. 'My wife ...' He did not finish his sentence, emptied his glass and spoke angrily. 'I don't know why you let that Lucinde drink here – or her friends.'

Monsieur Bernard shrugged his shoulders. 'Having Madame Nouzet as a mother-in-law'd drive anyone to drink. She treats Lucinde worse than a slave – never says a kind word about her or anyone.' He wiped a couple of glasses thoughtfully, searching through his limited vocabulary for a suitable description. 'She's the most unchristian woman I know.'

Arsac snorted. 'She goes to church often enough.'

'That doesn't make her a Christian.' After a moment's pause, Monsieur Bernard continued, 'Some of the men found Lucinde quite amusing at first – a bit of lively banter, some teasing – and of course there were several who took her advances at face value and went off with her.'

Arsac turned to the salesman. 'Now she's become a real nuisance. Lot's of the men think you shouldn't allow her in here, Bernard.'

'Oh, she's not all bad. If it wasn't for Lucinde, poor Tomas would've starved to death years ago.'

'He'd be no loss!'

'And there are quite a few families who've plenty of reason to thank Lucinde. Families who'll never be able to pay for all they get in Nouzet's shop.' Monsieur Bernard dropped his voice so Hélène had to struggle to hear what he was saying. 'Last week there was a nasty incident. Some of the wives came looking for Lucinde. They dragged her over to the fountain; one of them fetched a pail and, while the others held her down, threw water over her. You can imagine how Lucinde struggled, the language was dreadful and all the time the women were screaming, "Leave our men alone, we'll clean you up, you trollop, you whore," et cetera, et cetera.' Monsieur Bernard cast a quick look towards Hélène and continued, his voice even lower, 'I really thought they were going to throw her into the fountain, but she fought them off and ran away. Her clothes were soaked through, you could see everything.' The other two men chuckled salaciously.

Hélène stood up; the barman looked at her closely. 'Are you okay?' Hélène nodded, gripping the heavy baskets. Monsieur Bernard watched her leave with a worried expression.

The evening meal after a market day was a weekly treat for the family. Whoever had gone to town would recount all the gossip and the talk over their soup would be livelier than on other days. When Hélène came into the kitchen and saw Agathe and Philippe smiling expectantly, she ran to her room, banging the door shut.

The following morning Hélène left the house without eating breakfast. At lunchtime Agathe found Hélène standing in the kitchen garden leaning on her hoe, the robust weeds growing defiantly between the long lines of beets and cabbages.

'What's got into you, Hélène? You were supposed to finish this today but you've hardly started.' Agathe stepped fastidiously over the rows of vegetables. 'What happened yesterday?' She put her arm around her sister. 'Is something the matter?'

Hélène shook her head mulishly. 'Nothing. Nothing's different from before.'

Agathe's expression crisped, she stood with her arms on her hips. 'You're not still sulking over going away, are you?'

'Leave me alone, will you?' Hélène ran, careless of the tender plants, away from her sister down into the valley. It was well past supper-time when she returned and went straight to her room, slamming the door.

For three days Hélène did not eat; she kept to her room when she was not making a half-hearted attempt to weed the vegetables. On the fourth evening, after Philippe had stumped up to bed, Agathe asked through the closed door. 'You must tell me what's wrong.' She went in to the tiny room and found Hélène sitting on the bed, surrounded by scraps of cloth. 'That was your new frock! What are you doing?'

'Making dresses for the girls.'

'Why? It's far too good for them.'

Hélène's shoulders slumped. 'What's the point of wearing nice things?'

Agathe sighed, clucking her tongue. 'You must get over this, Hélène. You're making yourself ill and that won't do anyone any good.'

'I don't care.' Hélène shuffled away until her back made contact with the corner of the room. 'Go away, Agathe! You've got everything you ever wanted: Philippe, Berthe, Cécile, the farm. And what have I got?' Hélène gathered up the scattered remnants and threw them on the floor. 'Nothing! Not one thing – and no hope of ever getting them.' She pushed away Agathe's soothing hand. 'Get out of my room! Leave me alone.'

***

'I don't want to go to bed.' Berthe was usually a placid little girl who did as she was told but in the past few weeks she had become quarrelsome and whiny, infected by the tense atmosphere in the house. She put her arms around Hélène. 'You put me to bed.'

Agathe strode across the kitchen. 'No! You go to bed when I say so.' She grabbed the child, pulling her away from Hélène so roughly the little girl began to cry. Philippe hobbled out into the evening air.

'Why can't I put her to bed?'

Berthe struggled to escape from her mother, reaching out towards Hélène. Unable to get free, Berthe began to scream in earnest until Agathe smacked her hard and her howls subsided into a frightened whimper.

Hélène stalked over to Agathe, glaring at her. 'There was no need for that. Why not let me put her to bed if she wants me to?'

Agathe cradled her daughter in her arms; reaching out for the honey pot, she dipped her finger into the golden liquid and let Berthe suck the sweetness until she calmed down, saying frostily, 'Berthe's bedtime's nothing to do with you.' She bundled the small child into the box bed where her tiny sister lay. 'If you want to be helpful, you should do the weeding and not interfere with the way I'm bringing up my children.'

Hélène gasped at this injustice; involuntarily she raised her hand as if to strike Agathe. Horrified at what she was about to do, she ran outside. As she stalked up the hill, she tried to rationalise the surges of anger towards her sister which often overpowered her. The envy that had always been there had now been made much worse by the seething resentment Hélène felt at her own desolate prospects. She tried to convince herself that, at heart, she loved her sister, but Agathe's contentment with her lot and obdurate refusal to accept any change to their lives left Hélène feeling a bitterness that bordered on hatred.

When she returned an hour later, Hélène could see the glowing ash of Philippe's pipe through the gloom of the falling dusk. As she passed him he called out and, reluctantly, Hélène sat down beside him. Philippe spoke softly, 'Unless we get as good a crop from the garden as we did last year, we'll all go hungry when winter comes.' He did not look at Hélène and continued to pull on his pipe. ''Til my leg heals I'm afraid we're all relying on you.'

Hélène replied sulkily, 'Why can't Agathe do some of the gardening while I look after the girls? I'm sick of doing all the hard work.'

Philippe sighed. 'She says looking after the girls is hard work.' He laughed mirthlessly. 'I doubt you'll persuade her, I've haven't managed.'

Hélène nodded and quickly went inside. That night she said to herself, 'If only I could have my own baby. A child - then my life would be worthwhile.'

***

In the following weeks Hélène spent as little time as possible with the others. She avoided mealtimes, staying in her room or trailing down to the level strip of ground where the weeds continued to thrive. Bent over the rows of fledgling plants she pulled and tugged at the dandelions and creeping buttercup until, depressed by their tenacity, she would sit defeated on the damp earth, staring into space. At first Agathe's reproaches were fierce and angry until, intimidated by her sister's obvious misery, she stopped coming down to the vegetable patch and stood watching Hélène from the terrace, frowning with incomprehension and frustration.

As the days went by Hélène's clothes began to hang more and more loosely; her face, darkened by the sun, showed the sharp contours of her cheekbones, her eyes were dull. Each evening she would sit at the end of the terrace, shadowed by the clouds as they strayed across the moon, unaware of the warm breeze that stirred the sap-sated leaves, waiting until she could be sure Agathe and Philippe were asleep.

Day and night she struggled to find a way out of her situation. There could be no husband, no life away from the drudgery of the farm: her romantic dreams were just a silly girl's imaginings. The one hope that kept returning was that somehow she would have a child. A child would be a consolation for the life the war had destroyed – it would bring a joy for which she was prepared to endure the disgrace of being a mother without a husband. But where would she find a man to father this child? Unable to contemplate a relationship with any of the men she knew, Hélène relapsed into despairing self-pity.

One evening Agathe walked down the terrace to stand in front of Hélène, who was sitting on the stile leading to the upper fields. Annoyed at this intrusion, Hélène was about to jump down, but Agathe held on to the wooden struts so she could not escape. 'Philippe and I are worried about you, Hélène. Even though it'll be very hard for us, as soon as his leg's better we think you should go and live in Valence as you've always wanted.' She looked up at her sister. 'I'll ask the Curé if he can find you a job and somewhere to stay.'

Hélène turned away. 'Too late. The Curé's already spoken to me. He told me he'd tried to help another girl but couldn't find her any work. He said there were too many people leaving the Plateau.' Hélène continued bitterly, 'He also said it's God's will I stay here and it'd be a sin for me to leave because you need me, I must resign myself, et cetera - all the usual stuff he always comes out with.'

Agathe was silent for a long while. When she did speak, her tone was conciliatory. 'If you carry on not eating you'll get ill. I'm worried you won't make it through the winter.' She looked anxiously up at her sister. 'There's got to be something that can be done.'

'Not that I can think of.' Hélène laughed harshly. 'And I've certainly thought enough about it.'

'Why're you so sure?'

Hélène jumped down from the stile and faced her sister, glaring at her fiercely, her eyes burning. 'Because I want a child. A child of my own.'

Agathe put her hands on the wall to support herself, frowning at her sister with uncomprehending eyes. 'But you've got Berthe and Cécile.'

Hélène laughed cynically. 'Oh no, *you've* got Berthe and Cécile! They're not mine and you make quite sure I know it - and they know it too.'

Agathe was silent, taking in what Hélène had said. 'I don't think that's quite fair.' She thought for a while then spoke reluctantly, 'When we have another child, you could adopt it.'

'That wouldn't work, you know it wouldn't.' Hélène spoke with her back to her sister, 'You'd never be able to give up acting as its mother. Anyway, I want to be a real mother– to feel a baby kicking in my womb, to give it my milk, to know it's mine and no one else's.'

'But you're not married!'

Hélène dismissed this objection with a wave of her hand.

'Husband or no husband, to have a baby you have to have a father.'

'Don't I know it!' Both women stood looking across towards the moonlit hillside; a couple of bats swooped past and disappeared into the darkness of the woods, the crickets chirruped mechanically. 'I've considered every possible man around Saint-Agrève and there are none available, they're all taken. All of them – however awful.'

'What about Roland? You were keen on him once.'

Hélène snorted. 'He's not interested.' Hélène could see Agathe did not believe her. 'I went to see him. He made it absolutely clear he wants nothing to do with me.'

There was another silence until a thought struck Agathe. 'Is that why you wanted to leave here so much? So you could have a child?'

Hélène shook her head fiercely. 'No. I wanted to study, to teach, perhaps to write; all sorts of things I could only do if I was away from this place.

But if I have to stay here, then having a child would make it bearable.'

'I understand Hélène, but I can't see how ...'

Hélène spoke, her voice barely more than a whisper, 'There is one way. It'll shock you, but I've thought about it and I don't see it would be so wrong.' She took her sister's hand. 'If I went to bed with Philippe, once, at the right time, and became pregnant.' Agathe recoiled, her hands over her mouth. 'Let me finish, Agathe. It would only be once, just one time.'

Agathe gasped. 'You can't! It's a sin. A terrible sin.'

'It would be the creation of a new life – a life that'd be loved and cherished. That isn't a sin. France needs more children, the Curé himself said so.'

'But Philippe's my husband. It's his duty to be faithful to me. It would be horrible to think that you ...'

'I'm not suggesting having an affair with Philippe. I promise it would only be one time. I'm not trying to take him away from you.'

Agathe drew away, revolted. She changed tack. 'He wouldn't do it.'

'Even if you wanted him to? Even if you allowed it so I'd stay here and we could continue living together for always and I wouldn't be desperate to leave any more?' Hélène paused. 'It'd be the best thing for all of us.' She lowered her voice. 'I can't think of any other way.'

'But having a child outside marriage would be a terrible disgrace – for Philippe and me as well as you. And if people realised it was my husband, your brother-in-law, who'd done it ...' Agathe put her head in her hands. 'I couldn't bear it! It would be the worst shame of all.'

Hélène spoke quietly, 'I've thought of that. I would stay here on the farm. As hardly anyone visits us we could make sure that no one saw me while my pregnancy was obvious. And if you pretended to be pregnant, when my baby was born they'd never question that it wasn't yours.'

'More lies, more sin.' Agathe walked along the edge of the terrace towards the farm. 'You're asking for a terrible thing, Hélène.' She turned towards her sister, her voice high and determined. 'Your plan won't work. Philippe'll never agree. He loves me.'

'Then he might if you persuaded him.' Hélène ran after Agathe and took her hand. 'I think of Philippe as a brother, nothing else. He's yours. There's no need to worry; it would be only once. And then I'd have a child of my own and I'd be happy.'

'And if you didn't get pregnant?'

'Then that would be it. I promise.'

Agathe continued to stand looking out over the valley; she shivered as the cold sliver of the moon disappeared behind a cloud. 'I wish you hadn't said all this Hélène.' She spoke very quietly, 'Things won't ever be the same.'

***

For a few days after their conversation there was a strangely calm atmosphere on the farm. Hélène once more joined the family for meals and although she did not eat or talk much, it was apparent she was making an effort. Agathe, too, appeared to have changed; she included Hélène in looking after the two girls and even cleared the potato patch of weeds. Philippe was more cheerful as he was now able to walk without crutches, relieved the heavy splint had been taken off his leg.

The brilliant blue skies and balmy breezes of summer had solidified into a sultry heat that suffocated every effort. Each afternoon the air hung heavy with impending thunder and by evening a deep-throated rumble rolled around the valleys and jagged cracks of lightning fractured the sky.

As time passed, the mood in the house also darkened. As Philippe was chopping wood down in the bottom of the valley, he could see Agathe and Hélène arguing on the terrace but was too far away to hear what they were saying.

'Do you really want a child so much you'd risk the disgrace?'

Hélène shook her head. 'If we follow my plan there won't be any shame.'

'But if you ever wanted to leave the farm, you couldn't take your child with you.'

Hélène's eyes glittered. 'But don't you see, of course I couldn't leave because I couldn't leave my child - and that's exactly what you want, we're all in this together! We'd all get what we want.' She stood, tears glittering in her eyes. 'If not, my life means nothing to me. A child would give me something to live for - without that hope...' Her voice trailed away. She whispered, 'It's up to you; to end a life or create a new one.'

Agathe stood saying nothing for a long time. She turned away. 'I'll pray for guidance. God will tell me what to do.'

***

Late one afternoon thunder had brought a welcome rain that fell hard and heavy, bouncing off the cobbles of the courtyard. As Philippe stood sheltering in the doorway of the kitchen, he could see the two women quarrelling at the end of the terrace in spite of the downpour.

When the two women returned, Philippe glared at them both. 'What's going on? I'm not going to put up with this constant rowing any longer.'

'Agathe knows what's the matter – ask her.'

The meal was eaten in silence. After it was over, Philippe said to Agathe, 'You'd better come upstairs with me.'

Hélène put away the dishes and stood by the door watching the lightening as it turned the sky an incandescent white, the bright forks streaking down to impregnate the black hills. Through the window above she could hear Agathe's voice become louder, more insistent, but could not hear what was being said through the noise of the storm. Her heart beat violently and she felt sick, knowing her fate was being decided. There was a flash and a great roll of thunder, so close Hélène ducked inside and hurriedly closed the door. Now she could hear Philippe's voice above the din. 'How could you even think of such a thing?' Furious voices shouted simultaneously, a pleading note from Agathe, a long-drawn out cry and the bedroom door burst open. Hélène stood watching as Philippe dashed down the stairs and out into the driving rain.

In the hush that fell over the house, Hélène sat on the edge of her bed waiting for Philippe's return, listening to Agathe sobbing upstairs in her bedroom. It was not long before the thunder began again, rolling round and round the valley. Dawn was lightening the eastern horizon when she heard Philippe's steps on the staircase and the cold tone of his voice as he spoke to Agathe.

***

This was the agreed night. The two girls had been put to bed and the three adults sat round the table; no words were spoken nor looks exchanged. Agathe passed round the wooden board with the *picodon* cheese, but the other two shook their heads. From time to time a hand would reach out to the pitcher of wine and a glass would be refilled and emptied. Outside the lingering light of the autumnal sky had almost faded, but still the three continued to sit, silently drinking, unwilling to move. At last Agathe pushed back her chair. She stood for a moment, uncertain what to do – to kiss her husband goodnight, to bless them or to curse – each alternative flickered across her face. She took a deep breath and went outside, leaving the other two listening to the reluctant footsteps that took her up to her solitary bed.

Philippe went out to the yard; Hélène could hear the sporadic spurts of water as he washed at the pump. She went into her bedroom, quickly taking off her clothes and slipping over her head the clean white nightdress she had laid aside. She lit a candle whose comforting glow glanced off the brass bindings of the chest, the only piece of furniture in her room apart from the bed. Hélène brushed her hair, her hands trembling. The splashing of water seemed to last an eternity; she shivered. Far away an owl hooted for its mate.

It was uncannily still in the room as Hélène waited. She pulled the clean white sheets tighter, straightened the already-straight bolster, and went to look again at her reflection in the small fly-spotted mirror, noting the strange dark gleam in her eyes. Hélène heard the door of the kitchen close, her heart beat fast in her breast. She was shaking. An eternity passed before Philippe lifted the latch. Hélène stood facing him as the door opened.

Philippe stood on the threshold. In a low voice he said, 'I can't go through with this, Hélène.' She looked at him, uncomprehending, numb, and for an infinite moment neither moved. Despairing, Hélène held out her hand and took his, willing him to look at her, but he would not meet her imploring eyes. He continued to hold her hand but turned his face away. Hélène moved closer until she could feel the warmth of his body. They stood together awkwardly, closer than they had ever been before. The silence of the room enclosed them; the darkness beyond the slim pool of candlelight enveloped them.

Gently Hélène drew Philippe towards the bed, inch by inch, his face and body still turned away from her. She gently turned him towards her so they stood, body to body, the hard edge of the bed firm against the back of her thighs. The night was intensely quiet; there was no sound except the fragile whisper of their indrawn breath. Hélène dropped her hand from his shoulder, careful not to touch the bare skin of his chest, and took his other hand. She lay down on the bed, sinking into its rustling folds, Philippe stood, holding both her hands, his face still turned away. She pulled him down towards her so they both lay, parallel and separate on the bed. Neither spoke, the flickering light of the candle the only movement in the unstirring obscurity of the night. For a long time they lay unmoving, conscious of each other, listening to the rhythm of the other's breathing. Far away the owl hooted once more, the woeful sound fading into silence.

Hélène reached for Philippe's hand; stroking its rough texture and hard callouses felt strangely intimate. They lay for a while side by side until Hélène laid his palm tenderly on her breast, where it lay quiescent, separated from her by the thin cotton of her nightdress. Gently she held it there until the nipple hardened and he could feel the beginnings of her desire. They lay for a long time until Philippe responded, felt the shape of her breast, explored the contours of its softness. Hélène felt a wave of sharp, painful pleasure flood through her body; a moan escaped her, quickly stifled. Unnerved by the sound,

Philippe moved away and they lay apart once more, enclosed in the warm glow of the candle.

Hélène took his hand and once again, more confidently, guided him as he explored her breasts, her belly and further down, where he stopped. Hélène lay supine; the anticipation of his touch on her moist cleft was unbearable. She got up, lifted her nightdress over her head, her young body a shining silhouette against the gleam of the candle. As she lay down again, her hand ran over the firm muscles of his chest, stroking the wiry hairs that escaped from under the thick cotton of his underpants. She pushed the unforgiving material away until they both lay naked, untouching.

Hélène continued to stroke his chest, careful not to touch his upright penis, conscious of its power. Philippe at last turned towards her and, with eyes closed, ran his hands over her body, down, at last, into the softness between her legs. Biting her lips so she would make no sound, Hélène succumbed to the delight of his touch. For a long time they lay, hands moving gently over each other's body. From time to time Hélène opened her eyes, the enclosing shadows of her familiar room strange, comforting, safe – then closed them again to concentrate on the ecstasy of his caresses.

Philippe lay on her; he came into her with a great thrust of pain and rapture. As he moved slowly back and forth, Hélène felt a great completeness, the relentless, fierce rhythm building in her until she felt she could stand it no more. With a great shuddering explosion, it was all over.

Philippe slid out of her; for a moment he lay spent beside her, then got up, pulled on his pants and left the room. Hélène lay motionless; consumed, content, confounded by the beauty of their lovemaking. As she stretched out towards the other side of the bed where the rumpled sheets still held a little of his warmth, Hélène listened to the grating of the pump as Philippe worked its handle fiercely up and down, pained by his determination to eradicate any trace of her.

The candle guttered as Philippe made his way with heavy steps upstairs to Agathe. Hélène lay awake, remembering, recalling, reliving their lovemaking; above her she could hear the sobs of Agathe and the murmured reassurances of her husband.

Finally, the candle flared and went out, leaving only the deep silence of the night, the rustlings of animals, the lugubrious hooting of the owl, the creaking timbers of the old house. Holding her belly, Hélène fell asleep.

Chapter Twelve

Winter 1920–Spring 1922

Under the cold light of the moon the whole family tramped up the stony path to the Faugerons. Although Hélène usually dreaded a *viellée* with Philippe's family, the atmosphere at Les Laysses had become unbearable and she was glad to be spared another evening immured with her brooding sister and a silent, moody Philippe.

Gerard flung open the farmhouse door. 'Come in, it's freezing out here.' He herded them towards the fire, where Madame Faugeron and Sophie sat, their knitting needles barely pausing as Agathe and Hélène stooped to kiss them. Gerard put a protective hand on his wife's shoulder. 'Sophie's expecting again – I hope you won't mind if she stays where it's nice and warm.'

Monsieur Faugeron doled out the plum brandy for his guests and raised his glass. 'Here's to another successful year.' His smile wavered for a moment as he glanced at Philippe. 'I'm glad your leg's healed, son. I hope it didn't cause you too many problems.' He leant back in his chair, avoiding Agathe's stony glare. 'What a summer.

We've never been busier – took us all our time to get everything done.'

Madame Faugeron looked up from her knitting, her keen glance sizing up Philippe and Agathe, who sat side by side, unsmiling. 'And you two?' She changed rows with an irritated flourish. 'Any news?' She nodded towards Cécile, who lay asleep in Agathe's lap. 'She's over a year old; surely it's time to be thinking of a boy?' Agathe and Philippe remained silent.

Sophie directed a complacent smile at Agathe and said smugly, 'Maman's right, you should be thinking about having a boy sooner rather than later.'

Hélène interrupted. 'It's hardly a matter of choice – you can't just order a boy or a girl.'

Sophie snapped, 'What would you know about it?' and turned back to her knitting.

Madame Faugeron smacked her lips with satisfaction as she took dainty sips of cordial. 'Have you heard the latest about your friend Lucinde?' She looked at Hélène and paused for effect. 'She's had a letter from that husband of hers. It must be five or six years since he disappeared.'

Hélène opened her eyes wide. 'That's fantastic news – she'll be so pleased! Is he coming back to Saint-Agrève?'

Philippe shook his head. 'Surely he wouldn't risk it! He must know there're lots of lads who'd give him a pretty unpleasant reception.'

Sophie put down her knitting. 'It wouldn't just be the men! I know plenty of women who'd make sure the coward got what he deserved.'

Agathe remarked tartly, ‘Perhaps it’d be a good thing if he did come back; it might put a stop to her sinful goings-on.’

Madame Faugeron popped a roast chestnut into her mouth and masticated slowly before replying, ‘That’s neither here nor there; we won’t be seeing him again in Saint-Agrève.’ She looked round with a self-satisfied smile. ‘He’s in Canada!’ Gratified by their astonishment, she continued, ‘He managed to get to Switzerland, then made his way to Canada. He’s ended up in Quebec but can't afford to pay for their crossing, so they’ll have to wait another year.’

Hélène interrupted her. ‘But it’s great he’s alive. This’ll give Lucinde something to look forward to, some hope of happiness.’

‘Happiness? She was happy enough to go to the café and get drunk, waving the letter in everyone’s face. She should’ve known better. Her news didn’t go down very well. Roland Gounon and some of the others were furious – taking on about how he was a deserter and how they’d make sure he wouldn’t get away with it – and so on and so forth. Anyway, this enraged Lucinde so much she attacked Guonon and hit him with one of his crutches. Monsieur Bernard had to tear her off him and throw her out.’

‘Roland’s always making trouble.’

Sophie continued to knit aggressively. ‘A lot of the women are fed up with the way she pesters their men. They’re sick to death of her.’ With a grim expression, Agathe nodded in agreement. ‘She’ll come to a bad end, Quebec or no Quebec.’

Monsieur Faugeron turned to Philippe. ‘What did you make of Nouzet?’

Philippe pulled on his pipe. 'We were pretty sure he'd deserted. But to give him his due, he's done well to get to Canada; that must've taken some doing.' He spoke thoughtfully, 'I don't believe he was a coward, he just hated the war, couldn't stand being in the Army.'

Madame Faugeron turned her attention to Hélène. 'You're looking well. I see you've got over whatever it was that was making you look so thin and peaky.' Hélène blushed. 'A boyfriend perhaps?' Agathe interrupted brusquely, 'Where's Henri?'

Monsieur Faugeron and Gerard laughed. 'Out chasing girls. We rarely see him in the evenings nowadays. He's getting as bad as that Italian.'

Madame Faugeron's needles clicked away, only half hiding her satisfaction. 'He can't help it if the girls find him attractive. He's a fine strong boy.' She turned to Agathe, frowning. 'Daughter-in-law, I've a message from the Curé. He said he's not seen you at Mass for over a month, asked me if you weren't well.' Agathe flushed, biting her lip. Madame Faugeron raised her eyebrows, paused in her knitting and then shrugged. 'I said I'd pass it on so I've done my duty.' The emphasis on 'my duty' was not lost on Agathe, who hurriedly finished the slice of solid Savoy gateau that signaled the end of the *viellée* and stood up to leave.

Away from the warm fug of the kitchen the air was bitterly cold, and over to their right the Mézenc gleamed, its covering of snow a bright white against the deep blue of the night sky. The two women walked in silence, huddled deep in their thick shawls; Philippe strode ahead carrying the unlit lantern, the moonlight so sharp it was easy to find their way along the rocky path.

'Thank goodness that's over.' Hélène looked sideways at her sister, who ignored the overture. Hélène sighed; after a *viellée* at the Faugerons' they would shorten the long walk home with an analysis of the evening, their laughter soothing the irritations inflicted by the spiteful female Faugerons and their insensitive mates. Tonight they walked in silence.

When they reached the farm, Agathe put the two children to bed. As she tucked a blanket tightly round the sleeping Cécile, she cleared her throat. 'Well?' Hélène said nothing, but Agathe insisted, her voice tense. 'It's been three weeks.' Her lips tightened. 'This is hard for me, Hélène. If you're pregnant I'll need to know, it'll be up to me to fool people like the Faugerons. Don't forget that.'

Hélène stammered, 'I'm not sure.'

Agathe stood up straight, her eyes wide with relief. 'Then you're late?'

Hélène looked away, embarrassed. 'My periods aren't always as regular as clockwork.'

Agathe stood, eyes shut, fists clenched, straining to control herself. 'It's only fair you tell me as soon as you know.' She took a deep breath, seemed about to say more but turned on her heel and went upstairs.

In her bedroom Hélène took out an old exercise book from the brass-bound chest and ticked off another square. She counted the ticks again; twenty small marks on the page, four of them after the square she had coloured in. Hélène smiled and folded her arms across her stomach, cradling the infinitesimally small being she knew was growing inside her. As she looked in the mirror, she remembered the broken looking-glass and smiled; surely the baby within her was a sign that her seven years of bad luck was over.

Hélène waited for the others to fall asleep. She had been irrationally pleased that Philippe had not made love to Agathe since the night they had lain together, relieved to be spared a jealousy made more intense by her memories. Hélène knew she had to accept she would not make love to Philippe again – Philippe belonged to her sister and she had promised – but she was also aware just how much she wanted to experience again the tender excitement of his caresses.

***

Agathe wiped the sweat from her forehead as she came into the farmhouse, pulling feverishly at the padded sack she now wore round her waist whenever she went into Saint-Agrève. 'The sooner you have this baby the better. I'm sick of women asking me, "How're you feeling?", "D'you think it's a boy?".' She continued peevishly, 'I can't wait to get rid of this thing. It's so heavy and it itches horribly.' She sighed and poured herself a glass of water.

Berthe came running out of Hélène's room. 'Maman, something bad's happened.'

Hélène lay curled up on the bed, her face ghostly white, the bedclothes stained a livid red. Frightened, Agathe wiped away the wisps of damp hair that clung to her sister's forehead and shouted for Philippe.

Shooing Berthe away, Agathe put a large cauldron of water to heat over the fire and ran to get the old sheets she kept in a basket in the barn. Hélène's cries became louder as Philippe hurried into the kitchen. 'It's started. Two months early.'

Philippe stood, uncertain. 'Shouldn't we fetch Madame Bret?'

Agathe bustled past him. 'Don't be stupid! After all these months pretending it's me that's pregnant.'

'But surely...'

Agathe did not allow Philippe to finish his sentence. 'She's young and healthy. There's no reason to imagine it'll be complicated. We'll manage on our own.'

A loud shriek rent the air; Philippe winced. 'Is there anything I can do?'

'Draw a couple of pails of water and put them by the fire. Then leave us to it.' Agathe picked up the sheets and went into Hélène's bedroom.

All night Agathe sat with her sister, clasping the hand that wrung hers. The contractions were hard and frequent but by morning there was still no sign of the child. Agathe came out of the room haggard with exhaustion and worry. She sat down for a moment to drink the coffee Philippe held out to her. He stood up. 'I'm going to get Madame Bret. We could lose Hélène and the baby if we don't get help.'

Agathe looked at him, her eyes dark with lack of sleep. 'No, not yet. Her cries sound dreadful, but it's quite normal for labour to last for hours. We all have to go through this.'

By nightfall Agathe could not hide her alarm, Hélène was weakening as she pushed to no avail. Philippe sat outside but still the cries tore through the crisp air. In answer to his unspoken question she replied stubbornly, 'Hélène's adamant she doesn't want Madame Bret.'

'I don't care. Hélène needs a midwife and to hell with the consequences.' He looked sternly at his wife. 'I'll make Bret promise to keep our secret.'

'That's a joke! She thrives on gossip – this'd be meat and drink to her.' Agathe burst into tears, the anxiety and tiredness overwhelming her. 'I wish I'd never agreed to this. No good can come from such a sin.' Another cry roused Agathe; she got up wearily and went into the house. She came out again in a few minutes. 'She's determined not to have the midwife, whatever happens. After all the sacrifices we've made, she wants to keep trying.' Agathe dried her eyes. 'I think we should do as she says.'

'But what if she doesn't make it?' Philippe got up, anger and fear sharpening his words. 'This has gone on long enough. Hélène's in no fit state to make any decisions – and neither are you. I'm going.'

Agathe clung to his arm. 'No! There's no earthly way we can explain all this. For the last few months I've been going round pretending to be pregnant – I've lied to the whole town. The women will never forgive me. They'll make my life unbearable – and Hélène's.'

‘It’s none of their business.’

‘You know what they're like, they’re capable of anything. They’ll treat Hélène the way they treated Florence Dufour when she had a baby; they forced her to leave Saint-Agrève.’ Agathe paced up and down the terrace. ‘If people know it’s Hélène who’s had the baby and not me, they’ll want to know who’s the father and there’ll be plenty who’ll suspect that it’s you. The shame and humiliation would be unbearable.’ Agathe's voice broke. ‘Imagine what your family would say. It would be the end of everything. We couldn’t stay here if people knew what we’d done.’

‘Then we shouldn’t have done it in the first place. This’s all our own fault.’ Philippe looked coldly at his wife. ‘I can’t stand by and let Hélène suffer like this.’

Agathe eyes blazed, her voice rising hysterically, ‘So you do love her after all! You’re prepared to make it impossible to live here anymore because you care about her, not me.’

Philippe took hold of her shoulders, shook her gently and sat her down. ‘Agathe, you know that’s not true. I love you and our children more than anything else – but Hélène’s life matters to both of us – and the child’s too.’ He stroked her hair. ‘I’ll wait two more hours but if things don’t get any better I’m going to get the midwife.’

Weeping, Agathe went back into the farmhouse.

An hour later she shouted from the bedroom door, ‘It’s coming. I can see its head.’

Just before dawn, after two days of labour, a baby boy was born. Agathe washed the scrawny red infant, wrapped it in a clean sheet and laid it in the wooden cradle. For a while Hélène lay almost unconscious then held out her arms for the wailing child. 'My son,' she whispered.

Agathe cleared up the bedroom and went to sit by the fire with Philippe. She said quietly, 'It's a boy. What shall we call him?'

Philippe took her hand. 'That's for Hélène to decide.' Agathe burst into tears.

***

The summer was long and hot, the fields lay parched and the hay was thin and dry.

Apart from mealtimes eaten silently and in haste, the three adults were rarely together. Agathe made sure Philippe and Hélène were never alone and it was Agathe who now worked in the fields while Hélène stayed in the farmhouse, minding the two girls and looking after her son. She was enchanted by him: delighted by his smiles, she had to discipline herself not to spend hours playing with his tiny fingers; cradling him in her arms as he suckled at her breast gave her a sensuous pleasure; at night she would sit by the cradle looking down at the sleeping child, stroking his soft, downy head. During the day she worked hard, determined to keep her side of the deal with her sister, the infant strapped to her back in a large shawl, conscious of his every movement. As the months passed and Frédéric's character began to emerge, his strong will dominated the household - to Hélène's delight and Agathe's exasperation.

But it saddened her that Philippe took no apparent interest in his son and his withdrawal from the family became more pronounced than ever. He would only come into the kitchen at mealtimes, and long after Agathe had gone to sleep, Hélène would hear him climbing the stairs to their bedroom. Days passed without him speaking a word and Hélène dreaded the dark days of winter when all three would be cooped up in the house as the winds of the *Burle* swept across the mountains, bringing icy air down from the north. She caught herself looking at Philippe as he sat, smoking and drinking, wondering if he, like her, ever thought of their lovemaking. Only once did their eyes meet and a gleam of recognition passed between them. After that Philippe withdrew to the barn more often in the evenings, only sitting with the women when it was too cold to be away from the fire.

***

The snow was beginning to clear from the south-facing fields when Agathe told Hélène she was pregnant and that she was sure the child would be a boy. Hélène hugged her sister, and the two sat knitting in a more comfortable silence than they had enjoyed for over a year. That night Hélène lay awake, afraid to analyse her confused emotions at her sister's news as she held her own son in her arms.

Agathe's belly grew and became more cumbersome but she still insisted on doing much of the heavy work, mutely determined the other two should not be alone together. Both Hélène and Philippe told her to stop wearing herself out, but Agathe brushed away their concern and persevered, worn out and irritable.

Spring arrived with its endless tasks - and a persistent rain which made working outside impossible. The farmyard was treacherous with puddles of slimy water. Hélène was preparing the evening soup when she heard Agathe's scream and the clatter of a falling bucket. She ran out to find her lying on her back, the precious milk streaming into the stinking mud. Agathe struggled to get up but fell back groaning. Hélène yelled for Philippe, who came running. The two of them managed to get Agathe into the kitchen, where she lay struggling for breath, clutching her distended belly.

Philippe bent over her. 'I'll get Doctor Gounon.'

Agathe shook her head, the words coming as a whisper through clenched teeth, 'Madame Bret. Quickly. Something's happened to the baby.'

Philippe snatched up his jacket and ran out. Hélène sat holding her sister's hand as she twisted in agony. The rain relentlessly beat on the window. It was over three hours before Philippe returned with the midwife, both soaked to the skin. Madame Bret got to work quickly while Hélène stood by, useless and fearful.

In an hour it was all over. Madame Bret called to Philippe and they stood looking down at Agathe who lay barely conscious, her skin glistening with sweat. 'It's a pity she lost this one.' She folded the notes Philippe proffered, shoved them into her bag and turned to go. 'It would've been another boy.' She went across to look at Frédéric who was crying, desperate for the milk Hélène dared not give him while the midwife was there. 'He looks a fine fellow.' She turned to Hélène. 'He came too fast for you to get me, you said?' Hélène nodded. 'That's odd, her others weren't particularly quick in coming.' Madame Bret looked penetratingly at Hélène. 'Next time don't try and deliver it on your own.' She turned to Philippe, using the irritated tone she used when talking to men, 'She'll need to stay in bed for a good while, she's lost a lot of blood.'

Later that evening Agathe woke and began to wail. 'This is God's punishment for my terrible sin.' Her voice rose, 'I've prayed every night for a son, why did He give you a boy and not me?' Agathe clawed at her nightdress and threw herself on her knees, her voice high and hysterical. 'Forgive me, Lord.' She turned on Hélène. 'I should never have let you two come together. Every day I've repented, wishing it'd never happened.' Agathe beat her fists on the bed. 'I'm being punished because I didn't stop your evil plan.' Hélène stood in silent misery, not knowing what to do.

Philippe came in and took both Agathe's hands, holding them tight. 'Stop it! You had an accident and you fell. This has nothing to do with God or with punishment.' He held her in his arms until she calmed down. 'We'll have other sons. You need to rest and sleep.'

***

A week later Agathe was still confined to bed, her forehead feverish. 'I don't want you to go into town with her.'

Philippe sighed. 'We don't have a choice. You know the *foire aux boeufs gras* is the only time we can sell Eloise.' He took her hand. 'We've got to sell her; she's not given any milk for months. And you know I can't do it on my own.'

'I might be stronger by then.'

Philippe laughed gently. 'It's tomorrow. I have to get everything ready tonight.' He sighed again. 'Agathe, you don't have to worry about Hélène and me. It's the fever that's talking.'

The dawn was still a couple of hours away as Hélène and Philippe set off, the sleety rain making the track slippery and treacherous. Philippe led the way, sitting on the cart piled high with logs while Hélène followed, leading the docile beast. She patted her coarse, reddish pelt, remembering the innumerable times she had sat, forehead pressed against Eloise's warm flank, while her abundant milk squirted into the pail between her legs. For fifteen years Eloise had provided the family with nourishment and drawn the unwieldy plough across the recalcitrant fields. A wave of desolation caught at Hélène's throat; eight years ago she had tied white ribbons to Eloise's sharp-pointed horns for Agathe's wedding – a remote, unimaginable world full of optimism and happiness. Hélène walked onward, relieved she did not have to talk to

Philippe, on the rare occasions when they were alone she felt embarrassed and tongue-tied.

As Hélène handed Eloise over to Philippe, her sadness was mixed with an undefined sense of foreboding. She gave the faithful animal one last hug and quickly turned away. The cattle market in Saint-Agrève just before Palm Sunday was the biggest in the region, families with their beasts had come from all over the Mézenc and Hélène found it difficult to fight a path between the ragged lines of cows, whose owners stood bellowing their beasts' remarkable qualities. When all her cheeses had been sold, she went back to the square to find Philippe. It was drizzling and, as she walked through the cheerful throng, her gloomy mood intensified. The church bell tolled mournfully.

Passing in front of the café, Hélène tried to ignore the large group of men standing outside, drinks in hand, watching the goings-on in the market. She was annoyed and flustered when Roland called out to her. 'Hélène Vernot, I'm surprised you're not at her funeral!' Hélène frowned uncomprehendingly. 'God knows why you were so friendly with her, but I'd have bet good money at least you'd be there.' He looked her up and down, shaking his head. 'Haven't you heard?'

'Heard what? Who's died?' Taking hold of his arm, Hélène knew the answer. 'It's Lucinde, isn't it?' Roland nodded, eyebrows raised. 'What happened?'

'She went too far. Good riddance.'

Another man chipped in, 'She was caught in bed with the Giberts' son from up on the Chiniac. A lad of fourteen. He said she'd forced him to do it.'

Roland chuckled sardonically. 'Whether anyone believed him or not is another matter. Anyway, he cried his eyes out and made a great fuss, so his mother got extremely agitated and went round screeching to all the other women. It ended up with a gang of them getting together and storming off to find Lucinde. Everyone agrees the women dragged her to the fountain and threw her in but Tomas, who was hanging around as usual, says that some of the women held her down and drowned her.'

One of the men shrugged. 'You can't rely on anything he says.'

Roland continued, 'The women say she hit her head as she fell and it was an accident. Whatever happened, by the time Monsieur Bernard got the women off her and hauled her out, Madame Lucinde Nouzet was very definitely dead.' As he finished speaking the bell stopped and there was silence.

Hélène ran down the Grande rue wildly, forcing her way through the crowds. At the church door she caught her breath and opened it quietly. In the gloom she saw the plain wooden coffin unadorned by flowers standing on a bier in the centre of the nave. Madame Nouzet was sitting in a pew at the front of the church, alone apart from the Curé. Hélène sat down at the back near the door.

The Curé stood above the coffin, his voice reverberating through the empty church. 'Lucinde

Nouzet lies here, her short life taken from her at the tender age of twenty-six as a result of her unbridled self-indulgence. She lived a life of dissipation and sin; she seduced others to share her wickedness; she chose the way of the flesh and was unrepentant right to the end. The Holy Bible teaches us that the wages of sin is death and those who live a life of sin will be punished by eternal damnation. God will have no mercy on this woman who gave herself up, not to His ways but to the sensual delights of the Devil.'

Madame Nouzet's head nodded at each orotund condemnation as Hélène felt icy tears creep down her face, nauseated by the Curé's sanctimonious hypocrisy. Eight years ago Lucinde had been a spirited young woman with a thirst for life, now she lay unloved and unmourned, damned by a priest who could not resist the temptations of which he accused her. She tried to shut her ears to his pompous platitudes and recall the friend she had loved for so many years, but her thoughts kept returning to the baying women at the July celebrations and the muttered conversation of Monsieur Bernard. She shuddered, imagining Lucinde's impotent terror as the women surrounded her; their writhing, sweating bodies preventing any escape from their hate-filled faces and clawing hands. Hélène left the church, slamming the door behind her.

The rain had begun to fall in earnest. Hélène walked back to the square, her sombre thoughts jarred by the cacophony of cheerful calls, men slapping each other's palm in a '*patche*' to seal a deal, the low mooing of the beasts as they were led off to new owners – or to their slaughter.

Hélène found Philippe surrounded by a group of men, laughing and relaxed. It pained her to see him happy; for a long time there had been no laughter on the farm and she had forgotten how his face could light up with pleasure. As soon as Philippe caught sight of her, tension tautened his cheeks and his eyes lost their sparkle.

'Can we go home Philippe, if you don't mind?' He did not reply but gathered together his purchases.

There was an uncomfortable silence between them as they made their way out of the town, seated side by side in the cart, immured in their own thoughts. The rain was now beating in their faces, stinging and relentless; it was only when Philippe heard Hélène sniff and wipe her face with the back of her hand that he realised she was crying.

'Lucinde?' Hélène nodded. 'I'm afraid I can't feel sorry for her.' Philippe shook the reins.

Hélène wiped away her tears with the edge of her shawl. Her voice vibrated with indignation. 'You may not have liked her, but her end was terrible.' She spoke of the empty church, the satisfaction in Madame Nouzet's bobbing bonnet, the Curé's sanctimonious condemnation. 'What he said was dreadful. It gave him real pleasure to condemn her for eternity!' Hélène glared at Philippe, but he simply nodded his agreement – Philippe had no time for the Curé. 'If there is a God, surely He would forgive her? All she wanted was someone to love her.'

‘She had Marius. All she had to do was wait.’

‘But for most of the last eight years she didn’t know if he was dead or alive. That must’ve been dreadful. Then there was the loss of the baby. And all the time she had to put up with that awful old woman making her wait on her hand and foot while she said vile things about her. People should feel sorry for her!’

Philippe did not reply.

Hélène began to cry again, she wished Philippe would put his arm around her but their night together made that impossible. He flicked the reins again, looking ahead, guiding the bullocks along the rutted road through the rivulets of water that rushed down the hillside.

Hélène continued, her voice brittle, ‘It’s not just that she’s dead – but I believe those women killed her.’ Hélène’s voice shook. ‘Whether they actually did it by holding her under the water or because she hit her head, those vicious cows murdered her!’ Hélène shivered as the rain continued to fall.

Philippe spoke sharply, ‘Murder’s a very strong word. Don’t even allow yourself to think it, Hélène.’

‘But to be hounded to death by people who’re just as bad in their own selfish way. Lucinde was as much a victim of the war as Roland or …’ Hélène stopped herself. ‘It’s awful to think in a few months she’d have been on her way to a new life in Canada,’ Philippe quickly patted her hand then abruptly withdrew it and concentrated on driving the bullocks.

The rain had now become so intense it was hard to see more than a few metres ahead. Once they left the road, the track wound its way round the contours of the hillside and was awash with running water. The bullocks kept stumbling and Philippe reluctantly left the shelter of the tarpaulin to lead them, coming to a halt in a narrow gill where the spouting stream had washed away the planks of the bridge. He coaxed the beasts through the rushing torrent but, with their hooves slipping on the steep slope of the ravine, they could not pull the cart through the eddying mixture of mud and stones. Hélène climbed out and stood by Philippe as he tried to lead the animals forward, but the cart would not be moved.

'We'll have to push; the bullocks can't do it on their own.'

They stood side by side, shoulders jammed hard against the rough wood, the stream running over their clogs, soaking their clothes, tugging at Hélène's skirt. The cart resisted; they tried again, Philippe urging her to shove harder. Suddenly the cart lurched forward; Hélène lost her balance but Philippe caught her before she fell into the water. For an infinite moment they stood holding each other close – then leapt apart. Hélène held on to the cart to steady her racing heart, Philippe was already striding away from her.

When they reached higher ground, the two climbed back into the wagon. Philippe manhandled the heavy, sodden tarpaulin over them both and as he did so their eyes met. Unbreathing, unblinking, their eyes held steady, betraying with unequivocal certainty the depth of their desire. At last Philippe turned away. Hélène sat absolutely still as he took the edge of the water-logged canvas and pulled it over their heads. They stared ahead, silent, rocked by the uneven movements of the cart, Hélène's heart beating so fiercely she felt she could not breathe. She made no movement, willing him to respond to the exhilaration he had aroused in every nerve of her body. Philippe pulled the tarpaulin tighter around them, its weight forcing them together until they could be no closer. They sat side by side, rain pouring down their faces, conscious only of the closeness of the other's body burning through the layers of soaked clothing and, as the cart continued its ungainly progress, its slightest shift unleashed intense tremors of desire. Hélène licked the moisture that leaked over her lips; its salty taste told her she was crying.

Unspeaking, oblivious of anything beyond their enclosed world, they reached the gate of the farm. Without a word or glance, Philippe jumped down and led the cart into the farmyard, while Hélène hurried past Agathe into her bedroom.

Hélène stared at the reflection in the mirror, at eyes wide with a new knowledge; she put her hands up to her face. Agathe tapped at the door. 'Pass me your wet clothes; I've got some dry ones here for you.' Hélène felt her blood run cold and for the first time in her life she was afraid.

Chapter Thirteen

April–October 1922

It rained continuously for the next three days. Confined to the kitchen, restless children got in everyone's way and the sisters bickered over trifles. Hélène tried hard to ignore Philippe, but whenever he came into the house her heart leapt and in spite of herself she could not stop watching him. As he never returned her glances, her feverishness alternated with a gnawing exasperation.

As she put Frédéric to bed, Hélène held him tight and kissed him tenderly, her love for her son intensified by the new feelings she felt for his father. After the child had fallen asleep, Hélène lay awake, reliving that betraying glance, the acute awareness of Philippe's body against hers. Her fervid imaginings were interrupted by the small voice of her conscience, she silenced it fiercely. Her love was different from that of her sister; she could share with Philippe a physical passion that did not interest Agathe. All three would contribute to the happiness of the others; their love would be a perfect triangle that would satisfy them all. But the voice persisted. With a brusque stubbornness

Hélène refused to consider the consequences, convincing herself there would be none. Agathe must never find out, no one must ever know. Their love would be an inviolable secret between herself and Philippe. As dawn broke, she tossed and turned, doubting the intensity of the look they had exchanged, wondering if she had imagined that electrifying closeness.

On the fourth day the sun broke through the clouds and its warmth sucked steaming wraiths of mist from the soaked valleys. It was a relief to escape from the kitchen, where the shrill voices of children scratched at Hélène's nerves. Philippe returned at lunchtime, his clothes wet and muddy.

'I've been as far as the road, the track's a quagmire.' Philippe did not look at Hélène but at Agathe. 'The bridge'll have to be mended and I'll need Hélène to help me – those long planks are difficult to manoeuvre.'

Hélène felt her heart beat so strongly she was afraid the others would hear it. Agathe was silent for a while, and then nodded slowly. 'I suppose it's got to be done.'

The following morning Hélène walked beside Philippe, a length of rope slung over her shoulder. The sun was already high, the meadowsweet in the hedgerows gave off its heavy scent, birds wheeled and crowed in a brilliant blue sky and the leaves of the trees, drunk with sap, were a luminous green. Looking round at the burgeoning countryside, Hélène was intoxicated with the optimism of spring. 'It's all so beautiful.' She smiled at Philippe who smiled back, a rare pleasure lighting up his face.

The stream was no longer the brown torrent of a few days before but a clear brook that jumped and fell between mossy boulders. Far below the path, lying at various angles, were the beams that had constituted the bridge. Philippe knotted the rope round one of them; above him on the track Hélène pulled hard, but it was heavy and kept getting caught. Hélène clambered down. Philippe's hands brushed against Hélène's as they manhandled the heavy timber up the rough slope to the track, tripping, sliding, falling against each other. Wading across the stream, Hélène slipped and sat down heavily in the water, they were both laughing as Philippe helped her up. Hélène caught her breath as he pulled her towards him but he quickly let her go and they continued their work in silence.

At midday Hélène shouted down to Philippe, 'I'm starving. Let's find somewhere warm for lunch. I want to dry out a bit.'

They clambered upwards and came to a sunlit clearing with a view down the valleys to the Alps, a thin glistening line against the soft blue of the sky. Hélène laid out the food and the two sat on a bed of bracken, backs against an old chestnut tree, arguing amiably about the best way to tie the timbers together. Hélène lifted the edge of her sodden skirt and tried to wring out the water. She looked sideways at Philippe. 'Would you mind if I took this off?'

'Why not?' He sat watching as Hélène undid the buttons and the heavy garment fell to the ground. She picked it up and hung it over a branch, her lithe body stretching upwards, the wet cotton of her petticoat clinging to her thighs. She turned round, caught his glance and blushed. Hélène came back to where he was sitting and, misjudging the distance slightly, sat down. They were now very close, almost touching.

Hélène took a large bite of cheese and stretched out her bare legs. 'I love the sun. Everything looks better, tastes better.' She sniffed the air. 'Even people smell better. You for example - smell of ...' She stopped abruptly. The silence between them lengthened; became awkward. Both spoke at the same time, stopped and restarted simultaneously – laughed nervously. Again a silence fell between them as they sat looking ahead. Hélène made as if to get up: instinctively Philippe put out his hand to stop her and for a long moment they remained perfectly still until Philippe pulled her towards him.

Hélène lay in his arms and a new contentment overwhelmed her. She lifted up her face and kissed him, surprised that this should be their first kiss. Philippe undid the buttons of her blouse, nuzzling his face between the warmth of her bare breasts; he caressed her gently with his lips, pulling off his trousers as Hélène undid his shirt. When they were naked, Philippe stroked her, the thrill of his touch exciting, intoxicating. Hélène felt his hard urgency and stroked him gently as he quivered with pleasure. Clasped together, they rolled over so that Philippe lay on top of her, his body embraced by her legs; Hélène waited, tensed and expectant as he pushed inside her. Involuntarily they gasped, overcome by the completeness of their coupling. Unhurriedly and deliberately, with an intensity and silent purpose that excluded the rest of the world, Philippe coaxed Hélène's body to unbearable ecstasy. After it was over, Philippe held Hélène close; they lay still, listening to the murmuring of the woods and the tender songs of invisible birds.

Suddenly Philippe pulled away and sat up, looking down at Hélène with an anguished expression. 'I shouldn't have done that. I'm sorry. It mustn't happen again.'

Startled, Hélène knelt in front of him. She watched a spasm twitching the muscles of his cheek and stroked it gently. 'I love you, Philippe.' She kissed him. 'For the moment, that's all that matters.'

At the end of the afternoon Hélène jumped up and down on the bridge, testing its robustness. She glanced back at Philippe, who stood watching her from the bank, a rueful expression on his face. She ran towards him. 'It'd be so much better if we had a railing. Why don't we come back tomorrow?'

Philippe looked down at Hélène, and straightened up, his voice neutral. 'We can't spend any more time on it, the hay's ready for cutting. With this spell of hot weather we can't leave it any longer.' Hélène backed away, nodding sadly.

The sun had dipped behind the hill as they walked back to the farm. Hélène turned to Philippe. 'During all the years you were away didn't you ever feel tempted to ...' She did not end her question.

'No!' Philippe frowned, appeared about to speak, and then thought better of it. There was silence for a while.

Hélène spoke hesitantly, ‘In one of Francis’s letters he said he’d had a fight with Roland about me.’ Hélène paused. ‘D’you know what it was about?’

Philippe’s reply was terse. ‘Gounon made a remark that upset Francis.’

‘Did he say we’d made love?’

Philippe laughed cynically. ‘He didn’t put it quite like that. And he shouldn’t have said it, whether it was true or not.’

‘No he shouldn’t.’ There was a long pause. ‘But it is true.’

‘There’s no need to tell me.’

‘I’ve never spoken about it to anyone, not Agathe nor Lucinde.’ Hélène walked in silence for a while. ‘It was horrible.’ She took hold of Philippe’s hand. ‘Not like making love to you. That’s the most wonderful thing that’s ever happened to me.’

Philippe flinched and walked faster. 'It can't happen again, Hélène.' As they neared the bend before the farmhouse he stopped and turned to Hélène. ‘Agathe ...’

Hélène looked at him directly. ‘We both love Agathe. She must never, ever find out.’

That night Hélène could not sleep, she lay luxuriously reliving their lovemaking, murmuring to herself, ‘I love Philippe and he loves me.’ She shuddered at his insistence it would not happen again - but soon comforted herself. Hélène could not believe he would have the strength to resist making love to her; it was a craving that could not be denied. She bent over the cradle where Frédéric lay and stroked his dark curls, smiling contentedly at the sleeping infant.

***

Hélène had always enjoyed haymaking: the hot sun, the smell of cut grass, the cheerful banter over lunch with the men who moved from farm to farm. Alone in the barn with Philippe as they waited for the clumsy, overladen haywain to creak its way down the hill, Hélène threw aside her fork and came to stand close to Philippe; he ignored her and moved away. When Hélène reached out to take his hand, he jerked it away as though she had bitten him.

'Don't be a fool, Hélène.'

She strode away from him, pained by his resistance, frustrated that this new world was more complicated than she had imagined. 'I just wanted ...' She did not dare finish her sentence.

***

Days passed and, as Philippe appeared more remote than ever, Hélène found it hard to cope with the alternating violence of her hopes and the despair that overturned them.

The gold of the evening sun had just left the ridge of the hills across the valley; shadows slanted across the table strewn with the remains of supper. Philippe took out his pipe. 'I've just been over the Malleval hill to check on the rye. One of the terraces is in a bad way, must've been washed away by the rain. Unless we do something about it, we'll lose half the crop.'

Agathe looked at Philippe in surprise. 'But that's winter work. Can't it wait?'

Philippe shook his head. 'I don't think so. If we get any more rain, the whole lot's likely to come down and we'll need to get it mended before the rye ripens. A few days should do it if I've someone to help me.' Hélène could hear her heart beating.

Agathe pushed away the empty tureen and frowned. 'You know I can't! I couldn't even walk that far, never mind lift heavy stones. It'll have to be Hélène.' She looked at Hélène, who hurriedly gathered up the bowls and took them into the kitchen.

***

The basket with their lunch was heavy on Hélène's arm as they walked along the path to the far hillside, terraced by their predecessors over the centuries. The early-morning air was already warm and still, bright with butterflies that fluttered over the high banks of meadow flowers, joyful with swooping swallows and the cheerful rasping of crickets. Hélène moved the basket to her other arm, content to be with Philippe, who strode beside her in silent companionship.

Hélène chattered as she piled up the bulky stones. ''I adore Frédéric, he means everything to me.' She paused before adding wistfully, 'I'd thought being a mother would make my life complete but I'm afraid it hasn't.' She stood for a moment, eyes narrowed against the sun. 'I wanted to go to college so much, to study, to learn about the world.' Her voice sank low. 'I dreamt I'd live in Paris one day.' She stopped, looking sideways at Philippe. 'Don't you find life here dull and boring?'

Philippe smiled at Hélène. 'I've no desire to live in a town, thank you. Or to study, I'd quite enough of that at school.' The two sat down, their backs warmed by the hot stones, looking down the bare grass-covered slopes. 'I've always wanted a farm of my own.'

'But Les Laysses is yours now.'

Philippe sighed. 'I'd hoped we'd find a place where the farming's a bit easier. We'll never do more than scrape a living off this land. It's frustrating to know that however hard you work, you'll never make enough to buy much more than another cow to replace the one that's died.'

'Agathe doesn't mind that.' Hélène could not keep the resentment out of her voice.'

'Les Laysses is her home.'

'It would've been so different if Papa and Francis were alive.'

'It's hard for me to live here knowing I survived while they didn't.' Philippe drank from the bottle of wine, his face clouding over.

Hélène turned to him, taking hold of his hand. 'You still have nightmares about the war don't you?'

'Fewer than before, thank God. Memories fade.' He gave a rueful smile. 'Fade a bit, anyway.'

'I've always thought you should talk about what you've been through, not keep it all bottled up.'

Philippe made a face. 'You're more robust than Agathe, but I doubt whether there's any point.' He shuddered. 'I've tried hard to forget the horror of it – always being afraid and always having to hide being afraid; the filth, the noise, the stench, the sheer bloody insanity of it all. There's no need to share that.' He shook himself. 'Like everyone else, I thought things would go back to how they had been, that we'd just take up where we left off.'

'That's definitely what Agathe thought.'

Philippe looked reflective. 'She does – and to give her her due, she's really tried.' He paused. 'But it isn't the same as before. For those of us who'd got through the war more or less physically intact, we've changed in ways it's taken me a long time to recognise.'

'I didn't really know you before you went away. How've you changed?'

Philippe thought for a long time, eyes unfocused, facing down the valley. 'I'm much more cynical. I can't feel enthusiasm the way I used to. Take hunting, for example: I do it now because I'm expected to; I don't get any pleasure from it. And I'm not optimistic any more.' He shook his head with a wry smile. 'That may be just because I'm older, but during the four years of war so much that was good was wasted, lives thrown away for nothing.' He pulled at his pipe, his eyes narrow. 'The futility of it all undermines everything I do, any happiness, any sense of satisfaction – even any hope that the future will be better.' He sat forward, arms round his knees, his face drawn, eyes half closed. 'I spend a lot of time wondering what is the purpose of a life – is it only to feed ourselves, keep ourselves warm and dry, bring up our children? That's all I do and yet, like you, I don't think it's enough – every animal does the same.' Hélène nodded. 'And if I can't bring myself to believe I was saved for some special purpose, neither can I believe we're just pawns in the hands of a God.'

'As Agathe would have us believe.'

Philippe drank deeply. 'Life isn't better as a result of the war, in fact, it's worse – so I keep asking myself, what was all that suffering for? Perhaps wars don't have to be *for* anything, perhaps they just happen – but then why does something so dreadful have to "just" happen? Who knows?' There was a depth of sadness in Philippe's voice Hélène found hard to bear. He took another pull at the bottle. 'Seeing what Francis had to go through was very hard. He was so young, so unprepared for all the horror. He couldn't defend himself against it. And, ultimately, there was nothing I could do to help him.' He put his head in his hands. Hélène put her arms around his shoulders, cradling him, rocking him gently. After a while he lifted up his head, tears in his eyes, she kissed his eyelids tenderly.

They sat for a while, Hélène holding him close, feeling the tension in his spine as she stroked his back, murmuring into the warm mustiness of his hair.

After a while, Philippe sat up. 'Why'm I being so depressing? It's a sunny day – why waste it on gloomy thoughts?' He pulled Hélène to her feet. 'Come with me.'

They ran down the slope. The stream that ran through the bottom of the valley was lined with rowan trees whose slender trunks held aloft a tender curtain of leaves, dappling the ground with sunbeams. Philippe took off his clothes and jumped into the sparkling water. Hélène stood on the bank, entranced by the shimmering whiteness of his body, the body she loved but had never truly seen before. He splashed water at her, the droplets making rainbows in the still, warm air. Hélène squealed, quickly taking off her clothes to stand naked on the riverbank. Philippe stood up, the waters swirling giddily round his waist; she walked towards him and they embraced, the glacial water eddying around them. They held each other close; Hélène's cold nipples erect against his chest, his member long and hard pressed against her belly. Back on the bank, basking in the warmth of the sun, they made love slowly, tenderly, passionately. It was a long time before Philippe would allow them to come – drawing out a pleasure that was agonising, sweet, tantalising, eventually unendurable. He lay inside her, both feeling an aching completeness that neither wanted to end.

For two more days they half-walked, half-ran, to their secluded valley. Shielded from the searing sun, hidden by a screen of verdant leaves, they lay naked by the stream, making love passionately, uninhibited in their exploration of each other.

Encouraged by Hélène's adventurous delight, Philippe greedily explored new sensual pleasures that Agathe's dutiful acquiescence did little to satisfy.

Hélène sat in her petticoat as Philippe lay stretched out beside her, spent and fulfilled. She looked down at him tenderly. 'I love you, Philippe.' He did not respond, gazing upwards at the buzzard circling lazily overhead. Hélène tickled his nose with a long stem of grass and lay down beside him, her face almost touching his. 'Tell me you love me.' Philippe eyelids closed, his mouth crisped. Hélène persisted. 'Please.'

Philippe turned away. 'No Hélène.' He got to his feet and pulled her up; he kissed her on her forehead. Hélène felt the pricking of tears, but she kept silent.

Later that afternoon, sitting propped against the wall, postponing the moment when they would have to make their way home, Hélène asked wistfully, 'What would you wish for if you could have anything you wanted, however impossible?' She held her breath, willing him to say that he loved her, that he wanted a life with her. After a while, Philippe straightened up, grinning. 'I'd like one of these new machines, they call them tractors.' He smiled at her happily. 'That's what I'd really like.' He grew serious. 'And if I could have an even more impossible wish …' Hélène looked at him, eyes wide. 'I'd like to move to Canada.'

Hélène raised her eyebrows in surprise, trying to hide her disappointment. 'Canada? Why Canada?'

'Since we heard Marius was living there people have been talking about it. There's lots of good land, we could have a big farm that'd be a lot more successful and a damn sight easier to look after.' Philippe's smile dissolved. 'But that really is an impossible dream. Agathe would never even consider it.'

Hélène's tone was resentful. 'She'd say, "Who'd want to go to Canada?"'

Philippe laughed. 'Followed by, "We're much better off staying here."'

There was an uncomfortable silence between them. 'And she's right in a way. We've a lot to be thankful for.'

Hélène turned away from him. 'Have we?'

Philippe took her in his arms. She tried to push him away, but he held her close. In the middle of the open field they made love, silently, urgently, careless of anything but each other.

As Agathe ladled out the evening soup, she looked closely at both of them. 'I tried to come and see how you were getting on today.' A cold shiver ran down Hélène's spine. 'But I still haven't the energy to walk that far.' Agathe smiled. 'But I'm getting stronger every day. It won't be long before I'll be back to normal.' Filling her glass with wine, Hélène drank deeply, a mixture of fear and relief choking her. Agathe continued, 'How much longer will you be working on that wall? So much needs to be done round the farm.'

Philippe did not look at either woman. 'I reckon another day should be enough.' Hélène shuddered.

***

The sun still shone, the flowers still waved in the meadows as the gentle breeze passed by, the couple still splashed and bathed in the stream after making love – but the day's brilliant gloriousness was tainted by the knowledge that this brief interlude was about to end. As the time came to return to the farm, Hélène stood looking at the trampled grass, seeing the imprint of their bodies in the crushed flowers. She took hold of Philippe's hand. 'We've been so happy.' Her voice trailed away. 'I don't know when we'll be as happy again.'

'There's nothing I can say or do to alter the future, Hélène. You know that.' He looked down at her. 'We must be grateful for what we've had and not ask for more.'

Hélène pulled away. 'You know I'll never be satisfied with that.' They trudged slowly back to the farm while the old stiff silence returned to walk between them.

***

'So the missus's still poorly, Faugeron?' Roland leered at Philippe as he entered the café. 'I bet you're not too upset – gives you the chance to bang the sexy sister. Always said you're a lucky bastard.'

Philippe rounded on Roland. 'Shut up, Gounon, I've had enough of your filthy fantasies.'

Roland laughed with glee, turning to his companions. 'That hit the mark! Just look at his face – red as a turkey's wattle!' He grinned up at Philippe. 'What is it Faugeron, a bad conscience? Or are you jealous? You know I had first bite at that particular cherry and I've had first refusal since. Is that what's bothering you?'

Philippe strode over and grabbed Roland by his jacket, lifting him out of his chair so that his metal legs dangled helplessly. 'Sod you, Gounon; I've had enough of your nasty insinuations.' Infuriated by the cackling sniggers of the group, he shook Roland hard.

Monsieur Bernard came striding over. 'What the hell's got into you, Faugeron? You know how much he enjoys winding people up.' Philippe let Roland drop back into his chair and left the café, swearing under his breath as the guffaws of the men followed him, furious he had lost control.

Hélène stood by the fountain waiting, her empty baskets at her feet. As soon as they were out of sight of the town, she threw her arms around Philippe and held him close. She looked up at him, her eyes misty with tears. 'I can see something's the matter, has someone upset you?'

Philippe shrugged. 'Bloody Gounon. He's a complete bastard.' He paused. 'I don't think we should go into town together again. There'll be gossip.'

Hélène removed her hand. 'Sadly, I agree.' She sniffed. 'That poisonous Nouzet woman's such a bitch. Asked me why Agathe never comes into town these days. There was a group of her busybody friends in the shop, staring at me down their noses. I said she still wasn't well enough and they stood sneering at me. As I left, the Lafont woman took me aside to tell me I'd better mind my reputation. Frustrated old cows!' She walked on, swishing at the flowers with her empty basket.

'They're spiteful, but it hits home when we know their suspicions are justified.'

'Oh don't, Philippe. I can't bear all this!'

They walked on in a brooding silence. Hélène took hold of his hand, but there was no response, so she dropped it.

'So. what's the news from town?' Agathe sat under the lime tree as the distant shouts of the children wafted cheerfully from the end of the terrace. The lingering warmth of dusk drew out the languorous smell of the honeysuckle, while overhead came the contented droning of insects as they sucked the last sweetness from the lime blossom. Agathe had a large bowl of haricots on the table in front of her; taking a handful of the long, curved pods, she squeezed out their dark crimson beans. Hélène sat down beside her; Philippe brought a chair from the kitchen.

Hélène waited for Philippe to answer, but as he remained silent, she dragged herself away from her melancholy thoughts. 'The big news is that Marius has sent two boat tickets for Canada. He obviously hadn't heard about Lucinde, and Madame Nouzet's absolutely furious because she can't go on her own.'

'Be fair, the poor woman's bound to be upset; he can't come here and she can't go there so she'll never see her son again!' Agathe gathered up the empty pods.

Hélène shrugged. 'Which means there're two tickets to Canada going to waste.' She looked at Philippe who did not meet her glance. 'Wouldn't it be wonderful if we could have them and set off for Canada together?' She chewed on an empty pod. 'I'd give anything to get away from this miserable town where everyone pokes their nose into other people's business.'

'But who'd want to go to Canada? To go all that way with no idea what'd be facing you when you got there. We're better off staying where we are.' Hélène burst out laughing, but there was a bitter edge to her laughter. 'What's so funny?' Agathe looked across at her sister, smiling.

'Nothing – that's exactly what Philippe and I thought you'd say.' She looked across at Philippe, forcing him to take her side in teasing Agathe. 'We more or less got it right word for word.'

Agathe laughed happily. She pushed aside the bowl and took hold of each of their hands; she held them in silence for a while, before saying gently, 'I'm feeling so much better now. And I'm so glad we can still laugh together. It's like old times again.' She smiled at each of them in turn, her eyes misted with emotion. Hélène felt a flame of joy leap through her; they were, as she had wished, all three truly happy. As she beamed with pleasure, her smile froze as she watched Philippe raise Agathe's hand to his lips and kiss it – something Hélène had never seen him do before. It hurt like a great gashing wound. She gasped for air and ran into the kitchen.

That night Hélène heard the murmur of conversation in the bedroom above. She lay listening, knowing and dreading what was about to happen. The voices died away and, as her ears strained to hear, the familiar creaking began. Hélène stuffed a handkerchief into her mouth and stole quickly out of the house. At the end of the terrace she bent over, spewing out the evening's soup as she held on to the stile, sobbing.

Looking back at the dark mass of the farmhouse, Hélène turned and rushed wildly down the path leading to the woods. She ran on and on, her breath fighting her tears until she came to the terrace where, only the day before, she had made love to Philippe. It was dark and sombre, the stones they had put in place stood inscrutable in the cold gleam of the moonlight. Beneath the wall buttercups waved, their flowers lividly colourless, but Hélène could find no trace of the crushed grass where their two bodies had lain entwined together. Nothing remained: it was as though their lovemaking had never been. A wave of desolation overwhelmed Hélène. Under the icy indifference of the moon, she made her way slowly back to the farm, her heart aching with emptiness.

***

The following morning Hélène was in the barn milking Noemi, her forehead leaning against the passive beast, her tears absorbed by the comforting hide of the animal. When she had wrung the last drop from the pliant udder, she stiffened as she saw Philippe come into the byre; he hesitated before perching on the edge of the manger. They looked at each other with a silent antagonism and Hélène's heart sank when she saw the determination in his eyes.

'I'm sorry, Hélène, I can't go on. I hate myself for what we're doing. It's my fault, I should never have let myself ...' He stopped.

'Fall in love with me?' Hélène whispered.

'I love Agathe, Hélène. She's my wife. I hate all this lying and deceit.' He looked hard at her. 'It was terrible yesterday when she seemed so content.' Again he paused. 'So trusting of both of us. It brought home to me just how much we were letting her down. I can't go on, Hélène, and you must accept it.'

Hélène took hold of his hand, pulling him towards her, but he resisted. 'I won't accept it! These few weeks've been the only time I've been happy. I can't accept there'll be no more love, no more joy in my life.'

'Don't exaggerate, Hélène.' Philippe got heavily to his feet. 'If we carry on, we'll bring misery down on all three of us - and on the child.' He continued, his voice slow and emphatic: 'This is bound to end in disaster and must stop – for your sake as well as for Agathe's.'

Fighting desperation and anger, Hélène hissed, 'Then go to hell! I hope the pair of you rot in your own self-righteousness. Neither of you knows what the word love means.'

Philippe stood looking at her for a moment, his expression impossible to read. 'It's finished, Hélène.'

***

As the evenings shortened and the trees began to turn, Hélène's despair intensified. She dreaded the winter days when the three of them would be immured together, with all her senses reaching out to Philippe while he remained resolutely inaccessible. As she surreptitiously watched him, it seemed to Hélène that Philippe was unhappy too; he had returned to his lonely drinking, sitting for long hours outside the barn before clumsily climbing the stairs to his bedroom. In the darkness she relived their days on the hill, aching as she remembered the lovemaking and the talks – scouring her thoughts to see if there was anything she could have done to keep him. As the days passed she became more determined to rescue something from their past and to secure some hope for the future. She waited.

***

'Philippe's forgotten his whetstone.' Agathe pointed to the wooden pouch on its leather strap hanging by the door. She looked hot and cross. 'I suppose I'll have to take it up to the top meadow.'

Hélène quickly took it down. 'It's all right, I'll go.' She did not look at Agathe as she dashed out of the door. 'I won't be long.'

Philippe was the other side of the hedge, slashing at its lower branches with a sickle; he did not hear her approach. Hélène hurled herself into his arms; she lifted up her face, eyes shining, and kissed him, her arms wrapped round his neck, holding his face close to hers, triumphant when she felt the surge of his desire. All her body cried out to be joined with him, to have him inside her once more. She closed her eyes, her body melting as a long shudder of desire ran through her. Intertwined, they moved together until Hélène's back was against the trunk of a birch tree; she pushed aside Philippe's braces; he pulled up her skirt, lifting her up so that she could sink down on him. In a few moments it was over and they stood, conjoined, gasping for breath, eyes shut.

As she straightened her skirt, Hélène had tears in her eyes.

'It's been so long.' She stroked his face tenderly. 'I can't do without you – and you can't do without me.'

Philippe turned away from her, one hand supporting himself against the tree, his eyes closed. He cursed under his breath, shaking his head from side to side. 'I swore I'd never make love to you again.'

Hélène took his hand, but he snatched it away. 'We love each other Philippe – we can't help it.'

Philippe clasped his head and glared at her fiercely. 'Of course we can help it – we're not animals!' He wiped his hand over his face, his expression hard and resentful. 'Hélène, I can't and I won't live my life with a bad conscience.'

'A bad conscience is a price I'm prepared to pay.'

Philippe clenched his fists as he shouted, 'Well, I'm not! This won't work, Hélène and you know it. You must keep away from me.'

‘I didn’t come here to seduce you – it just happened. I long for you all the time.’ Hélène paused before saying acidly, ‘And I’ve no one else. I’m all yours.’

Philippe cursed. ‘Hélène, you know there isn’t any way that can be changed.’

Hélène was silent, moodily picking at the bark of the tree. ‘But I love you – and even if you won’t say it, you love me too. I accept we’ll have to keep it a secret, but even if we can only make love occasionally, like today, it’d give me something to live for.' She spoke sullenly, 'I’m not asking much.’

Philippe shook his head angrily. ‘I won’t live a life that’s a lie.’ He glared at Hélène. ‘I hate the idea of having secrets from my wife. That’s not the way I am.’ He turned away, speaking harshly, ‘If you won't let me alone, you must leave Les Laysses.’

Hélène grabbed hold of his arm. ‘But I can't! I can't leave without Frédéric. How could I live without my son - or without seeing you?’ She shook him fiercely, suddenly terrified. ‘Don’t send me away, I couldn’t bear it!’ Faced with Philippe’s obstinate silence, Hélène took the sharpening stone out of her pinafore pocket and threw it on the ground. 'That's why I came, damn you!' She ran off down the hill.

***

The brilliance of autumn had faded into the bleak precursors of winter. Slanting sheets of sleety rain gusted over bent backs as the three wordlessly harvested the potatoes. Hélène knew Philippe would never be hers; even if he loved her, he still loved Agathe more. But she longed for him. The smell of his jacket hanging by the door sent her into an aching fever; each evening she imagined his lean, naked body as she listened to the grinding of the pump and felt sick with desire. Despite his cold disregard, Hélène could not accept they would never make love again.

One evening, as she laid Frédéric in his cot, he held out his arms, held on to her, would not let her put him down. He smiled anxiously up at her, sensing her anguish and stammered, *'Maman, t'aime moi*?' Bursting into tears, Hélène held him tight, smothering his tiny face with kisses. She stroked his head until she was sure he was asleep.

But Hélène lay awake. In the room above she could hear the nightly sounds of Agathe getting ready for bed, the swishing of water as she washed, the careful sounds of clogs being lined up under the bed, the soft murmuring of her sister's prayers, the mattress rustling. Hélène waited to hear Philippe stumble upstairs. Time passed. Hélène thought she heard Agathe's gentle snoring and her imagination flew to Philippe alone in the darkness of the barn. She felt an overwhelming need to be with him; her body ached to hold him. Naked under her nightdress she could feel the insistent current of desire surge within her. Listening intently, she thought she could hear the sound of Agathe's regular breathing; she must be asleep. Hélène wrapped her shawl around her and let herself silently out of the house.

The night was pitch black and she could feel the clouds pressing down on the roof of the buildings. On tiptoe she made her way to the door of the barn, gently pushing it aside. In the gloom she could see the dark silhouette of Philippe, the glow of his pipe coming and going. She shut the door behind her and glided towards him. 'Agathe's asleep.' Hélène reached out towards him as she whispered, 'I love you.'

Philippe snatched away his hand. 'Go away, Hélène! Are you mad?'

'Please, Philippe.' Hélène was undoing the strings on her nightdress. 'Please, Philippe, I need you so much.'

'Leave me alone.'

'No! It's all right – she's asleep. I heard her. Please, Philippe, we have so few chances to be together.' Hélène drew the nightdress over her head so she stood naked in front of him. 'I love you. I'd do anything for you.'

Philippe took hold of her arms and shook her. 'I'm not going to make love to you.'

Hélène moved closer to him, her bare breasts pressing against his shirt, her arms around his neck. Philippe tried to move away, but his back was against the wall. He spoke desperately, 'Get away, Hélène. Leave me alone.'

'You want me – I can feel it.'

Hélène pulled Philippe closer to her; she entwined him in her arms and gently pushed him down onto the soft mound of dry grass. There was no sound apart from the rustling of the animals in the byre below; the darkness was all around them as they fell into the dusty heap of hay. Philippe resisted, struggled to get free but Hélène had wrapped her legs around him, her arms held him tight – she kissed his mouth, his chest, lower and lower.

A high shriek pierced the air, a bright light lanced through the barn. The beam pinioned Hélène where she lay, the translucent white of her limbs stark against Philippe's dark clothing. For one moment she held on to him, a fragile raft in this new world, but he slid backwards out of her embrace, knelt for a moment, head bowed, and then stood up, a black silhouette against the light. Hélène searched his face but only the plane of his cheek was illuminated, the caverns of his eyes impenetrable, fathomlessly deep. He backed slowly away, turned and left the barn. The barn door was slammed shut, the bar slotted into place, leaving Hélène in an inky darkness still resonating with the echoes of Agathe's scream.

Stupefied, numb with horror Hélène stared into the abyss, the chasm that faced her, the catastrophe she had created. Nothing would ever be as it had been. Her life had shattered. She had lost everything - Frédéric, Philippe, her sister, her future. Agathe would send her away; send her away without Frédéric, with nothing. She screamed silently, 'No, no, not that! Never again to see my son.' She knew it was hopeless to beg her sister to let her stay; Agathe would not forgive her for what she had done.

Hélène felt around the floor for her nightdress and put it on. She crawled into the hay and curled up, whimpering, unable to comprehend what had happened, unable to imagine what was to come. She shivered as the wintry night seeped through the thin cotton. Beyond her misery she vaguely heard noises; the scurrying of the *loirs* as they ran along the beams overhead, mice and rats rustling in the hay all around her. Hélène drew her nightdress tight across her legs. There was no other sound, and this scared her, her imagination filling the silence with horrors. She crawled towards the wall and urinated, scuttled crab-like to another corner. A *loir* ran over her foot; she crept further into the hay. Time extended indefinitely as she crouched, every muscle tense, waiting for Agathe to return, knowing her wrath would be dreadful. Cold sweat trickled between her breasts. She was mortally afraid.

The door was thrown open and a lamp illuminated the sinister shadows of the barn. Blinded by the light, Hélène heard Agathe push a heavy object over the threshold. A bundle of clothes landed at her feet.

'Get dressed.' Agathe's voice was raw, grim, bitter. Hélène struggled with the fastenings, fear making her fingers clumsy. When she was dressed, she crawled to kneel at Agathe's feet. 'I'm sorry, Agathe. I'm so sorry.' Hélène did not dare look at her sister.

Agathe seized Hélène's hair, pulling it hard so her face was dragged into the full glare of the lamp. 'Liar!' Agathe twisted her sister's head from side to side then let go, throwing Hélène to the ground. 'You disgust me.' Hélène was face down on the floor, moaning. 'You bitch, to betray me with my own husband. I gave him to you so you could have a son. I didn't want to, I did it for you – but that wasn't enough, you had to have him, too.' Agathe grabbed Hélène's hair again, jerking her head up so she had to face her accuser. 'I trusted you while you were opening your legs for him. You whore! You're worse than that slut Lucinde.' Agathe made an effort to control herself: she pulled Hélène to her feet, marching her to the door. 'I never want to see you again. Get out and never come back.' She shoved Hélène hard. 'Take it and go!' Hélène picked up the heavy case.

Hélène found the strength to look at her sister. Agathe's face was rigid with bitterness, her eyes red but pitiless. Hélène spoke in a whisper, 'Please forgive me.'

'God may forgive you but I never will. Never!'

Agathe pushed her out into the cold night air. Rain was falling, a thin, icy sleet. Hélène walked across the courtyard, past the closed farmhouse door; for a moment she stood in the beam of golden light that streamed from the window of the kitchen, its warmth still full of the familiar, which had now become a memory. Hélène's heart ached with unutterable sorrow; she turned to Agathe. 'Please let me say goodbye to my son. I beg you.'

'You have no son.'

Agathe stood at the gate, the light from the lamp playing over Hélène's bent back as she stumbled down the track, dragging the heavy suitcase. As Hélène reached the first bend, the light disappeared and she was left in the cold, wet night.

Her mind numb, rain and tears running down her face, step after step, she staggered forward.

When she reached the bridge, Hélène slumped to the ground. She hid her face in her hands, gnawing at her fingers so the physical pain might distract her a little from the dreadful horrors that faced her. She sobbed frantically, calling out her son's name 'Frédéric, Frédéric, my darling one, never to see you again'. She rocked herself back and forward, twisting her head from side to side in an effort to fight off the fears that assailed her. Then she sat staring into the darkness for a long time. She did not know where she could go, what she would do. She did not care.

PART THREE

Chapter Fourteen

March–May 1939

Hélène prodded the smouldering log. A flame flared for a moment; listlessly she poked it again.

'Leave that alone!' Hélène's husband shook his newspaper in irritation. 'Wood costs money. My money.' Albert Picot's reedy voice grated on Hélène's nerves; she let the poker fall so it clattered onto the hearth. The newspaper crackled sharply, followed by silence. Hélène gazed into the dully glowing embers, stifling her thoughts, waiting.

'Get me another brandy.' Hélène picked up the empty bottle and went out to the kitchen at the end of the corridor. The small room was dank, foetid with the gas that seeped from the bottle by the stove and the sour smell of drains. She reached into the cupboard over the sink and took out a bottle of cognac. A slight flicker of satisfaction passed over her face.

Hélène filled her husband's glass and left the bottle on the faded chenille tablecloth. She adjusted the guttering flame of the big oil lamp; its flame illuminated a room full of heavy, brooding furniture, each surface covered with a clutter of cheap Madonnas and miscellaneous saints, souvenirs from the many shrines her husband's late wife had visited. Hélène felt suffocated by the room's stale, stuffy atmosphere, isolated from the world by rusty velvet curtains festooned with tarnished tassels. From behind his chair, she looked down at the cadaverous frame of her husband and her face knotted with revulsion. As he replaced the half-empty glass on the table, she glanced at his flushed cheeks and refilled it to the brim. She sat down, waiting.

The clock on the mantelpiece struck nine, the notes lingering in the sterile air.

Picot lowered the *Gringoire*, the weekly newspaper whose neo-Fascist views were a mild reflection of his own. He took off his wire-rimmed spectacles, frowning. 'Who the hell cares if Hitler's broken the agreement he made at Munich?' He glared belligerently at Hélène, not expecting an answer. 'Why should France get all worked up if he's occupied some insignificant countries we've never hear of? I don't give a damn about Czechoslovakia or Romania.' Picot smoothed his wispy moustache. 'At least he's got the balls to face up to the bloody Communists – they're wrecking our economy with their endless strikes.' He sniffed. 'He's got the right ideas about a lot of things.' Hélène got up and stood looking into the dead fire so he could not see the loathing and contempt in her expression.

'Daladier hasn't a clue: last year he ordered a partial mobilisation – and now he's cosying up to

Hitler! They should make up their mind whose side they're on.' Picot smiled to himself, gratified to see the effort it was costing Hélène not to respond. He continued complacently, 'Thank God, I'm ready either way. I've bought as much grain and corn oil as I can lay my hands on.' He sniggered, 'If prices go up like they did in '14, I won't complain. That war worked out extremely well.' He sipped his brandy with satisfaction. 'Whatever they decide prices're bound to rise.'

Ignoring him, Hélène picked up her book. A hostile silence filled the room.

'What's that you're reading?' Picot leant forward. 'Give it to me.' Instinctively Hélène held on to the book before reluctantly letting him take it from her. He glanced at its title and threw it back at her. 'God knows why you're interested in Paris, you'll never go there. All this reading's just a waste of time.' He looked at her with disdain. 'Maria, may her blessed soul rest in peace, used to knit or sew in the evenings – she was always doing something useful.' He glowered at Hélène who sat tight-lipped, staring at the floor. He picked up his paper. 'There's no point in comparing the two of you. She was a saint, while you ...' His voice sharpened. 'God forgive your sins.'

Hélène smoothed out the crumpled pages and found her place; she turned away from her husband and continued to read. There was no sound in the room apart from the rustling of paper as Picot carefully folded the *Gringoire* and picked up the *Croix de l'Ardèche*, a local Catholic journal.

'Now here's something that'll interest you.' Picot glanced at his wife, his small eyes glittering with malicious delight. He straightened out the paper and read in his thin voice, 'The diocese of Viviers is sorry to announce the death of Père Montagnon, Curé of Saint-Agrève for the last twenty-five years.' He looked across at his wife, hoping for a reaction to this unexpected news, but Hélène maintained her blank expression and appeared uninterested. Picot snorted in annoyance as he pored over the article, nodding and grunting, 'Really!' from time to time. Hélène controlled her curiosity, ostentatiously turning a page. Picot cleared his throat and read out loud, impatient to provoke her into a response. 'Père Montagnon started his career in the seminary at Viviers. A brilliant theologian whose student treatise on the Pauline Creed was widely acclaimed, he was expected to rise to great heights. After the closure of the seminary in 1905, he spent some years at Privas giving spiritual guidance to the congregation of St Thomas. As a priest apparently headed for high rank in the diocese, or even in the wider Church, it was a surprise to many when he decided to leave the bright lights of Privas and dedicate himself to the rural community of Saint-Agrève.'

Picot put down the paper. 'I knew him, of course. Spoke a lot of good sense in his sermons and had a fine way with words. A clever man. Such a shame.' The sanctimonious tone was replaced by a salacious chuckle as Picot rubbed his hands together. 'But Père Montagnon was a naughty boy. Couldn't keep his hands off the female sheep in his flock.' He paused, savouring the memory. 'There was a good-looking woman in the congregation, fine figure, supposed to be a widow but no one could place her husband. Anyway, she took to confessing her sins – often. People began to notice. One of the old women who were always skulking about the church saw them at it in the sacristy. He'd got his cassock up by his armpits and she was kneeling ...' The lubricious smacking of his lips nauseated Hélène. 'The old biddy wrote to the bishop and before we knew it, he'd been transferred. A great loss in many ways.'

Picot looked across at his wife, his lips glistening with saliva. 'I bet he found plenty of sluts like you in Saint-Agrève willing to drop their knickers for their priest.' As Hélène did not reply, he picked up his newspaper and continued sententiously, 'I think you should pay for a Mass for his soul.'

Hélène burst out, 'Why? I've no reason to be grateful to him.' She bit her lip hard, furious for rising to his provocation. Denying her husband any sign of emotion had become Hélène's only source of gratification. In the early years she had fought him – sworn, shouted, even struck him – until she realised the violence of her response only increased his satisfaction. Over the years they had refined the arts of their merciless warfare: Hélène had schooled herself not to respond to his taunting, Picot had perfected the technique of needling her.

Gloating with triumph, he pretended to show surprise, his voice staccato, sarcastic. 'Of course you must be grateful. After all, it's entirely due to him that we're now man and wife.' He smiled at her, the thin lips opening briefly to show irregular yellow teeth. 'But more importantly for you, he was the only person our Magdalene could turn to in her hour of distress – wasn't he, my dear?' He poured himself another glass of brandy. 'You must give thanks for the compassionate Curé who sent you to me so you could look after my sainted late wife.' Picot crossed himself. Realising Hélène was no longer listening, Picot shook out his paper; when he next spoke his voice was thick and slurred. 'A Mass is the least you can do.'

Hélène sat staring at the dead fire, waiting.

When the newspaper slid to the floor, Hélène closed her eyes and breathed deeply, thankful for the brandy that gave a fleeting respite from her husband's calculated cruelty. She looked with disgust at the head lolling against the back of the chair, the mouth hanging open, the scrawny neck with its Adam's apple bobbing up and down as he snored. She wished he was dead like his old friend the Curé.

Hélène picked up the discarded newspaper. Seeing the Curé's name revived traumatic memories which came jostling and jangling out of her subconscious: the agonising walk from the farm, the rain lashing at her face, the dead weight of the case, her thoughts ricocheting from one searing loss to another. Staggering forward, without thinking where she was going or what she might do, she had made her way up to Saint-Agrève; it was still dark as she made her way along its unlit streets. Seeking shelter from the rain, Hélène had gone into the church and lain down on a row of chairs. The Curé had found her as he prepared for Matins.

He stood towering over her. With a bark of triumph, he took in her pitiable state. 'Ha! I know why you're here, Mademoiselle Vernot.' He gave another cynical laugh. 'I always knew it would come to this. I told your sister you couldn't be trusted, that you couldn't resist corrupting her husband but she wouldn't believe me, said you'd promised it would only be once.' He bent over so his face was almost touching hers and shouted, spittle flecking onto Hélène's cheeks, 'Your sister committed a mortal sin *for you*, she made a huge sacrifice *for you* – and this is how you've repaid her!' The priest dragged Hélène to the steps in front of the altar and forced Hélène down onto her knees, banging her forehead against its stone plinth. 'What you've done is unnatural, an abomination. Pray God for His mercy.'

When the Curé returned, wiping traces of milky coffee from his lips, his voice was brittle with contempt. 'You can't stay here; your presence defiles the House of God.' Hélène cowered away from him. The Curé raised his voice so it rung round the bare church. 'I have prayed to God for guidance and in his infinite love for sinners He has directed me to be merciful to you. I will write a letter to my old church in Privas asking them to see what they can do.'

'Please don't tell them.' Hélène's voice was small and pleading.

The Curé bellowed, 'Of course I must tell them! Why else would you be throwing yourself on their mercy? You've brought this on yourself because you couldn't control your carnal lust.' He rummaged in the pocket of his cassock, retrieved an envelope and a handful of francs. He held them out to her. 'There's a train for La Voulte around midday; change there for Privas. And pray God to forgive you for the terrible things you've done.'

After the priest at St Thomas's had read the Curé's letter, he made no attempt to disguise his disgust. The housekeeper led Hélène away to a bare bedroom, where she spent a sleepless night. In the morning she was summoned to the priest's study; he would not look at her, as though the very sight would infect him with her wickedness. He spoke sharply, eager to rid himself of Hélène and her sins. 'I'm sending you to the Picots. He's a pious man with a sick wife, so I hope he'll take pity on you. But be under no illusion, he'll expect you to work, and work hard.'

'I'm used to working hard.'

The priest picked up her hands and dropped them scornfully. 'In the fields. You've not worked in a shop before?' Hélène shook her head. 'Well, it's up to you. You've made your bed and now you must lie on it. And if your life seems hard, remember it's God's punishment.'

It was almost seventeen years since that dreadful day; seventeen years of suffering. Hélène accepted she had done a terrible wrong and deserved to be punished but her misery had known no bounds. Every day she tortured herself thinking about Frédéric, tried to imagine him as he grew up, tearful at the thought he would never know her to be his mother. Sometimes she tried to comfort herself by believing that the love between her and Philippe had been so great that what had happened was inevitable – but she knew that it was not so.

At first she had not appreciated how much the Picots enjoyed tormenting her. At the beginning, the pain of being parted from her son, from Philippe and the farm had numbed Hélène to their taunts and then, as the first agonies deadened into despair, the humbling consciousness of her guilt kept her from confronting them. Later, as the years passed, she had tried to escape from their sanctimonious viciousness but without money or friends all her attempts ended in failure. Bitter and resentful, she had found herself condemned to an unrelenting drudgery from which there seemed no prospect of deliverance.

***

Every day except Monday Hélène served in her husband's charcuterie, a substantial shop with a large window overlooking the bustling rue du Malconseil below the apartment in which they lived. The Caserne Rampon, the military barracks, was a few streets away and whenever groups of young men passed by, she would watch them in the insubstantial hope that one day she might see Frédéric. The mornings were usually busy but in the afternoons, especially on Wednesdays and Saturdays after the market had ended, Hélène sat reading the books she had borrowed from the library even though Picot objected, saying it gave the impression she was above serving in the shop.

Late one afternoon two young men came into the charcuterie joking and laughing, their new uniforms clumsy and ill-fitting on their tall wiry frames. Hélène's heart lurched as she recognised the patois of the Plateau. She looked at the taller, dark-haired youth and sank onto a chair as her knees gave way. The two recruits stopped their horseplay and looked at her in alarm; they were about to leave the shop when she managed to blurt out, 'Can I help you?' smiling apologetically. 'I don't often have the chance to speak patois.' Her voice shook as she formed the half-forgotten phrases. 'Where are you from?'

'I'm from Devesset, he's from Malleval.' The young man grinned at her. 'Villages near Saint-Agrève. D'you know it?'

Hélène nodded, trying to keep her voice low so as not to attract the attention of her husband, who eavesdropped on all her conversations. 'I know it well.'

The two young men smiled with pleasure. 'You've been there on holiday? It's very popular in summer.'

Before she could stop herself, Hélène replied, 'No. I used to live there once.'

The taller one raised his eyebrows. 'What's your name? Perhaps I could take a message to your family when we go back on leave?'

Hélène shook her head. 'None of them live there any more.' She wrapped up the pies they had bought and the two turned to go. Frantic at seeing them disappear, Hélène spoke urgently, without thinking, 'There was a family I knew well, the Faugerons. Would you know anything of them?'

The taller young man paused, his hand on the knob of the door. His face lit up. 'I'm Frédéric Faugeron; this is my cousin, Remy.'

Hélène held tight to the back of her chair, she continued recklessly, desperate to continue the conversation, to keep Frédéric from leaving so she could feast her eyes on him. 'I used to know Philippe and Agathe Faugeron. I was in the same class as Agathe.'

'They're my parents.' Frédéric's face clouded. 'My father's in good health but my mother died six years ago.'

He looked as though he was about to say more, but his companion clapped him on the shoulder. 'We'd better get back to the barracks – don't want to get into trouble so soon after arriving.' The bell on the door jangled for a long time after they had gone.

A painful blow in the middle of her back tore Hélène out of her thoughts. 'What's got into you? It's time to close the shop and you're just sitting here.'

Hélène got up quickly. 'I'm not feeling well.' She looked at Picot defiantly. 'I need to lie down.'

Once in the bedroom Hélène closed the curtains and flung herself on the bed; curled up in agony, she bit the pillow to stifle her cries. She had known immediately the young man was her son, the resemblance to Philippe was unmistakable and she had been moved beyond words to find Frédéric's eyes were the same dark green as her own. Hélène yearned to hold him; the ache of his loss that she had never been able to suppress overwhelmed her. But the tenderness in Frédéric's voice when he had said, 'My mother died six years ago,' had cut her to the core, and the unchallengeable truth that her own son did not know her, would never know who she was and that she would never be able to tell him, eclipsed all other thoughts. He had not reached his second birthday when she had – Hélène moaned out loud – when she had abandoned her child.

As she lay in the darkened room, Hélène's thoughts turned to Philippe. Over the years she had worn out her memories and it was an undeserved refinement of her punishment that she could no longer conjure up Philippe's smile or recreate his voice. Frédéric had restored her recollections and she could see once again the crinkles round Philippe's eyes when he smiled, hear the contentment in his voice after they had made love, stroke the contours of his cheek etched against a sunlit sky. She began to sob.

After a while Hélène realised she was crying too for Agathe, the sister she had betrayed, who had taken away her son and cast her out – but whom she had never stopped loving. That Agathe was now dead was an inconsolable loss, the impossibility of her forgiveness now certain.

***

As the days passed, her hopes of Frédéric visiting the shop faded and she began to fret. Desperate to see her son again, she decided to look out for him at the gate of the garrison in the early evening when the recruits changed duties.

Hélène made her way through streets bustling with people on their way home from work. She took up a position on the side of the square opposite the barracks, but it was difficult at that distance to recognise individuals as they emerged through the imposing gates and strolled beside the tall iron railings. She moved closer, watching the young men in their dull brown uniforms come and go. A group of soldiers stood near her, arguing fiercely.

'Of course we've got to fight Hitler! He's a maniac. He won't stop 'til he's taken over the whole of Europe.' The young man threw the stub of his cigarette on the ground, grinding it fiercely into the gravel. 'France can't just stand by and watch.'

The other soldier shrugged. 'The government doesn't agree with you – and neither do I. Bringing countries together to oppose Hitler peacefully's the only way. If we stick together with Russia, Britain and the rest even he wouldn't be so foolish as to take us on.'

'Don't be ridiculous! He destroyed Czechoslovakia and no one did anything – and only a week ago Italy simply marched into Albania. We need to stand up to the Fascists, show them they can't do as they like.'

'That's Communist propaganda! Whatever happens, we don't want another war.' The two moved away, still arguing. Hélène shivered, afraid for Frédéric.

For five days she waited in vain, avoiding the mocking stares of the young men, who assumed she was there for the same purpose as the groups of giggling girls who hung around the barracks. On the sixth day she saw him. A wave of pride poured through her as she watched the tall, handsome youth stride along the pavement; she smiled at his strength, the guileless vigour of his expression, the way he confidently swung his arms. Hélène walked rapidly towards him, but was overtaken by a young woman running headlong across the Champ de Mars who threw her arms around Frédéric and kissed him. Hélène stood watching, bereft, as they disappeared under the shade of the plane trees, chattering and holding hands.

A few days later Frédéric came into the shop. Hélène served him clumsily, her hands shaking – as he was about to leave, she came out from behind the counter and followed him into the street. 'I'm so glad you came back, I was hoping you would.' She smiled at him as he frowned, unsure what to make of her. 'Please tell me more about your family. I was great friends with Agathe for a while.'

'It's not easy talking about her.' Frédéric looked away. 'Even now I miss her – she was such a wonderful mother to us all.' Hélène swallowed, biting her lip to hide her agitation. 'It's been hard for Papa – he misses her too.' His words almost choked Hélène.

'She had two girls, older than you.'

'Berthe married a shopkeeper in Valence. Cécile died of pneumonia when she was only ten. Dorothée helps Papa with some of the farm work when she's not at school.' Frédéric looked sideways at Hélène. 'This can't be very interesting.'

Hélène took hold of his arm, thrilled to touch him, but he drew away. 'No, no, I'm curious.' She smiled up at him, but his expression was wary and her smile did not soften the distrust in his eyes. 'Who's Dorothée?'

'My younger sister.'

'How old is she?'

'Fifteen.'

'And has your father remarried?'

'No.' Frédéric was looking at her strangely, unsure what to make of this woman. Hélène wanted to ask him so many questions, but he was backing away from her, embarrassed. She reached out to touch him but he evaded her and said quickly, 'I must go.' He looked at Hélène, confused as to her intentions. 'If you tell me your name I'll mention meeting you to Papa.'

Hélène blushed. 'There's no need to do that.' As he got further away she nodded up at the shop sign. 'I'm Madame Picot.' Frédéric shook his head as though to clear his thoughts and walked swiftly away. At the corner he turned and, seeing her still standing there, broke into a loping run. Hélène felt tears spring to her eyes, she feared he had misunderstood her and would not come to the shop again.

That evening as she sat across the empty grate from her snoring husband, Hélène tortured herself with the thought that Philippe had been free for six years but had not made any attempt to find her. The Curé knew where she had gone; it would not have been hard for him to discover where she was. She winced; six years ago she had not been married to this odious man and would have been free to marry Philippe – or at least to be near him.

***

As the dreary days passed, Hélène became more and more obsessed by thoughts of Philippe. Each night she imagined herself walking along the track to the farm and holding Philippe once more in her arms. Each morning she awoke to face the undeniable fact that escape from Picot was impossible.

Desperate in her frustration, Hélène decided she must write to tell Philippe she was miserable and unhappy. After Picot had fallen asleep, exhausted by his loathsome attempts at intercourse, Hélène mercilessly scrubbed herself clean and crept down to the sitting room. As her frenzied pen covered page after page, she unburdened herself of all her love and despair. Rereading the letter, it struck Hélène with a shiver of fear that she no longer had any idea what effect such an outpouring of emotion would have on Philippe. The words of Frédéric haunted her: after six years Philippe still missed Agathe. The next night she tried again, writing a short note saying she had met Frédéric, was saddened to hear of her sister's death, would like to hear more news of the farm – and he should send his reply via Frédéric. Hélène's spirits rose as she slipped out of the shop with the envelope and dropped it into the post box.

Time passed slowly. Hélène calculated how long it would take for her letter to reach Les Laysses and for its reply to return to Frédéric; as that day came and went she added more days which turned into weeks, all the time attempting to fool herself with elaborate excuses. She spent long hours in anxious speculation as to why Philippe had not replied and came to the conclusion that involving Frédéric had been a foolish, even a dangerous, idea and that she should not have written at all. She regretted what she had done and became obsessed by her need to see Philippe.

One day Picot stormed back from church and shouted at her as she sat staring into space. 'So, you think you're too good to serve our customers! Madame Leclerc's just asked what's the matter with you – you've given her the wrong change twice – and she's not the only one who's complained.'

A week later, Picot burst into the kitchen where Hélène was washing up, a letter quivering in his hand. 'Now I'll have to go all the way to bloody Aubenas to sort out that crook, Mounier!' He slapped the paper angrily. 'He's saying he won't sell me any more pigs, but I can see through him as well as anyone. He's trying to keep hold of his animals in the hope that once war'll be declared he'll get a better price. The bastard!'

Hélène pinched her hands hard under her pinafore; she waited a moment so her voice would not betray her. 'Why can't you write and tell him?'

Picot swore with exasperation. 'What the hell d'you think I've been doing? I need to tell him face to face and if he sticks out, as I'm sure he will, I'll have to make a deal with him. Pigs are going to be worth their weight in gold as soon as we mobilise.'

Hélène said icily, 'Perhaps there won't be a mobilisation – no one but you wants war.'

'Don't be such a fool! D'you imagine the "pact of steel" is all about having nice little chats? Hitler and Mussolini mean business and the sooner our knock-kneed government recognises it, the better.' He looked down at the letter and pursed his lips. 'If I've got to go all the way to Aubenas, I might as well go on to Largentière and see what Roche has to say about corn. He dealt in a lot of black-market stuff last time and it'd be good to get him on side before the harvest. Together we could beat down the price before it's too late.'

'How long will you be gone?'

'A couple of nights. Dammit!'

That evening Hélène went to the kitchen, took a bottle of syrup of figs from the medicine cupboard and, holding her nose, drank all its contents. She spent most of the night in the privy and in the morning lay moaning with pain, clutching her stomach.

Picot glared at her, weighing up her condition, and swore. 'Damn you, that's all I need!' He took his watch out of his pocket. 'I've got to go. I'll put a notice on the door saying we're closed.'

The next day, before dawn, Hélène put on her Sunday coat and hat, forced down some bread and cheese and made her way to the station.

***

Hélène felt sick with nerves as she stepped down from the train at Saint-Agrève. She pulled fiercely at the brim of her hat so it hid her face and walked quickly up the road into the town. On the street leading to the square Hélène passed a few shops with shiny signs bearing unfamiliar names, but there were many more, like Madame Nouzet's store, that had been abandoned and stood forlorn with closed shutters and peeling paint. At the corner of the square Hélène hesitated, looking across at the freshly painted café, cheerful with a new green awning; she swallowed hard, afraid of meeting Roland. As she approached, Hélène was relieved to see there was no one apart from a group of young men gathered round an old Malterre motorbike, arguing. She went up to the bar; a woman she did not recognise served her a cool glass of beer.

'I'd like someone to take me to a farm near here – it's called Les Laysses.'

The woman nodded. 'I know where you mean – Faugeron's place,' and shouted to a tall, gangly youth, who swung his leg over the motorbike and loped into the gloom of the bar. 'At least it'll stop Jean-Pierre squabbling.' She laughed indulgently. 'Half the lads round here can't wait for the war to start; the other half say it'll never happen.' Hélène smiled palely, preoccupied.

Jean-Pierre grinned at Hélène. 'I'll take you – if you don't mind a bit of a rough ride.' Hélène looked askance at the machine. 'Otherwise you'll have to wait 'til the afternoon when Arsac comes back with his taxi.' Hélène nodded quickly: she had to be back in Privas that night – and if Arsac was the man she remembered, she wanted to avoid him.

As the bike swept along, for a brief moment Hélène felt a surge of exhilaration. She had never been on a motorbike before or travelled so fast, but as they left the road and began to bounce down the track to the farm, all the familiar landmarks – the wall where she had been trapped in the snow, the bridge she had mended with Philippe – overwhelmed her with memories. As Hélène took her hand from his waist to wipe away her tears, the young man turned round. 'Are you all right, Madame?' She nodded as he swerved back into the ruts that led downwards.

As they drew near to the farm, Hélène felt panic overtake her and she struggled to breathe. As a distraction, she enquired about some of the people she had known. To many of the names the youth gave the laconic reply, 'Dead.' When she asked about Roland Gounon, he shrugged his shoulders and did not answer. She repeated the question; Jean-Pierre took his foot off the throttle so the machine made less noise. 'He's ill.'

'What the matter with him?'

'He's gone blind and has to stay in bed. It's one of those illnesses men get when they go with bad women.' He pressed his foot down again so the machine leapt forward. 'My mother says he'd be better off dead.' Hélène felt a pang of sadness; she half-wished she could visit him, to give him some comfort, but that was impossible.

As they ricocheted down the track, tears blinded Hélène's eyes; she rubbed them away roughly, every glimpse of the beloved countryside too precious to miss. As they reached the final bend, Hélène tapped Jean-Pierre's shoulder. 'Please let me down here, I want to walk the rest of way.' He manhandled the machine round in the narrow space. 'Come back in a couple of hours.'

Hélène waited until the erratic throbbing of the motorbike had faded away and silence closed around her. In the windless air nothing moved, the buzzard lazily circling high above made no sound, the scent of the honeysuckle lay like a heavy haze over the hedgerows. She stood motionless until the intense stillness had seeped into her and calmed the rapid beating of her heart. A passing cloud made her shiver and Hélène forced herself to walk towards the farm, past the long roof tucked against the mountainside.

All the scenarios Hélène had conjured up over the last few weeks chased through her mind and a cold trickle of sweat crept down her spine. When she reached the wall of the farm, Hélène felt faint and steadied herself by holding on to its sharp granite stones. For a moment she was tempted to walk away, to stride back up the track and leave the past behind, but, taking a deep breath, she carried on, her legs unsteady. As she turned into the farmyard she stopped, absorbing the familiar smells of animals and dung; the clucking of hens as they picked and scratched; the dilapidation the years had wrought on the old house.

Philippe came out of the barn. Neither moved, their eyes locked together. For a long moment they stood, separated by the width of the yard, conscious only of each other, joined by an indefinable emotion that took away their breath and stopped their hearts. Hélène walked swiftly towards Philippe as though pulled towards him by some magnetic force; he did not move, his eyes did not flinch but stayed fastened on hers. His silence and immobility unnerved Hélène. Unable to read his expression, she stopped, as though the current that had drawn her towards him had suddenly reversed. They stood facing each other, trying to read the other's thoughts, to reconcile these new faces with the ones they remembered. Philippe's cheeks had been hollowed by years of hardship; deep lines were etched around eyes that had turned a lighter, more luminous blue. Hélène's hair had been cut short, its red curls forced into fashionable waves; her face, which rarely saw the sun, was pale and powdered, her lips emboldened with dark red lipstick. Tentatively Hélène held out her hand and together they walked down the terrace to the bench on which all three had talked and laughed so many summers ago.

For a long time they sat in silence, not knowing how to begin. Hélène cleared her throat. 'Did you get my letter?'

'Yes.' Hélène felt a surge of pleasure at hearing the deep voice, which had not changed, but this joy evaporated as Philippe asked, his tone neutral, polite, 'Why have you come, Hélène?'

Hélène fidgeted nervously with her hat and put it down on the bench. 'Because I wanted to see you. To find out how you were.'

Philippe looked down at the ground. After a long pause he nodded back towards the farm. 'As you can see, things've gone downhill a bit. It's been very hard.' Hélène waited for him to continue. 'Up here we've always had the weather to contend with, but over the last few years we've had to fight harder and harder to keep our head above water – and even then we keep falling behind. Everything costs so much.' He gave a half-smile. 'I still haven't got that tractor I wanted, though my brother hires me his reaper each summer, but it's not much use on our fields.' He sighed. 'I've had to put sheep on some of the terraced land; I can't manage to plough them anymore.' He paused. 'This winter's going to be a struggle without Frédéric.' Philippe sat, shoulders slumped, looking down at his gnarled hands.

There was a long silence. Hélène swallowed. 'Tell me about Agathe.'

Philippe's voice sank lower. 'I knew there was something terribly wrong for months before she died. She'd get up during the night and come back to bed exhausted. She wouldn't admit she was ill and kept going 'til the last few weeks, when she couldn't hide the pain any longer and just lay in bed suffering. It was a dreadful time for all of us.' He turned to look at Hélène, a glint of defiance in his expression. 'She forgave me, Hélène.' Hélène was silent. 'That meant a lot to me.' He looked out over the valley. 'For years I tried my best to make it up to her. It was difficult for her – and for me – but I deserved my punishment; she didn't. Eventually we found a way of being together, not as it once was, but good enough. Better than I deserved or hoped.'

'Did you ever talk about me?'

'From that night onwards your name was never mentioned.'

'Not once?'

'We never spoke about it or you.' Hélène felt her blood drain away, mortified to have been cut out of their lives so completely. Philippe continued, not looking at Hélène, determined to reach the end. 'When she knew she was dying, she took my hand and kissed it. She said, "You've been a good husband, Philippe, I know how much you've loved me. No one could ever have come between us." I asked for her forgiveness and she nodded, said she'd forgiven me a long time ago.' He smiled sadly. 'But I haven't forgiven myself, Hélène.' Philippe stopped speaking; there was a long silence. At last he roused himself and asked quietly, 'And you?'

Hélène's voice was brittle. 'I was sent to work at the Picots; serving in his shop as well as looking after the house and his sick wife. It was a miserable existence, but at first I was so unhappy their spitefulness just seemed part of my punishment. Later on, I realised I was powerless against them because they knew what I had done and that I was afraid of being found out.' She added bitterly, 'And, of course, their sanctimonious self-righteousness gave them a perfect excuse to torment me.'

'But you signed your letter "Hélène Picot".'

Hélène got up and walked to the edge of the terrace, when she spoke her voice was raw and harsh. 'In the end I hadn't a choice. If any man seemed to take an interest in me it wasn't long before he would stop coming to the shop and avoided me in the street. It was obvious Picot must've warned him off.' She continued, her voice high and hard, 'As his wife's various ailments got worse and she became even more vicious, I tried desperately to find another position, terrified of what would happen when she died, but whenever anyone agreed to employ me the offer would be withdrawn after a few days – no explanation given. Again, Picot must've said bad things about me. A month after his wife's funeral Picot told me I'd have to marry him because I couldn't live in his house unless we were married. I told him I'd never agree. He laughed and said he'd make sure I'd nowhere else to go.' Hélène walked back towards Philippe. 'I told him I hated him, he replied that feelings didn't come into it – he needed someone to do all the things a wife has to do and in return I'd have a place to live, food to eat – otherwise I'd starve. When I kept refusing, he threatened to tell everyone what I'd done and throw me out with nothing.' Hélène's voice broke. 'Within a month we were married and he could do with me what he wanted – and he did!' Hélène shuddered and shut her eyes. 'It wasn't just that he hit me – I could've put up with that – but at night he makes me do shameful, horrible things.'

Hélène brushed away her tears and sat down, her face drawn and hard. There was an awkward silence between them. 'I've been punished for loving you, Philippe.' She shook her head as if to clear her thoughts. 'I accept my guilt. I accept I had to pay a price – but to lose Frédéric and endure seventeen years of humiliation and torment? Must it be without end?' Eventually she turned to face Philippe. 'Six years. Why didn't you try to find me? The Curé knew where I was – he could've told you.'

Philippe shook his head. 'I didn't ask him.' He was silent for a long time. 'I didn't think it would be fair to Agathe.' He looked away. 'After she'd died the thought that she'd forgiven me gave me some peace. I'd got the farm and the children to look after; it was tough but at least the burden of guilt had gone. To look for you would've seemed like betraying her all over again.'

Hélène winced and was silent for a while. When she did speak, her tone was hesitant, not wishing to alarm him. 'I knew you'd try to repair the damage we'd done, so I put any thought of being with you out of my mind.' Hélène's voice strengthened. 'But once Frédéric'd told me Agathe had died, the hope of happiness came flooding back. I can't get it out of my mind. You can't imagine how much I've longed to see you!' Hélène turned to him impetuously. 'Are you glad to see me?'

Philippe sat frowning, thinking about his reply, and then he smiled as though the thought surprised him. 'Yes. Yes I am.'

Hélène leant towards Philippe and kissed him, an awkward kiss that did not last long. Philippe pulled away.

Embarrassed, Hélène walked to the end of the terrace, breathing in the peacefulness of the woods. She returned to stand over Philippe, who sat looking down at the ground. 'It's so beautiful, so calm – the world seems so far away.'

Philippe sniffed dismissively. 'Don't get too romantic, Hélène. It isn't always sunny and it isn't always summer.' He looked up, challenging her. 'Remember you were desperate to leave.'

'I was wrong! Living in a town is awful; you're always hemmed in by buildings that shut out the sun. Here you can see for miles, the air's so clean and everything smells so lovely. In Privas spring and summer come and go, but none of it matters.' Hélène bent down. 'I want to come back, Philippe. I want to live here again.' Philippe would not look at her, but shook his head; Hélène gently turned his face up towards hers. 'I'm so unhappy, Philippe. You can't imagine how dreadful it is living with that man.'

Philippe remained silent. Hélène fell to her knees. 'Let me come and live here, Philippe. I'm not asking for anything more. I just want to be here again.' He shook his head. She got back to her feet. 'Let me stay – as your sister.'

Philippe shut his eyes and turned away. 'I feel sorry for you, Hélène. I can see you're unhappy and I'd like to share with you some of the peace I've found – but you certainly can't live here.'

'I could stay in Saint-Agrève and come every day to help on the farm.'

Philippe laughed sadly. 'Don't be silly, Hélène.'

She took hold of his hand. 'You've been saying how hard it is to run the farm and it'll be even harder now Frédéric's doing his military service.

Why won't you let me help you?' Her grip on his hand tightened. 'I've thought about it so much. The only people who knew why I went away were Agathe and the Curé – now we can make up a story to explain where I've been and why I've returned.'

Again Philippe shook his head. 'There was a lot of gossip, Hélène. After telling people you'd found a job in Lyon, neither Agathe nor I ever mentioned you again, but we knew tongues wagged.'

'But that was seventeen years ago! Six years since Agathe died! We're older, different people. We can explain.'

Philippe laughed sadly. 'I doubt it, Hélène. Things haven't changed that much here, people will still talk.' He looked at her tenderly for a moment, and then turned away. 'Your life sounds awful and I pity you – but I can't help you.'

'Because of Agathe?'

Philippe nodded slowly. 'Yes, but also because you're married, Hélène. From what you've said, your husband isn't going to let you leave, however much you dislike each other.'

'Hate each other.'

'He'll never let you go.' He looked intently at Hélène. 'Don't forget, he knows what happened between us. He would use that against you – against both of us – and Frédéric.'

Hélène sat down hard on the bench, her head in her hands, sobbing, her shoulders shuddering. After a while Philippe patted Hélène's shoulder awkwardly. 'Come into the house and I'll get you a glass of brandy.'

Hélène hesitated at the threshold before walking quickly into the kitchen. She looked round, dismayed by the changes she saw. 'You've got one of those new stoves.'

Philippe smiled. 'Hardly new, it's been here for years. It was Agathe's pride and joy. It's very practical; it uses much less wood and gives a lot more heat.'

'But it was lovely to sit beside the fire, especially in winter.'

'We can open its door and see the flames.' Philippe made a wry face. 'But I agree, it isn't the same.'

Hélène walked over to the stove. Above the great beam hung a photograph of the family, the baby Dorothée on Agathe's lap, Philippe and Frédéric standing behind her, the girls sitting on either side. Agathe was slightly stouter but otherwise exactly as Hélène remembered. 'Where's the photograph of the wedding?'

'Gone.' Philippe hesitated before continuing, 'By the morning every trace of you had disappeared: the photograph, your sewing, knitting, the bowl you used for coffee.' Hélène steadied herself with a hand on the table. 'It was for the best, Hélène.' He poured her a glass of brandy. 'Drink this.' They sat down in their old places on opposite sides of the table.

Hélène kneaded her damp handkerchief. 'How was Agathe with Frédéric? Our son.'

Philippe smiled sadly. 'She loved him. I don't think she ever thought of Frédéric as yours, even at the beginning it was as though he belonged to all three of us. She cared for him, and he loved her.'

'D'you think he missed me?'

'He was very young, Hélène, only a baby. The two girls asked where you were – for a while.' He sighed and fell silent.

'He's turned into a fine young man. He looks so like you. I knew straightaway he was our son.' Hélène's faint smile faded. 'But it hurt so much that he didn't know who I was.' She smiled sadly, 'He didn't know what to make of me.'

Philippe stiffened. 'You can't tell him, Hélène. He was devoted to Agathe – he believes she was his mother.'

Hélène wailed. 'I know, I know. Hearing him say that was the most painful thing of all.'

There was a long silence. Philippe sighed. 'I'm worried about Frédéric and all the other young men, I'm afraid there's bound to be another war.' He took out his handkerchief and mopped his brow, 'In spite of all we went through.'

Hélène spoke hesitantly, 'Surely he'll be all right. We've got tremendous defences in place; the Germans'll never get through. It's not like last time – now we're prepared.'

Philippe shrugged, unconvinced. 'In my opinion we're relying far too much on our fortifications and not enough on artillery and airplanes. The Germans've got an excellent Army and they're very well equipped; if they attack the Maginot line it's likely to be a long-drawn-out struggle and if they attempt to crash through in the North it'll be a bloody fight.'

'Could you be called up?'

'Theoretically yes, I'm still young enough,' Philippe laughed humourlessly, 'but I wouldn't pass the fitness test.' He glanced up and saw the concern in her eyes. 'My leg still gives me trouble. Not enough to stop me working, but it wouldn't be much good for marching.' His face became drawn; Hélène could see how much he had aged. 'Frédéric reminds me of Francis sometimes – young, keen to fight, no idea what's facing him.' He patted Hélène's hand, speaking to himself, 'It mustn't be like last time.' Trying to lighten the conversation, he smiled at her. 'Perhaps you're right – our defences'll stop Hitler even trying.' He refilled her glass. 'Let's hope so.'

Hélène thought she could hear the thrum of the motorbike in the distance, but the sound faded. Afraid time was running out, she clasped Philippe's hand and pulled him to his feet so they stood close together. Once more there were tears in her eyes, but her voice was sharp and urgent. 'Philippe, I beg you, try and think of a way I could come here. We've both been punished for what we did and up 'til now I've accepted it, but it would be terrible to be so wretched for the rest of my life. There must be a way we can both find some happiness. You need me here and I want so much to be with you.' Hélène put her arms round his neck, her eyes beseeching him.

The sound of the motorbike was now quite distinct. Philippe gently disentangled himself. 'As long as you're married, Hélène, there's nothing that can be done.'

'But if I wasn't married?'

Philippe shook his head. 'But you are, Hélène.' He tenderly pushed her away as the sound of the motorbike died. 'And I can't see any way you could live here.'

'Would you want me to – if I was free?'

Philippe sighed. 'I don't know the answer to that, Hélène. I just don't know.'

She looked into his eyes. 'But you might? I can hope for that?'

'Oh, Hélène!' She clasped him in her arms and held him tight. Philippe pulled away, his voice hoarse with emotion. 'You'd better go.'

Hélène whispered, 'I love you, Philippe. I always have and I always will.'

Philippe walked with her to the corner of the farm. The motorbike was propped against the wall some distance down the track. Aware the young man was watching them, they shook hands formally, eyes locked, committing their changed faces to memory. Hélène walked backwards for a while, unable to break the bond that bound them together, her body aching to be with him, willing him to let her stay. The distance grew between them and Hélène finally turned away, her heart torn in two. When she reached the bike, she looked back and gave a small wave; Philippe remained motionless, infinitely far away. Hélène slowly climbed on the pillion, looping her arm around the young man. As the bike kicked and roared, Hélène twisted round, her eyes searching for a reprieve as Philippe was eclipsed by the rough stone walls.

Chapter Fifteen

June 1939

It was a sultry Saturday evening. Men jostled to buy beer in the crowded bars, raised voices vied with the clamour of many radios. Hélène walked home reluctantly, her eyes fixed on the granite pavement, struggling to quash the gloomy premonitions that darkened her thoughts. In the distance a band was playing; the insistent thump of the drums momentarily lifted her spirits and Hélène drifted with the general movement towards the Champ de Mars. Exposed to the callous glare of the sun, men in uniform and women in light print dresses moved mechanically round the bandstand, isolated in their separate worlds by the dogged beat of the music.

Hélène walked round the square looking for Frédéric. Young soldiers stood under the trees, arms twined around girlfriends; groups of youths dawdled along the pavements, shoving and punching each other as they unwillingly made their way towards the garrison's gates. She headed for the corner nearest the Café de Caserne, where she had caught a glimpse of Frédéric the day before. Hélène leant against a tree and, taking a handkerchief from the pocket of her cardigan, mopped the perspiration gathered at the neck of her blouse. A young man's voice reached her.

'There's the old biddy who's always hanging around. I can't imagine what she's thinking – she must know no one'll go with her.' Hélène lowered her head and hurried away, self-pitying tears pricking. In the narrow streets the air was stagnant, stiflingly hot. The doleful sound of a bugle fell in lingering waves over the town, recalling the soldiers to their barracks. It was too late to catch a glimpse of Frédéric.

Hélène reached the Place d'Église; not wanting to go home, she pushed open the heavy wooden door and entered the church. The chill, unwelcoming twilight lowered her spirits further. Undecided whether to stay or go, Hélène sat down, resenting the brightly painted Virgin and Child who stared, aloof and uncaring, up to a heaven in which she did not believe.

As Hélène pulled her cardigan tightly around her, an old woman edged out of the shadows and shuffled on painful feet up the aisle, snuffling in her eagerness to know who had come into the church at such a late hour. As her bent frame weaseled past, Hélène raised her head and nodded briefly at the familiar face, knowing she would inform Père Eyraud, who would in turn tell her husband.

As the sinister sounds of the old woman's footsteps died away, Hélène dug her nails deep into her palms. She wished Picot was dead. This was not a prayer; Hélène was not pleading with the unresponsive image of Christ. She shivered; she was afraid of Picot and afraid of what she might do.

Last week Picot had hit her. He had hit her many times before, but in the past Hélène had punished him with a wall of contemptuous silence, a refined form of denial she could sustain for weeks. This time her reaction had been involuntary and shocking.

It was early afternoon and the shop was empty. Hélène sat idly, her thoughts occupied by Philippe and Frédéric, she had not heard Picot calling from the kitchen – or had not bothered to reply – she could not remember. Exasperated, he had come into the shop and struck her hard on her shoulder; it still hurt when she brushed her hair. In that instant the long years of iron discipline had evaporated and she had cursed and lashed out, revealing all her revulsion. He had pulled her into the kitchen and shut the door. The claustrophobic heat, the slimy steam from the bubbling pans of greasy meat, his closeness in the tiny room, made Hélène retch; she vomited over a bowl of bloody offal and collapsed onto the floor. He had kicked her with unrestrained enthusiasm. Instinctively, Hélène reached for the rack of knives, twelve long blades energetically sharpened every day. Cursing, he had grabbed her arm and dragged her up the stairs to their bedroom, where he had left her, locking the door behind him.

The thought that her husband was the only obstacle preventing a new life with Philippe had turned Hélène's calculated hatred into a simmering rage and she was scared that if – when – Picot provoked her again, she would not be able to hold back its force. Sensing Hélène's implacable self-control had weakened, her husband now played a deadly game in the hope that, sooner or later, she would do something terrible and he could watch with self-righteous satisfaction as Hélène brought on herself a dreadful retribution.

In the damp, lowering church Hélène shuddered. She looked up at the unpitying stare of Christ; chilled by its haughty indifference, her thoughts turned to Philippe. It had been five unendurably long weeks. She was desperate to talk to him again: to learn if the spectre of Agathe would always come between them. Hélène shut her eyes, exhausted and bored by her unanswered questions – she would not see him again, she had no way of knowing.

The old crone materialised from the shadows, the lights in the choir were turned off, the silence broken by ostentatious sweeping, a pail clattered – the secular sounds echoed round the stone walls, disturbing the saints in their chapels. Hélène sat tight, knowing she had only a few minutes before the woman would sidle up to her, mumbling indignantly that it was time to close the church for the night. Hélène bent her head; for a precious moment she allowed herself to relive the walk across the farmyard, the quick, unsatisfactory embrace, her final sight of Philippe as the motorbike turned the corner. She imagined herself running over the hill down to the farm, arms outstretched, the wind in her face, the beauty of the tree-filled valley beneath her. Hélène ached to be with Philippe, to be at Les Laysses, away from this gloomy town. The stumbling, bunioned feet in their deformed shoes drew nearer; as the crone thrust her rheumy nose into her face, Hélène stood up. She moved away along the row of chairs, glaring defiantly at the lugubrious saints battling their own demons. Hélène left the dank obscurity of the church and walked out into the bloodshot flare of the setting sun.

The cafés were still full; through open windows a multitude of radios blared music into the evening air, far away Hélène could hear the dull beat of the band. Fragments of arguments caught her ear: war was inevitable, it was inconceivable, it was imminent, it would never happen. The church clock struck eight as Hélène entered the dark, narrow rue du Malconseil and turned the heavy key of her front door.

***

'Can't you see the shop's shut, Mounier?'

Hélène continued to clear away the trays of sausages as her husband stood, arms akimbo, in front of the stout, red-faced man.

Mounier cast a suspicious glance towards Hélène. Picot turned on her. 'Go upstairs.' Hélène hesitated, a bowl of *boudin* in her hands. 'You heard what I said, get out!' Hélène shrugged and left, slamming the door behind her.

Half an hour later her husband appeared with a satisfied smirk on his face. Picot pulled the brandy bottle towards him, filled his glass and drank off the cognac. He sipped his second glass more slowly, smacking his lips. 'Mounier's a fool. Thought he could put one over on me.' Hélène continued to read; she had no interest in her husband's business. Picot looked at his wife, eyes narrowed, determined to share his self-satisfaction, in spite of her indifference. 'It seems a handful of farmers offered him a good deal on their maize; being a greedy bastard, he couldn't say no, but at the same time he couldn't go to the bank 'cos he'd already borrowed a small fortune to buy the pigs. The devious shit thought he'd put pressure on me to lend him the money.' Picot rubbed his hands with pleasure. 'Anyway, I made him squirm! He was trying every angle he could, but he had to go fifty-fifty in the end – and pay interest at twice the bank's rate!' He chuckled mirthlessly. 'No one gets the better of me and it's about time the stupid bastard realised it!'

He finished the glass and poured another. Annoyed by Hélène's silence, he opened the paper and snorted with irritation. 'When's this bloody war going to start? We've got an agreement with the Russians, we're all clear what Monsieur Hitler can and can't do – and then the British go weak at the knees, whining on about being fair, et cetera.' Picot slapped the paper in exasperation. 'Everyone knows we're going to have to stand up to the Germans sooner or later.' He looked over at Hélène, who affected not to hear him. 'Our politicians are pathetic and the British bunch are even worse. The sooner we declare war the better. I don't give a damn whether we win or Hitler wins; here in Privas we're well away from any trouble. Dammit, money's the same whoever it comes from.'

Hélène ignored him but she was only pretending to read. The heat in the room was stifling, the thick curtains prevented even the breath of a breeze, the overstuffed furniture gave off a fusty smell that almost choked her, the untrimmed lamp flickered annoyingly.

Picot emptied his glass and lowered the newspaper. 'By the way, I had a conversation with Madame Leclerc this afternoon.' He bared his teeth in a quick grimace, his eyes icy. 'A very interesting conversation.' Hélène made no response. 'She asked me where you'd gone the other day.' Hélène involuntarily gripped her book more tightly. 'She said she'd seen you at the station.' Hélène forced herself to slowly turn a page. Picot's lips extended more widely. 'At first I was puzzled, but then she told me it was the day the shop was closed.' He looked closely at Hélène, who kept her eyes fixed on the page. Picot put down his paper and leant forward. 'In other words, while I was away in Aubenas.' He seized Hélène's book and threw it onto the table. 'Wouldn't you say that was interesting?'

Hélène replied as steadily as she could, 'How many times do we have to go over all this? I was in bed. I was ill. I didn't leave the house.'

Picot folded up the paper carefully, taking his time. 'She was absolutely certain it was you. Said you were wearing the hat you usually wear on Sunday and your brown coat.'

'Lots of women have brown coats.'

'That's true. But it's hard to explain the hat.' His tone hardened. 'You'd better come clean about what you were up to. I'm not bothered about your reputation, such as it is.' He spat into the empty fireplace and continued, his nasal voice grating on her nerves, 'But my reputation matters to me. I'm not going to allow you to drag me into a scandal.' Hélène started to get up but he roughly pushed her down into the chair. 'As you won't tell me, I'll find out for myself. Tomorrow I'll go to the station and make some enquiries. I'll take the hat with me.'

'You'll do no such thing!'

Picot sniggered with anticipation; now he had penetrated her defences he looked forward to probing this unexpected weakness. 'You'll give it to me after breakfast.' He took up the *Gringoire* again, rattling its pages with satisfaction. 'This might explain why you've been spending so much time in church recently. A bad conscience – that's probably it. I'll ask Père Eyraud on Sunday what you've been getting up to.'

'He won't tell you.'

Picot smiled condescendingly. 'I think you'll find he will.'

Hélène shrugged. 'My conscience is clear.'

'So you say, but I'll find out tomorrow who's telling the truth. I want to know what you were doing the moment my back was turned.' Picot took a big gulp of brandy and refilled his glass.

The muffled sounds of the church clock could be heard; mechanically Hélène counted the strokes even though she knew it was ten o'clock. Her husband lay splayed out in his chair; his breath, stinking of brandy, wheezed in and out, nauseating Hélène. The newspaper slid to the floor. Suffocating in the oppressive atmosphere, Hélène picked it up and sat fanning herself. She undid the top buttons of her blouse, reaching between her breasts with a handkerchief to wipe away the perspiration. She undid the buckle of her belt, wafting her dress to direct the stale air down onto her stomach and thighs.

Hélène sat looking at Picot, hating him. Every aspect of him filled her with disgust: the wispy hair he was too miserly to have cut, the pale, hairless arms, the grease-stained shirt, the greed, the unspeakable acts he made her perform ... Hélène felt sick. She turned away. Picot moved restlessly in his chair.

Despite the heat, Hélène shivered. Picot had questioned her over and over about the days he had been away, certain there was something she was hiding, determined to find an inconsistency that would prove she was lying. Up to now he had not succeeded, but Leclerc's accusation would be hard to disprove. Although it was unlikely anyone at the station would remember her, Hélène had had an argument with the man in the ticket office, who could not believe she wanted a day return. He had explained at length that it was a long journey to Saint-Agrève and it would be better if she stayed the night. Hélène had insisted; the man behind her had become irritated and rude; she had almost missed her train as a result. And she cursed her vanity. To impress Philippe she had chosen to wear her Sunday hat with its distinctive blue feather rather than the unremarkable beret she normally wore. If Picot did discover she had been at the station, he would certainly learn she had gone to Saint-Agrève and quickly work out who she had seen. Hélène shuddered; she did not know what he would do, only that it would be truly terrible.

Hélène closed her eyes. She must escape – but she had no money and nowhere to go. Philippe was right; Picot would stop at nothing to get her back simply for the pleasure of punishing her. If only he would die. She focused all her willpower as his breathing rasped and halted. Picot hiccoughed, a slick of saliva seeped from the corner of his mouth and the whistling snores started again. Defeated, Hélène desultorily turned the pages of the newspaper until her eye was caught by a headline; the guillotining of the murderer Eugen Weidmann would take place at dawn, the dreadful machine was now in place and crowds were already queuing to watch the spectacle. Hélène shuddered.

Gripped by her fear of Picot, Hélène's stomach contracted, the rising bile made her feel sick. She walked listlessly into the kitchen, filled a glass with water and slowly sipped the tepid liquid. Hélène returned to the sitting room with a full bottle of brandy and mechanically refilled her husband's glass. Picot was moving restlessly in his chair, twitching in some agitated dream. As Hélène turned away she felt a dragging at her skirt, she could see the prong of her buckle had caught in the frayed tablecloth. She tugged at the belt to free it but as she pulled, the lamp swayed, its heavy shade tipped towards her and toppled over as the shabby chenille tablecloth ebbed across the table and slid to the floor. Hélène caught her breath as the noise of breaking glass was muffled by slithering folds of material falling in green, undulating waves.

She froze, mesmerised by the small, frolicsome flames as they edged around the folds of material. Patches of cloth turned black, crepitated, shriveled, until brighter, stronger flames began to appear; soundless and innocent-seeming; they consumed the mottled fabric as it melted in the heat. The yellow flames eagerly devoured the dry brittle cloth and licked upwards towards the desiccated velvet of Picot's chair. Shaking herself, Hélène reached out to her husband, tapping him hard on his shoulder. He half woke, cursing, 'Bitch, leave me alone,' before subsiding into his stupor, muttering, 'Get away from me, you cow.'

Hélène stood immobile as the flames crept onward, silently gaining in height and intensity. She blinked, a shudder ran through her, she grabbed Picot and shook him hard; he lashed out, a flailing blow which smacked into her nose. Hélène staggered back, hands attempting to stanch the bright blood, whimpering with pain. Slowly she walked backwards towards the door, step by step, her eyes fixed on the leaping fire. All of a sudden there was a sibilant surge as the flames caught the brandy-soaked carpet and leapt high into the scorched air with a hiss of triumph. Frightened out of her trance, Hélène ran towards the kitchen. She fumbled under the sink for the metal bucket and turned on the tap, holding her breath with impatience as its measured flow poured unhurriedly into the receptacle, tense and unseeing as drops of her blood dripped, diffused and dimmed the clear water.

She could hear Picot shrieking, swearing. Leaving the tap running at its inexorable pace, Hélène ran down the corridor. As she reached the door she could see Picot stamping, slapping at the flames that licked lasciviously at his trousers. The rush of air from the open door inflamed the fire, which surged upwards, catching Picot's jacket. She watched as her husband beat at the flames that now surrounded him, screaming at her, his face twisted with fear and rage. Hélène stood in the doorway, her eyes fixed on him, but it was as though Picot was far away and the scene appeared unreal, imagined. As he lunged from side to side, she came to her senses and dashed back along the corridor. The pail was now almost full of water; she hauled it out of the sink and sped back.

The curtains were now a sheet of fire, the smell of carbonised velvet overpowering and sickening. The chair, where she had been sitting minutes before, was now a blackened skeleton, riddled with flames. There was a roaring crash as the curtains collapsed to the floor, the crackling of the flames grew stronger and louder, punctuated by more distinct detonations as the multitude of knickknacks fell to the floor or exploded. Picot was flailing his arms, writhing and twisting, dancing in an ecstasy of pain, beating at the flames licking at his jacket and up towards his face, his thin hair on fire. He staggered towards her, Hélène raised the bucket but the heat scorched her hands and the arc of water fell short, hissing and sputtering impotently. She ran out into the corridor, pursued mercilessly by the flames. Picot's howls of pain rose to a shriek of anger as he tried to follow her but was beaten back by the blaze. Cursing, he turned away shouting, screeching, swinging wildly at his burning clothes.

Hélène ran into the dining room. Sweating in the infernal heat, Hélène tried to open the double doors to the sitting room as Picot crashed against them. He swore at her, screamed in pain, shrieked for help – his voice shrill against the raging fury of the fire. He beat frantically at the panels, rattling the handle of the door, but the hot metal was unbearable to touch. The paint began to blister; in great welts it turned black, bubbled, burst in the heat. On the other side of the door Picot was so close Hélène could hear the agonised rasping of his breath as he fought the fire for oxygen. Hélène tried again to turn the doorknob, the skin of her hand searing in the heat. As the inferno intensified, Picot's screams rose higher and higher, his curses now mixed with demands, with threats – then promises of money and gold. Small yellow flames began to creep between the door and the architrave. As the wooden panels began to buckle, Hélène could see the fists of her husband as each blow cracked and splintered the burning wood. The pain in her hand became unendurable. She let go.

The door fell towards her; Picot, falling with it, lay at her feet. The sudden rush of flame caught Hélène before she could back away, singeing her hair. The fire raged out of the sitting room and Hélène rushed into the corridor, but it was already ablaze, with no chance of escape towards the stairs.

The carpet in the dining room was now a cauldron of flame. Hélène ran to the window, tugged at the heavy handle, which would not budge, rusted solid after so many years of disuse. She wrestled with it, tried to turn it, the crashing destruction of the fire surging behind her. With a last frantic effort, the mechanism gave way and Hélène pulled the window open. The inrushing air sent the flames soaring high to the ceiling. Her rayon dress melted in the heat; as it clung to her leg, Hélène felt a searing pain as the burning cloth welded with her flesh. She shouted for help. In the street below she could see a crowd of people looking up at her; she heard the splintering of the shutters as they broke into the building. Turning round, Hélène watched the dark shadow of her husband stagger blindly towards her, arms flapping feebly, flesh blackened and bleeding. Hélène waited until she saw him totter forward and fall, consumed by the leaping flames, finally silent. She scrambled over the iron balcony and jumped into the street below.

Chapter Sixteen

June–September 1939

Hélène felt nauseous from the anaesthetic. Where the molten rayon had been cut away her leg was piercingly painful; in the dim light she could see her right hand was a ball of bandages. As she struggled into consciousness, she heard two nurses talking in hushed tones at the end of her bed.

'Six murders! That Weidmann's got what he deserved.'

'They should've guillotined the other one along with 'im – he's just as bad.'

'They said on the radio it was bright daylight by the time he was executed – the crowd who'd gone to watch got a really good view.' The nurse giggled. 'I can't wait to see the photos in the *Gringoire*. Serve the bastard right!' The voice dropped further. 'What d'you make of 'er?'

The reply came as a whisper, 'She must've murdered 'im – why else would the Police've sent a copper to sit outside 'er door?'

There was a murmur of agreement and the two women left the room.

Hélène felt a clammy constriction round her throat, her stomach heaved and she shook convulsively. The police suspected her of murdering her husband; they would investigate her and her past, she would be found guilty and condemned to death, crowds would queue to watch her execution, glad she was going to die. Hélène writhed from side to side.

In the penumbra of the feeble bulb, Hélène lay quivering, her skin damp with dread. When she closed her eyes she saw the lamp slowly keel over, watched herself standing by the door immobile as the flames engulfed the body of her husband, apparently impervious to his screams of agony. She rang the bell and begged the nurse for a sleeping draught. For an hour or so she fell into a bottomless sleep, to wake screaming as the heavy blade of the guillotine was let loose and plunged down, severing her neck from her body. A nurse leant over her, hissing angrily, 'Stop making so much noise! You'll wake the other patients.'

Hélène did not dare call the nurse again. Her staring eyes searched shadows seething with spiteful spectres who taunted her. Her lips gibbered, her teeth chattered. The people in the street had heard Picot's cries, his curses, his shrieks; they would testify that she had killed him. Closing her eyes, Hélène saw the terrible silhouette of the guillotine, heard the cries of the blood-lusting crowd; she would die reviled, strapped into that dreadful machine. It would have been better to live a life of misery with Picot than this – but it was too late. What had been done had been done.

When the morning light finally crept into the room, a nurse entered, started violently and ran out. Just outside the door Hélène could hear her high-pitched voice. ‘She’s awake. She gave me such a funny look. I’m frightened to death! Thank goodness you’re here to protect us.’ The voice was lowered. ‘Did she really kill her husband?’

A man’s voice answered truculently. ‘She might’ve done. Can’t say ’til the sergeant comes and takes a statement.’

‘But you wouldn’t be ‘ere unless your bosses suspected something?’

The man’s voice sounded surly. ‘True enough, there must be something fishy.’ Hélène heard a sudden scuffle, a muffled giggle. ‘Perhaps you’d keep me company? I’m bored rigid stuck here.’

In the overheated, stuffy hospital room, Hélène lay shivering uncontrollably.

***

The sergeant was a large, once-handsome man. His carefully tended moustache flowed like a soft white fountain on either side of his full red lips; his hair, too, would have been silky if it had not been oiled and flattened so brutally. He sat down by the bed, carefully placed his kepi on the bedside table and solemnly took his notebook from the breast pocket of his uniform. He spoke formally, his tone neutral, professional. ‘Please accept my condolences, Madame Picot.’ He cleared his throat importantly. ‘Last Thursday there was a serious conflagration above the Picot charcuterie, rue du Malconseil, a conflagration in which your husband perished. The law requires me to carry out a thorough investigation of all pertinent circumstances in order to find out what transpired at your home that night.' Hélène nodded, holding herself rigid, trying not to show her fear. 'You must answer my questions honestly and to the best of your recollection, Madame Picot, otherwise you'll face severe penalties.' Again he coughed, pencil poised. 'Tell me, how did the fire start?'

Cold sweat beaded Hélène's upper lip; she wiped it away. Swallowing twice, she made an effort to appear calm and began to describe in a soft voice the account of events she had rehearsed.

'It was quite late in the evening. I'd just heard the clock strike ten; I was sitting reading my book. My husband was asleep in his chair. He would have a few glasses of brandy each evening.' Hélène paused. 'It was his only vice, he didn't smoke.' The policeman nodded briskly, indicating he wanted her to get to the point. 'A little later he got up to go to bed.' She shut her eyes, as if to imagine the scene. 'I can see it very clearly. He stood up, he was shaky on his feet and reached out to steady himself; his hand missed the table but grabbed at the tablecloth. As he staggered and fell, he pulled the cloth down with him. The lamp toppled over, then the bottle of brandy. I jumped up but I wasn't quick enough. He was already on the floor, the tablecloth was on fire and the flames had started to burn his clothes.' Hélène opened her eyes. 'That's how it started.'

'And then?'

'I ran into the kitchen to get some water, but the tap was so slow. By the time I got back, the room was full of smoke and flames, I threw the water over my husband but it wasn't enough, it was already hopeless.'

The policeman laboriously wrote this down then stopped to lick his pencil. 'Why'd you use an oil lamp? Your house must have electricity.'

Hélène smiled bleakly. 'My husband thought electricity cost too much. He believed the oil lamp was a lot less expensive.' She sighed. 'I didn't mind, a lamp gives a much pleasanter light.'

'You say he'd been drinking?'

'Yes, every evening. My husband worked hard and a few glasses of brandy after supper helped him relax. The brandy bottle was almost full. When it broke it soaked into his trousers. That made it much worse for him.'

The sergeant painstakingly wrote this down. When he had finished he looked closely at Hélène. 'Why didn't he escape into the corridor?'

'There was no point, it was already ablaze. There was no chance of getting down the stairs. I ran into the dining room to see if we could get out that way, into the street.'

'Which you did, but Monsieur Picot did not.' The sergeant raised his eyebrows, pencil poised above his notebook.

Hélène forced herself to look at the man directly; she raised her bandaged hand, wincing with pain. 'That was how I burnt my hand. I was trying to open the doors so he could escape. The handle was so hot I couldn't turn it, and in the end my hand was so sore I couldn't hold it any longer.' She paused and dabbed her handkerchief to her eyes. 'It was too late. The fire had taken hold and …' Hélène lay still, her eyes closed.

There was a long silence as this was carefully noted down. Eventually the sergeant raised his head. 'I understand you and your husband were both regular churchgoers?'

Hélène nodded. 'Every Sunday, sometimes more often. We both attended the *église* of St Thomas.'

The sergeant nodded. 'I go to the Temple myself, but I've been told by Père Eyraud you always attended Mass together. He was full of praise for your husband.'

The sergeant ponderously finished writing and closed his notebook. Hélène was relieved his questions were over but, as he sat staring into space, laboriously fashioning his conclusion, the lined face and narrowed eyes giving no hint as to his decision, a choking panic seized her. After what seemed an eternity, the sergeant leant forward, so close Hélène could smell the tobacco on his breath. 'One final question.' He looked sternly at her. 'In cases where only a husband and wife are involved, I have to ask, what was the state of your marriage? To put it simply, did you love your husband?'

This was one question Hélène had not anticipated; she shut her eyes, concentrating on her response. It was impossible to admit she did not love Picot, it would open up avenues of suspicion she wanted desperately to avoid – on the other hand, she could not bring herself to give him, even in death, the satisfaction of hearing her say she had loved him.

The sergeant gave a dry, embarrassed cough. 'I'm sorry, Madame, but it's a question we are required to ask under such circumstances. Your obvious distress is answer enough for me.'

He rose to his feet, towering above her, pushing his notebook into the top pocket of his jacket. Hélène lay looking up at him, trying to deduce a verdict from the sergeant's worn, inscrutable expression. He cleared his throat and spoke with judicial solemnity. 'From all the evidence at my disposal, it's clear to me this was simply a tragic accident.' He inclined his head. 'Please accept my condolences on the loss of your husband.'

The sergeant picked up his kepi and tucked it under his arm. 'I'll leave you in peace, Madame Picot. I wish you a speedy recovery.' He gave a brief bow and, as he reached the door, called gruffly to his officer to accompany him to the police station. Hélène burst into tears.

***

Two days later Hélène had another visitor, ushered in to her room with gushing servility by the matron herself. Picot's lawyer, Monsieur de Bonneville, was a tall elegant man who appeared ill at ease surrounded by the clinical paraphernalia of the hospital. He sat down gingerly at some distance from the bed, took off his hat and, unsure where it might be safe to put such an impressive object, placed it tenderly on his lap. He smiled urbanely at

Hélène. 'I bring you my sincere condolences, Madame Picot. Your husband was a fine man, a pillar of the church and one of our town's most eminent businessmen. He will be much missed by many.' The lawyer inclined his head graciously in Hélène's direction, 'Most of all by you, dear lady.' He paused as though in remembrance, then brought the uncomfortable silence to a close with a neat little cough. 'I'm afraid we must address ourselves to the sensitive subject of his final wishes.' He raised his eyebrows in an unspoken question, but as Hélène did not reply he continued, his voice carefully modulated, 'I'm sure your late husband must have made a will; such a careful man of affairs would be bound to have made preparations?'

Hélène replied cautiously, 'He did. He kept it locked in the sideboard.'

'Ah, as I feared.' Monsieur de Bonneville nodded gravely. 'Then there can be no question of finding it; the whole room was quite devastated by the fire.' He sighed. 'Sadly, he wouldn't leave a copy with me – he always insisted it wasn't quite finalised. Whenever I pressed him, he would make a little joke, saying there was no hurry.' The pale smile left the lawyer's face and he looked penetratingly at Hélène. 'Did he share with you his intentions?'

Hélène was silent and looked away. She knew perfectly well what her husband had intended. The silence extended and became awkward.

Monsieur de Bonneville stroked his hat thoughtfully. 'Given that there's no evidence he wished otherwise, the law states that you, as his only surviving relative, will inherit everything.' He smiled complacently. 'I'm sure that would have been his wish.' The lawyer resumed, in businesslike tones, 'Madame Picot, your late husband was admirable in many ways, but especially so when it came to managing his financial affairs. As I'm sure you know, he made a fortune during the Great War and, with characteristic astuteness, avoided the temptations that cost many people their savings during the depression and then the devaluations of '36 and '37. With great foresight he invested much of his money in property here in Privas – you are now the owner of about twenty premises, all of which bring in secure and substantial rents. He also bought gold, the most prudent of investments, which has substantially increased in value over the years.' Monsieur de Bonneville bowed his head in respect for this impressive achievement. 'Your grief, I am sure, prevents you from feeling any emotion other than sadness, but your late husband's financial wisdom might, in time, bring you some recompense for your incomparable loss.' He smiled at Hélène. 'Madame Picot, I am happy to tell you that you are now in possession of a fortune of approximately one hundred million francs.' He paused and smiled, anticipating her response.

Hélène stared at him. Eyes wide, she stuttered, 'I don't know what to say. My husband never talked to me about money.' Monsieur de Bonneville nodded, smiling. 'This comes as a great surprise.'

'Of course, of course. Completely unexpected.' Again the lawyer paused, stroking his hat absentmindedly. 'However, in view of the fact that war is, in my opinion, not only inevitable but also imminent, I feel it is my duty to impose further on your understandable distress at your bereavement and offer what little advice I may before the catastrophe befalls us. I would strongly recommend you do not sell any of the property. Whatever happens, it will give you a handsome income on which you can live most comfortably.'

Hélène raised her hand, indicating she wished to speak. Monsieur de Bonneville paused, frowning. 'I want to sell the apartment and the shop. I'm determined not to go back there.'

He smiled gently, relieved. 'That is quite understandable. The property is damaged, but not too badly and is in an excellent situation. I will happily arrange its sale for you.' He raised his eyebrows in interrogation. 'Might I enquire, do you have any thoughts about where you might wish to live?'

'I had thought of returning to live on the Plateau.' Seeing the lawyer's astonishment, Hélène continued hurriedly, 'It's where I was brought up.'

'Really!' The lawyer sat back, digesting this information, he shook his head solemnly. 'I'm surprised anyone would choose to live there. The country's so wild – and I'm afraid the inhabitants are almost as savage.' He shook his head and smiled at Hélène. 'I'm sure that when you have come to terms with your new situation, you'll find Paris or the Cote d'Azur much more agreeable prospects.'

He continued, his sonorous voice slipping over Hélène. 'I would recommend you leave the gold where it is – under the circumstances one cannot guess what the franc will do. Should you need capital, it is always possible to turn gold into cash.' The smooth voice paused momentarily. 'Over the last few months I understand your husband had purchased large quantities of oil, various grains and pork – you should hold on to these until, at the very earliest, the Army fully mobilises. I'm sure you'll find their prices will rise considerably and you'll make a handsome profit.' He smiled at Hélène unctuously. 'I'm sure that's what your late husband had in mind.'

'But that's profiteering!'

Monsieur de Bonneville frowned majestically. 'You may call it what you will, dear Madame Picot, but buying cheaply and selling dearly are perfectly acceptable business practices.' He brushed an invisible speck of dust from his silvery grey sleeve. 'I would be happy to advise you on the best time to sell these agricultural products to bring you the maximum advantage.'

He cleared his throat and hesitated before continuing. 'Finally, there is something else I feel I must say.' Once more he gave a refined cough. 'I must warn you, once the extent of your inheritance becomes more widely known, I'm afraid you will receive the attentions of various dubious characters. Obscure relatives will expect you to pay off their debts; friends you have long forgotten will be eager to lighten the burden of your grief in return for a loan; and undoubtedly there will be men who profess to have always loved you, or to have suddenly fallen in love with you, who would be honoured to spare you the loneliness of widowhood by marrying them. Do be on the alert, Madame Picot.'

Monsieur de Bonneville stood up, smoothed his gleaming hat, picked up his slender cane and bowed graciously. 'Forgive me for imposing my advice on you, dear Madame.' He took her hand, raised it a suitable distance, inclined over it, and straightened up. 'Once again, my condolences for your irreparable loss – and be assured my services are always at your disposal.'

After the lawyer had left, Hélène lay perfectly motionless, overwhelmed and unbelieving – the sum mentioned by Monsieur de Bonneville was beyond her imagination. Hélène had never had any money of her own, even after she had married Picot he had made her beg for every sou. When he was feeling particularly sadistic, he would unlock the casket in which he kept his documents and pore over his will, ostentatiously amending figures and making alterations. Hélène had been told many times that all his wealth was to be used to endow a stained-glass window in the church of St Thomas, dedicated to himself and his first wife. This had left Hélène unmoved; she neither expected nor wanted his money, and as soon as Picot realised this he had refined his strategy. He stipulated she was to be allowed to live in the apartment, which he knew she hated, and was to have an annual allowance that would prevent her from starving but not much more, an allowance that would cease if she remarried. Hélène remembered the smug smirk on her husband's face as he described these conditions;

gratified he could make her life miserable even after his death.

Hélène shut her eyes. The lawyer's words slowly germinated, the realisation she now had money of her own took root. She could afford a new coat, hat, dresses – as soon as she left hospital she would go to Modes de Paris, the most expensive dress shop in Privas. Intoxicated with Monsieur de Bonneville's news, Hélène allowed herself to dream: she could go on a trip to Paris; she could buy anything she had ever wanted – a bicycle, a car, a home of her own. She could buy Philippe a tractor; they could buy a new, bigger farm. For the first time since she had left Les Laysses, Hélène felt a flicker of happiness. She smiled.

That night Hélène had another terrifying dream. She was strapped to her bed and the nurses in the hospital were pointing at her, hissing 'murderess, murderess'. Hélène woke in the half-light of the hospital room, sweating with fear. The happy optimism of the evening had evaporated; in the bleak darkness she tossed and turned, prey to the dread that Picot would find a way from beyond the grave to destroy her.

However, as the news of her inheritance spread and the nurses' animosity changed into a fawning solicitude, Hélène's nervousness gradually disappeared and she tentatively began to adapt to her new life. A nurse brought her a copy of the local paper praising her bravery in trying to save her husband; even the ill-disposed Madame Leclerc came to offer an oily sympathy.

As she became more confident, Hélène's thoughts increasingly turned to Philippe. Her feelings had become more complicated since Picot's death. She loved Philippe, yearned to live with him and with Frédéric, but she no longer wanted to live at Les Laysses – the old farm was haunted by the shade of Agathe, it held too many sad memories. Forced by her injuries to spend many idle hours, Hélène indulged her fantasies: she lived contentedly with Philippe and Frédéric; they bought a big farm perhaps in the South of France or even in Canada; she married Philippe. Hélène was tempted to write to him, but did not dare give the nurses a letter addressed to an unknown man, afraid it would resuscitate suspicions not entirely dispersed by the sergeant's conclusion. She waited restlessly to leave the hospital and be free from the obsequious attentions of its staff.

***

After her release from the hospital Hélène moved into the undemanding comfort of the Hotel du Louvre, recommended by Monsieur de Bonneville as a suitable place for her convalescence. As soon as she had settled in, Hélène had written to Philippe, a brief message scrawled untidily with her left hand, telling him where she was and that her husband had died in an accident. Almost a month had passed with no reply and she led a lonely, purposeless life, unable to make any decisions.

One afternoon, lured outside by the gentle sun of late August, Hélène was attempting to read under the shade of a plane tree. Hearing agitated footsteps, she turned to see Madame Durand, the owner of the hotel, coming towards her across the gravel, her face furrowed with irritation.

'You've a visitor to see you, Madame Picot. A Monsieur Faugeron.' Hélène's heart leapt as her book fell to the ground. The woman stood looking down at Hélène, her lips pursed. 'D'you know this man?'

Hélène clutched at the edge of the table, feeling faint. 'Yes. From a long time ago. Bring him to me here, please.'

As Madame Durand stalked back to the hotel, Hélène quickly took a small compact out of her handbag and dabbed her face with powder, she redrew her lips with a newly purchased lipstick. She swallowed rapidly to keep down a rising nausea. Even though Hélène had spent days and nights rehearsing this meeting, she was afraid – in a matter of hours it would be decided whether she would begin a new life with Philippe or must learn to live without him.

Hélène gripped the table as Philippe nodded to Madame Durand and came towards her, hat in hand. His best suit of dark, thick cloth looked ill-fitting and uncomfortable; the bright sunlight cruelly laid bare the worn edges of its pockets and cuffs. Hélène got up clumsily; she walked towards him stiffly, her right leg dragging. They kissed on each cheek and, for a moment, Hélène held Philippe tight. They sat down on opposite sides of the green metal table, the spidery legs of their chairs rasping against the gravel. Hélène took hold of Philippe's hand; he returned her pressure briefly then withdrew his face grave. Embarrassed, Hélène twitched at the scarf wound round her head and laughed nervously. ‘My hair hasn’t grown back yet. I’m afraid I look a fright.’

Philippe made no comment and Hélène blushed. He took in the bandaged hand and the stick leaning against the table. ‘I read about the fire. How is your hand?’

‘Quite sore – I won’t be able to use it ’til the bandages come off. But it’s my leg that hurts the most. They’ve told me the skin'll never grow back properly.’

‘I’m sorry.’ Philippe fell silent. He looked back at the hotel, its four rows of windows with their neat shutters looking impressive in the sunlight. ‘This is very grand. It must cost a lot to live here.’

Hélène nodded. ‘Two hundred and fifty francs for full board for a week.’

Philippe looked shocked. ‘A fortune!’ He turned his hat in his hands, uncomfortable, unwilling to say more.

Hélène gave a short, tense laugh; she reached out as if to touch his hand and then withdrew. ‘I’m so glad you’ve come at last.’

There was a long silence as each waited for the other to begin.

Philippe spoke first. ‘When are you planning to leave here?’

‘In a few weeks, I hope.’

‘You’ll go back to your old home?’

Hélène shook her head vigorously. 'No! Nothing could make me. I hated the place even before this happened.'

'I see.' Hélène waited for him to continue, barely breathing. Philippe fell silent, twisting his hat in his hands. When he did speak, his voice was firm, as though he had reached a difficult conclusion. 'When I got your note I assumed you'd need some help, so I spoke to my brother Gerard to see what we might do.' Hélène's heart beat hard and loud. 'He'd heard about your accident. He'd kept the bit in the *Riverain Agricole* to show me.'

Hélène smiled wryly. 'The nurses cut it out for me. "*Hélène Picot, née Vernot, bravely tried to save her husband, who perished in the flames at their home above the well-known Picot Charcuterie, et cetera.*"'

Philippe nodded briskly and continued, 'It seemed as though your apartment had been badly damaged so I imagined you wouldn't be able to go back there.' Hélène held her breath, willing him to say what she longed to hear. 'There's no reason why you should've heard, but both my parents died some years ago, so I thought Gerard might have a room to spare. Since Sophie's death he's married again. Bernadette isn't perhaps the brightest girl, but she's kind. I think you'd get on well with her.' He smiled drily. 'Better than you would've done with Sophie.' Philippe looked directly at Hélène. 'It wasn't easy but I've managed to persuade him to take you in.' He smiled at Hélène, proud he had been able to help her. 'At least you'll have somewhere to live.'

Hélène shut her eyes and turned away, fighting for breath, her fists clenched. Philippe wanted her to live with Gerard, not with him. She remembered the claustrophobic woods shutting in the Faugerons' farm, the unwelcoming kitchen teeming with children. 'Why must it be with Gerard?'

Philippe's smile faded. 'Because he's the only person I can think of who's got any room to spare. It won't be easy for him to put you up – as he kept telling me! In return you'd have to help on the farm and with the children. Bernadette's got a small baby to look after and Sophie's youngest child is quite a handful.'

Hélène blurted out bitterly, 'I'm never going to be anyone's unpaid servant again.' She looked away. 'Agathe couldn't bear to live with Gerard and I could never stand him.'

Philippe's expression hardened. 'You said you wanted to come back. You said you missed working on the farm.'

'But that was with you! At Les Laysses.' Hélène took hold of his hand, her eyes full of tears.

'No! You know that's impossible.' There was an awkward silence. Philippe spoke more gently. 'Gerard has a wife, Hélène. That makes all the difference. You and I couldn't live in the same house.'

'There's Dorothée.'

'You know it's not the same.'

A waitress came over from the hotel to ask Hélène if she would like her afternoon tea. Hélène tried to smile. 'For two, please.' The couple sat in silence while the girl arranged the delicate tea service on an immaculate tablecloth and left them. Hélène wound the starched napkin into a tight ball under the table and cleared her throat.

'I've also been thinking what we might do.' She attempted to take Philippe's hand, but he turned away. 'I'm a rich woman now.' Hélène paused, anticipating a response, but Philippe's expression remained unchanged and inscrutable. 'I'm going to sell the charcuterie and the apartment. I'm told I should get a good price in spite of the damage.' Philippe did not look at Hélène; he sat very still, his gnarled hands folded over one another, brown against the stark white of the damask. 'But that's only a part of it – I've inherited Picot's entire fortune!' Disconcerted by Philippe's silence, Hélène continued, speaking rapidly, hurrying to get to the end – to his decision. 'I've thought so much about our new life together.' Tenderly Hélène put her hand on his. 'Remember our dreams from all those years ago? Now I've got enough money to make them come true! We can buy a farm with lots of land wherever we fancy. Frédéric can live with us. We could even go to Canada – as you wanted to do. I've been reading about it; there's lots of land available – we could build our own house.' Faced with Philippe's silence, Hélène's voice rose, vibrating with nerves. 'We could even get married – no one would know who we were. I'm sure Frédéric would grow to love me and we could be a family at last. Together, as we'd always hoped to be.'

Philippe pushed aside the fragile teacup, leaving the tea untouched. Hélène's face lit up as a new argument came to her. 'If we left for Canada soon, Frédéric wouldn't have to fight.' Philippe moved away, his chair scraping on the gravel; he put his arms on his knees and lowered his head. Alarmed, Hélène spoke even more quickly, hardly taking breath, 'In Canada no one would know us; we'd be free to do as we want. I've looked into the cost of the crossing, the prices of farms.' Hélène's voice dropped to a murmur. 'I've thought about it so much, Philippe. It's what you said you wanted.' When she had finished there was a profound silence.

Eventually Philippe spoke, his voice toneless. 'Frédéric doesn't want to be a farmer; he wants to be a lawyer.'

'Oh.' There was a long silence. The waitress came to clear the cold, unconsumed tea from the table.

When they were alone, Philippe looked at Hélène, a long, reflective gaze that made Hélène nervous; she could not read his thoughts, although she sensed he could see deep into her own. She twisted away, uncomfortable. 'Philippe, please think about my plan. It'd be an exciting new life for us both. We deserve some happiness after all we've been through.'

'You know I couldn't live on another man's money, Hélène.' Philippe's voice was gruff, his face stern. 'I'd find it humiliating.'

Hélène bridled. 'You don't need to see it in that way. Picot didn't acquire his money through honest work; he got it by profiteering while you were fighting in the trenches. It serves him right I've got it now. I've earned it after so many terrible years with that man. You must think of it as our money, not mine or his.'

Philippe glared at her, offended and angry. 'It certainly isn't mine and I'll have nothing to do with it! You may be able to justify living off the money of a man you hated – but I never could.'

'Oh don't look at me like that!'

Philippe picked up his hat. Hélène took hold of his arm. 'Philippe, please think about it. Don't leave me. I can't bear it if you walk away again. We've a chance to have a good life together while we're still young enough to enjoy it.'

Both sat still, Hélène's eyes fixed on Philippe, mutely beseeching him to accept, but he stared sightlessly at the blank windows of the hotel. The sun went behind a cloud and an eerie chill settled on the couple. After a long pause Hélène dropped her eyes and asked Philippe, her voice hesitant and low, 'Did you ever love me, Philippe?'

Philippe thought a long time before he replied. When he did speak, the anger in his voice had evaporated and he spoke as though to himself. 'I've never asked myself that question. Right from the start my feelings for you were mixed with guilt; the guilt was always there. After you left, the guilt was all that remained.'

Hélène stood up. She took a few agitated steps, and then came back, leaning over the table. 'When I came to see you that was all you talked about.'

'And Agathe's forgiveness.'

Hélène waved this aside and moved closer to Philippe. 'D'you imagine I didn't feel guilt too? For seventeen years I've paid for what I did, seventeen years of being separated from my son, thinking about him - and you - every single day, day and night. Whatever words priests use – expiation, atonement, penance – I've paid a terrible price. Surely after so much pain, so much torture, we've both wiped the slate of our conscience clean?'

There was a long silence; reluctantly Philippe looked up at Hélène. 'I always loved Agathe, ever since I was a boy. It never changed.' He looked away, toward the hills where the evening light was softening their gentle slopes. Hélène sat down, fighting tears. Eventually Philippe continued, his voice low, 'But with you I did feel something else. I can't explain it very well, but when I was with you the world seemed a bigger, brighter place where I could dream of a different life, and where those dreams might come true. With you I didn't feel imprisoned by the past, the everyday, the ordinary.' He looked down. 'You made me feel I could be happy.'

Hélène smiled sadly. 'It was the only time I've ever felt any joy.' She wiped away a tear with the back of her hand. 'But now I'm free to live as I want to. Can't we start again, Philippe, be together, love each other, forget guilt and sad memories?' He did not reply but sat with his head in his hands, shoulders bowed. The silence extended, Hélène sat looking at him, her eyes misted with tears as all her tentative hopes subsided into a sombre resignation.
At last she broke the stillness, speaking softly. 'Perhaps if things had been different?'

Philippe gave a half-laugh. 'Not only 'things', as you call them. I would've had to be a different person altogether.' Philippe cleared his throat; he sat up straight in his chair, his face grim as he looked at Hélène. 'So you don't want to come back to the Plateau?'

'I did want to.' She paused. 'I wanted to be with you, Philippe.'

'I can't have you living at Les Laysses.'

Hélène sat in silence for while. 'And I couldn't live with Gerard – any more than Agathe could.'

Philippe's voice hardened. 'I'll tell Gerard.'

Hélène felt a confused anger rise within her. 'You've told me so many times that life's too hard on the Plateau. Why won't you consider farming somewhere else?'

After a long pause, Philippe spoke softly. 'The farm and the Plateau are all I know, Hélène. They're in my bones. Now Frédéric's gone, it won't be long before Dorothée's independent, so I'll only have myself to look after and everything'll be a lot easier. The daily rhythms of Les Laysses have become part of me – I couldn't live anywhere else.' He continued quietly, 'You've changed, Hélène.' He smiled sadly. 'And I haven't.'

'I could buy a house and live nearby. I could come to see you and Frédéric from time to time.'

Philippe smiled ruefully. 'D'you really want that, Hélène? Within months you'd be as frustrated and unhappy as you were when you were young.'

Hélène sat back in her chair, defeated. The more she had come to terms with her new wealth, the more she realised she did not want to return to the harshness of the Plateau. She could not deny what he had said. 'Can I visit you at Les Laysses?'

'As Agathe's sister.' Philippe smiled at her cynically. 'But I don't expect you'll want to very often. You've other choices now.' He took his watch out of his pocket and frowned. 'I must go. I'm meeting Frédéric.' He stood up. 'Mobilisation can't be far off, it'll only be a matter of time before he's sent north and I want to see him before he leaves.'

'Can I come with you?'

'Of course not!'

Hélène replied fiercely. 'Why not? He's my son! I want to see him before he goes away. It might be the last ...'

Philippe interrupted her. 'You can't do that, Hélène! If you tell him who you are you'll confuse and unsettle him just when he needs to be strong.'

'I don't need to say who I am.'

Philippe leant forward, his face tight. 'Then why would you, a stranger, want to see him? What possible explanation could you give?' Hélène winced. Philippe spoke harshly. 'I won't let you destroy all the love Agathe gave him – as his mother.' He stopped, breathing heavily.

'That's a cruel thing to say!' Hélène began to cry. 'You've left me with nothing – not you, not my son, not even hope.'

Philippe bent over Hélène, his face so close she could see the grey bristles on his chin. 'You're being foolish and selfish! You've just told me you're a very rich woman. You're still young.' Philippe straightened up. 'Stop looking to the past for your happiness.'

Hélène put her face in her hands. 'I'm so lonely.'

'We're all alone, Hélène. We can't go back to the past and we don't know what the future will bring – especially with a war closing in on us. Remember when I married Agathe, how simple life seemed? We thought we knew exactly how our lives would be. Two months later everything had changed.' He spoke under his breath. 'I'd give anything to prevent Frédéric having to endure what we went through.' There was a long silence. Philippe gripped Hélène's hand tightly. 'Promise me you'll keep away from him, Hélène, I beg you.'

Hélène did not reply; she slowly withdrew her hand. Philippe was the first to look away; he made as if he would speak but instead picked up his hat and turned to leave. Hélène dropped her head into her hands, knowing she would not see him again.

When he spoke, Philippe's voice was cold, reflective. 'There's something I must ask you. I can't get it out of my mind.' He did not look at her. 'Was the fire really an accident?'

Hélène pushed back her chair so hard it fell to the ground; she limped quickly and erratically to stand in front of Philippe. 'How can you ask me that? What makes you think I could do something so terrible?' Hélène took hold of his arm. 'I loved you – my crime, if it was a crime – was to love you. Because of it I took something from my sister that I shouldn't have done – and I've paid for it. But to think I could have cold-bloodedly killed Picot!' She moved closer to Philippe, the words spitting into his face. 'He burnt to death – have you any idea how awful that is? To see his flesh blacken and disintegrate, hear his screams?' She turned her face away and her voice dropped to a whisper. 'Of course I feel guilty because I wanted him to die. Even when I saw him in agony, there was a part of me that hoped he would die.' Her voice strengthened. 'But that was only part of me. I did what I could to save him; it wasn't enough, but it was all I could do.' She looked at Philippe, eyes unflinching. 'I can't blame myself for being alive while he's not,' – her voice was barely audible – 'even if I am glad he's dead.' When she had finished there was a long silence.

Philippe nodded slowly. He took her hand. 'I'm sorry, Hélène.' There were tears in his eyes. 'I'm sorry for everything.' He turned quickly and walked away.

A few minutes after Philippe had left, Madame Durand bustled towards Hélène, her lips a tight line of disapproval. 'You've sent that man away, I see. Monsieur de Bonneville warned me you'd have strange men coming after you and your money.' Hélène was about to remonstrate with her in Philippe's defence, ashamed and hurt on his behalf, but she felt too drained, too exhausted. Anyway, it did not matter now.

That night Hélène's heart ached, but no tears came. She went over what Philippe had said. How could she ever have dreamt of finding happiness with Philippe? Philippe belonged to Agathe. He had always belonged to her sister. Exhausted, Hélène drifted into sleep. She dreamt she had gone back to Les Laysses with Philippe. They were sitting at the kitchen table facing the ugly black stove, Agathe's stove, they talked about the day just ended, the animals, the weather, their tasks for tomorrow. They had long ago exhausted all conversation about the past – there had been so little to say. They did not talk of the future because the future would always be the same as the present. They went upstairs and made love in the same bed where Philippe had lain with Agathe, Hélène conscious of Dorothée lying below, listening to the sounds they made.

A door slamming in the hotel corridor jolted her awake. Hélène tried to recall the once-beloved face with its gaunt planes, its clear blue eyes and, for a moment, she held it in her imagination, but then the image blurred, melted, faded away and she was left staring into the dark shadows of the room.

***

The atmosphere in the town grew gloomier as the rumours of war intensified. The streets were strangely subdued; people barely spoke, guiltily going about their business, reluctant to be away from their radios, their newspapers, their homes.

On Friday 1st September the tension in the hotel tautened as an ashen-faced Madame Durand opened the door of her office and said in a quavering voice, 'I've just heard on the radio, Hitler's attacked Poland! The army's been mobilised.'

The following day Hélène went to the garrison, where streams of sombre men were making their way silently through its gates. The town was eerily still; the cafés empty; in the market square a handful of old men stood talking in creaking voices. 'Now they've voted funds for the Army, the declaration must be days away.' Two women standing nearby began to cry.

On Sunday, Hélène went down to the salon as the majority of guests returned from Mass. Madame Durand joined them wearing her best black dress, the one she saved for important funerals. 'Great Britain has declared war. Our government has sent an ultimatum to Hitler demanding he withdraws from Poland. It will end at five this afternoon.'

At five o'clock the grave and silent guests were gathered in the hall of the hotel; Madame Durand emerged from her office and declared in a quavering voice, 'It's begun. We're at war. God help us all.'

***

Hélène came wearily into the bedroom; she took off her black straw hat and threw it on the bed. Hot and thirsty, she poured herself a tumbler of water, took a sip of the stale liquid and went to the window. In the street below groups of people were returning from the station, the faded tricolours clutched in children's hands drooping in the heat. She counted ten heavily laden cars moving slowly along the rue Cours du Palais, all with bulky trunks strapped to their roofs. She leant against the window-frame and sighed.

Hélène had got up early that morning. She had hurried to the Champ de Mars hoping to find a place where she would have a clear view of the soldiers as they marched out of the barracks, but she had been too late; a mute, jostling crowd, already two and three deep, lined the route. At ten o'clock the bugles had sounded, their mournful notes echoed by the wailing of infants. The garrison gates grated as they were dragged open, the sergeant at arms barked a command while the band struck up the 'Marseillaise', its strident notes passing over the sullen crowd. Hélène had tried to elbow her way through the press of waving women but could make no progress. The lines of young recruits moved in tight formation across the square, eyes staring straight ahead, rifles aligned across rows of shoulders. Hélène craned forward with the rest of the women, desperate to see Frédéric for one last time. She thought she saw him, but could not be sure; she pressed forward, but he had gone, ranks of other young men had taken his place.

Hélène jostled her way out of the crowd to join the flow of people who were trudging towards the station, but the surly melée could not keep up with the marching men. Desperate for one last glance, Hélène made her way down narrow side streets, but the mass of onlookers was thickly pressed and all she could see against the sunlit sky was the sinister glint of bayonets. The band was now playing 'Quand Madelon' and the old tune brought back a rush of memories from Saint-Agrève twenty years ago. A wave of anguish choked her; she leant against a wall, shut her eyes and, accompanied by the fateful tramp of marching feet, saw Emile, Roland, Marius and Philippe as they marched away to their terrible war. Drained of all emotion, Hélène made her way back to the hotel, the uncertain glimpse of Frédéric too fragile to become a memory.

***

Far away a church bell tolled for evening prayers. As its rolling notes died away, Hélène sat down in front of the dressing table, her reflected image staring deep into her soul. After a while she took a deep breath, left the room and went downstairs.

She found Madame Durand locking the big door with its stained-glass panels; without taking off her hat, the heavy woman sat down awkwardly on one of the unforgiving chairs that lined the lobby. She looked wearily at Hélène. 'What d'you want, Madame Picot? I'm not in the mood for more bad news today.'

Hélène swallowed hard and straightened up. 'I'm leaving tomorrow. There's nothing to keep me here now.'

Madame Durand shrugged. 'Where are you going?'

'North. Paris, probably.' Madame Durand shook her head slowly in disbelief. 'Don't worry. This time the Germans'll never get anywhere near Paris. I'll leave in the morning.'

Hélène packed her belongings in a small suitcase and snapped it shut. To calm the emotions that chased through her mind, she went to sit by the open window. Moonlight bathed the mourning town in its cool indifference; in the distance the etched hills reminded her of the young girl whirling round in her nightdress, swearing to find romance and adventure. For a long time she sat by the window dreaming of Paris. As the tranquil night subdued her memories, Hélène smiled to herself, welcoming the first stirrings of reawakened hope.

Embers of War trilogy

Desire and Despair is the first volume in ***Embers of War***, an epic tale evoking the bitter reality of conflict and its far-reaching consequences. The title of the second volume is ***Darkness at Dawn***.

1939. Hélène is now a wealthy widow recently arrived in Paris. She is charmed by Guerin, a ruthless seducer, and befriended by the sophisticated Touvigny as the city prepares for war.

One year later, Occupied France is a country torn between collaboration and resistance - a world where individuals are forced to choose between good and evil; whose decisions can lead to destruction or to a deceptive freedom. Repelled by the horrors of the Nazis, Hélène escapes to Vichy France where she witnesses extraordinary crimes and exceptional heroism. Isolated in the wild countryside she finds love - at the cost of a fateful compromise.

It is a gripping story of evil and tragedy, courage and passion, vengeance and survival.

In ***Darkness at Dawn***, Lesley Lever draws on extensive research to capture the danger, the senseless cruelty and the moral complexities of Occupied France.

Redemption is the third and final volume of the ***Embers of War*** trilogy.

It is now 1944, Paris has been liberated but France is shattered by the brutality of the Occupation: torn between demands for retribution and a desire for regeneration; learning to live with disillusion, yearning for optimism and hope.

Hélène has returned to Paris haunted by her longing for Léon, afraid past mistakes will destroy her new life. As she journeys through a ruined continent, love emerges out of misery and destruction.

It is a moving account of the heartbreak of love, passion and eventual fulfilment.

In ***Redemption***, Lesley Lever draws on extensive research to capture the hopes, the disillusion, the moral confusion of a continent wrecked by war and revolted by the horrors of the Holocaust.

Non-fiction by Lesley Lever

One Billion Girls examines the lives of girls from birth to eighteen. It reflects on the millions of girls in the developing world who are denied any freedom, whose sexuality provokes fear and harm, yet whose repressed lives are seen as normal - it also focuses on girls in developed countries whose choices are restricted by more subtle discrimination. Based on conversations with girls and women in eighty countries, the author's findings are reinforced by statistics which show a shameful picture of inequality and abuse. She challenges religious doctrines, tolerance of harmful customs and inadequate international efforts that leave hundreds of millions of girls living intolerable lives.

It is a story that has not been told. The daily misery of many millions of girls who are routinely abused in their home or in domestic service, who are denied an education, who are almost all married and mothers before they reach fifteen, is largely unreported and ignored by international institutions.

As the Chief Executive of the world's largest organisation for girls and young women, Lesley Bulman-Lever was inspired by many girls who were determined to change their world. This is their story.

If you would like to know more about Lesley Lever and her work you can visit her website, www.lesleylever.co.uk

36456896R00234

Printed in Great Britain
by Amazon